In a mote of dust
lies the end of the world.

Praise for
DUST

"Pellegrino has crafted a very intelligent novel
designed to scare the pants off readers.
Imagine *The Hot Zone* crossed
with a Stephen King novel."
San Antonio Express-News

"Fascinating."
The Denver Post

"An action-packed novel that will remind
readers of Michael Crichton."
The Midwest Book Review

"Thoughtful, carefully researched and really
scary . . . Pellegrino invents a great cast of
characters and keeps his readers guessing."
Rocky Mountain News

Other Avon Books by
Charles Pellegrino

Fiction

FLYING TO VALHALLA
THE KILLING STAR
(with George Zebrowski)

Nonfiction

HER NAME, TITANIC
RETURN TO SODOM AND GOMORRAH

Coming Soon

CHARIOTS FOR APOLLO:
THE UNTOLD STORY BEHIND
THE RACE TO THE MOON
(with Joshua Stoff)

CHARLES PELLEGRINO

DUST

AVON BOOKS  NEW YORK

A single leatherbound edition has been published by The Easton Press.

Excerpt on page 77 from *Insomnia* copyright © 1994 by Stephen King. Published by Viking Penguin, a division of Penguin Books USA Inc. Used by permission of the author.

AVON BOOKS, INC.
1350 Avenue of the Americas
New York, New York 10019

Copyright © 1998 by Charles Pellegrino
Inside cover author photo by Quintana Roo Dunne
Library of Congress Catalog Card Number: 97-26936
ISBN: 0-380-78742-3
www.avonbooks.com

First Avon Books Paperback Printing: March 1999
First Avon Books Hardcover Printing: March 1998

AVON TRADEMARK REG. U.S. PAT. OFF. AND IN OTHER COUNTRIES, MARCA REGISTRADA, HECHO EN U.S.A.

Printed in the U.S.A.

WCD   10 9 8 7 6 5 4 3 2 1

To the unfading memory of
WARREN LUFTIG

Hameth and Y'gre are flying tonight.

I will show you fear in a handful of dust.

—T. S. Eliot

Contents

Prologue: Satan's Black Pool   1

I Provocation

 1 Paradise Regained   9
 2 Awakenings   17
 3 Defining a Crisis   32
 4 City of Dreams   41
 5 Long Beach   44
 6 The Oracle   58
 7 Carnival   74
 8 Looking In, Looking Out   80
 9 The World, the Flesh, and the Devil   107
10 The Mad Room and the Phoenix Road   122
11 The Birds and the Bees   132
12 Crisis Redefined   173

13 Into the Belly of the Beast　　　　　　186
14 Darwin's Warm Little Pond　　　　　　194
15 Marching to Valhalla　　　　　　　　209

II Penetration
16 Clasp the Monkey, Saturn　　　　　　225

III Evocation
17 Ashes to Ashes: The Wings of Icarus　273
18 A Chronicle in Amber　　　　　　　　291
19 Return to Babylon　　　　　　　　　　304
20 Point of No Return　　　　　　　　　318
21 Sole Survivor　　　　　　　　　　　345
22 My Way　　　　　　　　　　　　　361
23 All Aboard for Ararat　　　　　　　369
24 Testament　　　　　　　　　　　　400

Epilogue: The Johnny Appleseed Voyage　409
Afterword: Reality Check　　　　　　　419
Selected Bibliography　　　　　　　　443
Acknowledgments　　　　　　　　　　448

Prologue: Satan's Black Pool

Autumn, 65,566,699 B.C.
Late Cretaceous Cycle
Phase I

They huddled on the floor of the forest, watching, waiting.

They were not quite mammals proper, for unlike many of their brethren they laid eggs in deep burrows and subsisted on roots.

They were not reptiles. They did not know the distress of chilling blood, so they felt no longing for the noontide sun, no impulse to move from the shadows.

They watched.

Across the great bay, smoke from seven dying volcanoes spread with lazy speed, obscuring much of what was to

1

be Manhattan Island and Nassau County. The bay was calm as an oil pool, and along the edge of the tropical New Jersey shore the pterosaurs no longer flocked, for all the fish were gone. It was mating season for the flying saurians, yet in large areas of the northern hemisphere, no pterosaurs sang. The root-eaters sniffed cautiously at the air and stiffened their whiskers.

They watched.

They waited.

An enemy, as yet unseen to the root-eaters, was approaching from the greater bay to the south—from the shores of an inland sea that, owing to the thick muds, or marls, now forming there, would someday be named the Marlborough Plains.

They moved among the palms as if they owned the Earth, a pair of ornithomimids—ostrich dinosaurs—with sharp beaks and swift, muscular hind legs, the scourge of New Jersey. The mother was about three feet tall at the shoulders and almost twice as long from beak to tail. Her child was only half as long, but he had no trouble keeping pace with her, trotting faster than any horse—now only latent in the root-eaters and their kin—could gallop.

The morning dew had burned off hours before, and the air through which they ran was now dry enough to evaporate their sweat instantly, stealing away excess body heat and keeping the two saurians from boiling to death in their own internal fluids. Their closest relatives were reptiles; yet, like a mammal, the mother attended to her child constantly, never venturing more than a few feet away.

Shafts of sunlight were still stabbing straight down through the tall palms when the pair reached the north shore and, in perfect unison, dug their feet in like powerful brakes, churning up clouds of dust and dried leaves.

From among the blue dandelions to the left there came a movement, and the larger animal looked in that direction, her eyes yellow and catlike, her long neck probing in sweeping arcs. She bent forward and, without removing her gaze from the dandelion patch, picked up a clam shell in three spindly fingers. She sent a message to her child, shifting the chameleon skin on one side of her body from a black-and-white zebra pattern to something vaguely hi-

eroglyphic. The child read the tapestry of lines and shapes on his mother's left flank as if it were a handwritten note.

Nothing hitherto seen upon the planet could be even distantly compared with the detailed communications now passing between the two saurians. Their skin shimmered in a million points of light, as if adorned with a cloak of microscopic gems. The colors included tanzanite blue, ultramarine pearl, ruby red, quartz white, and sapphire black. The child understood that he was to follow behind and watch very closely. With a blush, he signaled to his mother that he would obey.

She went directly to the mound of dandelions and began chopping at the ground with the sharp edge of her clam shell. The root-eaters, barely as large as the shell, refused to give up the mound. One of them reared up and hissed at her, then bit a finger. With an impartial swipe she brought the shell down across his midsection, cutting him in two. The other root-eaters got the message and scrambled down their burrows.

Even before she nudged the body with her nose, she could smell its bad odor. The root-eater was far from being a favorite food, but she scooped up the two halves in her beak anyway. Insect-eating salamanders, frogs, and the smallest and tenderest of the dinosaurs—these were among the mother saurian's favorite foods, but they were becoming scarcer with each passing week. And these were not all that had diminished as the summer wore on. Save for the occasional termite swarm, the clicking and buzzing of insects was to be heard no more, and the leaves of dandelions and poinsettias, palms and hibiscus, displayed no holes or blemishes. They seemed wrong and nightmarishly out of place in their perfection.

The mother crushed and shredded the root-eater in her mouth. Then, blushing red about her throat, she signaled to her child that it was feeding time. He came forward to nuzzle her, and when he opened his mouth she passed the soft meat into his throat, keeping only the bony and furry parts to herself. When he stopped feeding she resumed her attack on the root-eaters' burrows, slashing with the clam shell and digging with fingers until her paws ached.

The child watched, as finally, carefully, his mother

broke through to a little chamber strewn with grape-sized eggs. In their run for their lives, the furry animals had left behind a small but potent feast. As she inspected the eggs for hardness, she was pleased to discover that their contents had not been given sufficient time to grow; their yolks were still fresh and soft, still brimming with un-used nutrients.

She handed the clutch—all of it—over to her child; and when he looked up at her, blushing puzzlement in shades of citrine and topaz, she signaled to him that she was not hungry. It was a lie, of course. And watching her, as he swallowed the little banquet in two gulps, he did not guess at the hunger she was forcing out of her thoughts, for he had never seen his mother lie before. In this time of encroaching famine, she would take only as much nourish-ment as was necessary to keep herself alive, in order that she might keep her son alive.

(If only . . .)

It was the most pitiful sensation any thinking species— human or saurian—would ever know: If only . . .

If only nature, in some horrible spasm of malevolence, had not chosen this moment to spiral down into famine and chaos, then it would have been possible to believe that the root-eaters' kin might never have had a hope of overrunning the Earth, and that saurians, not mammals, were destined to put their feet upon the moon.

If only . . .

They continued their trek to the southwest, in search of food. Shortly after sunset they came upon a region of forest where the leaves were not unblemished and unholed. The mother stopped and grabbed a handful of foul-smell-ing soil, sniffed at it, and threw it aside. She shrieked a scarlet warning pattern on her left flank, and her son shrieked silently back at her.

A bright crescent moon was rising. Shafts of moonlight slanted through the naked, dead limbs of a tree, slanted through ten thousand naked trees onto ground that was leafless and rapidly eroding, filled with the stench of de-caying white webs. As they explored the dying forest the mother became aware of a soft sound behind her. She turned immediately, her large eyes ticking back and forth from tree to tree. She saw the wide depression over which they had just crossed, and which she had taken to be a dried lakebed, suddenly and miraculously refilling. The surface of the lake moved like a mist, but it was blacker than any mist had a right to be, and it ran like a flood tide.

She realized that they now stood on a hill turned suddenly into an island, with the false lake swirling just a few feet below, expanding its dimensions. Her skin brightened with horror, her feet felt like tightening springboards, and she wanted to flee. But she signaled to her child to stay on high ground, and she went closer to the lake; she did not know why. In a moment the lake was ankle-deep. It felt more like a thick dust than a fluid or a mist. It brushed over her feet like a living, breathing thing, and it tickled. In another moment it was knee-deep, and when she rubbed her leg with a hand, the tickling sensation— and her momentary hope of safety—ended with heart- breaking speed.

A sharp pain radiated from her legs as the lake, over- whelming in its force, closed on her, submerged her, bit into her relentlessly, and moved on toward the child. She managed one leap, a splendid but useless display in which her feet actually cleared the surface; but the substance of the lake clung to her in great black mats, and when she fell back again she disappeared in a terrible glut of blood.

It became a feeding frenzy, with the mother saurian's body drawing the tide away from her child and creating, briefly, a narrow path of escape. But he did not flee to save himself. He waited for her to resurface and stayed with her too long, not fully comprehending what death signified, unable and unwilling to believe that it meant the end of her.

If only . . .

I
PROVOCATION

What seest thou else
In the dark backward and abysm of time?
— WILLIAM SHAKESPEARE

Never look back. Something might be
gaining on you.

— LEROY "SATCHEL" PAGE

1

Paradise Regained

Late Holocene Cycle
Phase I
Midnight, Time Present

The volcanic islands north of the root-eaters' perch were long gone. For twenty million years, sediments from the eroding Appalachian highlands had piled up around them, forming the Raratan and Magothy layers of sand, silt, and clay that were the very foundation of Queens and Nassau counties. Even the mile-high glaciers of 25,000 B.C. could not shake this foundation. Instead, they plowed all the rubble of antediluvian New York and Massachusetts on top of it, and as the wall of ice receded across Connecticut, its streams of meltwater merged into a mighty river, deepening the rift between Long Island and the continent, to

9

carve the valley that, in an era of rising sea levels, became Long Island Sound.

On a barrier island known as Long Beach, all that remained of the glaciers was quartz rubble ground into a stretch of sand so white that had there been nothing more than starlight to see by, still it would have shone. From a stand of condominiums behind the boardwalk, from buildings named Ocean Club, Renaissance, and the Breakers, lights cast distinct shadows across Jeep tracks and footprints on the beach. There were only two places secluded from the light. One was under the boardwalk. The other was in the shadows of the great mounds upon which the lifeguards sat by day. Jon preferred the open spaces of the lifeguard mound.

But nowhere on the beach, this night, could he enjoy complete seclusion. A half moon was rising, 2,400 miles farther from Earth than it had been in 65,566,699 B.C., but just as bright. He could see Hel's face in the moonlight, pale, without detail. Planting a kiss on her forehead, he nudged her gently and, taking the signal, she craned her neck to kiss Jon on the lips. A blanket unfurled and a little pile of canned colas, candy bars, and a dark box fell out of it. They paid no attention to the spill. They just stood there above the night surf, hugging for a long time before bending down to spread out the blanket and pick up their belongings.

Hel found the dark box, and knew at once that it did not belong among the candy bars and colas, and guessed immediately what it had to be.

"You didn't!" she said.

"Happy birthday," said Jon.

And she was simultaneously smiling and weeping, even before she found the diamond ring inside.

"When?" she blurted.

"Soon . . . soon . . . I was thinking, after graduation next spring. Then Northrop-Grumman is sending me west for more schooling, and to work on the Powell launcher."

"The launcher? You got the contract?"

"We got it," he said. "What an amazing future our children will see." He pointed toward the sky, and Hel looked where he was pointing. Maybe someday . . .

Hel looked at him and she wished that he would always stay the same, that he would always be full of great hopes, that he would never outgrow the child in him. She had not been as lucky, having been told from earliest childhood that she was exceptionally stupid and could not possibly amount to anything of worth. But Jon had told her—and she would not believe it—that she could easily run rings around every one of his friends at the academy, and that in time he expected her to outclass him. "Mediocrity sees only itself," he once said. "Talent recognizes genius."

They embraced and kissed deeply, each believing that infinite possibilities lay ahead as a gentle breeze came up from the south and overhead the cold stars burned and just thirty yards away, what to all outward appearances was but a dirt-splotched stretch of beach came suddenly alive.

Within the splotch, sixty billion dark shapes moved busily to and fro—each smaller than a mote of dust and each sensing a change in the sand's rhythm. They did not see the couple, but they could detect their vibrations superimposed upon the steady break and drag of the waves. The vibrations summoned chemosensors into action—little pits running the lengths of their abdomens and enclosed by nerve endings—and now they could *smell* the couple. There was the unmistakable scent of skin and skin oils in the air, strongest just a few tens of yards to the east.

As sixty billion mouths and 240 billion pairs of feet suddenly quickened their pace, their owners had no way of knowing or understanding that many more of their kind existed than had existed for tens of millions of years. Nature's delicate balancing act was coming unhinged—again.

They existed to breathe and to breed. And to feed.

With no other purpose, and with cold indifference, they sniffed at the gradient and began to move as one.

Russ was finding it impossible to doze off in spite of the falling humidity. Tonight the air happened to be cool and dry enough for him to sleep with the windows wide open and to let the steady pounding of the night surf lull him into unconsciousness.

But always the insomnia gnome was present, gnawing

at the back of his mind with little rat's teeth, rarely allowing him the pleasure of total relaxation. It was trying to tell him something, he supposed. Trying to tell him he was bored. Bored with his job. Bored with Long Island. Bored with that chain-smoking bitch Pamela they were going to make him marry.

So he sat up in bed with four pillows propped behind his back, flipping from news station to news station, and finding very little to sustain his attention. It was a slow news week. Three hundred were killed today in the India food riots, but all anyone really wanted to report was that someone had finally shot the right Buttafuoco—

(boring)

Some biologist was doomsaying about acid rain and the great North American frog die-off—

(boring)

And the price of coffee was certain to triple by Christmas, owing to some sort of mite infestation in Colombia—

(irrelevant)

At last he found late night talk show host Joel Martin, who had been running a whole series of programs on "*Civilization: The Next Fifty Years.*" This time he had invited his most frequently heard-from but only rarely boring guest: Richard "Tuna" Sinclair, that crazy scientist who was always digging up the lost worlds of the Babylonians or the dinosaurs, while at the same time designing rockets. His only explanation for working in such seemingly opposite directions was that the past gave him signposts to the future.

(eerie)

Tonight, in what Russ liked to call Richard Sinclair's true Babylonian fashion, he was babbling on about some strange fossil discoveries in New Jersey. Russ tweaked up the volume.

"Now, the dinosaur-extinction puzzle goes something like this," Richard was explaining. "If you go anywhere in the world and start digging back to seventy million B.C., you will find all sorts of dinosaur bones. Above these bones, in a zone of rock dating to about sixty-five million B.C., you'll encounter an ominous layer, usually several feet thick, in which no bones of any kind are found. And within this layer, when you look very closely, you'll see the ash of a comet or asteroid bombardment. And above the ash comes a new layer crowded with the bones of ancestral sheep, camels, elephants, and pigs.''

"Fine," said Joel. "But what does that tell us about the future?"

"I'm getting to it. When we pick through those older, lowermost layers of rock very, very carefully, we begin to see evidence of a great change occurring all over the world. Across New Zealand and Antarctica, across Alaska and northern China, ice was beginning to form and, at least in a local sense, as far as those high-latitude locations were concerned, the tropical rain forests and all that lived in them went extinct—or, more accurately, they retreated toward the equator. This may explain why many of the dinosaurs were already gone more than a hundred thousand years before hell broke loose.''

"And, boy, how hell broke loose," said Joel.

"You bet," said Richard. "When the comets came down, the dinosaurs and most other heat-loving creatures were already being confined near the equator. And directly into this narrow confine, into Mexico in particular, came these earthshaking explosions. The Mexico impact alone would have put the entire Cold War nuclear arsenal to shame. If you were a burrowing mammal, you might have had a chance—living, as you were, in a ready-made bomb shelter. But if you were a surface-dwelling saurian and you happened to be living in equatorial Mexico, or in Brazil, or in California, you were probably a goner. In the absence of dinosaurs, America's mammals came up from their burrows and began, over the next million years or so, to spread, and to diversify, and to grow in stature and grace. I suspect that when the climate warmed and when it became possible to live again in Alaska and Greenland, these larger, newer mammals crossed over on land bridges to China and outcompeted what few dinosaurs had survived far from ground zero. The great dinosaur disappearing act would thus have been a two-step process.''

Richard's eyes had acquired the manic expression that had made him famous. A flash point had been reached, at which the man became self-sustaining and no longer needed an interviewer; and Russ's level of boredom went down a few notches, and he began to relax.

"A two-step extinction," Richard continued. "First a cometary anvil chorus, then a comet-derived mammalian swarm. It's a nice, tidy picture. But like most hot speculations, it's probably wrong."

"Probably wrong?" Joel exclaimed. "Your own pet theory?"

"Probably wrong," came the reply. "When Luis Alvarez first began studying the comet ash layer, he suspected that all the plants of the world had been virtually wiped out during the ashfall, and that a few burrowing mammals, and most of the world's insects, had outlived the dinosaurs by eating roots and seeds."

"You're not satisfied with that explanation?"

"No. Not now."

"Then Alvarez was wrong too?"

"Alvarez too."

The scream was shrill, distant, and very brief. He recognized it as a young man's scream, and yet it died so quickly, Russ wondered if he'd only imagined it. He clicked down the volume and turned his head in the direction of the window.

Motes of dust clung to the window screen. The only sounds were the waves pounding the beach, a few teenagers overstressing the swings in Magnolia Park, and the groan of wooden planks under a police car cruising the boardwalk.

All quiet on the western front, he told himself. Even the crickets seemed too bored to sing.

He shifted his weight on the pillows and raised the volume. Sinclair was narrating over pictures of something grotesque and antlike, magnified large enough to eat Russ alive in his bed.

"This one drowned in a pool of tree sap," said Richard, "tree sap that became the organic gemstone amber, providing us with little tombs tens of thousands of times older than any pharaoh's. Whole mountain ranges have come and gone since this insect died, about sixty-five point seven million B.C., right across the river, in New Jersey."

"Sixty-five point seven million B.C.? You mean, you can date it that accurately?"

"It's easy if you have volcanic rocks and comet ash layers to work with. This new amber deposit was tucked right below the comet debris fields, just inches below it. And the first thing you'll notice is that it's chock-full of insects—"

An amberized graveyard moved across the screen, as if an entire swarm had been caught in mid-flight.

"Now, here's the scary part: We've also got deposits that began forming just above the ashfall—only a few hundred thousand years later."

"Only!"

"You'll have to bear with me on this one Joel. Paleontologists have an odd way of viewing time. What's important and just a little bit crazy about the insects we're finding above the ash layer is that they constitute whole new genera, when we compare them with what was living before the comets, just a few inches below the ash. With the exception of cockroaches and termites and a few other oldies, almost all the insects that lived among the dinosaurs perished right along with them."

"So you're saying the comet impacts were more devastating than even Alvarez imagined."

"Shook the whole world's ecology from the bottom up, by the looks of it. And if it could wipe out something as resilient as the insects, it seems a wonder to me that *anything* survived."

The second scream came a little louder, but this time it was three or four voices crying out; a young woman had joined in.

Just some kids drinking beer and horsing around, Russ told himself. *Nothing to trouble yourself about.*

He nudged the volume up higher.

Richard was explaining how civilization had gotten only the merest taste of a cometary impact—a forty-megaton taste—in the wilderness of Tunguska, Siberia, in 1908. He then cautioned that what had occurred in the past was bound to recur in the future, and that with the human population spreading now even into Siberia, even a Tunguska event could no longer be risked.

"That's why we need the Powell launcher!" he exclaimed, and went into a monologue about something called Project Spaceguard and the Valkyrie Mark One rocket, with which it would somehow be possible to detect and destroy an incoming comet long before it got anywhere near Earth. It was all getting a little over the top for Russ, but it did not matter.

Richard did not know yet that many of his assumptions were wrong, and that Earth was only now about to yield up its secrets to him.

The next screams were louder, nearer, and more numerous. Russ shut off the volume and ran toward the window, where he discovered that he had not been hearing the shrieks of kids horsing around after all, but cries of pain and terror.

Below, under the floodlamps of Magnolia Park, he saw a girl rolling on the ground in what he first thought to be a wool sweater. Two bundles of clothing lay nearby, and within them, shreds of flesh moved. Only one of her friends still stood, and he, too, seemed to be wearing wool—black wool. Or red. Or both. The boy batted at himself as he ran, and screamed, *"Oh God oh God please get it off me oh no oh God oh no no noooo——"*

It seemed to Russ that the screamer might actually have made it out of the park had he not bounced off a fence post and crashed into a picnic table that likewise seemed to be covered with wool. The boy fell and did not move again.

On shaky legs, Russ backed away from the window, sat down hard on his bed, and began dialing 911. No sooner had the dispatcher picked up than he heard a movement behind him—but that was impossible. He had been alone in his bed all night, and there was a Medeco on his door.

When he turned, however, he realized to his horror that he was no longer alone in his bed, and that being bored had been the least of his worries.

2

Awakenings

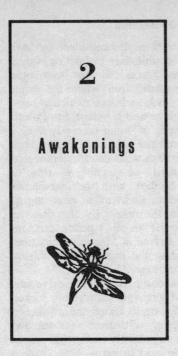

DAY 1

Long Beach was a compromise for Richard Sinclair. Although his wife, Dawn, had accompanied him on expeditions to Mongolia and Australia, she was a born and bred city woman and found it impossible to live more than a short train ride outside Manhattan. Richard, for his part, would have been perfectly content living in the outback of Australia; but he knew that he would have gone every bit as mad living in the confines of Manhattan as Dawn would have in Mongolia. Even Stonybrook and the Hamptons were too country for her. "Too many trees," she had said. "They attract insects."

So they settled in the little city of Long Beach, less than an hour's train ride out of Penn Station. Their hometown was cut off from the rest of the continent by bays and marshlands, and was accessible only by boat or bridge. And Richard liked it that way. Just a few steps from home lay the open spaces of the Atlantic, from which the winds brought clean air, on most days, and upon which no one had built cities yet—although he and physicist Jim Powell had been dreaming up methods of doing precisely that.

Shortly after Russ, Jon, and the kids in Magnolia Park had made their acquaintance with what newscasters would come to call the *motes*, Richard was speeding west out of Suffolk County's Viacom Studios, with the marshlands and pine barrens of the Ocean Parkway to one side of him, the Atlantic Ocean on the other. By the time he reached the Jones Beach Tower, the first police cars, responding to a 911 call, had arrived at Magnolia Park, and a new call was going out into the night: *"Two officers down. Require immediate assistance."*

By the time he had parked the car in his driveway, checked to see that his little girl was comfortably tucked in, brushed his teeth, snuggled up to Dawn and awakened her with his cold feet, another cry of distress went out, and the line to the state capital was suddenly alive with voices.

Prompt government action was to prove little, except perhaps how frail is the structure of civilization before the onslaught of nature. Upon receiving descriptions of unexplained deaths on Long Island, a governor's aide called the Centers for Disease Control in Atlanta, wasting more than an hour trying to pass along a vague, third-hand account of "carnivorous dust" to a woman whose specialty happened to be viral infections.

It did not matter.

As they spoke over the phone, the pitiless black pool came up from the shore, swarmed into the open windows of the two oceanfront condos on either side of Magnolia Park, up the walls of parlors, into bedding and night-clothes. But the dust of Earth—turned now into eighty billion sets of slashing fangs, and before sunrise into 120 billion—was not really the shatterer of humanity's dreams, the devourer of what Richard had seen as the coming Golden Age. The bureaucrats and the scientists would have to look elsewhere for that.

Dust was merely the putrefaction that spreads after the last breath has been drawn, the outward and visible sign of death's presence. And so, as Richard slept and the governor's aide pleaded for advice, the world of their commonplace habits and social order was dead already, although to itself alive-seeming still.

"Daddy, you're silly."

On the wide TV screen, Richard's allosaur lay on its back, yowling and kicking from the tail swipe delivered by little Tam's stegosaur—re-created in graphics so real as to render even the computer-animated marvels of *Jurassic Park III* badly drawn cartoons by comparison.

As cockroaches watched from a thicket of dandelions in the foreground, the dying allosaur coughed blood and was assailed by the pterosaurian equivalent of vultures.

"New life!" Richard called out, and the allosaur dissolved into a pile of crumbling bones, then to white powder—which was swept offscreen by a gust of wind. And then a familiar purple shape entered from stage left, a little surprise Richard had programmed especially for Tam, but which would not go into the final, commercial version of the game.

"I'm gonna get you, Steggie!" Richard called to the champion.

Nine-year-old Tam pointed her cyber glove at the screen, said, "It's clobberin' time!" and laughed. Before he could even duck, the purple, grinning *T. rex* was spouting blood from six wounds.

"I hate you," Richard chanted to the age-old tune of "This Old Man."

"You hate me," Tam chimed in—

And then, in two-part harmony:

"We're a dysfunctional family,

With a whip-smack, paddy-whack,

with a two-by-four.

No more purple dinosaur!"

"Whale kiss!" Richard called, and stuck out his tongue like Shamu, threatening to plant a long, wet trail of saliva on her cheek.

"Yuck! Gross!" Tam hollered. Kicking and giggling, she jumped away to the far side of the couch.

Richard put a finger to his lips. "Shhhh! Don't wake Mommy."

Tam looked sideways toward the hallway and the bedrooms, listening intently for sounds of stirring. There was only silence. Mommy was supposed to work "the graveyard shift" tonight, Daddy had said. Mommy needed her sleep.

"Sorry, Daddy," she said in a whisper.

"It's okay, bunch. Now, what say we tuck ourselves around some breakfast?"

Richard removed his cyber gloves, clicked on a music video, and scooped up a forkful of scrambled eggs. The eggs had gone cold and the orange juice was warming— too long neglected in favor of the video game; but for as long as Richard lived, whenever he looked back upon this simple breakfast, it would seem extraordinary to him that on this blackest of black Mondays he had done anything so ordinary as sip orange juice and play video games with his daughter, while only a few short blocks away the dark stain that was to bring calamity to everyone and everything he held dear had already begun the process of dissolution, spreading out of Magnolia Park and working its poison upon the skin of planet Earth. And it came to pass that breakfast was not all that Richard had neglected this morning. The very technologies he cherished, and which he was now advancing, were making it increasingly possible—if not downright attractive—to cut oneself off from the everyday world in favor of a world of one's own. He had spent his first waking hour surfing the internet to Beijing for the latest news on a nest of baby tyrannosaur skeletons, then to Colombia for a census of insects in a new amber deposit. All morning long, with but the most casual flick of his wrist, he could have tuned in to CNN and known immediately that something was amiss in his neighborhood.

In the end it was technology that defeated Richard, that brought the storm bursting into his house to find it still occupied, that divided his family for conquest by allowing him to go through this last morning of the old world in ignorance of the fact that on a nearby stretch of beach the crew of a news helicopter had stepped out to investigate a pair of dark, "mote"-covered objects lying intertwined at the base of a lifeguard stand, only to become mote-covered objects themselves. Beyond this carnivorous no-man's-land, scarcely wider than a city block, was a picket of roadblocks, and beyond them an ever-widening fringe of excitement in which firefighters, police officers, and neighborhood volunteers ran from door to door, urging evacuation. This fringe had not yet reached the Sinclair household, and in the world beyond—in the Carolinas and the Azores and in the Tigris-Euphrates valley—those who did tune in to CNN were inclined, at first, to regard the disturbance at Long Beach with nothing more than morbid curiosity. There had been plagues and rumors of plagues before: Ebola virus; the New Guinea laughing sickness; killer bees; a species of amoeba that could multiply in a man's head and devour the entire brain within two hours; the chemosynthetic agent that had transformed a woman's blood into nerve gas; a bacterium that caused cows, pigs, and several children to explode. . . . Each, in its own time, had been trumpeted as an advancing plague, the gravest ever to threaten humanity; and each, in time, had fizzled into nothing.

Crises were always good for ratings, and the media heralded them at every opportunity. Someone could always be counted on to come forth from the university world and magnify a killer bee, an exploding cow, or any other oddity beyond all rational proportion. Typically the crisis singers were self-appointed know-it-alls who did not. But it did not matter. Everyone looked important on television, and the networks were coming more and more to resemble a crisis-of-the-month club, with plenty of noise and entertaining fury being bantered about, and too much crying wolf.

So it was possible to believe during the first hours of the last morning of the old world—as Richard brushed his teeth and then, very gently, so as not to wake her, kissed Dawn good-bye; as Tam covered a plate of eggs and put it in the refrigerator for Mommy; as a helicopter news team made its first and only encounter with the motes and the world looked on—that nothing particularly earthshaking was occurring in Long Beach. The sudden appearance of the motes was dramatic, yes—perhaps even a little terrifying—but by no means a true crisis.

Today was a big day for Tam. Richard was taking her to the old nuclear research facility at Brookhaven, to show her the new dinosaur exhibit he had been helping to build—big enough and interactive enough to fuel any nine year old's sense of wonder. Using the latest scanners, she would be able to see through what appeared, from the outside, to be a rather ordinary lump of reddish-gray rock, but which was actually a baby titanosaur skeleton still curled up in its egg. On 3-D computer projections she could stretch the fossil skeleton into a life-size adult.

Another scanning device would permit her to see, in all its astonishing detail, the first little snippets of DNA recovered from the titanosaur's bone marrow. These had turned out to be regulator genes, and using them on a completely fleshed-out computer simulation, Tam looked forward to shrinking a titanosaur to the size of a sheep dog. "For those of us who never quite outgrew *The Flintstones*," Daddy had explained, "you can have Dino running around."

Richard wondered. For years he and biophysicist Jackson Roykirk had talked about resurrecting the extinct, of turning genetic technology into the ultimate paleontological tool, so that living, breathing dinosaurs could one day be studied face-to-face. But for all the talk, the ongoing translation of ancient gene sequences into computer-animated saurians, combined with advances in holography, were rendering the whole idea of dinosaur cloning unnecessary.

As if virtual dinosaurs weren't big and wondrous enough, Richard thought acidly; and as if Tam's sense of wonder really needed much more fueling. Every Daddy's girl was the sweetest, the most irresistible, the smartest; but Richard's little girl was all of these and more—perhaps even a little too much more. It seemed to him she was already getting too smart for her teachers, for her parents, and for her own good. He was beginning to worry, as he became acquainted with her school principal on a first-name basis, that she would need a great deal of looking after as she got older; for the road ahead was bound to be unusually bumpy. She was a stubborn and independent child, and while these qualities were advantageous under the proper conditions, in the real world of classrooms and offices they formed a double-edged sword. Like Daddy, she would probably stink at office politics, and live to rue it. And when he thought of the difficulties that lay ahead, he felt a measure of guilt for instilling these very qualities in her almost from the moment she was born. At three months, she had closed her fist around a jade charm hanging from his neck and given him by Dawn on their wedding day. He'd intended to pass it on to Tam years later, when she came of age; but try as he did, he could not make her let it go.

"Good, good," he whispered to her, and then, although he knew that she could not understand the words, he said, "Remember this: What you do not give back, no one can take away from you."

Today, as Richard closed the front door and Tam hurried across the lawn toward the driveway, she still had the jade charm. It hung from her neck on a silver chain.

The early morning air was wonderfully still, and the sun, just clearing a row of rooftops in the direction of Magnolia Park, already felt warm on Richard's face. He noticed, when he opened the passenger door and boosted Tam up and into the Jeep, that her shoes were soaked. His, too.

Something seemed not quite right, but when he looked across the front yard the only sight that caught his attention was a grayish layer of dew on the grass, the perfectly harmless remnant of a thick mist that had come up during the night. From the feel of the sun, he guessed the dew would be burned off before the first coffee break at Brookhaven.

Too bad there was a museum to be built, he thought. This was promising to be a beautiful beach day.

Later, when he'd had time to think about the last walk he would ever take out the front door of his house, he remembered the tall stand of pines near the garage, and he remembered the bird feeders Tam had hung in them; but he was unable to remember hearing any birds this morning, or any other stirrings except the faint but persistent whooping of police sirens and helicopter activity somewhere in the distance.

As Jackson Roykirk drove east toward exit 68 and Brookhaven Labs, tweaking an old Ramones album up to full volume, he was every bit as isolated from the news as Richard Sinclair.

Distractions were usually bad for science and family life. And because the most pressing distractions often involved high-tech toys and were actually fun, a great effort of will was required to weed them out of one's life. Jackson had discovered very early that it was easy to lose a whole morning surfing the internet, battling a never-retreating flood tide of new information. He solved the problem by making only the most infrequent ventures into the net and by building a digital wall at his end of the line to keep out all but a close circle of friends or persons bearing irrefutable news of such low-probability events as:

Ark of the Covenant, unearthing of
sound barrier, breaking of, by propeller-driven airplane in
    level flight
Jesus, Second Coming of
plesiosaurus, in Loch Ness, capture of
Roswell U.F.O., delivery to my office of

or his favorite,

Republican Party, entire, spontaneous human
    combustion of.

CNN and talk radio had also been weeded out of his morning routine. Instead, he enjoyed breakfast and music with his wife (she preferred Australian rock bands, he favored neo-country punk). It did not seem to matter that Jackson began his days cut off from the rest of the world. Any really important news would reach him quickly enough at the lab. Besides, some of his best ideas seemed to pop up after breakfast with Ann, while listening to the Ramones or the Good Rats and stuck in traffic on the Long Island Expressway. Hypersonic maglev trains, the Nomad space probe, and nearly two hundred patents owed their origins to "the Distressway."

Today it was the local economy that occupied Jackson's thoughts. In a few short miles he had passed a new Wal-Mart "super center" under construction and two billboards announcing the grand opening of yet another shopping mall. He wondered where the money to support all that hoped-for shopping was supposed to come from. Except for a wealth of ideas emerging from places like Brookhaven, Long Island produced and exported nothing. There was a time when the island had produced airplanes, submarines, and rockets—including the ship that landed Neil and Buzz on the moon. Now, it seemed, more and more people were employed behind counters in shopping malls, or derived their income from the building of the malls, so they could spend their earnings at the malls. Local politicians gave sweeping tax and utility cuts to the mall owners, so they could employ local salespeople, security guards, and construction workers, who paid for the privilege of employment with increased tax and utility rates, to make up for the cuts to the owners.

It occurred to Jackson that Long Island was evolving into a hundred-mile-long, twenty-mile-wide cat-rat farm. How do you raise the cats? Great idea: Just feed them the rats. And what do you feed the rats? Simple, you give them the cats!

Better hold your tongue on that thought, Jackson told himself. If the word gets out, and people realize that it might be true, they'll abandon the island in droves—

(yes, like rats fleeing a sinking ship)

—Right! Just go ahead and crash the Long Island tax base; and when you get that call from the governor, you can bet it won't be an invitation to play golf.

Jackson was still developing his cat-rat-farm theory of economics, and the traffic had scarcely begun to snarl up ahead, when he noticed that an E-MAIL ALERT was flashing on his notepad. Lifting the pad from the passenger seat and simultaneously snapping it open, he wondered, with a start, whether it was Jesus, a plesiosaur, or news from a friend.

The voice chip and the little flat screen called out at once: MESSAGE FROM KENNY WAYVILLE, WELLINGTON, NEW ZEALAND.

"Should I continue?" asked the computer.

"Go ahead," replied Jackson.

The machine told him that Kenny and Connie Wayville were now the proud parents of a boy, born 8:51 A.M. New Zealand time, weight six pounds nine ounces, length twenty inches. Both mother and child were healthy and happy and the boy was to be named Christopher.

This was the last good news Jackson Roykirk was to hear for a very long time.

Richard was falling behind schedule. Broadway, his usual route out of Long Beach, was blocked by police cars—which raised not the slightest tingle of concern in him, for in this city it was perfectly normal for whole avenues to be blocked off on any given day. Richard guessed that work crews were repainting already twice repainted parking lanes—or some such nonsense—and after uttering a string of words Dawn would not have approved of his teaching their daughter, he detoured north, then east toward Jones Beach, turning up the volume on an Elvis collection and making Tam wince. She pointed an index finger at her mouth and made exaggerated vomiting gestures.

"Give the King a chance," Richard protested. "He produced some good records in his time."

"What's a record?" Tam replied, making him feel as if he'd been born in the Silurian Period.

He turned the volume down for her; but he did not turn the recording off, and he did not learn (as he would have if he had ejected the disk and switched on the radio) why two news helicopters were racing overhead, whence he had come, or why he was noticing more cars on the road than were usual for this time of the morning—all of them heading away from the city.

Minutes later, as they drove through marshlands on the

Loop Parkway, Tam began displaying Daddy's e-mail on her laptop.

"There's a letter here from Uncle Bill and Aunt Janet," she announced proudly. "They're someplace. . . . sounds like two bagels. I don't know all the words, but something's bad."

"Let the computer read it aloud," Richard said.

Tam made a scrawling motion with her touch pen, and the voice program activated: "Message from Bill and Janet Schutt, isle of Tobago: Field season going poorly. Bad juju down here. All the native bats appear to be dying. Starving. We've seen only one or two vampires alive, and they're not even supposed to be on this island! I have some thoughts on this; but, Rich, this is totally whacked. I must speak with you ASAP. Message ends."

Tam felt sad. Uncle Bill had taught her to respect and admire bats; and his favorite lab specimen, Lestat—a large, fruit-eating flying fox—had taught her to *adore* them. Most children perceived bats as being cold and creepy; but Tam had come to know them as warm and alert animals, some as affectionate as dogs, others diabolically clever.

She remembered the story of the roost of vampire bats Bill had encountered on the island of Trinidad. No larger than baby chicks, they had learned to hop and chirp like chicks in distress, tricking mother hens to take them under protective wings by nuzzling against their nerve-sheathed brood patches and triggering an instinctive, irresistible nesting urge. The brood patch was also sheathed in blood vessels, and once taken under wing, the bats turned against their unsuspecting "mothers" with fangs so sharp that the hens could not even feel, much less comprehend, what was happening to them.

She looked at her father. "Is it true, Daddy? Vampire bats drink blood?"

Richard smiled. "Yes," he said.

"And the biggest bats eat fruit?"

"Right."

"And the rest?"

"Insects, mostly."

"Yuck!"

"Right. Yuck!"

"Uncle Bill's weird," Tam said, and began to sing the song Bill had taught her during his last visit.

"DNA—"

"P.C.R.," Richard joined in, to the tune of "This Old Man."

"O.J.'s blood was in the car.

Daddy's built a micro-M.R.I.—

Barney clones—that ain't no lie!"

They sang two more choruses. Then another. And another. And when he could bear to sing it no more, Richard turned up the volume on "Heartbreak Hotel," making Tam frown, as if she were being forced to drink something bitter; but aside from his daughter's apparent lack of taste in music, the rest of the trip was pleasant and uneventful. Richard did not hear it on his radio, or see it in his rearview mirror: Barely a minute after he crossed the Loop Parkway drawbridge, the giant levers went up and did not come down again. There was no longer a road home. Long Beach was now a city surrounded by a moat, and where the moat began, so too began the quarantine.

His name was Ed Bishop and unlike some of his colleagues he did not make a habit of cutting himself off from the rest of the world each morning. Nor was he particularly surprised by the developments in Long Beach. He had seen something like this coming for a very long time. That few of his peers believed him had as much to do with his religious orientation—they called him a "nature worshiper"—as with the fact that his official position at New Jersey's Lucent Technologies laboratory was "engineer," not "zoologist."

"The time has come," he called over the pad-link to his old friend Edwin Wilson, "to talk about many things—about frogs and mayflies and darning needles, but mostly about species diversity."

"Or its apparent decline?" his friend said.

"Yes. That might explain your new problem."

"*My* problem?"

"*Your* problem," Bishop said. "If Long Beach isn't a

job for the Centers for Disease Control, then who else's problem is it?''

''Just about everyone's, if your theory turns out to be right.''

Theory was not quite the proper word. Bishop had noticed some odd changes in a creek near his home, then in a local stream, then in a river—and he could not yet provide a detailed explanation, or even a testable one, for what was happening. Caddis fly larvae and dragonfly larvae and a lot of other aquatic insects had been declining in numbers for more than a year. This past spring, it seemed to him that only a handful of species had survived the winter, and now they, too, were almost impossible to find. Bishop's physician friend, Joshua Lederberg, had confirmed that the phenomenon was not confined to New Jersey's creeks and rivers. Lederberg's own census revealed similar declines of species diversity in Canadian and New Hampshire lakes. The frogs and salamanders—and now the trout—appeared to be in as much trouble as the dragonflies. Bishop and Lederberg could not discern whether aquatic insects and their predators had declined together—perhaps as a result of acid rain—or whether the decline of one group was triggering the decline of the other.

''Evolution is chaos with feedback,'' Bishop was often heard to say. Late at night, he liked to entertain thoughts of rendering evolution more predictable, of making population dynamics as exact a science as orbital mechanics. He sometimes believed he might turn the trick, if all the little bits of feedback could somehow be measured and taken into account. His supervisors told him he might just as well try doing magic.

''Has anyone been listening to me?'' asked Bishop. ''Anyone besides you?''

''I hate to say this, but except for one of my old students at Pacific Tech, almost no one at all.''

''I don't believe this, Dr. Wilson—''

Dr. Wilson—again. He kept calling him that in spite of Edwin's request that he stop. Although more than a decade had passed since Bishop last sat in his classroom, and notwithstanding Edwin's insistence that his student-turned-old-friend call him by his first name, Bishop discovered that he could no more stop calling him "Dr. Wilson" than he could stop calling his own father "Dad."

"I don't believe this," he said again. "Josh and I submitted our letter to *Nature On-line* more than two months ago."

"And they haven't published it yet—I know."

"Why not?"

Wilson shrugged. "Maybe you shouldn't have mentioned acid rain. Someone probably thinks you're crisis-crying. And for heaven's sake, Ed—why did you have to title it, 'Multiple Miseries Bugging Us All'? Too bombastic. And then there's Joshua's frothy conclusions—these *are* his words, aren't they?"

"Which ones?"

"The part about how we must make some sort of Golden Rule pact with the Earth while there is still time?"

"Yes, that's him."

"And this?" Wilson asked, and read from his advance copy of the letter: " 'If people are jolted by the arrival of increasingly resistant bacteria and viruses, by ozone holes and global warming, then they should be equally alarmed that the conditions could be ripe for other surprises. There will be more surprises because our fertile imaginations do not begin to match all the tricks that nature can play.' "

"I'm afraid that's a conclusion we both came to," said Bishop. "I stand by it."

"It's very poetic, Ed, but it's not science. Jesus, how do you test something like that?"

"You don't test it. It tests you. If our census reveals anything at all, it's that the whole world could be a test tube right now, and we're stuck in it."

There was a gloomy silence on the line while Wilson considered the image Bishop had just painted for him. Then, after a slight shudder, the CDC scientist said, "I don't like what you're driving at, and neither will anyone else."

"They don't have to like it—all I need them to do is publish it."

"Not to worry, old friend. I'm on your side. I found very little to fault in your census, save its title and your occasional lapses into editorializing and melodrama. But I'm afraid our little enigma in Long Beach makes even your editorial—''

''A little relevant?''

''A little interesting. Perhaps a little *too* interesting. As I said, no one is going to like it, but I'll try to filter your idea through Washington—it'll probably take two or three days to sink in—and then I expect you'll be able to come down and say I told you so.''

''Thanks for the suggestion; but I'll settle for just coming down and shaking your hand.''

Wilson laughed. ''Did you forget? We don't shake hands at the CDC.''

3

Defining a Crisis

On that hot last Monday of the old world, America was at work, in tens of millions, and at vacation in the countryside and in the cities—again in tens of millions—in trains, hydrofoils, airplanes, and minivans. Americans were busy trying to realize large ambitions or small ambitions or having no ambitions at all, happy or unhappy because they felt like ambitious dreamers or did not feel like ambitious dreamers. Wherever they went, leaving good families or bad jobs or good towns, they spoke excitedly or unexcitedly about the broadcasts from Long Beach, afraid or unafraid, because they believed in the latest crisis or did not believe in it, or because they did not know what to believe.

The President had believed, when he spoke with the New York governor earlier in the morning, that whatever was menacing Long Beach would, at worst, require him to decide whether or not to declare the barrier island a

National Disaster Area. Either way, it was bound to cost the insurance companies and the taxpayers a pretty penny before the mess was cleaned up—and sooner or later that was bound to cost votes.

Now the phone rang again. His notepad screen went on automatically with the phone's buzzing. Any call patched through to his office had to be serious; but it was not the red phone, thank God; not the bad phone, the one he prayed nightly about to an agnostic's Jesus—"just in case you're there"—hoping for God's good grace against its ever ringing. This was the white phone, the good phone.

"Amber Murdoch, here." His chief of staff. As the President had requested of her, this phone call was also connected to specialists at the Centers for Disease Control in Atlanta and to General Andrews in New York, who had recommended the quarantine.

"Yes, Amber?"

"I've been researching the situation, speaking with the experts"—she cleared her throat, and the President's notepad began to display enlarged images of bodies lying on the beach where the first news helicopter had landed—"and the one thing they all agree on is that we're not up against a new kind of virus."

The President breathed a relieved, "Thank God."

"Even so, it's not going to be a picnic," said Murdoch. "Here"—the view of the beach began to change—"the guys at Lucent have been able to stretch the video for us. Now, if we zoom in on that first body lying in front of the cockpit, you can make out the fingers of the right hand clearly."

"What's all that graininess?" Countless black spots covered what was left of the fingers, and the grains shifted with every new frame, as if the video had been stretched beyond its limits.

"Those," Murdoch said, "are not your usual video grains. They're quite real. We appear to be looking at some kind of insect swarm."

"Insects?" *How the hell did* that *happen?*

Andrews broke in. "We're not even certain they're insects, sir. Our Atlanta people tend to specialize in microbes. Things that *cause* disease. Unless we're talking about mosquitoes, tsetse flies, or some other infectious beast, it's just outside their realm of expertise. These things in Long Beach: They don't *cause* infection, they *are* the infection.''

Another voice broke in. ''Ed Wilson here. I'm what you'd call the CDC's resident entomologist. I thought they might be ants at first; but we've ruled out that possibility. We've since spoken with Dr. Coher at L.I.U., and we relayed to him the enhanced video. There's not enough detail to say exactly what they are, but Coher is placing his bet on arachnids.''

''Spiders? Is that what everyone's so afraid of? A bunch of spiders?''

''Something like that,'' said Wilson, more calmly than he felt. He had never quite outgrown his childlike love of the ''creepy crawlers,'' and he often spoke in a jargon that was bewildering to almost anyone who did not share his sense of wonder for the insects, who did not marvel over the empires that thrived at the base of a tree. He had half expected to embarrass himself before the President, and was both surprised and relieved to be speaking with a man who caught on fast and did not have to be told what entomologists and arachnids were. ''What we're looking at,'' he continued, ''is probably something very ordinary turned into a plague organism.''

''Back to my original question: How does something like this happen?''

''It happens all the time. Keep in mind that the littler forms of life have pervaded every nook and cranny of the Earth's surface. Even under normal conditions, if you examined any four or five city blocks in Long Beach or Manhattan or Washington, D.C., you'd discover that there are more arachnids in those few city blocks than there are people on Earth. Coher was telling me that whole ecologies thrive on the little flakes of dead skin that fall off us at night while we sleep. The sheets on your bed support a population of at least two million mites, and as we speak, hundreds, perhaps thousands, of them are feeding beneath the skin at the base of your eyelashes—but you do not see them or feel them and had I never mentioned them you would not even have suspected their existence . . . under normal circumstances.''

''I don't suppose,'' the President said, rubbing an eye with his free hand, ''that there is a way for me to list them as dependents on my tax return?''

The others on the line responded with hollow chuckles or with no laughter at all. The chief of staff put it bluntly: ''Dr. Wilson, you said this happens all the time? Plague organisms?''

''Sure. If the humidity and temperature line up just right, for just the right number of weeks, so that most of the eggs survive, and if there happens to be enough food to sustain a population explosion, and if, at the same time, a natural predator happens to be removed from the scene, you end up with the plagues of locusts that have been terrorizing people since biblical times or with a ten-mile-long swarm of army ants devouring farmlands and farmers along the Amazon River.

''No one is quite sure what conditions are necessary to create these sorts of population surges, but it looks to me as if Long Beach is very good at something other places are bad at. We've got records of a slime mold coming out of the ground, growing into chicken egg–sized blobs, and spreading all over Long Island in 1973. The media had a field day with that one. They even got U.F.O.s into the act before it was all settled. In 1979 there was a plague of yellow jackets. Like the blobs, it threatened to spread statewide. In 1991 it was fleas. The whole town had to be fumigated. In 1994: mites. There's a report of pine trees being eaten to their bare limbs in a single afternoon.''

General Andrews's worried voice came then. ''So if you're going to have a plague in New York, it's most likely to begin in Long Beach?''

''I think so,'' said the entomologist. ''The old adage that lightning never strikes twice in the same place is a total fallacy. When lightning strikes a tree, that's because the tree happens to be the tallest object (and hence the best conductor) around—which means the conditions are right for it to get struck again.''

Andrews whistled. The governor and the President had thought him at best a tad hasty, at worst a tad paranoid, in pressing for the quarantine. Now he was beginning to view automobiles and parkways as disease vectors every bit as devastating as tsetse flies. Long Beach had four choke points: four bridges spaced at intervals averaging two miles between the Lido marshes and the Atlantic Beach toll gate. He hoped that all his assumptions were correct and that he had bottled the source of the infection up tightly before it could spread. He hoped so, but he really did not think so.

"Well, that much is settled," the President said. "We'll keep the quarantine."

"Just as a precaution?" said Murdoch.

"Yes. I'm sure we can wipe out a nest of bugs in only a day or two—and hopefully by tonight. But in the meantime I don't want a panic out there. I expect people outside the quarantine will be fleeing by dinnertime, if they're not hauling up stakes and leaving the state already. And God only knows what the survivors are thinking inside, behind those four raised drawbridges. Even a mile away from the swarm, where they might be considered safe, they must now be acutely aware of no more food coming by truck across the bridges, and if they begin to perceive this as a crisis stretching into days or weeks, then by midnight every supermarket and corner grocery store in town could become a war zone."

And the President began to suspect that no city, no matter how civilized or proud or pampered, could be more than two or three meals away from anarchy.

"I'll have to go on TV within the next three hours—*have to*. And I want to be able to tell them truthfully, especially in New York, that the quarantine is only a precaution and that the situation is under control. Now, the question of the hour is: Can I say this truthfully?"

"That depends," said Wilson.

"On what?"

"On what killed those people, for a start. And how fast we can kill it."

The chief of staff said, in her soft yet commanding tone, "If we have to, we can send men in with flamethrowers. It's a quick and dirty approach, but it should get the job done."

"If we have to," said Wilson, ". . . should work."

"By tomorrow morning at the latest," said Andrews, "and preferably by sunset today."

"Should work," the entomologist repeated. "Yes . . . if you're in a hurry . . ." He trailed off into thought, and no one seemed to notice that he had left his sentence unfinished. He frowned. Somewhere in the back of his mind, he knew that he had forgotten something, or overlooked something, or misunderstood something. It was the striped abdomen of a wasp that kept leaping up out of his subconscious—the stinging plague of the 1970s—something about wasps and bees that must not be forgotten, overlooked, or misunderstood.

"How soon can we sample and identify our . . . adversary?" asked the President.

"We've had a lucky break," said Andrews. "They've got an experimental blimp docked at Brookhaven, right where all the best diagnostic equipment happens to be. They're loading her right now—the fastest airship ever built, and damned near the biggest."

"How soon can it be there?"

"We can have the ship stationed over Long Beach within the hour; we'll have a firm diagnosis within two, two and a half hours at the outside, certainly in time for your speech."

Another voice entered the discussion, Leslie Wells on the com-link from Brookhaven. She had a background in insect pathology. She also had a well-known passion for spiders. "If they're arachnids, we should be able to clear the problem up quite easily. Spiders and mites hate detergent. Wipes them right out. Ordinary dish-washing fluid mixed with water should do the job in only a few minutes. No flamethrowers required, Mr. President—"

"Oh, morning, Leslie!"

"Good morning, Dr. Wilson. How do *you* read the evidence?"

"Certainly not microbes. Probably not insects. I agree with Coher: We must be looking at a swarm of spiders or mites. Mites would be my guess."

"Yes," said the pathologist, "it's just an isolated freak occurrence, Mr. President. I'm placing my bets on a species that came in with foreign produce, then found itself in a strange new environment with all its natural predators missing. In any case, you should be able to lower those drawbridges by breakfast.''

Reluctantly, it seemed, Wilson disagreed. ''I wish I could be as sure that this is going to be nothing more than an isolated incident. It's true that Long Beach has a history of getting struck by lightning, but certain information makes me wonder if this lightning strike might turn out to be the leading edge of a more widely spread storm.''

''You mean,'' the President said, ''like the statewide plague of wasps in seventy-nine, or the blobs of seventy-three?''

''I'm not sure, Mr. President. Every crisis has to start somewhere, so it might just as well be Long Beach. My worry is that even if you go in there with a tanker full of detergent and wipe those things out completely, you may be removing a symptom but getting nowhere near the cause. Long Beach isn't the only strange incident I've heard about lately. I don't know if it's new insecticides or what, but you'll notice quickly enough, if you go looking for them, that butterflies are virtually extinct this year. And just last week, lightning bugs entered the endangered species list. Lightning bugs, of all things—they used to be everywhere!''

''So, you don't think Long Beach is going to be a unique event?'' asked Leslie Wells.

''I have a friend—in fact he's the fellow who produced the enhanced video at Lucent. Bishop is his name. He's the only person I know who was not at all surprised by Long Beach. He says it may be an unanticipated effect of acid rain, or some other poison, but the net result is a decline in species diversity—which could trigger massive replacement events by the hardiest of the remaining species.''

The President looked at him quizzically.

''*Plague organisms,*'' Wilson emphasized. ''Swarms. This might be what happens when—if Bishop's population dynamics are correct—we begin to lose dragonflies, butterflies, frogs. . . .''

''Frogs!'' said Leslie Wells. ''I've heard about that.

And it makes no sense. Frogs have always been nature's great survivors. They even came through whatever killed the dinosaurs. But now they're just dying off—everywhere.''

"Any explanation?" asked the President.

"Not a clue," said Wells.

"And the bees!" Wilson added. "All of a sudden I'm getting calls from beekeepers—more and more of them every day—wanting to know if anyone at the CDC can explain why their hives are dying off. I've got dead bees arriving by the boxload—and the strangest thing: When I dissect them, I'm finding bee tracheae infested with parasitic mites. They've literally choked to death on mites.''

"Bee-eating mites?" said the chief of staff. "Is that what we're facing? A new species of mite?"

"No," said Wilson. "They're the same mites you'll normally find living inside bees. But they've grown completely out of control, much as the strep bacteria lining your throat will grow out of control if you are weakened by a flu virus. My guess is that the mites began multiplying because the bees were already dying from something else. The first rule of being a good parasite is not to kill your host. There's usually a balancing act involved—a sort of unspoken treaty between you and your host's immune defenses. If you kill the goose that lays the golden egg, more often than not you'll end up trapped inside the dead goose and starving to death.''

Wilson was an imaginative man who had just frightened himself. Long Beach . . . the frogs . . . the bees . . . could that be? Could these incidents be merely the first rumblings of an approaching storm, a black and terrible storm? He was reminded of the first ominous bump, six years earlier, just before the Beijing earthquake broke both his legs and killed a hundred thousand people. But, no—it couldn't be *that* bad.

"We need more evidence," Wilson continued. "We don't have all the science yet. Long Beach should tell us what we need to know.''

"How far"—the President seemed to choke on the word *far*—"How far is Long Beach from midtown Manhattan?"

"Twenty-five miles due east, sir."

"Shit."

"May you live in interesting times"; so went an ancient Chinese curse that on first hearing was designed to sound like a blessing. There was no question that something *interesting* was happening on Long Island, and no question in the President's mind that the media were going to make a major crisis out of a—what had the entomologist called it?—a plague organism? A plague organism in such proximity to New York City?

This was notoriously and most popularly a time of crises, most of them false; but the President did not know yet whether or not the Long Beach plague would turn out to be the genuine article. Wiser men than he had said that during a false crisis we always knew, to one degree or another, what was going to happen next, while during a true crisis—the bombing of Pearl Harbor, the bombing of Hiroshima, the orbiting of *Sputnik,* the explosion of *Challenger*—we not only knew nothing of what tomorrow might bring, we knew something much more frightening and more interesting: that nobody knew. Truly nobody.

"You should be able to lower those drawbridges by breakfast," Leslie Wells had said. So had Pliny the Elder spoken to his woman servant in A.D. 79, during the first rumblings of Vesuvius: "It's just a little volcanic dust. We'll have it cleaned up by dinnertime, my dear." If history served the President correctly, he knew that Pliny the Elder was still a permanent resident of Pompeii. But, no— it couldn't be *that* bad.

Yet by Thanksgiving the red phone would be ringing, and by New Year's Eve he would be dead.

4

City of Dreams

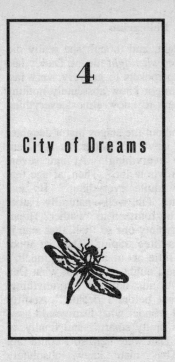

Tam watched excitedly as the research city of Brookhaven came into view: weirdly shaped buildings containing particle accelerators, DNA scanners, museums, and magnetic "bottles" where the search was now under way for a means of transforming antimatter into a practical, star-crossing rocket fuel.

The buildings were not all that looked weird. Anchored in a soccer field, the *Bluepeace* blimp resembled a wingless space shuttle eight hundred feet long. Tam knew that Daddy and his friend Jackson had been at work on the airship for as long as she had been alive. They had invented the carbon strings that held the ship together without any need for . . . something called girders, Tam remembered. Girders. This made it able to lift up more people and cargo, and Daddy was helping Jackson make rockets, too, that had strings in them. He said strings would make rockets ultralight, and though she really did not understand what the word *ultralight* meant, Daddy had explained that it would help rockets to go very, very fast and very, very far. Daddy might know absolutely nothing about music, but he did seem to know almost everything else.

There was an old saying about the stages that a daughter passes through in how she views her father. At age four, "Daddy knows absolutely everything!" At age seven, "My Daddy knows a lot, a whole lot." Then, at age ten, "My father doesn't know quite everything." By age twelve she has progressed to "Oh, well—naturally Father doesn't know that either," by fourteen to "Father? Hopelessly out of date," and by twenty-one to "Oh, that man is stupid—two-plus-two-equals-three stupid." Then, at about twenty-five: "He knows a little about it, but not much," and five years later, "Maybe I ought to find out what Dad thinks." Thirty-five years: "I must not rush into anything. Let me get Dad's assessment before I decide." At fifty she may be heard to say, "I wonder what Dad would have thought about that. He was pretty smart," and finally, at sixty, "I'd give anything if Dad were here so I could talk this over with him. That man knew absolutely everything!"

Tam, always ahead of herself, was now moving just beyond the third of these eleven stages. When the Jeep turned left toward the cafeteria and the public areas, she perceived a hive of activity at the base of the blimp. Usually people moved slowly at or near a laboratory. Daddy had always told her that *Rule Number One* in the lab was, "Never move fast. That's how accidents happen." Yet men were running from cars and trucks with big boxes in tow, and literally throwing them through the open doors of the ship's dining saloon.

For a fleeting instant she wondered if something had gone wrong with Daddy's strings, and if that might explain all the running and throwing. The rest of the day would be mostly a blur to Tam. Later, it came back to her only in snippets. She remembered Jackson waiting for them at the front door of the museum, telling Daddy, "We've got a problem." And she vaguely remembered halfheartedly tampering with regulator genes on a holo projection, asking the computer for advice on how to turn a dinosaur hatchling's skin purple, while little pieces of Daddy's conversation with Jackson reached her. . . . "My wife, my wife . . . still back there . . . you *must* put me on that blimp . . . I can help . . . I know the town . . . I know the airship inside and out . . . You've got to send me back . . . Got to!"

She could not recall Daddy hugging her good-bye, though she knew he must have done so before Jackson took her for a walk outside the museum and tried to explain that something bad had happened in Long Beach and that Daddy was going back with the blimp to find out how bad it really was.

Tam had only one question for him: "Is my Mommy hurt?"

"We don't know," came the reply. The words hit her like a punch in the stomach, burning that moment forever into her brain. She remembered the airship—nearly a sixth of a mile long—passing directly overhead as a surge of fear and adrenaline brought up her breakfast. Then, as Jackson knelt down to wipe her mouth with a tissue, and as the blimp's stern propeller and attitude control jets died off in the distance from a dull hum to nothing, Tam noticed something strange in the pine barrens that surrounded the museum. She heard a chipmunk in the distance, at least a hundred feet away, rooting around in a thick bed of pine needles. The sounds were crisp and sharp-edged, even at a distance, and Jackson, too, noticed that something was wrong. They seemed to realize at the same instant that the reason one little chipmunk could appear to create such a din was because there were no other sounds in the woods. None at all. No buzzing insects. No chirping birds. Nothing.

5

Long Beach

The *Bluepeace* blimp was never meant to generate a profit for Richard, or for any of her other builders or sponsors. She was officially on "permanent loan" to the Brazilian government, which was permitted to keep all the profits generated by this luxury liner of the air. It seemed to most people a bizarre if not scandalous arrangement, but only on first hearing. The airship *Bluepeace*'s mission was to save the Amazon and other waterways from human depredation, and the only way of accomplishing this was to make them too valuable to lose.

The deep ocean explorer Jason Bradley had realized that it would be far cheaper to build a touring, state-of-the-art airship and give it away than to write regulations, send in the U.N., hire lawyers, draw lines across the forest floor and along riverbanks, and to risk the inevitable exchanges of gunfire that would accomplish little except the hiring of more lawyers. And, as it turned out, the people who could most afford the *Bluepeace*'s exclusive staterooms were often the ones with the most incentive for slashing and burning the forests and silting the waterways. They were the ones who needed most to be dragged from their offices and sent cruising in an airship through Peruvian mountain passes, to be lowered on giant inflatable rafts for an overnight camping excursion in the treetops of the Amazon rain forest, and then to cruise, at treetop level, the Amazon itself.

Of course, there had been the problem of convincing the public that a helium-filled airship would not repeat the *Hindenburg*'s closing act. The point had been made, and made again, that the *Hindenburg* had been equipped with gasoline-fired engines, a kitchen in which food was constantly being fried—even a smoking room—and yet some cynical Nazi got the brilliant idea that they could fill that ship with explosive hydrogen gas and everything would be all right. The point made, the *Bluepeace*'s first season had proved so successful that she was now booked for the next two years and still booking.

To relieve the pressure—and to generate more profits—two additional airships were now about to be built, one as a permanent loaner, the other to be financed by Brazil.

So many Amazon-based purses were now being filled that the industrialists, sensing a mother lode of tourist dollars, could afford to send the airship back to Brookhaven for a major upgrading. A minisub had been bought from Japan and was being refitted so it could serve as a touring submersible, to be lowered from the *Bluepeace*'s undercarriage during cruises to the Galapagos and Antarctic shores.

Richard regretted that he had not suggested writing into the loan agreement a stipulation that one month out of each year be reserved for scientific expeditions, because the airship would soon be the finest oceanographic research vessel afloat. Built mostly from cornstarch derivatives—which Richard and Jackson had fashioned into light yet astonishingly strong filaments and hull sections—the ship had an unprecedented capacity to lift heavy equipment, dining saloons, staterooms, and people. Her single, solar-powered propeller gave her almost unlimited range and, unlike a conventional research vessel, she never had to ride out a storm. Graced with pressurized and heated cabins, she could climb from the ocean at the first call from a satellite, warning of an approaching hurricane; and her passengers could watch from on high, in brilliant sunshine, as the storm's steepest cloud banks passed more than a mile below.

"Perhaps next time," Jackson had said. "Perhaps next time we'll remember to write expedition time into the contract."

But Richard was not thinking about expedition time, as he sat in the dining saloon, with two men checking the cooling system and oxygen feeds on his plastic space suit, and with Leslie Wells unfurling a makeshift microscopy lab behind him. His helmet lay on the table, and he stared out a long row of windows overlooking the Southern State Parkway, thinking of Dawn being overtaken as suddenly as the helicopter crew in Leslie's video, almost losing his composure, then forcing himself to think of something else.

It can't be that bad, he told himself. *It's just one of those scary moments, like the night Tam disappeared and you called in the police to scour the neighborhood and all the while she was curled up in a small corner of the basement pantry, sleeping. You'll see, the swarm never even reached the house, or if it did, Dawn got out in plenty of time or buttoned herself in real tight.*

The panic attack began to subside.

You'll see, he repeated inwardly. *By lunchtime this will be just another science project.*

Just another science project . . . Jason Bradley had once compared Brookhaven National Laboratory to the best bar in every town. It was a well-known fact on expedition ships that, after a month out at sea, people who had gotten tired of one another after living together in close quarters day after day always went their separate ways the moment the ship docked in a new town. Yet by ten o'clock that night everyone invariably began drifting into the same bar, because after going their separate ways, each crew member stopped in the first bar he could find, and after a while he would begin asking people where they would recommend going next, and of course the final place was always the best place in town and by midnight the whole crew would be together again. The only real difference between Brookhaven and the best bar was that people like Richard Sinclair, Jackson Roykirk, and Jim Powell had not begun as members of the same crew. Brookhaven was just the point at which they all seemed destined to collide.

There were certain teachers about whom the same thing could be said. Richard's personal favorite was Doc Wilson, who had once put a protective wing over him and directed him toward the City of Dreams. It seemed to him that almost everyone who was anyone in the sciences had somehow known Wilson, at one time or another, as "teacher."

For Richard, life had been a search for good teachers. Fortunately or unfortunately, he never quite fit in with the university world, where one was always under pressure to choose some obscure branch of some narrow field and become the world's leading expert on, say, the evolutionary significance of the slug's anus or the environment inside a burning cigarette.

Richard's worst stroke of luck came when he found himself in a department whose members actually published papers with such titles as, "The Form and Function of the Barnacle Penis," "Homosexual Rape in Acanthocephalan Worms," "The Hagfish Slime Gland: A Model System for Studying the Biology of Mucus," "How Does the Toad Flip Its Tongue?" "Some Thoughts on the Jugular Vein of the Giraffe." In the midst of such hyperspecialization, Richard's own conversations tended to jump without warning from some aspect of deep-ocean biology to cryovolcanism on a moon of Saturn, then back to the high seas and deep under them. And where ideas about dinosaur DNA and antimatter-fueled rockets were supposed to fit in with any of this was anyone's guess. His supervisors all agreed that he had to go. The only question that divided them was, "This shooting off in all directions like a jet boat without a rudder: Is he trying to show off or is he just plain crazy?"

By the time he flopped up on the steps of Brookhaven, he arrived with the distinction of having had two of his laboratories smashed to pieces by angry colleagues. By that time he was beginning to regard himself as an unwanted freak; but with Wilson's help, he had found at last, in the City of Dreams, a circle of polymathic misfits just like himself, all of them one another's best teachers (and students), all of them exploring the sciences for the sheer, rip-roaring fun of it.

All, it seemed, except Leslie Wells. She had arrived from Pacific Tech only a week ago, for what was originally to be two or three lectures and a look at the new DNA "readers" and "printers"; but recent developments seemed bound to keep her on Long Island for a while.

She struck Richard as belonging to that species of scientist who took the mere label "scientist" as an opportunity to pretend they were superior to the rest of humanity, and who wore the badge of Darwin and Einstein with an attitude of "those of you who think you know it all can be very annoying to those of us who really do." Fortunately, they were a rare species; but whenever Richard found a specimen, it seemed always to turn up in the university world—and for some damned reason, it was too often elevated to an administrative position, where it could do the most harm and give scientists a bad name. Richard had a name for her species. He called them university brats.

Leslie, for her part, regarded Richard as a man educated beyond his abilities, and had wasted no time in telling him so. She felt justified in her grudge against Richard. A year ago she had discovered an intact dinosaur virus, and had wanted to clone it for more intensive study. But Richard intervened and stopped her project dead in its tracks by crisis-crying about the dangers of resurrecting a virus that had been out of circulation for more than sixty-five million years.

"What if it got out of the laboratory?" he had said. "What if it happened to be lethal to birds, or to the reptiles, or to any other close relatives of the dinosaurs? You could shake the whole world ecology from the bottom up." He spoke these words half angrily, half jokingly, and Leslie could not quite tell if he was being serious when, smiling indulgently, he had said, "What is this? If we're not smart enough to clone a dinosaur, let's aim for a simpler target and clone a dinosaur virus instead?"

"But the odds!" Leslie had argued. "My lab is sealed tighter than the Lunar Receiving Laboratory. The odds of a saurian virus getting out, and on top of that being lethal to present-day life, are as low as your odds of walking up to a Las Vegas slot machine and hitting the progressive jackpot on the very first try."

"Precisely my point: Someone does that about every other week. Now tell me: Does the world really need dinosaur chicken pox?" He had laughed; but she took it as a gesture of arrogance, as an intended affront. As Richard himself was quick to admit, he seemed to be missing that little internal radar most people took for granted, the one that told them, when they detected a raising of the brows or a slight drop of the jaw, that they had offended someone and should tread lightly. If he had just let his argument stand on its own merit, rather than fashioning it into a joke at Leslie's expense, she might even have sided with him and there might now be no hard feelings between them. The idea of accidentally wiping out the world's bird or lizard populations had seemed far-fetched to her at the time, but now she was having ideas of her own that sounded even more far-fetched.

Something about the present crisis, the real crisis, worried her more than Richard's imagined crisis of a year ago. If she had not been prevented from disturbing the sleep of a saurian virus, and if it *had* gotten out of her laboratory, and if it *had* proved deadly to birds or reptiles, then perhaps future history might now be changing. Outwardly she voiced the hope that the Long Beach problem would be wrapped up before breakfast, but inwardly she echoed the same worry Wilson and his friend Bishop had expressed: that the deaths might be symptoms of a larger problem. This brought to mind what now ranked as the strangest analogy she had ever made: She recalled the physician Jesse Stoff's discovery that certain inflammatory diseases could prevent the development of cancer, and she wondered if a resetting of Earth's ecology by her saurian virus might have similarly prevented the present crisis, if only Richard had been right, if only the virus had gotten out, and if only Richard had not stopped her.

(If only . . .)

Richard was testing his suit's com-link with Jackson, back at the lab, when he felt sudden pangs of hunger. He asked a member of his checkout team to mix him an Instant Breakfast in milk and coffee.

Leslie shook her head. "I guess even geniuses have to eat."

"How is it that I always seem to attract people like her?" Richard whispered to Jackson. "And how is it that I always manage to bring out the worst in them?"

"Ah," said Jackson. "It's because you always talk about so many strange things."

"But you're always talking about the same strange things!"

"Yes. But I'm seven feet tall and weigh three hundred pounds. I'm more intimidating. People will always think twice before they smash up one of my laboratories."

One of the engineers brought him a steaming drink and as he sipped, he noticed that Leslie was running footage of the mote-covered helicopter crew on her notepad. He ran a hand over the white plastic covering his legs. "I wonder if they'll be able to eat through this?"

Leslie shot him an icy grin. "You'll find out soon enough."

From A deck forward, the copilot called over the intercom, "Long Beach bearing five minutes directly ahead. We are approaching from the northeast. Instructions?"

"Come in as low as you can over Magnolia Park," said Leslie. "I want those high-resolution cameras running as soon as we reach the edge of town. Give us as close a shot as you can get without snaring us in the treetops."

An instant later, Richard heard Tam over the com-link. "Find Mommy," Tam demanded.

Mercifully, Jackson asked someone to take the girl back to the cafeteria. Even if her mother had survived—and as yet no one had been able to reach her on the phone—no one really wanted Tam to see what was approaching on the view screens.

At six hundred feet, the ship printed a shadow longer than its altitude on the channel between Long Beach and Long Island. Richard saw, as the pilots continued to push down the altimeter, that the quarantine could not possibly hold. Magnolia Park was located on the south side of town, and hundreds had fled north to the raised drawbridge at Long Beach Road. Now, dozens of those fleeing hundreds were paddling across the water on surfboards, tire tubes—anything that would float. On the other side, in Island Park, men dressed in what were either hunting outfits or army uniforms appeared to be ordering the paddlers back. Richard could not be certain, but he thought he saw occasional puffs of gunfire.

A heavy thud above one of the windows told him that someone below was indeed firing guns. It was common knowledge among blimp pilots that even under the best of circumstances, Americans liked to use airships for target practice. Usually, by the time the average bullet climbed high enough, air resistance and the pull of gravity had shaved off so much of its forward velocity that it simply bounced like a pebble off the blimp's hide—and even if it was strong enough to punch through, there was no chance of making a puncture large enough to cause a meaningful leakage of helium.

Richard could not be sure which side was firing at him, but he did know that quarantine was beyond ridiculous, if not beyond constitutional rights. It was at best absolutely ineffective. Gazing west, from a height of five hundred feet, the seaside city looked to him like a toy town with a church steeple, a train station, a school yard, and tiny toy mansions with private docks in their backyards. The trains were still in the station, but the toy boats were all gone. If there had ever been a legitimate concern about people spreading the motes out of Long Beach, it was already too late, because the city's wealthiest citizens, and their closest friends, must have sailed away the moment the bridges went up; and Richard imagined that they must now be scattered between Amityville and Manhattan.

National Boulevard passed below, and Richard traced the roadway through the south side of town, where it met Penn Street. His eyes followed Penn westward, finding the neighborhood surrounding his house—utterly lifeless, as if it had been abandoned for centuries, or millennia.

For Leslie, who had no family members on the ground

below, the approaching swings and slides of Magnolia Park were merely pieces of an archaeological puzzle waiting to be solved. For one fascinatingly terrifying and beautiful moment, the deserted boardwalk looked as ancient to her as Thera's West House or the walls of Tutankhamen's tomb. She wondered if Spyridon Marinatos or Howard Carter had felt as she did now.

Attitude control jets slowed the ship to a hover as it nosed over the top of the Renaissance building and cast Magnolia Park into shadow. The floor of the park still appeared to be covered with wool. Leslie swung a telescopic lens toward the beach, where the helicopter sat, its blades still idling.

Her notepad displayed what the lens saw. The body nearest the cockpit had undergone a transformation. The fingers of one hand—which had still been fingers two hours ago—now showed only bone.

"Stupid," she said. "To judge from the positions of the bodies I'd say they came down gung ho into the middle of a nest with their blades whirling full throttle. By the time the cameramen stepped into it, the blades were already sweeping shovelfuls of the things into the cockpit and over the pilots' clothes. . . . The poor bastards didn't have a chance. . . . And I'm counting six . . . make that seven more bodies in the park . . . and two near a police car. Its engine is still running. . . ."

"What's your diagnosis?" a voice called from Washington. It was Amber Murdoch, and her voice was dry. "Do you still think it's mites?"

"Certain of it," Leslie said. "These—what's the media calling them?"

"Motes."

"These so-called *motes* are really an arachnid swarm. *Mites.*"

So this is it, Richard thought: Operation Scrub. After all the necessary information was gathered, the *Bluepeace* would fly along the mite perimeter. Gallons of dish-washing liquid had been added to the airship's ballast tanks prior to takeoff, and by now it was sure to have mixed thoroughly with the water. Soaping the perimeter would, in theory, box the enemy in, creating a line it could not possibly cross. Then, as the bridges were lowered and the survivors were allowed to exit, their clothes would be doused and stripped off while behind them, fire planes doused the buildings inside the *Bluepeace* perimeter, and then, just for good measure, everything outside. By morning, according to Leslie, a room-by-room spraying of the affected area "should put the crisis well behind us."

As Leslie told it, everything was certain to turn out quite satisfactory.

Except that Richard recalled reading somewhere that spiders and mites sometimes spun little streamers of web that carried them aloft like windborne sailors . . . like dandelion seeds . . . like contagions. . . .

The western wall of the Ocean Club condominium was great looping tendrils of blackness through which only an occasional patch of light stucco showed. Billions of the little monsters covered the windows and balconies of the Renaissance; and Richard guessed that, if Operation Scrub did not work as well in practice as it did on paper, soon there would be hundreds of billions. Perhaps hundreds of trillions.

In the park below lay seven bundles of bones wrapped in shirts and pants and skirts. Richard understood that the Ocean Club and the Renaissance alone must contain more than three hundred skeletons. Many of them would be found in the elevators and stairwells; and it was in the stairwells, he knew, that the bright flame of civilization must have died first—in the stairwells, where men and women by the dozens had abandoned their beds and fled as one for the imagined safety of the streets. Those who reached the steel doors of the ground level first were pressed in the awkward attitudes of sudden death by the unrelenting avalanche of desperate, mite-bitten bodies that swept down from above. Richard tried, unsuccessfully, to force from his mind what it must have sounded like. *My God, my dear God,* he thought. And it became possible for him to believe that whatever was happening here was but a foretaste, that something had broken loose and was waiting to eat the world.

It was very easy for him to believe in nightmares as he

flew over Laurelton Boulevard and saw that it was dead. Then Penn Street—dead. Then Lafayette.

The *Bluepeace* dropped three glue-tipped anchor lines near the intersection of Lafayette and Penn, where all the surrounding lawns and driveways appeared to be covered in sheets of living black sand. The fourth, and final, anchor splattered down from the starboard bow, striking hard against one of Richard's pines, spreading over its base, and hardening instantly. Like the three that had preceded it, this sticky bomb trailed a long thread from the *Bluepeace*. As a precaution against any mites trying to sneak up the lines, guards at the bow and stern were continually spraying their end of the anchor system with jets of steam.

Richard snapped shut the sealer on his helmet, heard a hiss of air from his backpack, and felt the gurgle of cooling fluid beginning to circulate through a thousand feet of little tubes lining the inside of his suit. The fluid puffed up the plastic around his elbows and knees. It constricted his ribs and diaphragm enough to make breathing difficult, but encased as he was in a sheath of plastic, without a good cooling system he would be as a man strolling down a beach in a wet suit on a summer afternoon: cooked by sunshine and his own body heat in about fifteen minutes.

Leslie made sure the sample tray strapped to his waist was secure. "We'll need this back quickly," she said. "There won't be much time for sightseeing."

Richard tugged at his harness. "Understood."

"Ready?" called a voice over Richard's com-link.

"Ready when you are," he radioed back.

There was a whining sound: the tether reeling him down to the street. As soon as he felt his feet touch the ground, he unstrapped the harness. It dangled four feet above a turn-of-the-century road whose every red brick was crawling so thickly with mites that there appeared to be no place he could toss a dime without hitting a hundred of them. They swarmed over his boots in a second, and even through the thick plastic of his suit, he thought he could hear them moving out there.

"Hop to it," Leslie called through the com-link.

Bending on restricted joints, he vacuumed the mites at

his feet into the first of three sample chambers in Leslie's tray. As his helmet's camera automatically registered the time and place of sample number one, the swarm covered Leslie's tray and the fingers of Richard's right glove.

Monitors in the dining saloon showed that his breathing was quickening and that his heart had skipped two beats as he rose on unsteady legs and began walking in the direction of his house.

Halfway to home he knelt down to take sample number two from a skeleton clothed in a terry-cloth robe and slippers. The bones were stripped so clean that not even threads of tendon remained to bind them together. They simply appeared to have been flung across the sidewalk in the shape of a human body.

At Brookhaven, Jackson Roykirk viewed the street remotely through Richard's camera. He counted exactly six piles of clothing. Only six. Jackson could not understand why there were not more bodies on the lawns and the sidewalks. If you're being eaten alive in your house, he reasoned, your first, purely pain-driven response is to get the hell out of there. Penn Street should be strewn with bodies—*strewn* with them . . . unless they were all caught by surprise in their homes and were overcome so quickly that there was no time even to run outdoors . . . or unless the neighborhood had been evacuated before the menace reached them. Jackson thought about that for a moment and began fearing for Richard that the latter explanation would not hold up. Certainly there had been no evacuation in progress when the crisis first manifested, a few blocks away, in the neighborhood of Magnolia Park. Almost everyone had been home, then, and indoors; yet the streets there looked just as empty.

Jackson wanted to ask Leslie if she really thought mites could bring on death so quickly, but he knew Richard would hear the discussion over the com-link and he kept the question to himself for his friend's sake.

But Richard had already asked himself the same question, and was arriving at the same inevitable explanation for the apparent rarity of death in the open. The unburied dead lay everywhere, he told himself. Behind every closed door he passed.

Leslie had also reached this conclusion, and as Richard approached his house she told him to drop what he was doing and return to the ship at once.

"Two samples will be enough," she called through his suit radio. "The President has to make an address and we need whatever you've got—pronto!"

For long seconds he said nothing. He just stood on his front lawn, watching the ascent of the first dark specks to reach his faceplate. He fought hard to keep a grip on his composure, to think clearly; but through the faceplate he saw that his entire lawn—and the brickwork and the red tiled roof were black with them. For one surreal instant he tried to convince himself that if she had been very quick, Dawn might have fled the house in time, or closed the doors and windows and sealed herself safely inside. What got in his way, as a light midday breeze shifted the *Bluepeace* and caused the nearest anchor line to resound like piano wire, was the flutter of curtains behind the open bedroom window, and his last memory of her lying barefooted and barebacked in their bed.

Finally, he bent down on one knee and filled the third sample chamber. By this time the mites were sweeping over his helmet, obscuring his view and driving home the message that to fall and puncture his suit in Long Beach would be no less lethal than on the surface of the moon. When he tried to wipe the mites away with a gloved hand, his faceplate smeared with a reddish-black paste.

For a moment he was puzzled, and began rubbing harder. Then he stopped in horror and realization: The mites were engorged with human blood.

Like his daughter, Tam, Richard blocked large parts of Black Monday out of his memory. He could not recall being reeled in on the harness and, while still dangling below the dining saloon, being blasted with jets of live, sterilizing steam. He knew that he had been required to strip down and toss the suit overboard while a scrub team doused him with detergent. He knew that the harness and all four anchor lines soon followed his isolation garments to the streets below, but he could remember nothing except little snatches of conversation, mostly Leslie on the com-link to Washington. "Estimate fifteen hundred dead, Mr. President. ➤. . We're soaping the perimeter now . . . venting off some helium to maintain heading. . . . Have identified four species, so far . . . among them the common bed mite."

He remembered Leslie frowning. "Impossible," she said. "Bed mites are completely harmless. I'm afraid I've been oversimplifying events here. I was expecting to find a jungle species that managed to hitch a ride on a banana boat, then simply ran amok on a continent where it had no natural predators." Her voice rose to a seemingly hysterical pitch. "I was expecting to see a replay of what happened in Australia when rabbits were let loose, with nothing around to prey upon them, and they became a single mass of crop-devouring flesh twenty miles long. But I'm seeing nothing comparable here, nothing foreign, nothing that doesn't ordinarily belong."

She shook her head. "Snap out of it, Richard. We need every opinion we can get."

But Richard could not snap out of it quite yet. There were no words to describe his pain, no words except an endlessly replaying *NO* in his head, as if *NO* could somehow remove from his reality the loss of the woman he loved. But *NO* was not strong enough, and every minute the reality settled deeper into him, biting down, biting down hard. During one of those minutes he had thought of banishing the reality by leaping from the *Bluepeace*: a short fall to the nearest street or rooftop—thirty-two feet per second acceleration—just four or five seconds, he calculated, and then soothing black nothing.

He would have thought longer and harder about the jump, but the thought that stopped him was little Tam without Mommy *or* Daddy.

"Richard . . ." Leslie called.

But he did not hear her. He felt like a rat in a cage, as he sat at one end of the dining saloon, with his back to the wall, shivering violently. How could he possibly tell a child of nine that her mommy is dead? All he could do was try to stop his imagination from conjuring pictures of what lay beyond the open window and the fluttering white curtains.

6

The Oracle

Deep in the trenches of the Pleistocene epoch, nearly a half million years ago, intelligent life was a mere blemish upon the planet. On the Canadian ice fields and across the Mexican rain forests there were no traces of humankind at all, and over most of the great wilderness that was to become Europe, Africa, and Asia, one would have searched for the elephant hunters in vain. Only in a few isolated locations did they gather into lairs made up of as many as forty or fifty individuals. Near the Nile Delta, members of one little tribe left their footprints on a shore that no longer exists. They fashioned dome-shaped huts from reeds, learned how to bring down a hippopotamus with flint-tipped spears and flay it to the bone with oyster shells.

Humans, too, were flayed to the bone. No archaeologist could quite explain why, but many skulls showed signs of intentional defleshing with primitive tools. The emerging picture of the first minds to awaken on Earth was of tribe chasing tribe with weapons of flint over deposits of copper, oil, and titanium. The combined population of all the human tribes then numbered only a few thousand people, but copper, with its promise of better spears; oil, with its promise of rapid global transport; and titanium, with its promise of hypersonic flight, guaranteed that the blemish would spread out of the cellars of time, covering Earth from pole to pole, growing from a few thousand individuals to the multiple billions.

Among those multiple billions, Jerry Sigmond had grown up with his own dark blemish, had climbed out of his own deep trench. His mother had been a teacher of reading-disabled and hyperactive children, home whenever he arrived home from school, loved by all who knew her. His father was a carpenter who never, ever violated a contract or cut corners behind a client's back. He, too, had always been home for Jerry, and had been loved, it seemed, by everyone except Jerry himself.

Childhood was agony for him. Every Sunday his mother's kitchen became a gathering place for aunts, uncles, and neighbors who hugged one another upon meeting and departing, and who laughed boisterously over coffee and donuts. He grew up in a home surrounded by love; but in the end it made no difference. The blemish was within him, a darkness hidden in some aberrant bit of DNA and determined to grow with time. Jerry Sigmond was a man demonized by his genes, possessed by them, as if by the demons of old.

Adelle Sigmond had tried to teach her son that his purpose in life was to go to the grave able to say he had hurt no one, helped many. His job (and in the world of Adelle and Jack Sigmond, everyone had work to do, *God's* work), was to shine a little light into other people's lives, wherever and whenever he could. To Jerry, his parents' approach to life's challenges was at best naive and disgustingly sentimental (if not downright wimpy), and at worst (in the real, natural-selection, dog-eat-dog world of corporate America), a sure setup to be taken advantage of. By the time he was sixteen, Jerry was blossoming into a dedicated type-A overachiever, thankful to his parents only for the wealth of brainpower he had inherited from them— a wealth he had watched his mother squander needlessly, spending years blazing new trails into the minds of dyslexic children. He had listened to her going on and on, with all the excitement of a woman who has picked her nose and found gold instead of mucus, about how for some of her students the hopelessly scrambled words might be understood if only they could be passed through the fingers instead of the eyes. Teaching Braille to the sighted? Who would have thought such a crazy thing, and then thought to ask if it was just crazy enough to be right? Who but his mother?

He would not squander his own gifts. His job, his mission in life, was to rally the lazy, sheepish masses to his call for the promise of a perfect world, the world as it ought to be, according to Jerry Sigmond. He had a practiced, fine-tuned ability to cloud men's minds and reshape them to his own will. He could steal from you and even if you caught him red-handed he could look you in the eye with such honesty and kindness and speak with such calm conviction that within minutes you would begin to wonder if what appeared to be thievery was in fact nothing more than a misunderstanding or a mistake. Only those who knew him long enough to know that he had no old friends ever came to understand the real Jerry Sigmond.

"Sincerity is the key," an old grand master of comedy had said. "Fake that and you've got it made." Jerry Sigmond took George Burns at his word.

As a teenager he began studying his parents as if they were insects under his microscope, trying to learn from observation alone how to act in a manner that made people feel immediately at ease with Jack and Adelle, that made total strangers take a liking to them within seconds of first meeting them. He spent whole afternoons standing before the mirror in his bedroom, practicing Jack Sigmond's warm smile, and adding to it his mother's perfect blend of burning intelligence mingled with just a hint of naivete. It was an illusion, of course—nothing less and nothing more—but by the time he entered college, he was getting very good at it.

The last day of the old world caught Jerry Sigmond in a bar at Kennedy Airport. He was scrawling bank transfers on his notepad when the city of Long Beach, barely seven miles away, fell to the mote plague. Jerry had just lost a very profitable, nationally syndicated radio show, and might even lose his freedom, if he could not continue to stay one step ahead of the law. Throughout life, even after one colleague or another inevitably caught onto him, even as in every workplace he entered there eventually emerged a new scandal, he had managed to shine through. Like his dentist friend who had been accused of sedating and then fondling his patients, only to become a prized rock video guest star and return home one day to find his business tripled, Jerry discovered that even bad publicity was good publicity. And thus did he parlay his involvement in no fewer than four highly publicized felonies into credentials for hosting a talk show. He did, after all, live in a country where calling someone an egghead, or a computer nerd, or an Einstein had taken the flavor of an insult. America was becoming the perfect environment for the flourishing of a modern-day pirate who wore a business suit, knew how to romance the media, and who always looked clean-cut. The great Jerry Sigmond—too clever and charismatic for his own good, or for anyone else's.

"A dreamer of the day," Thomas Lawrence would have called him. The archaeologist-turned-revolutionary had observed that, "All men dream but not in the same way. Those who dream at night awake in the morning and consider their dream but vanity. But those who dream during the day are dangerous because they can act upon their dream, eyes opened, and make it possible."

Jerry Sigmond had dreamed a great dream. He saw his own hand and heard his own voice reaching out across immensity, and heard the luckless multitudes calling his name. Across America, the people were looking with horror at their economic future. Like most self-appointed oracles, Sigmond's brand of "leadership" consisted of observing very carefully the mob's wave of emotion, then riding the wave, cresting it to magnify his own illusion of authority. Few seemed to take notice that he was always short on solutions, long on lists of people who could be

blamed for everybody's problems. About the time Jerry
Sigmond learned that Florida's apiaries were dying off—
and, knowing that oranges were totally dependent upon
bee pollination, developed a strategy for making a "killing" in citrus futures—he was targeting what he called
"the unnecessary funneling of tax dollars to the intellectual elite: the eggheads, the computer nerds, the
Einsteins."

And the most dangerous cut of all was that some of the
"Einsteins" had indeed built for Jerry Sigmond the very
targets he needed to destroy them. These included an investigation of penile frostbite "as an unforeseen hazard
of jogging," another that concluded, "the introduction of
hydroelectric power into the Sahara Desert awaits only the
introduction of water," and a doorstop-mass tome leading
up to three reasons why "nuclear war may not necessarily
be desirable."

Strangely, Jerry Sigmond had overlooked these targets.
His first attack was against an obscure entomology paper.
He derived a great deal of pleasure from poking fun at a
poorly worded passage in the paper's Methods section:
"Beetles which seemed to be moving normally were
counted as alive, beetles moving but unable to walk were
counted as moribund, and those not showing movement
within three days as dead." Had he read deeper, he might
have derived a more serious message from the paper; but
he ignored it on his way to more important concerns about
people working in the natural sciences in general, and the
evolutionists in particular—the latter being an unpopular
minority among his listeners. And thus did he blame evolutionary preaching for everything from teenage pregnancy
to "America's turning away from God."

Up till that last week of the old world, Jerry Sigmond
had been vigorously, indeed happily, attacking a genetic
experiment at one of Edwin Wilson's labs. The scientists
had managed to shift a single regulator gene in African
green monkeys, causing subtle changes in brain chemistry,
and turning heterosexual males into homosexuals. It was
a major discovery: If the tweaking of a single gene could
control something so basic to primate behavior as sexual
preference, might the alteration of other genes just as eas-

ily be applied to the artificial boosting of human intelligence, or to the reduction or elimination of such emotions as hatred, or even to the enhancement of altruistic behavior? And if so, might humanity be on the verge of controlling its own evolutionary destiny? The real issue—which Jerry chose not to address—was, Whom should the public trust to control such technology? The government? Private industry? The military? The church?

None of the above?

Jerry Sigmond was not interested in real issues. He was interested in spite and envy. He was interested in *killing* Wilson's studies of genetic predetermination, simply for killing's sake.

"So there you have it," Jerry had told his radio audience, "a welfare state for the eggheads. After years of research—after six years of our government lavishing pornographic sums of money on Wilson and his ilk—what have your tax dollars bought? Scientists now tell us that they can take a perfectly normal monkey and turn it into a homosexual.

"Now, doesn't that just warm your heart?

"Perhaps the only real monkey in this picture is the one the Wilsons of this fine nation have made out of the taxpayer."

It all played very well to Jerry's listeners. It did not seem to matter to any of them that he had simply recolored Wilson's work to make it look like a cartoon, and then criticized it because it looked like a cartoon. The trick was rendered childishly simple when the targeted work involved monkeys. No skilled marksmanship required; the arrows simply fit very nicely into the holes Jerry made for them. Nor did it matter to his audience that he had been using his radio show as a means to devise and promote a fraudulent investment scheme. On the day of his dismissal, he had taken calls from an airline pilot who called him a great American and said, "We're right behind you". . . from an unemployed engineer who shouted, "Atta boy, Jerry! Keep up the good work!" . . . from a pediatrician who said, "My husband and I listen to your show every day, and we just wanted to say, keep at it and don't let the eggheads bully you'' . . . and from a score of others expressing similar sentiments.

Oh, yes, it all played very well for Jerry Sigmond; and the music might have lasted forever . . . if only he had not gone just one step too far, casting himself as the nation's most brilliant marketing strategist . . . if only he had not gotten a little too carried away with that ridiculous land-grab deal on the Isle of Luna . . . if only he had known when to stop. That was the problem with Jerry: He had a way of getting his way, but he did not know when to say good enough was good enough.

So much for his rallying call to a perfect world. The law was closing in, thwarting his plans, tormenting him; because he knew that whenever great men, such as he, dared to dream great dreams, inevitably there were those who stood in their way, held them up to scorn and ridicule, and attempted to drag them down.

"They laughed at Plato," he had announced during his farewell broadcast. "They laughed at Alexander, Washington, and Lincoln—great leaders all." What he failed to mention was that they also laughed at Bozo the Clown. Yet that was the way of it at a time like this. That was the way of it for a modern-day pirate who had learned to play the game of celebrity, in a society for which celebrity status was becoming far, far more important than substance.

He would be back, he knew. Like Richard Nixon and more than a dozen pirates before him, he knew that he could count on people's short memories and on a God-given human laziness that would prevent the majority of his audience from ever taking the time to read the relevant documents or penetrate into the details of his fall from grace; and in time, he knew, he could romance the many who rallied to him against the few who had exposed him. In time, he would render all documentation against him meaningless on account of its existing largely unread. And next time, it was going to be different. Next time he would come back to stay.

In the meantime, he would have to hunker down and satisfy himself with smaller dreams. He was like a dark malignancy forced back into remission, rejected by a healthy boost to the world's immune system, but always waiting for the system, once he ceased to fight it, to be lulled by his apparent absence into delusions of complacency, and ultimately into a moment of weakness. In a world enclosed by satellites, radio waves, laser relays, and the internet—in a world that had become a single, living membrane of human thought—it was easy for a wild cell such as Jerry Sigmond to make a comeback, reproducing its way of thinking throughout the body politic, spreading its black poison from the very center of society.

Jerry Sigmond was only marginally aware, as he shifted 20 percent of his savings to a numbered, nameless account in the Dominican Republic, that fifteen hundred people were unaccounted for in Long Beach and presumed dead. On the wide screen behind the bar a presidential announcement had just concluded. The situation was said to be completely under control and the quarantine would be lifted by morning. Jerry did not care about the fifteen hundred. So long as the "situation" was under control they weren't important to him. That last 20 percent—now, *that* was important. Measured against the 20 percent, not even his two little girls mattered. They and their mother would soon be left destitute, and their mother now mourned, as if by death, the loss of the kind and loving man who used to bake pastries for her and put homegrown hibiscus flowers in her hair. He had been replaced by a cold and dangerous man who would steal from his own children, if he thought he could benefit by it, and who seemed incapable of putting himself in their place and comprehending the pain he was inflicting.

Vanora Sigmond wondered if such change had really been possible. She did not believe that a sociopath could simply hatch full grown from a truly decent man, and she began to face the dawning realization that the sweet and charismatic man she married might never have existed at all. From the beginning, she had felt that no matter how well she came to know him, she could only know him so far. It seemed to her as if only six inches below the surface of his personality lay a thick eggshell through which he would never allow ingress. It was clear to Vanora now— as clear as all tragedies were when viewed with twenty-

twenty hindsight—that everything outside the shell must have been a facade, a very convincing fake, and that the true man was hidden deep within.

He had been there all along, watching and waiting. And when the time was right for Jerry Sigmond, the egg hatched.

Vanora and the girls were alone and bewildered. All alone, now. But if the lessons of the past eighteen months had made nothing more clear to them, it was that there was something in this world even worse than being alone. There was being alone with someone.

And now everything was becoming so much clearer to Jerry, so delightfully clear. He was alone and on the loose. The hatchling was loose.

He regretted that he would have to disappear for a while into the woodwork. Living under a shroud of false identities, he would be forced to drive one of those older model cars no one remembers five seconds after sighting them. Until the police, whom he regarded somewhat as America's ever-watchful immune system, could be lulled into complacency and forgetfulness, he would have to adopt a much lower standard of living than the one to which he had grown accustomed. His wife and daughters, knowing only that he had suddenly vanished with all their savings, would be left to the peculiar torture of guessing, during the months to follow, whether he was dead or alive. But he was not troubled. If all went according to plan, his involvement in yet another scandal could be turned into just one more qualification for celebrity, an actual plus on his resume.

Above all else, Jerry Sigmond prided himself on being a can-do type of guy who, if the situation required it, could charm the tusks off an elephant. And if his charm did not work, and his plan fell apart, he always had another plan in waiting. His talk show career and the Isle of Luna scam had been a backup plan to a previous failure of charm, and his present disappearance was simply a backup plan to his backup plan.

Nothing to worry about, he thought—not for the all-American can-do type of guy. Nothing to worry about at all, except for the fact that his flight to London had already been delayed more than two hours without adequate explanation, and the red WARNING box on his notepad now indicated that boarding might be delayed an additional six hours. Already he was concerned that the glitch had made him stay put in this bar long enough for the walls of justice to begin closing in on him, and that kind of failure was not an option.

Using the same false identity codes that had initiated his transfer of funds, he canceled his London reservation and scrawled "Air France" on his notepad. *Why not?* he asked himself. *Paris will do just fine at this time of year.*

A red panel stopped him. It appeared in the upper left corner of his pad, flashing in bold yellow letters: "NO BOOKINGS POSSIBLE AT THIS TIME."

"Why not?" he scrawled back, and the computer answered, "Quarantine of Kennedy and LaGuardia airports."

(Whafuk?)

"Quantas," he wrote.

"NO BOOKINGS POSSIBLE AT THIS TIME," came the reply.

The fringe of excitement was spreading in great ripples out of the Long Beach roadblocks. It had crossed county and state lines and, assisted now by CNN, was leaping the Atlantic. In Europe, the ministers of Transport, Finance, and Health no longer looked on with morbid curiosity. Someone had used the phrase "plague organism," and the TV behind the bar showed an American plane at De Gaulle Airport being refueled upon landing and sent home to Kennedy without its doors allowed to open.

At last, the events unfolding on the wall screen behind the bottles of Kahlúa and Sambuca became important to Jerry Sigmond. He now took real notice of the aerial footage showing the downed news helicopter in Long Beach. The chopper had finally run out of fuel and the blades had stopped idling. As the camera panned west, toward the abandoned lifeguard stand, it passed the skeletons of a would-be engineer named Jon and his would-be wife. Someone at CNN enhanced and recolored the scene with hues of crimson over black, turning it into a logo, of sorts, backed by an ominous music score.

As the logo faded to gray, an aging Ed Nash came

on screen. "At twelve-o-five, let's go to our Washington correspondent, who is standing now in front of the White House. Anything new on your front, Bob?"

"Well, Ed, just a moment ago, Chief of Staff Amber Murdoch confirmed what she called numerous casualties. She could not confirm numbers, or give any indication of what percentage were wounded as opposed to dead; but she did say that in talking with the President this morning, he had agonized before making a decision to enforce a quarantine of Long Beach. He had agonized over the possible loss of life if the barrier island were not quarantined, and this morning he was gratified that the casualties were minimized and that everything was done, in terms of planning, to contain and eliminate the mote outbreak. That is what Murdoch said. But again, at this point, we don't know precisely how many were killed or wounded.

"A few moments ago, Dr. Edwin Wilson, a biologist from the CDC, arrived at the White House. He is sitting down with Murdoch and the President's science advisors for a working lunch."

By now Jerry Sigmond was leaning forward in his seat, taking in every word. His pad flashed a red and yellow message: "Thai Air—no bookings possible at this time—"

He paid no attention. Nor did he take notice of the four uniformed men standing outside, two at each door. One of them, so as not to draw attention, muted his wrist radio. Jerry's backup plan to his backup plan was falling apart fast.

The Washington correspondent smiled. "Later in the day," he said, "Murdoch and the secretary of state will get together with the President as he continues to receive updates on the ongoing cleanup in Long Beach.

"So far, while the initial word here in Washington was pretty upbeat, there seems to be a sense of caution setting in overseas. Although the reports about ending the outbreak are positive, several European ministries have made pronouncements that we have a long way to go. This perception has already eroded confidence in the U.S. dollar, which has declined during the past two hours more than five percent against the pound, the franc, and the deutsche mark. Given these sorts of aftershocks, people know here that they could be in for a slightly longer haul than they perhaps thought.''

A hand grasped Jerry's shoulder, startling him. The man with the wrist radio—presumably a cop—said, ''We want to speak with you, Mr. Sigmond.'' Behind this man stood a second officer, holding a notepad displaying Jerry's most recent publicity still, morphing to match his changed hairstyle and hair color, and the beard he was trying to grow. *The game is over for now,* he told himself. Positive identification was unavoidable. He saw his own fingerprints and DNA signatures at the bottom of the display. If only he not spent too many hours shifting and disguising his funds, if only he had managed to sneak away to Europe, there would have been plenty of time to hack into the repository at One Police Plaza and rewrite his DNA profile.

(If only . . .)

Jerry spotted two more officers, one at each exit, and shook his head. He never would have believed that his plans could have been so easily thwarted by a bunch of bugs. And for the first time in recent memory, he realized that he had just about run out of backup plans. His immediate future diverged in only two directions: to piss the police off, or not to piss the police off.

He smiled his friendliest, talk-show-host smile, and even the burly officer with the wrist radio seemed to have been caught off guard and made to feel comfortable in his presence. One could not blame Vanora or anyone else for being fooled, for failing to see through the facade sooner, because Jerry Sigmond had perfected his act. With nothing more than the expression in his eyes, he could put a guest at ease before going on the airwaves to the world, even if that guest's worst nightmare had been standing to speak before a group of only a dozen people. With that same expression, he could make an arresting officer feel, upon first meeting him, as if the two of them had been friends for years.

''I've been expecting you,'' he told the burly man. ''I'll be no trouble for you.'' He moved his arms slowly away from his body, palms out, as if to convey that he bore no weapons or ill will.

The burly officer returned a benign smile. "Jerry Sigmond?" he asked.

"Yes."

"I'm Detective Nelson Guzman. This is Detective Vince Cardillo. We understand you've had a little trouble with the Isle of Luna, sir."

"Well, I guess you could call it a little trouble," Jerry said, and shrugged. "I guess you could call it a *whole lot* of trouble, to be honest."

"I understand," Guzman said, with a light Dominican accent. "What started out as a good idea just got a little out of control, huh?" he added sympathetically.

"Yeah, that's about the sum of it." Jerry was pushing fifty, according to Guzman's notepad, but the innocent expression on his face reminded the officer of the time his nine-month-old son had randomly pushed a set of buttons on his TV, hopelessly reprogramming the machine; and when he yelled, the child had crawled to him and hugged his leg, looking into his eyes with an expression that made it impossible for him to get angry.

"I expect you'll have to read me my rights," Jerry said.

"Yes," Guzman spoke in a soft, unhappy voice. "I expect I will."

So this is where it had all come to, all those years of careful planning. Bracing himself for yet another fall from glory, Jerry gazed back along the stream of time, back across the diverging path that had made him an oracle of the airwaves, back across at least a dozen other decisions branching off to roads not traveled. Somehow the branching roads seemed to him like links to alternate realities, lives he might have lived if his luck had not run out at each juncture and backup plans had not been forced upon him. In each of those alternate realities he saw himself as a man commanding ultrasaurian wealth, treated with the respect and admiration such wealth brought. It should have been—*would* have been—if not for a path that had directed his life down a never-ending cycle of crashing, burning, and rising again to face the next crash. And to make matters worse, he could see the precise moment of decision that had condemned him to experience life via the phoenix principle.

It had been fifteen years now since he had begun his public attacks on Wilson and the other money-sucking eggheads; thirteen years since Richard Sinclair became science's darling of the talk show circuit, and began stealing the limelight.

Jerry had made it his business to become Richard's "number one fan," to learn everything he could about him; and when he failed to find even a hint of scandal, he used the airwaves as a forum to give the impression of scandal where none existed. The effort failed. Richard disarmed him by inviting the press to scrutinize every facet of his own life. They found nothing. Absolutely nothing.

There, the matter might have rested, should have rested; but Jerry, as usual, carried it too far. He continued to press the character issue, until at last Richard challenged him to a duel: polygraphs at ten paces.

Jerry declined, and so did his ratings . . . for a while; yet he could count on the public's ten-minute memory span to buoy him swiftly to the top again. It would have happened that way—it should have happened that way—if not for Richard Sinclair.

As Jerry told it, "Richard did not know when to stop." In Jerry's world, it was Richard who pressed the issue too far.

Slime, Jerry reflected. *The bastard actually called me slime. On national television!*

"And let me tell you something," Richard had said. "I've seen bacterial sludge dredged up from the bottom of the Atlantic that I would regard as being more highly evolved than Jerry Sigmond—or at least more attractive.

"But when you are troubled by slime, you automatically know two facts. One: Slimy people tend to do a lot of nasty things that they don't want their enemies knowing about. Two: They make lots of enemies.

"Once you know everything there is to know about slime, including (most importantly) who its enemies are, all you need to do is let its enemies know everything you know. It's simple. It's logical."

And it worked, unfortunately. Jerry found himself pitted against an opponent who was, by nature, an information-gathering machine. That's how the laser plan was revealed to the judges and the media. It almost ruined him—almost, but not quite. And, oh—what a lucrative idea it would have turned out to be, if not for Richard's meddling.

Jerry had learned of a student who'd won a local science fair. Her gadget delivered pulses of light so brief and so concentrated that, with nothing larger than an ordinary battery pack in its clip, it could burn holes through sheet metal. It was small enough to be handheld, rendering it a formidable weapon, but Jerry Sigmond had a better idea. He befriended the girl, and pointed out to her that if the laser could be adjusted to burn only in the infrared, rendering its beam completely invisible, like the beam of a TV remote . . . and if it could be rebuilt in such a manner that rather than being held like a handgun, it could be aimed with the precision of a rifle, from as far as two miles away . . . and if its power requirements could be still further reduced, so that it would merely sting flesh, rather than singe or burn through it, then a trotter at one of New York's racetracks could easily be thrown off pace, and disqualified at will, and no one would ever be the wiser.

It was just another good idea that got a little out of control. One, two, maybe three races and both of them could have walked away with tidy little nest eggs. But six races later (plus two ill-timed boasts from Jerry's protégée), the secret became vulnerable to discovery. In very short order, the ever-watchful Richard Sinclair caught on to the scam and passed the news along to no fewer than three of Jerry's former associates; and for years afterward, even as the scheme—"Jerry's delightfully clever scheme"—gave a boost to his popularity, his life was never entirely his own.

Jerry Sigmond's hands were cuffed behind his back as Guzman, Cardillo, and two other detectives led him to the exit. News cameras were already gathering outside the bar. Jerry held his head high, and cast an expression that said he had nothing to hide.

He said nothing, and no one asked him to, and he realized with a start that the cameras were not aimed at him. The reporters were here to cover the story of planes being grounded by—what was the word? Motes? The cameras panned across crowds of stranded passengers, half of them craning their necks to see monitors, the other half pounding their notepads for flight information. On a TV screen overlooking a poor imitation of an outdoor Paris café, the Viacom network was rerunning portions of a recent interview on the subject of insects and spiders, featuring none other than Richard Sinclair.

The hairs on the back of Jerry's neck bristled. One day he would show Richard who was boss. One day he would show even these two cops with whom he was required to act so pathetically cordial. One day, Jerry decided, he would show them all.

They ushered him into a blue and white car with a chrome crash cage and no door locks on the inside. Yet strangely, he did not feel alarmed. Jerry began to sense the compass of his future life. He must reclaim his status as an oracle—and not just any great oracle of the airwaves—but, rather, the greatest oracle of all time. Perhaps this new "plague" was a tool with which he could accomplish just that. Smirking inwardly, he remembered Adelle's admonition: "When life hands you lemons, make lemonade!" Maybe, just maybe, these little "motes" were the most potent lemons that had been put on his plate in quite a long time.

Jerry smiled to himself and sat back. Whether or not he had escaped to Europe, the plan was very much the same; and he firmed a resolve never to depart from the direction the fates were pointing him.

Survive.

Rebuild.

Grow.

Come back.

Avenge.

All of which meant a lot of waiting, and watching, and plotting. It meant a more intensive scrutiny of whatever new roads lay ahead; a search for new opportunities disguised as a lot of hard work. But Jerry Sigmond was not afraid of hard work. Jerry Sigmond did not worry, as the police car sped him down Rockaway Boulevard toward whatever future may be. Like all gifted abominations, Jerry Sigmond was a can-do type of guy.

7

Carnival

Jerry Sigmond was not the only man who came to Kennedy Airport that day, hoping to duck the police and planning to fall quietly off the face of Earth. Like Mr. Sigmond, Jake Hoffman was, at first, too preoccupied to devote more than a passing thought to the outbreak, for he had no friends, family, or business interests in Long Beach. Even so, the motes came into his life with the same suddenness of sunset in the tropics, and plunged his plans into total darkness.

He was a tall man, clad in inconspicuous browns and off-greens. He had been seen, but barely noticed, by Detective Guzman, playing outside an arcade with his two little girls, at about the same time Jerry Sigmond was trying to rebook

on Quantas. To all outward appearances Jake was an ordinary
father, taking a short break between connecting flights. His
girls were three and five, and Mr. Hoffman appeared to be
devoted fully to them, perhaps even a bit too fully. If one
looked just a little closer, he became, at second glance, a
cruel, unsavory creature. His name was not Mr. Hoffman.
He had left his wife in Bangor, Maine, and was abducting
their two children to Paris, where he was planning to raise
them under an assumed name.

His escape was proceeding much more smoothly than
Jerry Sigmond's; in fact, Jerry Sigmond was providing a
much welcomed diversion for the police. Jake was also
better prepared than Sigmond. His identity, and the identities of little Wynne and Michelle, had been flawlessly
rewritten and quietly reregistered, from Scotland Yard to
One Police Plaza. Neither his wife nor the authorities
would be able to find him—until or unless he decided
otherwise. For good measure, he had, like Sigmond,
cleaned out all the family accounts, leaving his wife barely
enough money to pay next month's bills and buy a plane
ticket, much less to hire lawyers and detectives.

He had laid his plan out months in advance, laid it out
with attention to every detail. Then out of nowhere—out of
the deep impersonal nowhere—came the Air France cancellations and the sudden closure of De Gaulle Airport to all
American traffic. He joined the hundreds of displaced business people and vacationers who lined up before every available ticket counter in search of alternate routes through
Europe, until Wynne and Michelle became too bored and
too hungry and too cranky for him to continue the effort,
and until it became clear to Jake that any further effort was
like protesting against the winter snows in Alaska.

Still, he had plenty of cash on hand. If circumstances were
changing, he would simply adapt his plan. He did not let the
quarantine cost him his control and seemed every inch a
man in command of his situation. This was a frequent role
for Jake, but by no means his only one. What he truly had
in common with Jerry Sigmond was that one could look at
him and try to guess from appearances alone the measure of
the man, and be wrong by a country mile.

After the realization that his journey to France had, at

least for that day, been interrupted, he decided to try again in the morning and went about the task of finding a hotel room for the night.

Then came another change of plan. Hundreds of others had arrived at the same realization, and the same solution—hundreds of others before him. All of the hotels within sight of the airport were booked full. The nearest vacancy was nearly five miles away, in Queens, and he soon discovered that there appeared to be a conspiracy, among both innkeepers and cab drivers, to price-gouge the daylights out of every stranded traveler they could find.

Jake began to worry, as a yellow cab carried him and his two girls down Rockaway Boulevard: If the quarantine and the price gougers kept him here too long, his money and his luck might begin to run out before he got anywhere near setting up shop in France. He thought of the times he had spent listening to the shell game and freak show criers at the Hancock County Fair and whispered to himself, "It's turning into a fucking carnival!"

DAY 1, 2:40 P.M.

Richard felt nothing. No sorrow. No anger. No more of the pain that had made him want to sacrifice himself to gravity. Nothing.

The mind is a monkey, he told himself. Though he had tried to deny the reality—

"*Mommy!*" Tam had screamed—

—acceptance had taken hold of him, stealthily, unexpectedly. Between the moment he told Tam that Mommy was gone, and the barely remembered telephone call to Dawn's sister in Tucson, the screams inside his head had given way to numbness. Richard could appreciate the evolutionary significance of the brain's downshift to neutral. Nice defensive mechanism, he thought distantly. He felt as if he had been led in a drunken stupor from the *Bluepeace* into a world turned topsy-turvy, yet at the same time he felt acutely aware. Time seemed to have stopped for him; but he knew that it must be passing anyway. Until the numbing calm settled over Richard, his world had begun to resemble what King, the twentieth century's Poe, once described as "a malign carnival where the people on the rides were really screaming, the people lost in the mirror maze were really lost, and the denizens of Freak Alley looked at you with false smiles on their lips and terror in their eyes."

"No!" Tam had screamed. *"Not Mommy! Not Mommy! She's at home! She's okay! No, no, no, no, no! Not Mommy!"* She shook her head. Her straight black hair flew back and forth across her face, reminding Richard ever so briefly, and painfully, and absurdly, of the time he and Dawn had taken her to the carnival, to the rides, and the bright lights, and the mirror maze.

He cradled her in his arms until she cried herself to sleep, or more to the point, fainted away from exhaustion.

"I want Mommy," she had sobbed over and over.

"I want her, too," he said, rocking Tam gently in his arms.

"I want my room," she had said, fussing at great length about the small, dreary quarters assigned them at the Brookhaven guest house. "Why can't we go home?"

"Because the house has bugs in it," Richard explained. What else, he wondered, do you tell a nine year old?

"Tam, somehow we'll get through this," he had said with all the force of a guarantee. "Somehow it's gonna be all right." But he did not believe for a nanosecond that it was ever going to be all right. How many adults, he wondered, had uttered those same powerless words to the children of Auschwitz and Armenia, Palenque and Masada, Pompeii and Thera? It was an old habit—as old as the dinosaurs, for all Richard knew. It was the illusion parents created when life took a horribly wrong turn; it was the greatest, most ancient lie of all.

"It'll be all right," he told her, knowing that the light had gone out of the center of their lives, knowing that without Mommy, neither of them would ever be as happy again as they had been up till about eight o'clock this morning. But for now it was just ever so slightly all right. The numbness had taken hold of Richard. Sleep had taken Tam. Merciful numbness and sleep.

Richard noticed that along with anger and sorrow, the

numbness seemed to have swept away all the other emotions, even love. A quick inventory of his feelings revealed nothing except a sense of duty for his daughter. He felt like an automaton; and in this peculiarly cold and calm shock state, he realized that it was possible even to begin setting the compass for their future life, to begin planning to share housework and schoolwork without Mommy.

This isn't so bad, Richard told himself. And the thought surprised him. He could go on like this for days and days, feeling absolutely nothing. What troubled him was the nagging possibility that whatever combination of adrenaline and endorphins was coursing through his arteries and shutting down the most sensitive parts of his brain had probably bought him only a brief respite. He would not go on like this for days and days. His emotions would return, he knew; and when they returned, they would pay him back for this quiet interlude, pay him back with interest.

With that thought, all the moisture went out of his mouth. His tongue felt as dry as Egyptian limestone on an August afternoon, and suddenly he was craving Tam's favorite drink: ice-cold Cherry Coke mixed with orange juice. He thought of walking to the cafeteria but then thought better of it. Oranges were becoming as scarce as horse's toes and hen's teeth these days; the price of orange juice had soared so high that the cafeteria only supplied that bad-tasting powdered stuff the astronauts used to drink. No good, he thought. It just wasn't the real thing. Ordinary Coca-Cola would have to do.

He walked across the room, grabbed a can from the minifridge, and popped it open. As he sipped, he thought about citrus crops failing, and bats dying, and mites crawling all over Long Beach. But the bats . . . some part of his mind insisted that he should be thinking about the bats, and that he should have returned Bill Schutt's call. He knew that some bats were pollen eaters, others were fruit feeders. A few hunted for blood, while others homed in on flying insects with their radar. Hadn't Bill said that most of the island species were insectivores? And hadn't he heard somewhere that allergy sufferers never worried about living near citrus farms because orange blossoms did not release airborne pollen? Yes, he was certain of it. Citrus trees depended exclusively upon insect pollinators—bees, mostly—for the fertilization of their flowers and the production of their fruit.

He felt a touch of panic. He did not know why; but now that part of his mind which had become preoccupied with bats and bees was locking on Tam as the central and most threatened part of a strange new picture that was trying to take shape inside his head; and it was a big picture, though still misty and quite vague; and something in it was definitely after Tam.

She sniffled once or twice, but otherwise her face was pale and calm, without expression.

Sleep, the healer of wounds, Richard thought. A place to make repairs, and to hide.

He brushed the hair away from Tam's eyes and shrugged. Would she, too, be paid back with interest? Was Mommy already visiting Tam in her dreams? Sleep has its house, they say. And who had said that? Richard asked himself. Jesus? The Buddha?

Richard knew the worst part of sleep. He had known the death of his own parents, and he knew from experience that Dawn would come to them both while they dreamed. It tore at him, every time he thought of Tam being held by Mommy in her sleep, being rocked back and forth with her cheek on Dawn's shoulder, perhaps even being told, "Shhhh . . . It'll be all right," and then waking up cold and bewildered and feeling the warmth of her suddenly gone. Gone forever.

Even Richard's long-lost dog, Pervert, sometimes returned in his dreams and broke his heart. They would be running together through the old sandlots where condos now stood, and in his sleep Richard never questioned the nature of the miracle that had brought his childhood friend back to life. He just accepted the miracle . . . until he awoke, wondering where his old friend had disappeared to, and then realizing.

Richard did not cry easily, yet every time he awoke from the dream, his eyes filled with tears—which gave him cause to truly dread Dawn's return. Pervert was only a dog. Losing Dawn was going to be ten thousand times worse.

8

Looking In,
Looking Out

DAY 1, ISLE OF TOBAGO,
THIRTY MILES NORTHEAST OF TRINIDAD

The village was slowing down from its early morning
surge of activity to the slumber of midafternoon. Most
people on this part of Tobago put off their lunch hour
until the hottest part of the day. This was when radios
began blaring loud music, when hammocks were slung,
and even the children slowed down from their play. Nothing ever happened with great speed in the village even on
the coolest afternoon. The prevailing mood was one of
timelessness, cultivated over many generations of village
life. Most tourists who came upon the town simply drove
in one end and out the other, following their road maps

to more exciting parts of the island, looking smugly down their noses at the little backwater, mistaking the peace it might offer for boredom.

Bill Schutt was among the very few outsiders who stopped, stayed for a while, and who so loved the leisurely pace and weathered charm of the village that he sometimes wondered whatever in the world could possibly make him leave its protective quiet for Bloomfield College and the never-ending adrenaline rush that was Manhattan.

The villagers, for their part, liked the Schutts. On Saturday nights Bill and Janet could hoist White Oak rum and sing with the loudest and hardiest of them. Bill's strange little ballad about Barney the purple dinosaur had become a reluctant favorite; although after only two Saturday night steel-drum jam sessions it had acquired a few new verses that his old friend Richard would never allow him to sing within earshot of Tam.

Tropical zoologists, they had come to the island to investigate complaints about vampire bats attacking cows, making entire herds sick. But that was next of kin to impossible. There were no vampire bats on Tobago. Anyone who worked with them knew *that*.

The problem was that the vampire bats didn't know any better and were here anyway. Bill and Janet had strung fine-mesh nets in the forest; and on an island that should have supported seventeen different species of bats—nonbloodsuckers, all—the Schutts came up empty every time. Bats, it seemed, no longer lived on the island, save for occasional sightings of *Desmodus rotundus,* the common vampire. The insect and fruit-eating species were simply gone. Erased. All of them, apparently.

Bill decided to skip his lunch and siesta today. Instead, he searched the thick underbrush near the edge of a rain forest, trying to solve a mystery. He was among the first to realize that his world was tilting irrationally, that his people were entering a future shrouded in uncertainty, where nothing was as it first might seem. The island was becoming, for him, a place strewn with the fragments of a giant jigsaw puzzle, and the picture he was beginning to piece together in his head scared him.

He knew that on island habitats, with every grain of

pollen most likely to be blown out to sea and lost to the ages before it happened upon another island, almost all the fruit-bearing plants depended on insects, rather than wind, to propagate the next generation. He also knew that the dropping of undigested seeds in the guano of fruit-eating bats guaranteed the renewal of the rain forest. The guano even served as a ready-made package of seed fertilizer. It was a convenient arrangement, but it was moot. Bill suspected that if he searched the forest very carefully, he would discover that precious few berries had been ripening this season. The fruit-eating bats were gone and presumably dead—starved, probably.

He also knew that on the mainland a swarm of six million free-tailed bats could eat a quarter million pounds of insects in a single night. But *Tadarida* (a native of Tobago as well as the Venezuelan mainland) was nowhere to be found. In its absence, Bill would have expected to see ballooning populations of insects on the island, including fifteen or twenty extra tons of mosquitoes—but they, too, were nowhere to be seen. Now, in a four-stage argument, the puzzle pieces came together, and he could begin to construct a hypothesis about what was happening on Tobago.

Three details he knew: The fruit-eating bats, whose food source depended upon the presence of insects, were gone; the insect-eating bats were gone; the insects themselves were gone. This led to a fourth detail he did not know before: All or most of the insects had been wiped out, at least locally, essentially pulling the rug out from under the island's ecology; whereupon the bats became the first noticeable casualties of the insect die-off. First the insects, then the bats; even though Bill had not been there to see the progression, it must have happened that way. Logically it almost had to.

But *Tadarida* was only among the first noticeable casualties, Bill reminded himself. There were bound to be more. The thought that frightened him was that it did not seem to be a local phenomenon, restricted only to this island. He could understand a local insect die-off causing insect-eating bats to either starve or migrate to other islands in search of food. But he could not explain how the exit of *Tadarida* and the fruit-eaters would attract flocks of blood-feeders from Trinidad and Venezuela . . . unless something was turning the ecology upside down in those places, too—forcing the vampires into an island-hopping exodus in search of new food sources.

He wished he would hear from Richard—at least a confirmation that he and the family were all right, if not an opportunity to compare notes. The "mote outbreak," as CNN was calling it, had been the lead internet topic all afternoon, and Bill wondered—

(Could there be a connection? No, that's way too speculative. Crazy. I won't believe it.)

—why no word from Richard? All he knew, from his notepad, was that his e-mail transmission had been received somewhere on the road between Long Beach and Brookhaven, that Tam had acknowledged the signal, and that Richard's family must therefore be all right.

Bill emerged from the rain forest onto a patch of slashed-and-burned, grass-covered land. At the edge of the clearing he smelled something, then saw something. The only living souls for miles around seemed to be a herd of cows. They watched dumbly as he knelt down in the grass and prodded a dead bat with a stick. *Lasiurus borealis*, Bill told himself. Female.

Her stomach, distended with decay, was almost as large as a child's fist. It made her appear to be better fed than she must have been at the hour of her death. Bill knew the common red bat to be a solitary insect hunter that could be captured by setting up mist nets just before dusk, approximately an hour ahead of the feeding surge that most of the island's bat species undertook. In the Caribbean, *Lasiurus* specialized in the early evening insects that came out while the other bats were still at rest, sleeping and digesting the previous night's meal. Bill was impressed by nature's order: The forest fed in shifts; but now something was toppling that order headlong. As he prodded, thick mats of skin and red fur sloughed off the bones, releasing wisps of stench from inside. But there were no fly larvae, Bill observed—no maggots wiggling through what had to be more than an ounce of decaying, sun-warmed meat; truly a fly banquet. In these parts, maggots alone could dispose of an entire cow carcass in less than a week. Yet this poor creature had been lying on the ground for at least two or three days, and no flies had come—*where the fuck were the flies?*

When he flipped the bat over with his stick, he saw that no beetles had come. No ants, either.

The cows, observing him, looked sickly and restless, an occasional belch their only comment. Bill, lost in thought, took no notice of them. His imagination crawled back again onto that same, *way* too speculative limb. This time he did not recoil from the question. This time, he lingered: Did the mite outbreak in New York mean that whatever was happening here had already spread across continental distances? Could that be true?

He realized that he had to get through to Richard, *had* to compare notes with him; absolutely had to. If his hunch was correct, a Pandora's box was being smashed open, and he began to suspect that very soon he would not be worried about strange bat migrations. Not one damned bit.

"Bill?" He was still crouching in the grass when he heard Janet's call. There was a dirt road at the far end of the field. A pickup truck had just rattled by, turning Bill's view of her shadowy, as if she were a ghost. She waved a ghost shape over her head, and as she stepped out of the dust cloud, it resolved itself into a notepad.

"What've you got?" she shouted.

"A bit of a mystery," he called back. "Dead bat, no scavengers. What've *you* got?"

"A bigger mystery," she said. And when she knelt down beside him she flipped open her pad. More than a dozen e-mail messages scrolled by. None of them was from Richard; but each of them added a new piece to the puzzle, making the picture a little bit clearer, and a little more scary:

From Deedra and Karen, Smithsonian Institute for Tropical Studies, Costa Rica: Janet, it's confirmed. All the insectivorous bats have either died off or migrated out of Belize. Vampire bats also appear to have deserted the region. Of possible related interest, Colonel August Schmitt, a local rancher and amateur lepidopterist of some renown, notes that our butterfly populations appear to have been decimated.

From Arthur and Elizabeth in Colombia: Cannot follow up on your queries about whether or not bat populations are declining. We're much too busy here. Trying desperately to save our farm. This season's coffee harvest all but destroyed by plagues of fruit mites. Economic disaster of the worst kind.

From Darren and Sakiko in Venezuela: Confirmed. All bat populations, including vampires, missing. Ranchers here are reporting hundreds of cows dead from prion disease. A mystery: This particular prion disease is believed to be insect borne, but we are unable to identify the carrier species because our insect populations appear to be every bit as absent as our bats.

From Farouk, Marie, and Pete on Trinidad: Sorry to report that we are preoccupied with an outbreak of mad cow disease. Have identified vampire bats as probable new route of disease transmission. P.S.: We are up to our necks in vampires.

From Kim and Chris in Guyana: Disturbing developments. Facing possible loss of ranch due to illness affecting all our cattle. It's beginning to look like economic Armageddon down here. Regret that I cannot afford the time that will be required to set up nets and answer your questions about bats.

The only good news was that the sugar crop was said to be booming. Of course it was, Bill told himself. There were no insects around to bore into and munch on the sugar cane. A cheery thought, made all the more alarming by a vague P.S. from Kim about some sort of ritual slaughter in the outback of Guyana. It sounded in some ways every bit as gruesome as Long Beach, except that it involved far fewer people, was a lot bloodier, and on account of Guyana's long history of strange religious practices, was being attributed by the authorities to voo-doo cults.

Bill wondered.

He pulled a handkerchief from his back pocket, wiped the sweat away from his face, and was amazed to see that he had failed to take notice of the streamers of dried blood staining a cow's legs.

What on Earth—?

Janet looked where he was looking, and she saw that all the cows had bled—most from their legs only, some from their legs and their bellies. *Desmodus rotundus,* she concluded. Really vicious little beasties. They fed in packs, like miniature wolves; but they did not behave as one would have expected a winged adversary to behave. Their attack strategies were not based first and foremost upon flight. They *ran* on the ground, like spiders; and when they were close enough they scrabbled up your legs, and from there they could climb or claw their way to any perch they desired. Their remarkable agility on the ground was combined with stealth and cunning, and with incisors honed sharper than the finest surgical tool—so sharp, in fact, that when they slashed through your skin, individual cells would be cut in half and the nerves would register no pain. They could penetrate the arteries in your ankles and you wouldn't even know it.

"Desmodus?" Bill asked.

"That would do it," Janet replied.

They crept toward the herd for a closer look. The cows shifted uneasily but did not move away. Bill's eyes ticked back and forth, analyzing the blood trails. He guessed that the cows had been attacked shortly before dawn, and had stood here bleeding long past sunrise. It was typical for the victim's blood to be everywhere after a vampire attack because the bats' saliva was laced with anticoagulants, which prevented the natural clotting response. Even after a relatively minor attack, the blood simply kept flowing from the wounds, usually for several hours. Vampire bats were among the sloppiest eaters in all the animal kingdom, not only because of their grisly dietary habits and the nature of their spit, but also because their kidneys were extraordinarily efficient. With the first gush of blood over the taste buds, the kidneys shifted into maximum over-drive, began concentrating the blood solids and nutrients, squeezing out the water and dumping it instantly. As the bats clung to their prey, drinking—drinking deeply—they urinated. The urine was a watery, paler shade of scarlet, and it stank; but Bill neither saw nor smelled any sign of it in the field. The cows' legs and bellies should have been smeared from stem to stern with dried rivulets of urine and blood. To judge from the large number of puncture marks, had the bats clung on even for a few minutes, the cows should have looked as if someone had tried to butcher them where they stood. Bad as the attack was— he counted more than a dozen bites on one leg—it seemed peculiarly bloodless.

It was as if a bat pack had merely alighted, punctured the flesh, sipped the blood, and, perhaps finding it distaste-ful, moved on without taking enough even to kick the kidneys into action. Evolutionary biologists were often re-quired to draw volumes of information from mere scraps of bone, causing them to develop the very modes of think-ing that brought endless delight to Agatha Christie and her fans. The detective in Bill took note that the cows' noses were running thickly with mucus, and their eyes were al-most rheumy enough to be pasted shut, as if they were fighting off a severe flu.

What had the reports from Venezuela, Guyana, and Trinidad said? Cows, sick and dying? When he added this to what he knew about vampire bats, the thought sickened him. He knew that vampires would not feed on sick ani-mals—which explained why the bat pack had not stayed long enough to leave traces of urine: Something else, per-haps the last insect alive here, perhaps even the first vam-pire to reach the island, had infected them. He knew that vampire bats could not store fat in their bodies—which meant they needed fresh blood every night or they died. And he knew that this herd's attackers, even if they had failed to locate healthier cows elsewhere on the island, might still be alive and well fed, because one feature vam-pires shared with humans was the ability to behave altruis-tically. If you happened to be a vampire bat and you were unable to get a blood meal last night—not to worry, fella; your pal would vomit some of his meal into your mouth.

Aw, isn't nature wonderful? Bill thought ruefully. He knew that the displacement of forests by cattle ranches in Venezuela, Guyana, and Trinidad had made fresh cow blood as accessible to vampire bats as milk cartons and prime ribs were to people. As the ranchers increased the population of cows, they unwittingly lured the vampires out of the woods, and their population exploded as well. No one had asked what would happen if the bats' primary food source became sick; but Bill was certain that sickness had forced the vampire migration he was witnessing on Tobago; and he knew that here, too, cow blood was becoming tainted. Now he began to see what was to come.

Janet saw it, too; and the thought frightened her. "They'll just keep migrating, won't they?" she said hopefully. "Rather than feed on sick cows?"

"Or they'll stick around and look for healthier blood," Bill said. "Switch to a different flavor."

"People?"

He looked at the bite marks on the sick cows and grimaced. There were a lot of the little monsters out there these days. By everything he knew, more than the world had ever seen before. And they were roosting somewhere, roosting by the tens of thousands, sleeping in little clusters under eaves or in caves—but now, Bill guessed, they were hungrier than usual, and—

"It'll be dusk in a couple of hours," Janet warned.

Bill glanced up toward the sun. "Better tell our neighbors to hang double layers of mosquito netting over their beds tonight, and to button up their doors and windows real tight. Just in case."

"And tell them to tell their friends."

"Maybe," Bill said, trying to shake off the grade Z horror movie that was playing in his head.

"And maybe we're exaggerating," Janet said, trying to sound hopeful again. "Probably we're overreacting. I think what's gonna happen is that a lot of people are going to think we're pretty silly when they wake up in the morning." But Bill looked over his shoulder at the insect-eater whose starved, decaying body had attracted no maggots. And he began wondering what sort of ecologic train wreck could account for plagues of hungry bats and mites, and he wished more than ever, as the horror movie in his head began to gain momentum, that he would hear from Richard.

"You can't fool yourself," Bill said. "So don't try fooling me. This could get really ugly, really fast. You know it. I know it. In a month or even a week, this part of the Caribbean could become a place no sane person wants to be caught sleeping in, or around."

"All these islands? Half the Caribbean?" Janet shook her head. "No, it just can't be *that* bad. Can't be."

"It might be a lot worse than half the Caribbean," Bill said. "We could get on a plane for New York tomorrow; but I doubt we'd be leaving the problem behind us. I think Long Beach makes that clear enough."

Janet stood stunned for a moment, as if her husband were a crazy man; then the wall of denial crumbled and she began to see that the problem really could be spreading halfway across the Caribbean, or worse. "What's causing it?" she said at last.

"Such a little thing," he said, a slightly manic grin breaking across his face. "Almost the littlest things in the world—insects. You'd hardly even think to look for them on a normal day. But they're dead, Janet. Dead, or dying, or hibernating somewhere. And it's not just here, in the Caribbean. It's happening in New York, I think. It could be all over the world."

"No," Janet said. "That doesn't make any sense."

"I'm afraid it's the only thing that does."

Four hours later, and two thousand miles northwest of Tobago, dusk was descending upon Newbern, North Carolina. The beekeeper left the dirt road and ducked into the woods to his left when he heard a soft rustle. Human or animal? He had to be careful. If he was caught poaching from the quarry again, they'd probably confiscate his entire collection. Old Mr. Ames, in charge of mine security, had caught him red-handed last time and hauled him into court. The beekeeper still did not understand why Ames or anyone else would get so hot under the collar about a few fossil seashells and shark's teeth. This was a phosphate mine, for crying out loud! With their trucks and cranes and high-pressure water hoses, the miners were flushing ocean sediments out of a mile-wide pit, then hauling the phosphates away to make fertilizer, or to give magazine pages and book covers their glossy finish. The shells, teeth, and occasional whale vertebrae were mere refuse washed out with the till. They were valueless to the mine owners, unwanted, and bound to be buried in rubble and floodwaters as the cranes and hoses moved on.

Ames, the beekeeper heard, liked to boast in the local bars about the day he "busted and burned" the poacher. Ames joked about how, when asked to explain what he had been looking for in the phosphate pits, this "weird old beekeeper" opened up trays of fossil shark's teeth in the courtroom and began a crazy lecture about how this whole county had been under the ocean millions of years ago. A self-taught paleontologist, the beekeeper knew now that he must have been mad to show the teeth, or to speak so lovingly of his hobby. He realized, too late, that his enthusiasm could be contagious. One of the mine owners had been present in the courtroom, and his eyes opened wide when he saw a shark tooth wider than the span of his own hand. During recess, the owner had lunch with the judge, and an offer was made to drop all charges if the beekeeper allowed the phosphate miner and three company executives to have their pick from his collection.

And so it went: "I'll take that one . . . that . . . that one . . . and that . . ." Years of careful searching, and his finest specimens were snatched away in a single afternoon.

"I wasn't there to see it," Ames was often heard to brag, "but they tell me the old beekeeper sobbed like a little girl when they took his fossils away."

Well, Ames would never catch him again. Last time it had happened only because he allowed himself to become too distracted by the Miocene whale jaw he'd dragged out of the pit. The old guard must have spotted him from the road, then hid in the woods and crept up on him as he passed by.

"Well, Ames, you won't get me again," the beekeeper repeated to himself. "What right have you, anyway? God put the seabed here fifteen million years before the likes of you came along with your cranes and hoses and threw a fence around it. Nice tooth I've got here—better than any of the ones your friends stole from me—so I guess the score is just about even, now. But I'll get myself a bunch more before I'm through with you bastards. What else is there at a time like this? I'm broke. No more bees. All my hives are dead.''

His footsteps came to an abrupt stop. The rustling noises had started again. Ames? And the beekeeper made what he knew to be a stupid attempt to blend motionlessly with some tall bushes.

The rustling rose and ebbed, but the sound that froze him like a statue was what he thought to be—*swore to have been*—a low moan. Ames?

He closed his fingers tighter around the tooth, welcoming the weight of time in the heft of a fossil, welcoming most of all its power of distraction. Eight inches long—at the very least, he told himself. Even ''Jaws,'' the great white, possessed teeth no bigger than a shot glass. Whoever owned this must have been a *real* monster.

His thumb ran over a crescent etched into the flattest part of the tooth—a sucker mark about the size of a half dollar. It was a clue to what the shark had bitten, and formed part of a picture in which the tooth had actually been torn from the monster's mouth. The beekeeper recalled seeing photos of these same sucker marks on the hides of sperm whales. This sperm whale–sized shark, and the great sperm whale itself, shared an appetite for giant squid. . . . The woods remained silent, but something still prickled the hairs on the back of his neck, so he continued to stand motionless, watching and waiting. He listened for the snap of a twig under work boots, for thorns scratching against blue jeans, or any other signs that Ames—or, God forbid, Ames and one or two of his drinking buddies— was on the prowl. But the rustling noise, and all other noises, it seemed, had stopped. The beekeeper crept forward again, half wishing he could throw Ames to the great sharks, deciding to stay as far as possible from the dirt road, and peering into the woods ahead. They were dark and deep, darker than they had any right to be and—

He froze.

Yes, there had been something rustling here; but it was not a man. And, yes, Ames had been here, too; but he no longer looked like a man. During what must have been a brief but terrifying struggle, Ames had stumbled out of his shoes. His right eye was covered with mites. The left was gone. His left cheek had been eaten, and from where he stood the beekeeper could look inside and see a carpet of mites in the shape of a human jawbone and teeth.

Something under Ames's shirt gave with a wet blatting sound, and the beekeeper watched in silent disbelief as the guard's diaphragm suddenly caved in and most of his innards flowed out his back.

The beekeeper decided it was time to leave. *Screw the tooth*— He tossed it away, finding it suddenly too weighty a liability—then wheeled and ran whence he came, his shoes barely touching the forest floor.

He finally began to scream when he saw the way blocked by a flood tide of mites, and imagined the millions of them turning their heads and looking at him.

Half a world away, racing west to east, an aging KH11 satellite plunged through the line of shadow that bisected China, then downloaded what it had seen to an American aircraft carrier that waited fifteen hundred miles aft in the Indian Ocean. Some of the satellite's systems had begun to show signs of senescence; but its infrared sensors, augmented by onboard photomultipliers, could still magnify starlight ten thousand light-years away or detect the glow of a cigarette on a Himalayan trail. Even after the last of the electrical cells eventually burned out, or were pelted at hypersonic speed by meteors and flecks of paint from other spacecraft, the KH11 would be whirling around and around the world, for the next five million years. It would still be there, long after the works of Shakespeare, Darwin, and Plato ceased to be even a memory.

The KH11 would outlive the pyramids and the Sphinx. Perhaps even the Mount of Megiddo.

And certainly the *Nimitz*.

Fifteen hundred miles aft, the line of shadow was retreating toward India, bringing dawn with it. Still shrouded in darkness, the little steel control van of the American aircraft carrier *Nimitz* was alive with activities, each orderly in itself, the whole *surprisingly* orderly for such cramped quarters. Microdisks were being plugged into slots, coffee was poured, and infrared maps were made on a wall whose entire surface was a bank of laser TV screens.

The expression on Tom Dettweiler's face was one of puzzlement creased with worry. Under cover of night, and between KH11 flybys, heavy vehicles had attempted to sneak over hard-paved roads; but they had left unmistakable—albeit rapidly fading—infrared patterns on the ground, patterns that pointed like ghostly white fingers toward transport ships arrayed along India's east coast.

Madness, Tom told himself. Do they really mean to carry through with this threat?

"Looks like the doves are all about down on power," Scorp called from the flyer's station. "I've managed some extended flight operations, but they should have collected more than the necessary information already."

Tom nodded agreement as he watched three red dots on the main map. The dots, marking the doves' estimated positions, moved imperceptibly north and west, like the minute hands of three large clocks. They also moved silently, not yet daring to reveal their presence through an all too conspicuous but sooner or later all too unavoidable electromagnetic shout of collected data.

Satellite reconnaissance could accomplish only so much. Mostly, it identified which patches of land needed to be looked at in more detail. Contrary to popular belief, one could not read license plates from orbit. The same earthly atmosphere that had for centuries obscured the giant volcanoes of Mars from astronomers trying to look out into space also raised havoc with spy satellites trying to look in. Clear views of Mars were obtainable only if the planet happened to be directly overhead, with the least amount of obscuring air between the observer and the observed. The same rule applied to space-based observers: There was plenty of detail if you happened to be looking straight down; but the more you increased the angle between the satellite and its target, the more atmosphere you had to peer through. Five seconds of optimal viewing, and then the air itself began to act like a badly cut lens, through which the picture worsened in direct proportion to how long and how hard you looked.

Most of the world's governments knew this, and had learned long ago to synchronize their more covert activities with the ninety-minute orbits of the "spies in the sky." Hence the fading infrared tracks. Someone had gotten a little too hurried and literally burned some rubber as the satellite approached. By aid of the doves, Tom expected he would be able to find the hot but hastily stealthed engine that had made the tracks.

"Okay," Tom said. "Let's have it."

"Here it comes," Scorp replied, and pulled back on the toggles. At precisely that moment, the little winged robots nearly six hundred miles away climbed straight up. They had been skimming low over the Indian countryside for more than eight hours, gathering and storing information. Every radar system in the country seemed to be active—which was something new—but radar was no threat to the doves. They were built of radar-absorbing plastics and balsa wood, cut at such odd angles that what few radio waves were reflected from their surfaces ricocheted straight up, or down, or off to the side—in every direction except back at the radar source. Tom had designed each of his doves to have the radar cross section of a mosquito and, powered by batteries, to have the infrared cross section of a moth.

Usually, doves behaved like homing pigeons, but tonight's flock had been sent on a one-way mission. A very expensive decision, Tom thought, but it was the only way to effectively double their range. As the first of the doves rose on the *Nimitz*'s horizon, it shone, in one radio band, brighter than the Crab Nebula pulsar. There was no way the Indian military could have missed it, but it did not matter. In less than a quarter second, the robot had completed its data dump. One three-hundredth of a second later, the computer at the flyer's station verified that all data had been received intact, except for dropouts in some of the soil scans, and one two-hundredth of a second later the probe rebroadcast its agricultural file. When confirmation of receipt came in—still within that first part of a second—the computer initiated an electrical surge that turned the dove's innards into sheets of expanding flame. Everything the fire touched flashed out pallid white and sent forth new bursts of flame. The propeller exploded into two thousand pieces, each trailing sparks as it fell. For long seconds the dove's presence was made visible for thirty miles in every direction; but this, too, did not matter. Tom had designed even the robot's computer to break up into thousands of flame-consumable parts as it dropped out of the fireball. For sleuths and would-be techno-thieves, nothing except dust would reach the ground.

After the fireball appeared, Indian radar and missile batteries began a more intensive search of the sky, but to no avail. Twenty-three seconds after the first data dump, the second dove announced its presence, faster than any human could respond, and completed its transmission, faster than any missile could fly to it. A minute later, the third dove blazed forth.

Through the years, Tom's robots had allowed him to probe the interior of a Japanese sub bearing two tons of Axis gold and intact World War II documents three and a half miles down on the bed of the Atlantic. He had seen the *Titanic,* the *Cinque Chagas,* and what little remained of a Cold War–era Soviet vessel that had been consumed by a nuclear-tipped missile or torpedo hurled against it by its own navy—for reasons which, to this day, no one had explained. But none of these places, in terms of sheer strangeness, quite matched the pictures flashing across the array of screens in the control van. It was not the extraordinary number of Indian Harriers in the air, carrying air-to-air missiles and auxiliary fuel tanks for maximum endurance that worried Tom. Nor was it the ground-based forces converging toward rendezvous with a fleet of missile-armed destroyers, or the new pickets of mobile radar systems arrayed on the ground. Rather, it was the ground itself.

Now he could see the desperation in this land: an ever-worsening war between Hindu and Muslim, fueled by hunger and rampant unemployment, fueled by runaway inflation, fueled by—by what? Every way the doves had turned their electronic eyes, the ground appeared to be dead. All the rice fields, all the tea, all the grain—all appeared to have been smitten by the plague of black fungi that had begun to spread only three months ago, seemingly out of nowhere. So far, it appeared to be contained within the boundaries of India. Pakistan and the island of Sri Lanka were agricultural paradises by comparison—which explained why a disintegrating Indian Parliament had annexed them. War and rumors of war were always healthy distractions for political leaders who found themselves standing on shaky ground.

As far as Tom could tell, from the Ganges to Madras there was nothing to stop the proliferation of leaf and root-rotting fungi. They dominated the Indian peninsula with all-embracing thoroughness, seeming intent on converting the nation's plant DNA entirely to their own. For a time, fungicides had seemed the obvious solution, but the fungi spread faster than new chemicals could be manufactured. And by May it was clear that the chemicals themselves presented an intractable problem: How to poison an exploding population of fungi without also poisoning the soil and water in which their spores lived, and the plants on which they fed, or the people who fed upon the plants.

By early June more than two thirds of India's harvest had disappeared. Now, the doves revealed, all the corporate farms had simply shriveled up and died. On some of the mountain roads it was no longer necessary to look for the faint infrared signatures of tires printed on the pavement, because military vehicles had printed actual tire tracks upon thick beds of outwash mud. As the plants withered and the roots lost their grip on the soil, the rains began to erode parts of India down to bare earth and clay. The annexation, Tom concluded, was no mere testing of the other side's force of will, no mere flexing of muscle.

At the flyer's station, a young recon expert fresh out of Rensselaer Polytechnic Institute surveyed the ravaged farmlands and arrived at the same conclusion. "You don't suppose there's still a chance they're bluffing?" he asked.

"It's desperation, not machismo," Tom said. "History teaches us that war is extremely unlikely so long as each side has a reasonable standard of living, so long as each side has too many good things that it doesn't want to see destroyed. A few shadowy figures moving heavy equipment around doesn't worry me or scare me, all by itself. What I want to know is the conditions the shadows' families are living under. Are they well fed? Do they have clean drinking water? I get worried when I see an adversary who has nothing to lose. That's the one thing every man should be afraid of.''

Scorp nodded agreement. "It's a healthy fear, if you ask me.''

"What do you think will happen with them?'' the President said. "Can you give me probabilities?''

The admiral sighed. Always probabilities. Never a yes, a no, or a maybe. This president wanted everything laid out in probabilities, as if the politics of war were a science. But he knew what the President wanted, and was prepared for him.

"My team in the control van is giving it better than a ninety percent probability they'll invade,'' the admiral said quickly; and his voice shot up from the *Nimitz* on a narrow shaft of infrared light, touched an orbiting satellite, and was relayed earthward on a beam that was no wider than a church door by the time it reached the receiver at Camp David, from which the signal was routed north through a closed, fiber-optic line. Traveling at the speed of light, the words reached the Oval Office one twenty-fifth of a second after being spoken aboard the bridge of the *Nimitz*. The lag between questions and answers was perceptible only when viewed in the time frames of the computers that relayed the words, but in human time frames the phenomenon passed without notice.

"So the annexation is real,'' the President said. "Any predictions on what will happen if we stand in their way?''

"I'll give you a statistical certainty they'll fight us,'' the admiral answered uneasily. "And a good five percent chance they'll go nuclear.''

"But that's crazy. They'd have to be crazy!''

"You need to understand just *how* crazy the situation is right now,'' the admiral said, and he began to explain what Tom Dettweiler and the dove flyers had seen. The

President stopped him after only a few sentences, at the part about how the soil was more badly ravaged than anyone in India had let on, and how both American intelligence and CNN had failed to reveal an economy so badly shaken that the country could no longer afford to import replacement grain from its neighbors. He interrupted the admiral just long enough to summon his chief of staff and the CDC entomologist from their working lunch turned working dinner. When they arrived, the admiral began telling his story again. It took barely more than seven minutes. He ended with video footage of a man rescued from what his dove flyers had at first taken to be a badly disguised screen of mine-laying boats but which had turned out to be a tiny fleet of refugees. "We used to be a city of engineers," the elderly man with the bony knees said. "But go there today and you will find yourself in a place where there is no food, no work, and always the sounds of gunfire and children crying. You will hear the shouts of mothers and fathers. They are cursing, abusing. Cursing even God. And this is the end for us. This is the first time I hear Muslims, Hindus, and Christians who curse their gods."

When the report was finished, Edwin Wilson and Amber Murdoch said nothing. They just looked, wide-eyed, from the notepad screen to the President, and back to the screen again.

The admiral saw grave concern in all three of them, perhaps mingled with a hint of fearful prediction; but in Wilson's eyes he saw the faintest glimmer of something else. He sometimes observed that same twinkle in the eyes of his robotics people, down in the control van. It was the excitement of a child with a new puzzle to solve.

"Professor?" the admiral asked with genuine curiosity. "What's your take?"

"I was just . . . well . . . thinking about wasps, dead bees, and dinosaurs."

The President and the chief of staff looked at Wilson as if he had just joked during a eulogy, but the admiral seemed to understand. "Go on," he said.

"The Indians appear to be convinced that Sri Lanka has miraculously escaped the plague, that all the farmlands between Kandy and Colombo will somehow remain immune or uncontaminated indefinitely, and that annexing the island is nothing more than annexing the corner grocery store in time of need. And part of me has this terrible feeling that what we're seeing in India is merely a dress rehearsal for much of the world during the next few months, a drama for which the curtain may already be rising in America."

"What?" the President said. "That can't be right. It can't be *that* bad. Because if it's that bad—then Rome falls."

"Let's hope not," the entomologist said. "But when I have fears, I worry that the only difference between India and the rest of the world is that India simply got an earlier curtain call and perhaps a different plague organism than everybody else."

"Probabilities?"

"I'm guessing better than a five percent chance that it's global."

"Five percent?" the President said. "That's not so bad."

"Not so bad as what?" Wilson asked uneasily. "The probability that a large meteor will strike Earth sometime during the next fifty years is far less than one percent, yet we are spending billions on Project Spaceguard, and few among us will argue that those precious resources are being wasted. Need I remind you that you won this office by a margin of less than five percent, and that you won because your opponent advocated clearing the national debt with a five percent increase on every home owner's mortgage payments."

The President shrugged. "Okay. If that's your meaning of five percent, what do you suggest we do about it?"

"There's nothing much we can do, except hope that India and Long Beach are biological aberrations, and cling to the ninety-five percent probability that I'm wrong."

"What do dinosaurs have to do with any of this?" Murdoch asked.

"Yes," the admiral added. "I'm curious about that myself."

"They may have everything to do with it. I mentioned

Project Spaceguard. It grew, in part, out of the Alvarez team's discovery that a couple of large comets struck Earth almost sixty-five million years ago, about the time the dinosaurs went extinct. At first glance, it looks like a tidy cause-and-effect relationship, except that when you look a little closer, you see that an awful lot of dinosaurs went extinct *before* the bombardment. An awful lot of insects, too.

"And the same thing happened about thirty-three million years later, except that this time it was mammals who suffered most conspicuously. We call this the Terminal Eocene event—and right along with the mammals went a whole slew of insects.

"Here's another puzzle: Fifteen million B.C., another asteroid strikes Earth, carves out the Reis Basin in Germany, turns graphite into microdiamonds, covers the world in a cloud of ash. No mass extinctions associated with it, though. About eight hundred thousand B.C. the same thing happens on what was then Australia's west coast, only this explosion is even bigger. Pieces of the Australian countryside are steam catapulted into space. Molten black glass rains down like bullets across most of Indochina and as far away as Russia. And again, the mystery: no mass extinction."

Wilson looked around the room. He had them hooked, and the admiral sensed that he knew it. "I've always found science to be a lot of fun," he continued. "Sometimes it's like actually living through a detective novel, in which the riddle of the dinosaurs becomes the ultimate whodunit. But the fun and games are going out of it very quickly for me. Not to sound melodramatic, but it's like trying to solve a murder and discovering that you're dealing with a serial killer, and that you may be next on his list. If this is the case, then the mysteries the paleontologists are uncovering may be important to our very survival as a species. Now, think upon this: a little more than sixty-five million years ago—mass extinction . . . thirty-three million years ago—mass extinction. Given those numbers, we may be just about due for another. For all we know, Earth could be about to shake us off like a bad case of fleas."

"But there's a big difference here," the chief of staff

objected. "We're a hell of a lot smarter than whatever mammals were killed off thirty-three million years ago. And we're certainly a lot smarter than the dinosaurs."

"It may not make any difference," the entomologist replied. "Our civilization is a few thousand years old, and has always lived in the shallows of time. Our paleontologists have only begun to scratch the surface of deep time; but the dinosaurs *lived* in deep time. And they were swallowed up there, in the depths. And we don't even know what swallowed them."

The room went quiet again, and it would have stayed that way for a long time if the front desk had not cleared through a code-yellow call to the President. On one of his five notepads, the White House science advisor's name flashed bright yellow. The President put her on the speakerphone.

"What is it, Mary?" the President asked.

"There's been a—" She puffed hard and dropped off in mid-sentence, as if she were unaccustomed to strenuous activity and had just run up several flights of stairs.

"A second outbreak?" the President guessed.

She caught her breath and told him to activate another of his notepads. She patched through CNN footage of a mite-infested tract of forest. A header at the bottom of the screen identified the place as Newbern, North Carolina. "These things couldn't have spread out of Long Beach and grown to such numbers in a single day," she concluded. "I mean, they just *couldn't* have. Whatever is causing this must have been festering in both places for a while. This isn't just an infection sending out microbursts of destruction. Long Beach could be everywhere by now. Mr. President, we have quite a problem here. Even if the casualties can be kept small, nobody knows what kind of fear this will put into people.

"What happens when you have to worry that the common, everyday mites living in the leaves on your front lawn, and in your bed, and on your skin, may grow out of control at any moment and do a piranha job on you . . . And the banks! If the mites grow out of control, and the panic grows out of control . . . Wall Street has never faced anything even remotely like this before."

"Except perhaps the CAIDS scare," Wilson noted.

"Right," the science advisor said. "Just the mere mention of casually acquired immune deficiency syndrome tumbled the Dow Jones more than six hundred points in a day. And that was mythology. This is reality."

"But it's just mites, right?" Amber Murdoch asked. "You just bomb them with soap wherever they pop up and be done with them, right?"

"No, that's not right," the admiral said. "Not if the 'mites' are just an eight-legged variation on India's theme."

"What would cause fungus and mites to start eating everything in sight?" Murdoch asked. "I don't understand."

"Nobody understands yet," Wilson said. "That's what we have to find out: What's causing these symptoms."

"And if you find the cause, do you think it can be cured?" the President asked.

"I don't know."

" 'I don't know' isn't what I need to be hearing right now," the President said.

"Would you prefer I bullshit you?" the entomologist replied.

The President shook his head apologetically.

"Dr. Wilson . . ." All eyes turned toward the science advisor's screen. "We'll need someone in Newbern at first light. Have you ever worn a space suit?"

"No."

"Well, if you're willing to do this, we'll have to train you through the night. And then come dawn we'll be sort of lowering you into a snake pit with zero sleep."

"Oh, I wouldn't worry about me getting clumsy down there. I expect my own adrenaline will keep me wide awake."

"So you're willing to go in there?" the President asked.

"Willing?" the entomologist shouted. "Just try to stop me!"

Later, alone at his desk, the President clasped both hands behind his neck and swiveled his Teflon-reinforced chair—a relic from the Reagan administration—to look out the wide windows of the Oval Office. The night lights of Washington were pleasing indeed, and gave no hint of the latest mote outbreak just a few hundred miles south, or the long new day of famine that must now be striking across the Ganges River.

The world outside actually seemed peaceful, even utopian, unless one took notice of the faint ripples and distortions in the view—a relic from the ill-fated Clinton administration. The aluminized permaglass was not only capable of stopping a bullet, but any would-be Oswald out there in the night, taking aim, would be unaware that his view of the President was being refracted a foot and a half to the left or right of where he was. *All well and fine,* the President thought, *unless the would-be assassin was smart enough to cobble together a portable laser.* A pulse of light, unlike a bullet, would simply correct for the refraction, tracing the image of the President back to its actual source. And it could be fired from five miles away.

Even the least paranoid of his advisors had warned him that it would be safer to leave the Oval Office to the historians and spend his presidency at Camp David, with its more easily guarded perimeter. But the President liked doing business face-to-face, rather than on notepads, and whenever possible he wanted instant, in-person accessibility to the Senate and the House of Representatives. His successors, he knew, would become increasingly withdrawn from their constituency, until at last they were seen only on notepads and on television, and he wondered if it might one day be possible to generate virtual national leaders who in reality did not even exist, except as charismatic, computer-animated figureheads fulfilling some ruling party's agenda.

The thought chilled him.

He longed for the days when men armed with stinger missiles did not have to be posted atop the White House. He had heard stories about how Truman used to take long strolls, without a care in the world, through crowds on Pennsylvania Avenue. There had been a time when children gathered Easter eggs on the White House lawn, and the historians said Calvin Coolidge used to take early morning swims in the Potomac. They also told him that about 1628 B.C., on the Isle of Thera, none of the homes had locks on the doors, though they were multistoried, centrally heated dwellings filled with great works of art; yet here he sat, behind refractive, bullet-resistant windows with the Secret Service planning to replace the roof-top stinger array with a new system of laser defenses and—he laughed—and they call *this* an advanced civilization.

For better or for worse, he was stuck with it; stuck with this civilization, stuck with this job. He was what the author of *Childhood's End* had once called "the kind of president America so sorely needs, if you take pause to consider that there are some jobs which should never be given to people who volunteer for them, especially if they show too much enthusiasm." What the writer had in mind was a man who would be drafted by his party on the basis of qualifications alone, and who would have to be shoved kicking and screaming into the Oval Office.

Two more years, the President thought. Just two more years till the next primary, and maybe then the party and the voters would give him time off for good behavior. Maybe then he could think in terms of settling down and starting a family. In the meantime, as he had once remarked to a reporter: "I simply do not have time to get involved in my own personal life." He was not joking. He barely had time for a cat. There was only the presidency.

Something chirped on the desk behind him, and he turned to see a SEARCH COMPLETED card flashing at the top of a notepad. He scrolled down a long series of North American crop reports, finding no signs of fungal infestation or failures of any kind except in the citrus industry and . . . good thing we got rid of the honey subsidy, he thought. But all the grain crops were doing just fine. Indeed, a bumper crop of such great proportion was anticipated that corn and wheat were already taking a nosedive on the commodities markets. Dow Chemical was taking a hit, too, he observed . . . in the insecticides division . . . because farmers had stopped spraying their fields . . . as if there was no longer a need for insecticides . . . no need at all.

What was it the old entomologist had said about dead bees and dinosaurs? But, no—it just couldn't be that bad.

Yet a part of him kept going back to the afternoon, when he was about eighteen years old, walking alone on Hilton Head in a knee-deep surf that just couldn't have looked all that bad. But a wave caught him off guard anyway and drew him into a long, exhausting fight with an undertow. He had done everything the experts said you ought to do in such situations: don't panic, don't swim against the tow, in a headlong, futile dash toward shore; but rather swim parallel with the shore until you are out of the tow's grip.

And just when he thought he was safe, he realized he was not alone in the water. A dark brown shape, not much larger than he was, but *appearing* to be much larger, shot by, a half dozen feet on his right side, and circled around to his left. Its fin never broke the surface, nor did it so much as nudge him with its nose; and yet nothing, man nor beast, had ever made him feel so helpless before or since. He had a notion that if he panicked, the fish would sense his quickening heartbeat and home in on him, that if he splashed wildly toward shore, the savage brain might interpret this as the struggle of injured, easy prey. An inner, instinctive voice commanded him to proceed slowly, gracefully toward the shallows, and outwardly his mind fought against a grim certainty that just before he reached the line of white foam where the waves were breaking on the beach, and he could stand, and run, he would feel his foot being snagged in a vise and shaken violently from side to side.

He was getting very much that same creepy feeling tonight, a feeling that he was being pulled into deep water; and there were dark shapes circling in the undertow, darker than he cared to imagine right now, darker than he could imagine.

''Somehow we'll get through this,'' he wished he could tell his people. ''Somehow we'll get back to the shore. Somehow it'll be all right.''

Richard guessed that if someone had told their college buddies, more than fifteen years ago, that today he would be drawing up plans to coax extinct DNA back to life— to raise the dead, in a manner of speaking—and that Bill would be one of the world's leading authorities on vampire bats, they would have said, "Yeah, that sounds about right."

Richard's notepad indicated another e-mail message from Bill, but as yet he had not even read it, and felt no motivation to do so in spite of the URGENT blinker that had been tagged on. There were bigger issues on his mind. Tam. Sleep did not seem to have its house after all. His little girl had awakened after only two hours; and as soon as she remembered where she was and how she got there, she ran to the sink and vomited—again.

By now there could not have been anything left in her stomach. Her favorite dinner—buttermilk pancakes topped with strawberry syrup and sour cream—had gone untouched. He did not blame her. The numb state, as he was coming to call it, had spirited their appetites away, along with all their emotions . . . along with *most* of their emotions. Tam was now beginning to express anger.

"You *lied* to me," she shouted, recalling the night she had dreamed up invisible demons' arms stretching out across her sheets and trying to drag her underneath the bed. "You and Mommy told me there were no monsters— *no real ones*—but real monsters hurt Mommy, didn't they?"

Richard lowered his head and offered no reply. He tried to put an arm over her shoulder, but she pushed him away.

"Tell me!" Tam raged. "M-motes! Monsters! They're real, aren't they? Tell me!"

"Yes," he whispered. "I'm afraid they are."

"Then why did you say there were no monsters?"

Richard shook his head. "Because it used to be true," he said. His face was an expressionless mask. His voice was without life.

"It used to be true," he said again.

9

The World, the Flesh, and the Devil

DAY 2

Bill and Janet had never heard of vampire bats swarming upon and killing humans. Certainly, they never expected to witness and document such a case. Schools of airborne, blood-sucking piranha—they were the denizens of monster movies, not the real world. Yet dawn on Tobago brought with it shrieks and wails, and news of entire families massacred in their beds. One of the bloodbaths had occurred only a short walk down the road from the Schutts, at the nearest plantation.

This time the bats *had* clung on long enough to trigger

their kidneys to a rapid-water-dump response. Their urine was everywhere. Janet noticed that the floor and furnishings were smeared also with a dark, tarry substance. She recognized it immediately as feces, and like the urine, it stank of blood.

It was, Bill would e-mail Richard later that morning, "a horrifying experience. As soon as we stepped into the house, we were taken from our peaceful, paradise island existence and cast into a strange new world that shifted psychotic, as if we stepped into a Dalí painting. Everything seemed at once familiar, yet unfamiliar. There was the wide-screen TV, the cereal boxes set on the kitchen table for the next morning's breakfast, the dishes cleaned and left to dry in a rack beside the sink . . . the crib in the youngest boy's room, the model space shuttle in the eldest's . . . and the whole of it covered in rotting brown blood and urine. The smell was awful, the sort of stench that should have attracted whole armies of flies. And that was the most unfamiliar part of all. We saw none. That is what you have to remember, Richard, if you are receiving this. No flies!"

Only the eldest son had made it as far as the kitchen. The other four members of the Colbert family were lying in or very close to their beds. The attackers themselves had disappeared, and the fact that there were no dead or injured bats lying near the body of the eldest son—who must have been covered with them at the moment he tripped over a chair—confirmed for Bill their identity.

Ounce for ounce, *Desmodus rotundus* was the strongest bat in the world. Slamming into a chair and crashing onto the floor just wouldn't be enough to kill them. One could probably stand on them, although few were inclined to try, and they would get up and scramble away.

Bill guessed that hundreds, perhaps thousands of them, had crept under doorways and through windows into the Colberts' house. If you did not close those windows and seal the cracks under the doors with duct tape and they wanted to get in at you, they would invariably succeed. The big question on Bill's mind was, Where had they gone? Unlike their insect-eating cousins, their roosts were not confined to caves. There had been a long history of bat purges in the tropics, usually triggered by a random vampire-induced rabies death. In the past, while misguided government officials blasted and poisoned caves, killing millions of beneficial bats, the vampires had roosted in trees, under bridges, or in the basements of the officials' own houses. Like their mythical namesakes, they slept by day; and Bill guessed that they must now be roosting in diverse, and interesting, places. Bats were, after all, among nature's great infiltrators.

Bill remembered hearing about an amazing plan in which bats were to infest and destroy Japanese cities during World War II. Miniature incendiary bombs with timers were glued to their bodies. The bats were, in effect, the world's first attempt at constructing a smart cluster bomb. The bomb housing was a giant bat cage with fall-away walls and floors. Dropped by parachute from a plane, just before dawn, it was designed to open up at fifteen hundred feet. Seeking refuge, the bats would enter houses and factories, flittering onto wooden eaves and into dark corners where explosives and uranium oxides were stored, or into the beds of Hirohito and Yamamoto themselves, where they would blaze forth as six thousand tongues of well-placed flame.

The bomb worked well. Too well. When it was tested over New Mexico, some of the little winged bomblets went astray, descending into a newly constructed Air Force base and reducing every building, every airplane, and much of the scrub brush surrounding the base to cinders. A second bomb was quickly assembled; but shortly before it was to be dropped on Japan, it was rendered obsolete by the first successful test of the atomic bomb—a lucky break for the bats; not so lucky for their human captors. The Air Force never built another bat bomb, and save for a few people like Bill Schutt, the story had all but disappeared into history.

Where, he wondered, was *Desmodus* hiding?

"Bill?" Janet called. "I think you'd better have a look out the window."

He looked toward the place where Janet was pointing. Five people had been slaughtered inside the house, yet just outside, in the open air, where blood seemed as easy for the taking as walking into a grocery store, all but two of the Colberts' cows were still standing. None of them— even the two dead ones—showed any signs of having been fed upon this past night by *Desmodus*. Three of them stood shaking their heads violently from side to side, as if deliberately trying to make themselves dizzy. Two others made loud choking sounds. The rest, watching listlessly, responded with an occasional, sickly ululation.

"Dead by Sunday," Janet concluded. "The whole herd. Mad cow disease. Brain rot."

"But that's carried by flies, isn't it?"

"I think it's spread mostly by contaminated food, and maybe by horseflies."

"And there are no flies."

"Then it's as our friends on Trinidad suggested: The disease must have jumped vectors," Janet said. "Maybe it's jumped to a new carrier species." She could not turn her eyes away from the cows. "Wipe out the insects— wipe out the most common vectors of disease—and you're threatening the livelihood of an awful lot of disease organisms."

"That's a hell of a natural selection filter."

"You bet," Janet said. "It's Darwin's theory meeting Murphy's law. Any disease organism that *can* survive in the spit of a migrating bat population *will* survive. Anything that can go wrong, will."

Oh, my God, Bill thought. *Don't let what she thinks is happening really be happening.* But when he thought of the puzzle he had begun piecing together over the corpse of the red bat the day before—first an insect crisis, then a bat crisis—he knew that she was probably right. If the insects were disappearing, a lot of insect-borne diseases would disappear right alongside them . . . except for a lucky few that happened to possess the necessary biological equipment to ride along with other species. And so it came to pass that a prion disease had jumped from insects to bats; and in the Schutts' emerging picture, as the bats fed on the blood of cows, they were unwittingly poisoning their own food supply. Vampire bats would not feed on sick cattle, Bill knew; so as the prions had switched to a new disease vector, so too was the vector switching to a new food source.

Bill looked around the blood-and-urine-spattered room and shook his head. "They're roosting again; but they'll be back at dusk."

"I'm afraid we've just bought into a growth industry," Janet said.

Bill tried to stifle a laugh. "What have we got here? Bats? Death of cows? Flesh-eating mites? What next? Frogs?"

It was a joke, of course. Bill was always good for a joke, no matter how grave the circumstances. Even as fear began to constrict his throat he managed, as an afterthought, to off-load from his pad, with his morning e-mail to Richard, a message he had saved from a fourth grader who liked to write poems about bats:

> There once was a bat who ate bugs.
> He never, ever did drugs.
> He had really small eyes
> and liked mosquito pies.
> In his spare time he liked to soil rugs.

Just two days earlier, Richard would have immediately burst into laughter, but not today. Bill's joke about frogs, dead cows, and the Book of Exodus, especially, would provoke no laughter. Thus far, only a privileged few aboard the *Nimitz*, in the White House, and at Brookhaven Labs knew how a spreading black growth threatened to turn India, Pakistan, and Sri Lanka into a mass grave. The fourth plague—and there were six more yet to come.

The numb state came and went, but mostly it stayed with Tam, like a loyal dog. It pushed back her pain and her anger. It left her feeling as if all the horrors were not really happening to her—as if she were merely playing a cameo role in someone else's nightmare.

She never did go back to sleep, that first night at Brookhaven. Neither did Daddy. And strangely, neither of them felt particularly tired. Or hungry.

Numbness. Sweet numbness.

It allowed her even to accept that Jackson and some of the grown-ups had been yelling at Daddy, yelling something about "pulling your head together . . . serious business . . . pay attention, already." It allowed her to accept, without emotion, three or four other things the grown-ups had never meant her to hear, but which were spoken within earshot anyway. . . . There was no cause for concern about hazards to health arising from decaying bodies in the part of Long Beach referred to as "ground zero," because there were only bones picked clean and dead, soap-bombed mites. . . . The death toll in Long Beach had now topped three thousand, apparently because as many people were killed in the panic-driven rivers of stalled traffic that had backed up behind the raised drawbridges as by the mites themselves. . . . There were more mites breaking out somewhere. . . .

Numbness. Sweet numbness.

It allowed her even to play, after a fashion, with Georgiana—another child of Brookhaven, and another Long Beach refugee. But Georgiana's story of survival was quite different from Tam's. Georgiana's family was still intact, having been far away in a place called Trinidad when Long Beach fell. Georgiana said something had made her father decide to leave Trinidad in a hurry. Something scary. Something to do with bats.

That made no sense at all. Tam liked bats, and she could not understand why a grown man would be afraid of them.

Georgiana said there were a lot of things to be afraid of. She told Tam her father had noticed all the ants on Trinidad were gone. "This is very bad," Georgiana explained. "You won't believe how much the world needs ants. Even the deserts are full of ants. Even in Iraq there are ants."

"How do ants get in a rock?" Tam asked.

Georgiana, who was a couple of years older than Tam, laughed. Tam did not, even after her friend explained the accidental joke. Tam did not think she would ever laugh again. Georgiana sensed this and, trying to ignore the little twinges of guilt—

(Why did my family survive and not hers?)

—attempted to provide a distraction by downloading her entire ant library into Tam's notepad. She called a picture onto the screen, in browns and greens, showing a large colony of the South American ant known as *Brachymyrmex*. She then scrolled at psychopathic speed through nearly ten thousand species of increasingly larger ants, until at last the entire *Brachymyrmex* colony was scaled to actual size, standing on the head of the Bornean carpenter ant.

Tam muttered a faint "wow."

A little box appeared on the screen, quoting the Bible: "Go to the ant thou sluggard; consider her ways." Thus did King Solomon speak to a lazy subject, in praise of the harvester ant for the industry she displayed in building underground granaries. In certain trees, the ants, in their quest for shelter and food, ate or drove off invading insects and mites. They transported the seeds, aerated, and even fertilized the roots. Georgiana displayed close-up pictures explaining why the warm, moist ant tunnels did not fill up with fungi and bacteria, though providing the perfect environment for runaway growth. The ants possessed special glands that were constantly dripping chemicals, lethal to any fungi or bacteria that threatened them or their host plants. In return for shelter, nectar, and a few seeds, the ants behaved like white corpuscles. They literally became their host's immune system.

"A superorganism," Edwin Wilson had called the typical ant colony—and a picture of him appeared on the screen.

"The superorganisms make no concessions," the picture said. "They understand no mercy or variance given on their behalf, and will always be as elegant and pitiless as we now witness them, until the last one dies."

Tam wrinkled her nose disapprovingly. She did not understand many of the words, and on an impulse she grabbed control of the notepad from Georgiana. She began scrolling through the morning's e-mail, and stopped at a new message from Uncle Bill, only to find more words she did not understand, and a poem. There was something about mos . . . qui—mosquito pies! Yuck! She'd have to ask Daddy if there was any such thing; but someone had taken him away to a room where they were going to watch Georgiana's much-loved ant expert put on a space suit and go for a walk through the North Carolina motes.

Georgiana grabbed the notepad from Tam and put Wilson's ant lesson back on the screen. The entomologist was showing pictures of a fenced-in section of forest slowly dying off near Brookhaven National Laboratory during the 1950s. The scientists had irradiated the forest with gamma rays. For comparison, Wilson showed pictures of a similar patch of forest in which all the ants had been removed. The fates of the two forests were identical in every way except one: the irradiated forest began to recover as soon as the man-made stressor was removed; the ant-cleansed forest did not.

Tam made another grab for the notepad, but Georgiana yanked it away.

"If all of humanity were to disappear," Wilson explained, "the remainder of life would spring back and flourish. The increased rate of extinction and the deforestations now under way would cease, the damaged ecosystems would heal and expand outward. If all the ants—and nothing except the ants—somehow disappeared, the effect would be exactly the opposite, and catastrophic. Species extinction would increase even more over the present rate, and the land ecosystems would shrivel even more rapidly as the considerable services provided by these insects were pulled away—"

Tam got a hard grip on the notepad, this time. "It's mine," she said, and cut the Wilson lesson short, in favor of the video game file.

Edwin Wilson was running a little behind schedule. The final checkout of his space suit had taken longer than anticipated. It was older than the one Richard had worn in Long Beach the previous day. Its pumps and circulators made the inside of his helmet sound as if he were standing in the middle of a packing factory. Even after his harness was unhooked and winched up into jets of sterilizing steam and the helicopter had pulled away beyond the tree line, a reduction in the level of noise was barely noticeable.

He could not turn his head without turning his entire

body; and everywhere he turned, the forest was shrouded in black. Mites roiled over every leaf, displaying for him the curious blend of wonder and obscenity one encountered only in nature. He stood in the heart of the no-man's-land, in a Twilight Zone between beauty and horror, the living and the dead. If he tore the suit, the little black horrors would spill inside, erasing his world, turning it into theirs.

For close on a full minute, as the monitors at Brookhaven and Atlanta showed his heart thudding ever faster and perceptions of time began stretching to their outermost limits, he radioed back nothing. He simply stood in the small clearing, looking at the mite-crusted twigs and trunks, and at the three bodies that had shown up as infrared stains during the night. When successive satellite and helicopter flybys were viewed by aid of time-lapse photography, the infrared heat sources began to move, seeming somehow to have been reborn into a ghostly new life-form. As they cooled, they spread like the pseudopodia of giant amoebae, across dozens of yards of ground. Wilson had seen the films, and guessed immediately what was happening. The mites, as they stole away with their victims' flesh, also carried off some of their heat.

All that remained was hair and bone and loose cloth.

"One deer, two people," Wilson said at last. "Collecting sample number one."

He bent down and activated the first of three sample chambers in his tray, and noticed that the mites were already swarming over his feet. They were all the way up to the silvery band of sticky tape he had wound around his right ankle, so he could quickly tear off a length and make a patch should he tear a hole in his suit. There were a thousand ways of ripping his suit, a thousand mite-covered twigs pointing out at him from the underbrush.

He held the sample tray close to his faceplate. The morning sun was still low in the sky, and almost all of it was blocked by the trees, and what few shafts of daylight slanted uninterrupted to the ground were mostly absorbed by the mites. And still, even in this cold, dark place, the air in his suit felt as if it were above ninety degrees and there was enough light for him to see that the mites held few surprises for him.

"I don't have a microscope here," he radioed, "but I'll tell you now, when we compare them with the Long Beach samples, we're gonna see that they're nothing new to us. They're common, already-known mite species. All of them. I'll stake my reputation on it."

"Then you agree they just didn't spread out of Long Beach?" the President's science advisor asked.

"Certain of it," Wilson said. Which still left the question—the one he did not want to voice openly on any radio frequency—What *did* cause common dust mites living harmlessly in the leaves of the forest, and in our carpets, our beds, and our skin, to suddenly explode to such outrageous numbers and do a piranha job on us?

"Going after sample number two," Wilson announced, and began exploring the forest. In his avoidance of brambles and branches, he realized that he was moving more slowly than the most cautious deep-ocean explorer.

Deep ocean . . . and suddenly he was reminded of sponges—of all things!

Yes, sponges. He reminded himself that what they had in common with dust mites was that he'd once found it difficult to imagine a more benign life-form. Sponges comprised a large part of the world's reef ecosystems, providing shelter for fish and small crustaceans and filtering their waste products out of the water. Yet during the 1990s, in a small Mediterranean cave that had been flooded by the rise of Ice Age waters, something almost as strange as the motes had turned up. The cave was found to be almost totally lacking the sorts of nutrients necessary for the flourishing of sponges, but the walls and ceiling were covered with sponges anyway. Divers found the floor to be littered with the shells and bones of those few crustaceans and small fish that had wandered into the cave. Faced with a sterile environment in which sunlight did not support the growth of algae—which formed the basis of the Mediterranean food chain—the sponges had undergone a change of habit. Their glassy spicules became long, adhesive-coated hooks, from which the occasional straggler from the outside world could not possibly escape. Once snared, the straggler was slowly enveloped in migrating, corpuscle-like sponge cells and digested alive over the course of two or three days.

The harmless filter-feeding sponge had become a carnivore, and the lesson for Wilson was simply this: Given enough variables in nature, whatever nature needed to do, it invariably did. Given such examples as the sponges and the mites, nature might even appear to act consciously, deviously. It was an illusion, he assured himself, albeit a very persistent one.

His faceplate was fogging up, making it even darker inside his suit, just dark enough to allow the first little fingers of claustrophobia to caress his spine and move unexpectedly—gently, even—to his ribs, where they began to squeeze. His breath caught on the next two intakes. He pushed his face against the bubble, rubbed the moisture until he could see clearly again, and turned up the electric blower until a little blast of cool air tugged at the hair on his forehead.

There, that's better, he told himself. It meant more drain on the batteries, but under normal use his backpack had a life span of seven and a half hours. With the air-conditioning on high, he was down to about three hours. But he did not worry; he was planning to be out of here within twenty minutes.

"Are you all right, Dr. Wilson?"

"Yes. Just fine," he answered back.

Someone in Atlanta, monitoring his heartbeat and respiration, was concerned. It must have gone off the scales, Wilson guessed. There was no telling in advance who was going to "go buggers" in a space suit. Wilson recalled the unusual intensity with which the leader of the training team had peered into his eyes the first time the helmet closed over his face. The man was looking for the faintest glimmer of fear in him, for a widening of the pupils, for signs of unusual sweating, or his breath beginning to catch on every hitch. There had been no warning signs. But that was a practice session in a laboratory setting. If he had begun to panic, then, if he had begun to scream and claw at the seals, trying to pull the helmet off and let the fresh air in, there were a half dozen people standing around him, and no mites.

Here, he was on his own.

Here, he was discovering that adrenaline alone was not the cure-all he had hoped it would be. He found it more exhausting than supportive, and he wished they had let him have some coffee. But, no—that was against regulations. As the prep team told it, his suit was equipped with a urine collection bag fed by a rubber receiver which covered his penis. The "rubbers," in a tradition going back to the *Apollo* astronauts, were available in only three sizes: "extra large, immense, and unbelievable." The checkout crew told him that Buzz Aldrin, when he stepped away from the Lunar Module, immediately lost control of his bladder and became the first man to pee in his pants on the moon. More than a billion people had been watching, but only Aldrin knew what they were really seeing. They warned Wilson that his suit could easily handle a loss of bladder control, but that there was no collection system for feces. Coffee, they said, when combined with excitement, could trigger involuntary defecation. The warning reminded Wilson of the old joke about "farting in a space suit," except that the stink and feel of feces streaming down his legs could, in their own turn, trigger vomiting; and vomiting in a helmeted space suit was not nearly so funny as it was deadly.

"Picking up sample number two," he radioed, and squatted down on the "motescape"—

And then he saw the shark's tooth. He bent forward and picked it up. It was the largest he had ever seen. Maybe even worth keeping, he thought, if we can steam-clean it along with this suit—but then he thought better of it. As he tried to shake the mites off the fossil, they clung to his gloves; and when he glanced down he saw that the plastic on his legs and chest was completely covered with them, and the claustrophobia gnome was once again trying to close her gentle fingers around his ribs.

He jerked his head back and stood up quickly. Letting the tooth drop to the ground, he made his peace with the gnome, walked off toward the trunk of a tree, and raised his sample tray.

"Sample number three and I'm out of here," he said.

The light seemed to be dimming again. They had reached his faceplate, and Wilson was reminded once more of the cave and the sponges . . . of darkness . . . and carnivores. He cranked the power up another notch, and the backpack sent cooler, drier air roaring around his face.

There . . . that felt better. He could think again more clearly—he could hold back feelings of mites closing in on him, could divert his thoughts to cracking the secret of whatever had caused this runaway population boom.

"Finished?" This call came from the helicopter.

"I think so," Wilson said. He touched the tray to a mite-covered piece of bark and sucked a thousand of them into the third chamber.

"And none too soon," he said.

"That's unlike you," a voice called from Washington.

"Well, walk a mile in my moccasins and you'll see what I mean."

"Impressions?" Leslie Wells asked this question.

"It's not the mites that have gone wrong," he said. "It's their surroundings."

"Pretty strange conclusion, don't you think?"

"What I'm seeing around me is pretty strange. These mites, like the ones that have been choking the honeybees to death, were always present in the environment. You can bet on it. It's something to do with the bees themselves, with the forest itself that's gone all to hell. Something we're missing."

"Such as?"

"Such as the bees themselves weakening, or dying, or letting their eggs lie dormant. Such as this mass die-off of butterflies and fireflies we're hearing about, and maybe a whole lot of other insects we haven't heard about yet, simply because they're less noticeable. Yes, it could be something like that. Something strange."

"Could a single disease or toxin cause all that?" Leslie asked.

"In theory, perhaps. But in reality"—he had to shout over the din of his backpack and the approaching helicopter. "In reality there isn't a single virus or poison in all the known world that could account for this."

"Yes," Leslie said. "It sounds impossible."

"Impossible maybe—"

He stopped.

"—but here it is, all around me. Some controlling element—a predator, perhaps—has been removed from the mite's environment. Now, don't ask me what kind of little beastie, insect or otherwise, chews mite populations down to size. It must be something we haven't seen before. I think only two or three people in the whole world have ever made a study of mite ecology. Compare that against ants. We know a lot more about ants"—his breath caught —"we know ten thousand species of ants, and we know there are tens of thousands of species yet to be known. In the world of mites, the only things we could have missed are a couple of mile-long elephants."

He looked up and saw two men armed with steam hoses lowering the harness to him; but rather than fill him with relief, the helicopter, closing off the sky, made him feel even more claustrophobic. He shrugged the feeling off and continued to talk, even as the faceplate darkened with a thick, new wave of ascending mites and he began to realize that the harness, descending toward the center of the clearing, was becoming difficult to see.

He wiped a hand across his faceplate, fighting off the urge to let instinct take over and send him running blindly after the harness. Twenty thousand little bodies smashed and smeared across his field of vision, leaving a translucent, crescent-shaped window through which he could see—just barely see—his lifeline hovering in the air. He managed to keep his composure and walk slowly forward through the encroaching darkness of yet another wave of ascending mites.

"I don't know what eats mites," he quavered. "But I do have a good idea what should be keeping those fungi under control in India. Ants. Fungus gnats. And—"

His world went black. He smeared them away, created another translucent window; and when he looked down, he saw that they were as thick as wool on his chest. New surges of adrenaline shot through him like shock from a live wire, and his brain began snapping facts together faster than ever before in his life, looking for ways out of the forest and simultaneously sending up warnings that might save his friends, just in case there was no way out. Somewhere on the floor of his skull, computations that normally took an hour were conducted in a second without his even knowing it; and in this instinctive, adrenal shock state, a second really did seem an hour.

"My God! It's the fungus gnats!" he shouted.

"What?" called Leslie. "I'm not sure I understand."

"They're dead, I tell you! All the fungus gnats are dead!"

Darkness closed in. He rubbed another mite-smeared clearing into his faceplate, but again the darkness closed in, again, again, again. The helicopter pilot saw that he was in trouble and tried to bring the harness nearer to him, but the line circled behind and thumped hard against his backpack. Wilson's subconscious conjured up an image of something large standing behind him in the dark . . . stalking him. The image welled up in him like an awful alarm bell, and raw, murderous instinct took charge. He bolted forward, arms outstretched, bounced off a tree trunk, and screamed. His left side came down hard on the bones of Mr. Ames. He felt the old guard's ribs and a smashed piece of pelvis bite deep into his suit, stood up in the dark, ran headlong through some brambles, bounced off another tree trunk, came down on his left side once more, heard another row of ribs snapping—this time his own—rolled, rose to his feet again, tried as best he could to make another run for it, caught his foot on a rock, fractured his ankle, and hit the ground with a sickening crack that told him his faceplate was now wide open.

Two hundred miles directly overheard, a spy satellite, its lenses trained on the still cold, early morning ground, recorded an infrared, ameboid shape spreading from the place where Wilson's faceplate had been. Four hundred miles away in Atlanta, mission controllers had been monitoring biomedical data coming cross-country from Edwin Wilson. They watched the rise in Wilson's pulse rate, a rise that continued for forty-two seconds, then stopped abruptly. Fortunately, mercifully, someone had remembered to switch off Wilson's voice outfeeds.

10

The Mad Room and the Phoenix Road

The cell was small and completely bare. The bed was a concrete slab, the toilet a concrete box with a hole in the top. There was no window—not even a slit with bars to let the sun in. The single fluorescent light, recessed behind a sheet of permaglass in the ceiling, burned dimmer than the moon.

Across the room, opposite the concrete bed, a window-wall of solid permaglass separated him from the guard walk, and the world beyond. Through that window-wall, food trays entered and left via what Jerry Sigmond had come to call "the airlock." He thought he had never seen such a sterile and uninviting place in his life. It was the sort of place that had driven the late O. J. Simpson to bouts of wild-eyed, manic laughter (and as one urban myth had it, some years after they set him free, the "late" O. J.

walked off into the Mojave and was never seen again; but for all anyone really knew, he was wandering the desert highways right now, still giggling to himself).

Jerry understood that there were worse fates than being driven out of his mind by loneliness.

There was being driven out of his mind *by* someone.

It had taken every semblance of warmth and down-home kindness he had stolen from Jack and Adelle to charm Cardillo and Guzman into arranging solitary confinement. He thought that deep down he might actually have tricked the younger cop. The jury was still out on the burly Dominican. But they no longer mattered to Jerry so much as his jailers, and he was certain he had gotten Amy, the guard with the bad complexion, on his side. Already he knew that she was studying hard at night school, hoping to earn the degree she had forgone when she decided to marry straight out of high school . . . he knew that her husband of twelve years had left her . . . that she had frequently listened to the *Jerry Sigmond Show*. Already, he had gotten her to open the door, just a crack, just enough to allow Jerry Sigmond to crawl around inside her skull. He really did not care a rat's sphincter whether or not Amy and the cops liked him—except to the extent that by making them like him, even making them feel sorry for him, he might convince them to grant him favors.

The manipulation seemed to be working. On his very first day, he had managed to attain "protected" status. His private suite was cramped and too warm and too dark, and thus did little to alleviate the numbness that was trying to creep into him. It wasn't much, he admitted, but he'd take it.

He'd take Amy, too, before this was over, take her completely and inescapably into his web. She was the sort of woman no man would glance at twice on a busy street—which made her easy prey to the attentions of a handsome celebrity, and Jerry Sigmond knew it. Jerry Sigmond was counting on it.

As Edwin Wilson bled under the morning sun and another dove left the *Nimitz* and a hot, fungus-laced wind swept into Pakistan, Jerry stood before the floor-to-ceiling wall of permaglass and positioned himself under the fluorescent lamp so that he could see his reflection. For the next twenty minutes he practiced his gestures, his mannerisms, and his smile. That warm, inviting smile.

As soon as Amy reached the airlock, Jerry began his act. Across the cell, presenting only his back to her, he stood looking at the blank wall above his bed as if he were studying a window that looked out on the world. Long after she had placed his breakfast tray in the airlock, he continued to study the wall, giving her the impression of a contemptuous indifference to her presence. It filled her with disappointment. The oracle had more important concerns than a starstruck jailer; she was suddenly quite sure of that.

Silly girl, she told herself. *What were you thinking?*

Then he turned and looked at her with a blank expression that broke unexpectedly into a warm smile of recognition and welcome; and by the power of sheer contrast to the dejection of a moment before, he lifted her spirits instantly, shocking her; and Amy's next shocked thought was: *Why, he wasn't ignoring me after all. He was simply lost in his worries. He* is *glad to see me. I just misread him, misunderstood him—*

"Amy!" he said. "Good morning!"

She glanced down, fixing her gaze on the biscuits, the juice, and the sheaf of writing paper in the airlock. He did the same, and when she overcame her momentary shyness and looked up, his smile had become even warmer, almost fatherly. He stepped forward and spread out his hands, as if genuinely apologizing for her discomfort.

"I'm sorry," he said, relishing her confusion. "As you can gather, I've got some serious troubles on my mind."

"I understand," Amy said. "If there's anything I can do—within reason—that will make all of this any easier, just let me know."

"That's a deal. But I'm afraid you don't really understand what's happened to me. There were a lot of people who wanted to see me taken off the air. Now they've got their opportunity."

"You mean the scientists?" Amy asked.

"Yes. They didn't like me criticizing them."

"One of them is dead. You've mentioned him on your show. Wilson, I think."

"What?" His smile was gone. "How?"

"There's been a second mote outbreak. North Carolina, this time. Wilson went in. There was some kind of helicopter accident—"

"North Carolina? How the hell did motes get all the way down there?"

"That's anybody's guess. It's all they're talking about on CNN, on UPN, CBS—"

"Not good news for the stock exchange," Jerry said, and became downcast. "And *Wilson*. Unbelievable news," he added with quiet sincerity. "A terrible loss."

"Terrible loss?" Amy asked. "I'm impressed. Listening to your radio show, I wouldn't have imagined you cared whether he lived or died."

Jerry nodded his head, very slowly. "Oh, I cared very much whether he lived or died," and he chuckled to himself, inwardly, recalling the words of Thomas Gray: "Where ignorance is bliss, 'tis folly to be wise."

Not much of a eulogy, Jerry thought. But it served him well.

"You're too kind," Amy said harshly. "He was hellbent on stopping you, wasn't he?"

He looked at her warmly, conveying patience. "Many people wanted to muzzle me. But I never wished any of them to die for it. The difference between me and the Edwin Wilsons of this world is that I would have gone to the wall for their right to free speech. But they would not have done the same for me. While it's true I found almost everything that came out of these evolutionists' mouths offensive, I always tried to remember that we are living in America.

"What I'm telling you, Amy, is that in America we must stand even for the rights of people who express ideas we hate. The test of freedom means nothing if we apply it only to people with whom we agree."

"So you're trying to tell me this is all a censorship issue? That your being here is simply a setup? Some sort of conspiracy?"

He nodded again. "All anyone could *really* find to complain about was the Isle of Luna scandal. And let me tell you something: That was no scam. A couple of people in my organization might have gotten a little greedy; but if *you* had invested in it, I'd be telling you today to hold on to your shares. They'll make money one day. Lots of money. And that's the gospel truth."

He took a cup of tomato juice from the tray and sipped. When he looked up, he made sure to be smiling gently at her again. He wondered if Amy might be able to see through his smile. He would have to be very careful with her. She was homely and love-starved, and she was many other things, but stupid was not one of them.

"Rumor has it you've a lot to be ashamed of," she said. "They say you've destroyed people's lives."

"Do you always believe the last thing you heard on CNN? You're an educated person, for crying out loud. Please—take the time to penetrate into the details, to find out if what you've heard is a fact and not a fiction, before you join the wrecking crew. Didn't CNN, just last week, criticize the Canadian prime minister for conducting nuclear tests in the South Pacific?" Now his smile broadened, demanding an answering smile—which Amy did not deny him.

"Canada doesn't have nuclear weapons," she said.

"Exactly. And how many people do you think know that? How many do you think actually took the time to check the facts?"

"But we can't really blame them."

"Yes we can!"

"I'm not so sure about that. I don't think society can work that way. There has to be a certain amount of trust or it all falls apart. You can probably get by if you check about ten or twenty percent of the facts, but if we didn't believe *anything* we heard, everybody would be spending a hundred percent of their time checking up on everybody else, and all banking transactions, all industry—every business in the world—would come to a screeching halt. For society to work smoothly, we must be able to take, on good faith, about eighty percent of what we are told."

All the better for a skilled liar, Jerry thought, and then thought better of letting the thought slip out.

"Percentages," he said. "Now you're beginning to sound like the President," and he raised one brow approvingly.

Amy let out a laugh.

"And what have your bosses been telling you about me? That I'm some sort of monster?"

"Something like that. A madman. A born sociopath."

"Ah, Wilson's 'bad seed' theory again," he said, and he suddenly held up his right hand, pretending it was gnarled with age, and he pointed in her direction and let loose with a very convincing impression of Bela Lugosi: "I have no home. Hunted! Despised! Living like an animal. The jungle is my home. But I shall show the world that I can be its master!"

She laughed again, and he began to wonder how she would answer if he inquired about her religion and the depth of her conviction. He had occupied himself with a wonderful and delightfully secret hobby, back in his university days, before Richard and the Wilsons of this world began to butcher his dreams. The hobby had begun as a means of earning walking-around money, and it worked best with people who called themselves atheists. Such beliefs were most easily brought into the open during barroom discussions, and once Jerry found a mark willing to proclaim from highest authority that there was no Allah, no Rama, no Jesus—nothing except space-time geometry, death, and tomorrow—Jerry would press a little deeper, getting his mark to proclaim with equal authority that there was no such thing as "the human soul."

Whereupon he produced a one-page bill of sale, governed by the laws of the State of New York. It was a simple transfer of ownership contract, perfectly standard in every way, except for one peculiarity: The property being transferred, for the sum of one hundred dollars cash, was the "transferer's immortal soul for all eternity," with the stipulation that the transferee, "effective from the date of transfer, is sole owner of all rights including transfer or sale to third parties of transferee's own choosing."

Jerry had no difficulty finding a slightly arrogant mark

who could be pressed to agree that a hundred dollars was a very good price for something that did not exist. Always he made sure the mark was sober before signing on the dotted line and affixing a little pinprick of blood (a legally binding DNA signature, and the seed of superstition) to the contract. There was no thrill or sport in his hobby unless his mark was sober. No legality, either. Jerry knew that he could actually survive a lawsuit if the mark complained, especially as the contract did not even define what the transferer's "immortal soul" was.

As a final, vital detail, he left each transferer with a wad of cash, a copy of the contract, and a business card displaying his voice mail number.

What, he asked himself again, was *her* religious upbringing? Protestant? Catholic? One or the other, he guessed. There was something distinctly Irish about Amy. They exchanged another glance, and for Jerry the expression that had tracked across her face became a revelation. For an instant her eyes betrayed hope, and something else; and in that instant, he understood that she was beginning to trust him. From this moment, she would not just take 80 percent of what he said on good faith. She was now as high as 90. Perhaps 95.

"Who was it who said, 'Freedom of speech is life itself?' " he asked.

"I don't know," Amy said.

"Ignorance is the soil in which belief in miracles grows."

"Ingersoll."

"So, you *are* widely read. Good. The same man also said, 'It's what we don't know that will get us all killed.' If I remember correctly, he was talking about a word you brought up not two minutes ago. You said something about a conspiracy. What did I say, on my radio show, about cancer, AIDS, and all those other diseases that once brought immeasurable suffering to the world?"

Suddenly Amy's smile was gone, as if a mask had been torn away, showing what Jerry took to be a recollection of personal loss. He noted the change in her, and filed it away for future reference. By tomorrow, he thought, I'll have her 98 percent.

"Amy?" he prompted.

The smile returned, then slipped again. "You said . . . all those so-called secular humanists, all those Einsteins who were talking about building spaceships and bringing us into a genetic frontier—"

"Right! If the money-sucking vampires were smart enough to lay out plans for how to clone a dinosaur, and to figure out how to build an antimatter rocket—"

"Then cancer should have, by comparison, been an easy nut to crack."

"Now you've got it. While they were wasting our tax dollars turning green monkeys gay, I'll bet you they were sitting on a cancer cure for decades. Genetic frontier indeed! It wasn't until they could legally corner the market on designer genes that we began to see the so-called frontier. Until then, treating a disease with body-ravaging drugs was far more profitable than curing it."

Amy's smile had slipped away completely, leaving only anger and confusion, and a sorrow that filled Jerry with a horrible glee—which he concealed behind a mask of fatherly composure.

"Do you really believe they did it?" she asked, failing to ask herself how many of Jerry's accused had lost parents and siblings, spouses and children, to cancer while supposedly hiding cures. "Is it really possible that our scientists sat on cures for decades, until all the proper laws had been lobbied for and set in place? Until they figured out how to patent DNA?"

"Why should it matter what I believe? What do *you* believe? That's what counts. It's your job to go out there and penetrate into the details, to research all the immuno-genetic advances of the past two or three decades. Ask yourself: How many years has it been since a doctor first billed a patient for genetic surgery on an in vitro embryo? It's in the library. Go find it. Then ask yourself how scientists could have accomplished such a feat and *not* known, at the same time, how to beat cancer. What I'm asking you to do is go out there and look through back issues of all the major science journals."

"You're asking a lot," Amy said. "To understand half

that stuff, you'd have to work your way up to a Ph.D. in biochemistry.''

''It won't be necessary to go that far, but I *am* asking you to expend a fair amount of effort. I'm asking you to inconvenience yourself a little. Is that too much to ask?''

''No . . . but—''

''And am I correct in guessing that while the eggheads were redesigning monkeys and drawing up plans for a real-life *Jurassic Park*, someone you loved died of cancer?''

She nodded.

A hundred percent by next Tuesday, Jerry thought, and he found himself remembering how every one of his ''transferers,'' after a week or two, or a month or two, called his voice mail number. Every one of them.

Usually they left recorded messages, explaining in unmistakably embarrassed tones that, after having had time to think about the transfer of ownership, they'd like to return the cash for the privilege of tearing up the contract. He'd ask them what was in it for him if he allowed them simply to give back his hundred dollars, and he explained that maybe he'd *consider* it for five hundred. And Amy was on the verge of calling him friend and teacher. She was, after all, seeing the better side of Jerry Sigmond, a face as radiant as the summer sun burning off the morning dew, but—

He had always enjoyed watching the transformation of people who were totally materialistic—and who did not give a damn about what they had sold him—into sniveling little marks who were genuinely worried about the fates of their immortal souls. A few became religious, even fanatical, which merely increased the price on the deed of transfer. From these poor souls he was able to extract not only money but favors. He toyed with them, made virtual slaves out of them. Two of his marks had been Wall Street executives. They arranged, for Jerry's benefit, an insider trading deal that had yielded a small fortune in silk futures. Two or three others, he suspected, might even be coaxed to kill for him; and he told himself: *When I die and go to hell, I will be a prince in Satan's court.* That was also Jerry Sigmond; but all except a select few had ever learned, and by the time they did, it was usually too late to profit from the lesson.

"Do your homework," Jerry continued. "Walk that extra mile," and he guessed that if he really worked on her, he could get her to walk an extra ten miles for him, maybe an extra fifty, and perhaps even to walk it on her knees.

She nodded again, and tried to smile.

"It's hard to be proud of this country anymore. We've become a nation of sheep who, somewhat out of fear but mostly out of a desire not to be inconvenienced by a little extra work, will surrender our freedoms one by one. It's too much trouble to do one's own homework, to form one's own opinions and stand for them; so when the sheep see someone like me being shouted down, they say, 'I'll look away . . . I'll look away . . . I'll look away.'"

"You look away at your own peril."

He studied her eyes. *Ninety-eight percent, for sure.*

"And if what you say is true," Amy said. "If it's true about people just wanting to shut you up, then if they can drag you down so easily—"

"Then God help us all," he finished for her.

"Yes. God help us," she said, and glanced down at her watch. "I . . . must go."

"Understood. You've got other cells to visit."

"And already I'm behind schedule." She turned and pushed a tall rack of breakfast trays out of view, and something in her expression told Jerry that her opinion of him had just dropped a couple of notches.

Damn! he thought. *Back to 90 percent. Was it something I said?*

She was almost out of view when he said, "There is one little thing I've been wondering about. One last question."

Amy turned to look at him. "What's that?" she asked. He was smiling at her again. That charming smile.

"Do you believe in God?" Jerry said; and his smile widened.

11

The Birds and the Bees

In France, the quarantine was failing.

Of course, it was failing. The Schutts could have told them it would never work. Even a child could have seen the storm coming; and many a child did see, as they stood with their parents in the huge, arena-like terminal through which De Gaulle Airport's escalator tubes ran. Tugging excitedly at their parents' shirts and skirts, they pointed at the wire-mesh netting that formed a dome over the "arena," and asked why dozens of dead birds lay sprawled atop the dome. The parents, already frazzled by canceled vacation plans and by an ever-accelerating chain reaction of diverted flights, shrugged at the birds and hurried on to more important concerns.

*   *   *

When Richard emerged from the building, his face was ashen, as if he had just been punched in the stomach. He walked across the lawn, stopped at the edge of the pine forest, and tried to choke back tears. It seemed as if everything that could possibly go wrong was doing so. Janet Schutt could not have put it more aptly: This is what happens when Darwin's theory meets Murphy's law. The day had begun with Tam's refusal to eat, followed by news of the North Carolina outbreak, followed by calls from Dawn's sister in Tucson, explaining that she had spent most of the night trying to make her way to New York, but found that due to a sudden rash of passengers canceling their travel plans to what many were beginning to perceive as "the East Coast plague zone," the flights themselves were being canceled. That, Richard guessed, was bound to cost someone a great deal of cash before the crisis was over—which was perfectly fine with Richard: He felt so miserable himself that the thought of airline executives sharing even a fraction of his misery made some small part of him smile acidly.

And now his teacher, the kindly old "ant man" Edwin Wilson, was dead. Richard had sworn that the next time they met, he would honor Wilson's request to call him by his first name. Like almost everyone else who had come to know him, Richard had found it difficult to think of Dr. Wilson as anything other than teacher . . . mentor . . . second father. . . . But a promise was a promise, and . . . and now Edwin was gone. And still, the day was but beginning.

"What can happen next?" he said to the impassive sky, and was surprised by the crispness with which his own voice carried among the pines. There was something unsettling in that crispness, as unsettling as the slight quiver in Jackson's voice as he described the chipmunk he and Tam had listened to the day before.

Richard searched the trees with his eyes, and focused his hearing, and realized that there were no birds.

What can happen n—

He wished he had never asked the question, and as he turned and headed back across the lawn, he made a vow

never to ask it again. Ever again. And then he was at the
steel fire door. He kicked aside the brick he had used to
prop the door open, and after he allowed it to slam shut
behind him, he did a most extraordinary thing, when he
came to regard it in calmer moments: He made doubly
and triply certain that the automatic latching system had
bolted the door from the inside. His most primitive instincts told him—told him repeatedly—that something was
waiting out there, something that aimed to hurt his child.
Instinctively, he began to secure the nest.

Seventy-five miles west, something strange was happening to the New York Stock Exchange.
The Newbern outbreak had been smaller than the one
in Long Beach and had occurred in a more rural part of
the country. On first reading, the statistics did not look all
that bad. Only three men and one deer were confirmed
dead, and this time, the quarantine went in only one direction. People were free to leave the affected area through
specially designated "soap-down stations"; and as the
Eighty-First Airborne Division soap-bombed the Newbern
mining district, effectively cauterizing the outbreak, it became clear that the planes were far less successful in stem-
ming the growing perception that America's East Coast
was blossoming into a plague zone than they were in
bringing the mites under control. Los Angeles International
became the first American airport to resist letting westbound passengers deplane until they, their baggage, and
the planes themselves had been gassed with some as yet
unspecified anti-mite agent. With guaranteed delays of several hours, and exposure to potentially hazardous chemicals thrown into the bargain, those who did not absolutely
need to fly west canceled their reservations—the tens of
thousands of them. In addition, overseas air transport out
of the eastern United States was becoming increasingly
blockaded by European and East Asian nations. An economic flash point had been reached, at which the flames
of dissolution became self-sustaining and began to spread.
Barely an hour after the L.A. International announcement,
Amtrak imposed an identical de-miting protocol on all
westbound trains. By mid-morning, airline and rail stocks

had started a precipitous slide, checked only slightly by a small percentage of stock traders who had not shown up for work and whose phones went unanswered. They were the small percentage most surprised and most disturbed by news that millions of mites *normally* inhabited their carpets and their beds. Guided by a new species of paranoia, they started actually to feel uncountable little bodies pressing against their skin, as they loaded their families into cars and drove toward the imagined safety of the West.

Behind them, a tremor ran through the commodities markets. During the previous month, those who bought futures in honey and held on to them too long had been wiped out financially. During the previous two weeks, Florida citrus, too, had become first a commodity in short supply, and thus very expensive, and finally a nonentity. Some, like Jerry Sigmond, had foreseen the citrus boom and bust following close on the heels of the honey crash, and had profited immensely as prices climbed during a short-lived trend of increased demand. Other buyers, unlike Sigmond, cursed themselves for joining the tail end of a buying frenzy instead of the front, and cursed themselves again as they rode the downturn. Those who did not sell their Florida futures before the citrus crop failed completely—much like those heavily invested in honey futures a month earlier, or those invested in Chinese silk the previous spring, or those invested in clothing and computer parts from India the previous winter—were taking devastating financial hits.

Now, as the men and women who watched over the big boards and notepads of the stock exchange received news that the California citrus crop was coming up short, the novices among them awaited the inevitable buying trend, force-fed by rocketing wholesale prices. A new wave of price increases was coming, undeniably, but the California citrus investors came only in a trickle. What had worked once for a few sharp-witted Florida investors—a chance to make a lot of money for a little while, even as the harvest failed—had turned out to be a good idea that, like most good ideas, would not work more than once. Seasoned Wall Street bankers knew what was about to happen in California, even before the scientists guessed it. Their knowledge was reflected in the fact that the most experienced investors were bailing out of California citrus futures as fast as the novices were buying in.

Richard never ceased to be amazed by the human mind's ability, on surprisingly short notice, to fit even the most earthshaking events into the backdrop of everyday existence. He had heard the story of the child who, about a month after the very first moon landing, was asked by a reporter if he was going to watch the *Apollo 12* mission on TV. The child responded, "Of course not. I saw that show already." Only a few years later, when the first photograph of Mars was about to be transmitted live from the *Viking 1* robot, the broadcast was interrupted by regularly scheduled reruns of *Magilla Gorilla* cartoons. And within hours of the *Challenger* explosion, jokes, of all things—dozens of them—had sprung up all over the world. Richard decided that these behaviors were all variations on the numb state. Though becoming bored with the fantastic or laughing at a tragedy might seem crazy when viewed from a historical distance, it was, perhaps for those actually living through the events, an ancient and instinctive attempt to preserve the organism by preserving its sanity.

Richard thought about that often, after he walked into the cafeteria and found Tam and Georgiana laughing together over a notepad video game. Tam's appetite seemed to have returned. She and Georgiana had concocted a breakfast cereal from crushed graham crackers mixed with bits of Hershey bars and hand-shredded marshmallows.

Well, and why not? Richard thought. The numb state cracked faster in children, didn't it? Of course, it did. Even in war zones, while the adults huddled together wringing their hands, children could often be heard at play in the ruins. Tam was simply more adaptable than he.

As soon as he entered the room, she dropped what she was doing, ran to Richard, and gave him a big hug. Before Black Monday there had been a sparkle in her eyes that was now absent, and Richard wondered if he would ever see it again—

(maybe she's not as adaptable as you'd like to believe)

—but she was smiling again, and able to laugh again, and even if that sparkle had disappeared, smiles and laughter were little blessings nonetheless. These days, Richard would settle for any tiny scrap of happiness he could get.

He put a hand on Tam's head and ruffled her hair. And he told himself, *Somehow it'll be all right.*

(Won't it?)

Not if that silent forest across the lawn was any indication. It scared him, prepared his mind, on some unconscious level, for reception of the idea that there was a much larger picture to be grasped than mere outbreaks of flesh-eating mites seemed to reveal. Jackson and Leslie had been attempting to pry this fact under his cranium for some twenty hours, now. Wilson had come to this same realization, and had said so before he died: It wasn't the "motes" that had gone wrong, it was the forests and the fields that surrounded them. Richard did not always agree with Wilson, yet he had always looked up to him as "teacher." Like any good teacher, Wilson had always demanded that he ask questions: "It would be inappropriate to instruct you not to question my work, for that is the first thing every good scientist is supposed to learn—to question virtually everything."

Richard did question everything; but he had learned, after a while, to question Wilson less and less. Too many of the old man's strange ideas had turned out to be right, and perhaps his last words were precisely the shock therapy Richard needed. If he was right this time, something really big was afoot, the biggest thing ever.

He lifted Tam up and cradled her head against his shoulder. Perhaps Jackson was right, too, Richard conceded. This was not a time to become absorbed in grief and self-blame. It was a time for paying attention. Hadn't Bill e-mailed something about all the insect-eating bats dying in the Tobago forests? Hadn't there been a tone of urgency in his message? Yet Richard had left the message unanswered.

"Georgiana," he said, putting Tam down, "ask the pad if there are any new e-mail messages from Bill Schutt."

She scribbled something on the screen, and two new

windows appeared. "Two came in this morning," she said, reading. "One is really long and . . . oh, no."

"Let me see," he said, and pulled a seat alongside her.

"Me, too," Tam said, and jammed in next to her father.

Richard took the controls and began scrolling. Much of it read like a report to a science journal: too many big words for the children. But the part about a house spattered with rotting blood was understandable enough.

"What's *Desmodus?*" Georgiana asked.

"Vampire bats," Tam said.

Georgiana continued to watch Richard scroll down through Bill's report. She was able to pick up only a sentence here and there. Finally, she turned to him and asked, "What's this stuff about insects and the forest?"

"I wish I knew."

"And Dr. Wilson?" Georgiana said quickly. "He's in a forest now? Right?"

Richard hesitated. "I think so."

"Is he all right?"

"I guess we'll see." He paused, closed the window, and slid the notepad toward Tam. "I gotta go."

"Dadeee!" Tam yanked at his shirt. "Stay."

Richard stood up. "I've got to get back to Jackson and the others. I have to call Bill and Janet."

"What's so important?" she protested.

"Later," Richard said.

And as he stepped into the hallway, Tam called after him, "Your friends must be the luckiest people in the whole world. They get to have you all day and I'm lucky if I get you even for an hour!"

He heard it, every word of it. And it stung deeply. And with the sting came realization: His numb state had developed its first crack. This was his second small blessing of the day, though it came disguised as a painful sting. If nothing bad could get through his protective barrier, nothing good could get in either.

Tam was chipping away at the shell.

Tam was exactly what Richard needed: a daughter smarter than himself.

*　　*　　*

At 11:30 A.M. local time, word began spreading, among the people who manned the stock exchange computers, that they had better switch their notepads to CBS, where it seemed an investigative reporter was making a terrifying connection between mite outbreaks, citrus crop failures, and rumors that the Indian grain blight was far worse than anyone at CNN had been letting on. A file photo and a map showed the aircraft carrier *Nimitz* poised between India and Sri Lanka; and a voice overlay, reported as a radio plea from central India, cried, "There is nothing to live for. There is nothing to eat."

Marvin Tobis, a trader for Prudential Securities, shook his head. "Irresponsible bastard," he said. "I'll bet he never even made an effort to confirm that the call was not a hoax. Anything for a breaking story, that's the name of the game. Anything to be the first to announce the next so-called crisis."

"You think it's all made up?" the man next to him said.

"It's bullshit," Tobis said. "He should live to rue it."

Which, in fact, he would, by day's end. Although this was the very height of the tourist season, within ten minutes of the broadcast, CBS/Disney stocks began an unprecedented slide. The parent company was heavily invested in East Coast and Caribbean resorts, and rumors of a worldwide plague—even unsubstantiated rumors, when coupled with an escalating logjam in the nation's transportation systems—became a noose around the neck of CBS (not to mention the investigative reporter who had unleashed the plague rumors).

The London and Paris markets had already closed at the time of the broadcast. The Hong Kong, Singapore, and Tokyo markets were still hours from opening; but when they opened, and when computer projections showed America's transportation and entertainment stocks following the same path to destruction as its relatively insignificant commodities, confidence in the dollar was bound to weaken. Some would buy in at what promised to be attractively low prices, but most would sell, for it was impossible to ignore how greatly the Wal-Marts and service industries depended upon reliable transportation systems. A domino effect of unemployment and eroding tax bases loomed, as large and readable as a billboard. By the time the London and Paris markets opened tomorrow, Tobis guessed, American treasury bills might be only slightly more popular than a nest of plague mites.

Barely two minutes after Richard left, Georgiana's father arrived and broke the news of what had happened in North Carolina. Tam winced, and her eyes flashed anger. Georgiana's beloved "ant man" was "hurt very badly" and would not be coming back. That's what they had tried to tell Tam about Mommy, but she knew that when the motes were involved, "hurt" meant *dead*.

Georgiana's father took her, sobbing, into the hallway and tried to provide some comfort, leaving Tam all alone and in a dark mood, with her daddy's notepad.

Georgiana had learned a little trick—a joke, really— from an older friend, who in her own turn had probably learned it from an older friend. The kids at school were always passing the latest hacking programs back and forth in secretive, electronic conversations that spread faster than lunchroom gossip. Alone and lonely, Tam began cruising the lab's electronic highway. If she was really good at it, she told herself, she might even tap into the meeting room Daddy had run off to, and be able to spy on him. As she cruised, the lab's computers occasionally threw up roadblocks and challenged her, but the trick Georgiana had learned at school seemed to be working. The machines let Tam through, for she knew how to speak their language. Soon, Tam and the lab's computers were sharing the same joke.

Richard felt as if he had awakened from a bad dream, or a bad dream within a bad dream. The crack in the barrier between numbness and reality had brought him back to the world of human emotion, but he no longer wished to be human. He wished that with the wave of a magic wand he could be more like the mythical, emotionless Klatu. Being human bore too great a price—

(Dawn . . .)

—he broke down in the hallway, retreated to the seclusion of the nearest bathroom, and doubled over—

(I am in control of my emotions)
—in great, heaving sobs.

(Dawn!)

No point in letting the others see me this way, he decided. No point in alarming them; he closed the door behind him and vomited into the nearest urinal. There was precious little left in his stomach. Ever since Long Beach, nothing except Coca-Cola seemed to be staying down, and then only for a short time. But at least it kept him from dehydrating. And it did contain what, for Richard, seemed to be the two major food groups: sugar and caffeine; and by comparison to his failed attempts at keeping down a few bites of pancake, strawberry syrup, and sour cream, Coca-Cola tasted a lot better coming up.

(Dawn?)

How long had she been gone? A whole month? It certainly felt that long. It felt as if a whole lifetime had passed since he last saw her; but it was only a day, by everything his memory and his watch told him. Only one little day. Time suspension . . . if not for the overwhelming sense of loss, he might actually have enjoyed the illusion.

For no particular reason, he was suddenly angry with himself, and then sad again, and then he knew that the crack was trying to yawn wide open. He went to a sink in the corner, brought himself to utter the words, "I miss her," and surrendered all control.

Richard stayed there for a long time. When he stepped into the hallway his face was freshly washed. He was puffy eyed and shaken, but feeling more normal. He passed a vending machine, bought two new cans of cola, and took them with him to Jackson's office. Leslie Wells was there, with Jackson, bending over a trio of notepads and a little mountain of journals. Richard put one can down on a stack of books, opened the other, and said, "I owe you guys an apology. I'm ready to really work on this thing now."

"It's okay," Jackson said. "We know this has been tough on you. But we could really use your help." He pointed at the screens. "We've got more trouble."

"That's nothing new."

"*Big* trouble," Leslie emphasized. "We just got a report from Jim Powell. He's rather frantic right now."

Jim? Frantic? In all the years Richard had known him, he had never heard the like. Richard shook his head. "Jim's in Vancouver. What's wrong in Vancouver?"

"Everything," Leslie said. She handed Richard a transcript of Jim's report. "You can start by reading this."

It was only six pages long, a very quick read; but by the time he finished, his hands were shaking.

Now Georgiana could understand, to one degree or another, what Tam must be going through. The "ant man," whom she had looked up to with the same reverence that some of her classmates heaped upon rock stars, was gone. All that remained of him were books, laser disks, and a wooden pencil he had used during one of his visits to the lab. Her father had brought her to Brookhaven to get Wilson's latest ant book signed, and when no one was looking, Georgiana snatched the pencil (*Edwin Wilson's actual pencil*). She could not stop herself. After she got home, she noticed little bite marks in the wood—just like the scars she nibbled into her own No. 2s when she was nervous (Edwin Wilson was . . . *human*).

When Georgiana returned to the cafeteria, she found Tam hunched over the notepad. She had hacked into the lab's conference lines, with all the skill of a Stealth fighter pilot. Georgiana sat down beside her and watched approvingly. Tam was a quick learner. All her concentration seemed to be bundled up in this single task; but it only seemed so. Without turning her eyes away from the pad, she asked, "What's it like, do you think? Being dead?"

Georgiana frowned. "You mean, do I think there's a heaven?"

"Yeah."

"I don't know. My father says heaven is a place we wouldn't like, if we knew all about it right now while we're alive, but that after you're dead and you get there you really don't mind."

"You mean, like maybe it's all dark and nothing?"

"Yeah, but it's such a complete nothing that you really don't care."

"Daddy thinks maybe people come back after a while," Tam said, deriving more comfort from that thought than from Georgiana's dark nothing. "He believes in re— in . . ."

"Reincarnation?"

"Right."

Tam made some quick scrawls, defeating another computerized challenge. A ghostly face appeared on the screen, then disappeared in a wash of static.

"Here," Georgiana said, "let me try." She barked some orders into the notepad, and the resolution improved enormously, showing a bearded figure. Georgiana shrank it to a picture within a picture, the larger picture showing Richard, Jackson, and that new scientist from California.

"Ha!" Tam exclaimed. "We're in."

"Who's the guy with the beard?"

Tam smiled. "That's Uncle Bill, the vampire bat guy. And—wait! Here comes something else."

Another figure came on-line, blurry. Georgiana shrank him down inside a little window within the picture, moved his window next to Bill's, enhanced it, then adjusted the contrast and brightness. She recognized him immediately. They both recognized him.

"Oh, we've hacked into pay dirt this time," Georgiana said.

Tam drew her breath in astonishment. "You don't think we can get into trouble for this?"

"We'll worry about that tomorrow," Georgiana said. "This is the biggest score, the biggest score ever." With the help of a little electronic gossip and BNL's Nomad-frame computers, they were able to eavesdrop on the white phone itself. The newcomer on the screen was none other than the President of the United States.

"Jackson—I'm worried about that CBS reporter."

"I know, Mr. President—but what can we do? I suppose there will be plenty of other people piecing together the same scenario soon enough."

"I've been watching what's happening to the airlines," said the President, in a slightly ominous tone. "People west of the Rockies are under the impression that it's just an East Coast problem. They seem to believe that if they can avoid travel to the infected areas, they can avoid whatever is causing the mite outbreaks.''

''They're misinformed,'' Leslie said. ''The infection is all around them, from the remotest campsite to the most opulent executive suite atop the Transamerica building. Even without Tobago, Vancouver makes that understandable enough.''

On the other end of the White Line, the President shook his head, very slowly. Yesterday, Wilson said the probability that the problem would become global was about 5 percent.

Then it became 60 percent.

And then . . .

Jim Powell had transmitted helicopter views of Vancouver Island, from which the bloom of algae, protozoa, and putrefactive bacteria was horribly visible. It came down with the rivers and appeared to be expanding out of control, a hundred-mile-wide stain on the Pacific, the color of old blood. Those few shellfish strong enough to survive the red tides were rendered inedible. No one knew for certain what was happening to the bass, trout, and tuna. They seemed simply to have abandoned the region.

''I'm afraid this is not a freakish, isolated occurrence that is going to go away,'' Jim had reported. He then noted how a friend of his in Bangor, a forensic entomologist, was suddenly finding it impossible to do his job. Insect larvae and egg stages were valuable tools for fixing a murder victim's time of death, because blowflies, beetles, and ants were typically the first to arrive at the crime scene. Within minutes, they began feeding and laying eggs. But now, almost overnight, Jim's friend was finding one crime scene after another completely free of insects.

Mystified, Jim had hiked into the forests, following a hunch about the source of the red tides. He found the forest floor littered with the corpses of starved animals—birds, mostly. Their bodies should have been infested with maggots, but there was nothing to remove the accumulating dead except bacteria and fungi. Every rain filled the streams and rivers with bacterial runoff and spoiled flesh. The waters were too fertile, too overburdened with nutrients. The resulting population explosion of microbial life (and its residua) was consuming all the oxygen and choking off the lakes and reservoirs. "The fishing industry is history," Jim's report read. "And the water company is working overtime, pumping tons of chemicals into the storage tanks just to keep the drinking water safe. You can actually gag, these days, just smelling the chlorine in a glass of water. I'm living off canned sodas."

"Damndest thing I've ever heard," the President announced. "Right out of the Book of Exodus: rivers turning to blood, stinking of rotting flesh."

Watching from Tobago, Bill Schutt bowed his head. He had made a little joke about the Exodus plagues only a few hours earlier. Now he did not find it very funny.

"So, what have we got here?" the President asked. "Crop-eating fungal blooms in India. Seas of bacteria in the West. Bats in the Caribbean. And in the East, the common bed mite, the archetypal scavenger, undergoes a massive population explosion and becomes carnivorous."

"That's right," Bill said. "You might want to think of all these population blooms as opportunistic infections."

"Caused by the removal of something from their environment," Jackson added.

Bill nodded.

"And after comparing notes," the President said, "you're all convinced that the missing element is fungus gnats, bees, ants, and the like?"

"Certain of it," Bill said. "That's why there were no flies at the farmhouse this morning. That's why all the insect-eating bats have died here, and why no maggots are feeding upon their bodies. It's the same thing with the birds in Vancouver. And it's exactly what Edwin Wilson was trying to tell us before the mites got him. There's very little room for doubt: What we're facing is a mass die-off of insects."

It was the classic "good news, bad news" situation. *No more fleas, flies, or cockroaches?* the President wondered. *What's so bad about—about what? Crops dying in India? Mites and bats going crazy? And they say it's spreading? Correction: They say it's already spread.*

No more insects . . . it should have been good news,

until one really took pause to think about it. The next thing the President had to think about was naming a scientific nerve center to handle the crisis. Since the nature of the emergency was biological, it seemed obvious to him that any solutions would be born of biotechnology. The City of Dreams was number one in that field—equipped, as it was, with the world's most sophisticated micro-MRI scanners and computer-driven DNA editors. Moreover, the city's team had already passed its first test. In only twenty-four hours, Jackson Roykirk, Leslie Wells, and their contacts abroad had managed to identify the cause of the plagues. Who better to coordinate work toward a cure?

But how in the world did one concoct an antidote against something like this—against the death of insects? The President grinned nervously. "Are you sure we can't make this any stranger? Maybe toss in another element?"

"Oh, there'll be a new element," Leslie warned. "There'll be quite a few of them before this is over."

Richard grimaced. "I'm afraid I have to agree with her." He caught her by surprise. "It'll get plenty worse before it gets better."

"Better, Richard?" Leslie had never expected to hear Richard Sinclair agree even halfway with anything she had to say. "It may not be getting better for about four million years."

Richard looked down at his shoes, as if searching for a counterargument. He said nothing.

"Okay," the President said. "How high up the food chain do you think this is going to reach?"

"I wish it were all so simple as a mere food chain," Leslie said. "People have gotten used to planting ant baits and Roach Motels in their houses. We've sprayed millions of tons of insecticides on our fields to keep out the locusts and the beetles. We've poisoned the ground beneath our homes to keep out the termites. We've been at war with the insects since biblical times. And we've never really paused to think that it is they who take decaying plants and animals into the ground and break them down into fertilizer for the next generation of plants. And I don't think anyone has seriously considered, up to this moment, how insects might exert control over populations of mites and the bacteria of decay, preventing them from becoming plague organisms. We've all been brought up to think of *insects* as the plague organisms or the bringers of famine and economic loss. But we've had it backward all along. I think we begin to see now that the insects are really civilization's first line of defense against plague and famine.''

"If they're dying,'' Richard injected, "or if they're somehow going dormant on us, it will be as if the Earth's immune system has been pulled away.''

The President whistled. "Dear God. I never thought of that: how much we might need the very creatures we've been trying so hard to kill. Did we finally win the war? Is that what happened? Did we destroy them all?''

"I wouldn't give ourselves that much credit, Mr. President. I don't think it's anything we've done. The truth of the matter is, we probably don't even count. I doubt if all the insecticides we've ever used have resulted in the extinction of even a single insect species.''

"Then what's happening?''

Leslie took one of Richard's sodas and popped it open. "You probably have to track back quite a long way,'' she said, "to the two greatest mysteries in the history of this planet: the origin of life and mass extinctions. I think Wilson's dead bees, and Jim's missing maggots, are giving us a unique opportunity to study the latter.''

"You can't be saying that what happened to the dinosaurs was—but that's crazy! An asteroid killed the dinosaurs. Everybody knows that—''

Jackson broke in. "Alvarez published the asteroid extinction theory in 1980, and by now everybody believes it. But that doesn't mean everybody is right.''

"Okay,'' the President said. "What makes you believe that what's happening to us today happened to the dinosaurs sixty-five million years ago? This is all theoretical, right? I mean, if I walk into Congress talking about maggots and dinosaurs, one of three things is going to happen to me—all of them bad. I need something a little more concrete. I need—''

"We can give you better than a twenty percent probability on this,'' Leslie said.

The President flinched. "That high? This insect scenario?"

"We're willing to stake our reputations on it."

"Okay . . . so you say something like this happened before. What does the fossil record tell us? Where's the evidence?"

"That's my territory," Richard said. "And Bill's." He scrawled something on one of the screens and a graph came up. A geologic timescale at the bottom ticked off 500 million years. The President counted twenty peaks and troughs, each peak representing a mass extinction. Two of the larger, more recent peaks coincided with the Cretaceous-Tertiary extinction (ending about 65 million B.C.) and the "terminal Eocene event" (about 33 million B.C.). But they told only part of the story. The largest peak of all marked the Permeo-Triassic boundary, near 250 million B.C., which ushered in the reign of dinosaurs by sweeping the decks clear of nearly every other species then on Earth. It was followed, almost 33 million years later, by the Triassic-Jurassic extinction.

"What we're looking at is a brief history of post-Cambrian life," Richard announced. "Right now, the sun and Earth are moving through the galaxy at about five miles per second. We've traveled almost thirty-nine hundred light-years since the dinosaurs died. What this chart tells us is that we're mere newcomers, having climbed aboard only about a light-year upstream. We've had congressmen walking around Washington for years preaching about how we must save the planet, 'save Spaceship Earth.' They've got it all wrong. The ship was afloat for nearly four-and-a-quarter billion years without dinosaurs, four and a *half* billion years without us; and no matter what happens to us, it will sail for billions of years more. It's not the ship that's in trouble. It's the passengers."

"You remind me of something Cousteau said," the President reflected. "Something about how God, when he met man in Eden, commanded us to replenish the Earth and subdue it. But in order to do that, we have to remember that the Earth has a life of its own. These peaks and troughs of yours would seem to bear that out. They look just like the peaks on an EKG; but they're really the pulse of the Earth itself.''

"And you'll notice," Jackson added, "that the pulse beats every twenty-eight to thirty-five million years—"

"It's a lot closer to thirty-three million years," Richard corrected.

"Which means," Jackson continued, "as Wilson has suggested, we could be due for the next pulse about now, give or take a million years."

"Or just a thousand years," Bill said.

"Or just about now," Leslie said.

The President swallowed hard. "Which makes the question of the hour: What causes the pulse?"

"Oh, many different forms of bad luck," Richard guessed aloud. "Draining of the continental seas, fluctuations in solar output, the odd comet impact—and then, maybe once in a while, two or three bad events line up together, so that one day the seas retreat from North Dakota and the dinosaurs are standing up to their knees in snow on a salt flat wondering how life could get any worse for them and when they look up into the sky—what do they see but a comet about to strike the Earth.

"Now, about that comet: Some years ago, a fellow named Michael Rampino suggested that our solar system's passage through galactic dust lanes could be the main, forcing factor. I tend to agree with him. Such a passage would bring in a lot of extrasolar comets—stardust, if you will . . . " He drifted off into thought.

(from the dust of the stars to the dust of the Earth . . .)

"You will note," he continued, "that at least nine of the peaks on my chart are approximately synchronous with the formation of large impact craters—such as the alleged dinosaur killer on the Yucatan Peninsula—and also with giant lava flows that may well be a result of the impacts." Richard called a new picture onto the screen. "Now, the solar system makes one complete orbit around the galactic center every four hundred million years. Let's call this the galactic year. Our passage through a dust lane occurs roughly every thirty-three million years. You might call these passages the galactic seasons. The cometary bombardments are thus our galactic winter—maybe. It seems to work into a nice, tidy picture; except for one thing I just don't understand.''

"Only one?" Leslie said.

"Periodic impacts cannot paint the whole picture. Nature seems to abhor simple, black-and-white solutions. So, naturally, we've had the odd spring or summer impact that did not coincide with the thirty-three-million-year cycle— including the Ries Basin event of fifteen million B.C., and the Australian impact eight hundred thousand years ago— and no winter of mass extinction followed either of them. This seems to hint that if a comet or an asteroid strikes during ordinary biological times, maybe nothing much happens at all. But when I look at what happened during the last days of the dinosaurs, and at the end of the Eocene epoch, I see a lot of species disappearing *before* the bombardments, as if a particularly severe autumn had preceded winter, as if something had already softened the biosphere in preparation for the comets.''

"Okay . . ."

"So, mass extinctions are not the sharply defined, overnight die-offs most people would expect from comet impacts and volcanic lakes. The terminal Cretaceous and the terminal Eocene impacts had precursors. It's what I like to call the *Fantasia* Theory."

"Fantasia?" the President asked. "You mean, as in the Disney cartoon?"

"Exactly as in the Disney cartoon. Near the end of Stravinsky's *Rite of Spring* sequence, we witness the crash of entire ecosystems and the slow death of dinosaurs as precursors to a major geologic catastrophe. I don't know how Disney got that idea, but he seems to have grasped the reality long before we scientists dug up the actual clues.''

Richard displayed yet another series of graphs and pictures on the screens. They were excerpts from a paper he and Powell had been drafting for *Nature*, in response to a preprint they had received bearing the cheesy but hauntingly prophetic title, "Multiple Miseries Bugging Us All."

"Here's part of a census we've compiled on insects in amber." The left-hand side of the screen began scrolling down, showing lists of italicized names. "Bottom line: Seventy million years ago, just ahead of the dinosaur extinction, only half the world's insects belonged to families known today, and none to known genera or species. Now, when we compare this to nuggets of amber dating from sixty to forty million years ago''—the right-hand side of the screen began scrolling—''we find that practically all the insects belong to today's families. About half belong to modern genera and a few even appear to be present-living species. The change is complete after the Terminal Eocene extinction. Suddenly, virtually all of them belong to modern genera, and most to modern species. Until today, I believed this to mean the insects simply suffered through the extinctions with everyone else. Now, looking around, I begin to wonder if they may in fact be the very precursor we're talking about.''

''The cause of the suffering,'' Bill injected.

''Twenty percent probability?'' the President asked. ''A twenty percent chance that the dinosaurs died because the insects disappeared . . . for a while . . . and that the insects are disappearing again?''

''Twenty percent, or better,'' Leslie said.

''There's more,'' said Richard. ''Several major groups, including marine corals, oysters, and squidlike fossils called ammonites were, like the dinosaurs, depositing fewer and fewer species in the fossil record during the years leading up to the end of the Cretaceous period. Again, the picture we're getting is that all was not business as usual before the comet struck.''

Richard let that sink in for a moment, while he called his first graph back onto the screen. ''Now, Mr. President, remember the Permeo-Triassic extinction?'' he said, pointing to the highest peak. ''It, too, falls within our thirty-three-million-year cycle and it, too, is associated with massive volcanic upheavals, probably triggered by yet another hammer blow from space. This happened about 250 million years ago; and when Henk Visscher of the University of Utrecht began looking at the sediments immediately below and just slightly older than the volcanic catastrophe, you know what he found?''

''That something was already going wrong before the end of the Permian?'' the President guessed.

''Yes,'' Richard said. ''Something was going very

wrong. Visscher has uncovered something exceedingly rare in the fossil record: layers of ancient ocean sediment so well preserved that you can slice through them micron by micron, revealing intervals of time as small as ten thousand years. In doing so, he has unearthed a strange and perhaps timely scenario: During the thousands of centuries leading up to the volcanic ash layer—which now marks the boundary between Permian and Triassic time—fungi began to comprise more and more of the spores and pollen blown out to sea and preserved in ocean sediments; until at last they became the sole trace of plant matter at the boundary. Visscher believes that the continents were littered with dead, fungus-encrusted wood for as long as a million years before the volcanic boundary formed—which begs the question: Why were so many rotting trees lying around for so long?"

"For lack of termites?" Bill guessed, and then thought better of it. "But that's impossible. Termites survived. They might have evolved a few new species, but termites are still with us!"

"What if they somehow declined in numbers, to near extinction? Or went dormant?"

"Wait a minute," the President said. "Have termites been with us that long? Two hundred fifty million years?"

Bill smiled. "They've been with us a lot longer than that. Four hundred million years; probably longer."

"And you'll notice," Richard said, referring to his graph, "that the extinction pulse intensifies after the appearance of the insects."

"Yes," said Bill, "but that could easily be a result of imperfections in the fossil record. The further back in time we try to look, the more blurry the picture gets."

"Good point. Okay . . . but while we're talking about imperfections in the fossil record, let us also start thinking about the imperfections in our questions about the record."

"Looks like we've stepped into a biological free-fire zone," observed Jackson. "We'll have to rewrite the textbooks."

Leslie thought: *If anyone's left alive to read them,* and began to sweat.

"Now," Richard continued, "if I can put forth a good

guess—just a guess: What if the insects, and perhaps a few other old animal groups—such as the sharks and certain amphibians—adapted to the thirty-three-million-year cycle by becoming scarce, or going dormant, and riding the bombardment out in very small numbers?''

''But that's the antithesis of evolutionary survival strategies,'' Bill objected. ''You want to spread out as widely as possible, keep your numbers large, seep into every nook and cranny in the world, and guarantee that a few of your kind will survive.''

''What if a few of them already are in the nooks and crannies, somehow hibernating safely beneath our feet?''

The President wanted to know about sharks and amphibians. ''What do *they* have to do with anything?'' he asked, and Bill explained that sharks and frogs, like insects, had a long fossil history and appeared to be moving now toward extinction.

''But I thought frogs were being killed by acid rain,'' the President said, ''and the sharks by overfishing.''

''I wouldn't be so sure of that,'' Richard said, and gooseflesh broke out on Leslie's arms.

Bill shook his head. ''I just don't buy this theory,'' he said. ''Something just doesn't fit. I mean, we can be sure enough that the insects are vanishing, and that they've probably performed this vanishing act before—but going dormant in the ground? For a hundred thousand years or more? There's no evidence that they've any such capability. It has to be something else. Maybe they die off only briefly, like bamboo.''

''Yes,'' said Richard, and then, after a pause, ''could be!''

''Very good,'' Leslie said, nodding. ''I was thinking about that myself.''

''Well, it *might* be,'' Bill said. ''The bamboo die-offs come at a much smaller frequency, and work on a smaller scale, but they might help us to understand what's happening, at least by analogy.''

''Explain,'' the President said.

''Every hundred and twenty years, China's bamboo forests die, setting off an ecological powder keg by pushing most of the species that depend on the bamboo—and the species that depend upon those species—close to the edge of extinction, and occasionally right over the edge. The 1960s die-off nearly took out the last pandas. There was also a mysterious failure of crops, a major economic collapse, and an exodus of people into Hong Kong from the southern provinces.

"No one knows why bamboo does this. The best guess I've heard came from paleontologist Stephen Jay Gould. He saw it as a devious little trick of nature, played against bamboo's dependents—birds and insects, mostly. The periodic die-offs reshuffle the whole forest ecology, in effect resetting the tempo of evolution. As for the bamboo trees themselves: They manage to survive through . . . "

"Yes?" Richard said.

"Through the dormancy of their seeds."

Richard squinted at Bill. "Yes! I've seen this before. In the tomb of Tutankhamen, wheat seeds stored as offerings in sacred urns sprouted after more than three thousand years in the dark. And in the pharaoh's bandages there were beetle eggs—probably also thousands of years old— that hatched when brought out of the tomb into a more humid environment. So maybe we really do have evidence of dormancy over great periods of time."

"I've seen another example," Jackson said. "Insect eggs are everywhere: in the soil, in the air we breathe— sometimes we even gather them on our skin and pass them back and forth in handshakes. Now, go to an insect collection in any natural history museum in the country, remove a butterfly from one of the boxes, and look at it under a microscope. Do you know what you'll see?"

—and before anyone could even put forth a guess—

"You'll find at least one or two beetle or fly eggs on their wings," he answered for them. "Some of those butterfly collections are more than a hundred years old. A dried butterfly, like the body of a mummified pharaoh, will last almost forever so long as the air inside its container is rendered poisonous to museum beetles. Usually this is accomplished with a steady supply of naphthalene. Ordinary mothballs. But every once in a while a curator gets careless and fails to notice that the naphthalene has evaporated; and then, often within a few months, the wings and the thorax begin sprouting butterfly-munching insects—no matter how well sealed the container had been. The eggs simply wait for their surroundings to become more friendly, for the poisons to disappear, and then the grubs hatch out.''

''Chinese bamboo . . .'' Richard mused. ''During the past two thousand years or so it must have been transported all over the world. What happened during the last die-out, Bill? Did the bamboo die everywhere all at once?''

''Oh, there was a little lag time here and there, but it was essentially simultaneous from Japan and France to North Carolina and Russia.''

''So the timing of the bamboo cycle was probably set millions of years ago, deep within the plants themselves.''

''It appears that way,'' said Bill.

''So,'' Richard continued, ''somewhere in the DNA of every bamboo shoot, a genetic clock ticks away even as we speak.''

''Probably.''

''And the insect die-off—or dormancy, or whatever it is we're going through—could be simply a larger variation on the bamboo theme?''

''So what are you saying?'' the President asked. ''That things are going to hell now? That no matter what we managed to make of our civilization, whether we were virtuous or evil, we were going to catch it in the neck anyway because some sort of genetic time bomb was hidden under our feet even before we existed. My God . . . Where's the sense in that?''

''So much for the anthropic view of the universe,'' Bill said. ''It all comes down to what Gould tried to tell us about our place in the history of life: 'We are of it, not above it . . .' '' and then he trailed off, thinking again about bamboo trees. They were—like wheat, corn, and rice—grasses. The grasses had appeared at the end of the last major extinction cycle, about 33 million B.C. Descending directly from bamboo, they advanced like a wave across Africa's semi-arid plains, differentiating into new species, including barley, sugar cane, and common lawn grass.

"Even before we existed," the President had lamented. Bill had a good grasp of the timescales involved, and the extent to which such seemingly irrelevant underlings as grasses and insects held command over human affairs. Bill's ancestors had not even begun making tools by the time of the grass outbreak. They had probably not even stopped crawling around on all fours; but they were destined to follow the grasses out of Africa, destined to help propagate them across the rice fields of China, the wheat fields of Kansas, the lawns of suburbia, and the cow pastures of Tobago. In their own way, the descendants of bamboo had enslaved the descendants of dryopithecine apes, until at last they became a living green carpet spread across entire continents, manicured, watered, bred, and fertilized.

(of it, not above it . . .)

Fascinating, on the one hand; yet on the other, Bill glimpsed a disturbed and disturbing universe. He suspected that as the grasses spread, small arboreal animals came down from the trees, moved onto the savannas, and grew in stature. If his suspicions were correct, then the ancestral vampire bats, as well as his own dryopithecine forebears, owed much to the aftershocks of the terminal Eocene extinction. Thus, about the time the grasses began their takeover of Earth, *Desmodus*'s ancestors would have been feeding on small birds and other tree and bush-dwelling animals—which were easily overpowered; and then came the Miocene epoch. On the newly emerged savannas, and in the forest refuges they surrounded, a spasm of explosive evolution produced birds and mammals as large as condors and cows, rendering the old attack strategies all but useless. A lone bat could no longer ambush a prey animal and kill it in a single assault. Bill had once heard evolution described as chaos with feedback—wherein variation produced the raw materials for change, and natural selection decided the winners and the losers. If, in the evolutionary arms race, your prey grew too large for you to slash down, then nipping it became your last, best hope of not becoming another casualty in nature's extinction lottery. Natural selection therefore worked toward the emergence of anticoagulants, self-honing supersharp teeth, and such altruistic behaviors as sharing blood with your neighbors.

The origin of the vampire bats was thus one of the latest ripples in Darwin's pond; triggered, perhaps, by a ripple of newer, larger prey species; triggered by the origin of the grasses; triggered by—by what? By a cometary bombardment? Or by the death of insects? Or by a combination of both in which the comet arrived only to find an already ravaged Earth?

But slow down, Bill told himself. *You're getting quite ahead of the game.* Even if insect disappearances have occurred in the past, could an absence of insects really cause so much mayhem?

Of course it could, he thought. Evolution is not godlike. It makes . . . "mistakes," he thought aloud.

"What?" said Leslie. He barely noticed that she had been speaking and that he had interrupted her.

"Evolution makes mistakes," he said. "For every species living today, thousands have lived in the past—and died there; they simply dropped off into the fossil record, into the dust bin of history. Mistakes are bound to happen, given enough time. Mistakes must happen, because it is the mistakes themselves that are the motor of change in evolution. It is the fate of all species, including us, to eventually become extinct." He stopped and tried to picture himself reading through successive layers of rock, as if he were reading the pages of a book.

"If extinction did not occur," Bill resumed, "the fossil record would be the same all the way down. All the successful species would dominate and last forever, meaning that *Tyrannosaurus rex* would still be here, and we would not."

"I doubt that," said Richard. "*T. rex* was probably a successful replacement for an even older failed model. If not for a previous wave of extinction, even the tyrannosaurs might never have shown up."

"But how?" Jackson asked. "How can the tempo of extinction possibly be set by insects?"

Richard bit nervously at his upper lip. "*That's* the question," he said. "I'm sorry, Bill, but I'm not ready to buy into your genetic clock theory just yet. Time bomb genes;

they suggest some sort of internal design, or program—which brings us to the question of a programmer or a purpose; and *that* begins to reek of divine intervention."

"Then perhaps you wear the badge of Darwin with too much pride," the President suggested. "Watch that; it can dull your vision. You've already said that dinosaurs and humans arose as the direct results of previous mass extinctions. What this tells me is that every end presents opportunities for new beginnings. Maybe Dr. Schutt's genetic time bombs exist as a means for guaranteeing that these ends will occur."

"Life is more complex than even Darwin imagined," Jackson added. "For hundreds of millions of years, plants and animals have shrouded this planet like a giant living membrane. Maybe, in ways that we've barely begun to perceive—much less understand—the world ecology creates its own order."

"So, what you're suggesting," Richard said, "is that natural selection works not just on individuals but on the whole interlinked ecology at once."

"Right . . ."

"In which case," said Bill, "the largest organism on Earth is Earth itself."

Richard shook his head. "That bothers me. It borders too much on the metaphysical."

"Oh, not at all," Bill said. "Think about what complex interactions of life must go into building an ecosystem and then think about DNA as not only the planet's ultimate survivor but its ultimate parasite. For billions of years it has managed to maintain essentially the same chemical structure. DNA did not know that we were coming, and does not care whether it lives in you, or in a mule, or in a honeybee before it passes over to the next generation."

"In other words," Jackson said, "we are just one of the many costumes that DNA will wear."

"Right. Insect, dinosaur, man—it's all the same to DNA. Everything we do in life works in the best interests of our nucleic acids, not us. From the moment of conception, all your genes have been doing is orchestrating the construction of a brand-new body, with no purpose other than to live inside your cells for a few decades and to produce a new reproductive system, so they can eventually abandon ship, moving on with the first diploid cell of the next brand-new body just as your own body begins to age and develop leaks.''

"So the history of life on Earth is reduced to a never-ending symphony," Richard said, and his face brightened with realization. "A symphony written on nucleic acid and performed by protein." He then let out a weak laugh, never having thought of his sperm as lifeboats before.

Jackson grasped it next. "So, if DNA works in its own best interests, then the fate of individuals, even the fate of a whole species or a class of species, becomes much less relevant than we have been led to believe."

"Maybe," Bill said. "And maybe in such a symphony, we aren't meant to be heard at all."

Silence.

They were really trying to silence Jerry Sigmond, to cage him up and muzzle him once and for all time; and to one degree or another, they were succeeding.

Jerry did not like what he saw and heard on CNN; not one damned bit. Amy had persuaded his keepers to install a TV on the other side of the permaglass wall, and now he wished they had not. He could no longer bear to watch. In the Caribbean and South America, whole herds of cattle were being wiped out by a strange, as yet unidentified bat-borne disease. Brazil's coffee crop was failing spectacularly, and the tourist industry everywhere was a shambles. Many people—a great many of them—would soon be going out of business; and Jerry knew, better than most investors, that it was possible to roam the stock exchanges betting on other people's misfortunes. He could have been cleaning up right now on the coming failures.

But not to worry, Jerry told himself. *What was it Mom had said—Adelle, with her sickening Ann Landers philosophy?* "Most people are like tea bags. They don't know their own strength until they end up in hot water."

Jerry had gotten into and out of hot water many times before. This was just another kettle, and not nearly so hot a kettle as the one he found himself in when a man he'd driven to the very brink with grief and paranoia tracked him down like a dog and, at gunpoint, vowed revenge for what he believed to be the total loss of his immortal soul.

If not for a serendipitous jamming of the weapon, it would all have ended for Jerry Sigmond, with headlines of an up-and-coming talk show host's career cut short by an assassin's bullet.

And it should have ended that way, when one stopped to consider how easily Jerry moved a crowd, or a mob, with his words. The future outlook might have been brighter for everyone if it had ended that way, but it did not.

Leslie, feeling more and more like an outsider, watched the notepad conference with a mixture of admiration and dismay. Richard's voice was quickening, as if a kindling temperature had been reached. Bill's, too. Jackson's, too. *They're feeding off one another,* she thought; and somehow Richard appeared to be a catalyst for the feeding frenzy. Leslie could no longer view him as a man educated beyond his skills; the sheer grit he had displayed in taking the Long Beach "mote walk" had already scored him a couple of points. Even after she ordered him back to the ship, he had continued to gather vital data. If nothing else, she was forced to admit that Richard Sinclair was no coward. She was also willing to concede that he possessed more than a lion's share of brains.

And willpower.

She knew that, try as he might to pretend he was all right, he must be fucking far from all right; and yet he was able to throw himself with uncanny intensity into solving the riddle of the plagues. He approached this riddle with a quirkiness that was both inspiring and disconcerting. Richard was famous for connecting seemingly weird and unrelated facts together at a moment's notice, then suddenly reversing position on old theories, including his own. Except for this odd group of polymaths, Leslie Wells and almost every other researcher had found his behavior jolting, and had disliked him for it; and the arrogant bastard always seemed happy to return the sentiment. Oh, yes—he with the sharp, fast tongue. When he became excited, Richard spoke too quickly to be understood; as a colleague once said of his lectures, "Try to imagine Robin Williams talking about dinosaurs and space probes after chugging down a dozen cups of coffee—that's Richard Sinclair."

Now, witnessing him in action, she realized that when Richard got together with Jackson Roykirk or Jim Powell, the result was never Richard plus Jackson being next of kin to one plus one equals two. It was more like Richard and Jackson squared, a third entity that was really neither of them, nor both of them. And now, with Bill added to the equation, the entity was *cubed,* and this was next of kin to chaos. They appeared to be wrapping their minds around one another's thoughts and churning out arguments—and answers to counterarguments—even before Bill, or Jackson, or Richard could get whole thoughts out in sentences. There was something contagious about this way of thinking; despite her feelings of alienation, despite her growing fear of the future, Leslie felt herself being drawn into the flash point, irresistibly, like a moth into a flame. And she wondered how she had come to be here at all, with this odd congregation, scaring the daylights out of herself. Would that she had lingered just a little longer at the birthday party of a friend's child, she would have missed her flight from California and forgone this horror show . . . for a little while longer.

"At this point," Richard announced, "I'm just about willing to concede that if we look to the end of a geologic period, and we look to a comet as the reason for the end, we're probably looking in the wrong direction. So what do we have here? Did we really waste all our time planning Project Spaceguard so we could watch the skies, when we should really have been watching the ground? Was *Tyrannosaurus rex* really brought down by the grasshopper and the ant?"

Richard was now paddling in reverse, stirring up questions that appeared to support Bill's genetic clock, or time bomb, theory. "Now, does natural selection act only on individual genes, or is it really shaping everything all at once—molding the entire biosphere? And if so, do individuals count for anything in this picture? Anything at all? Maybe not, given a fossil record that shows most insect species going extinct right alongside the victims of their ruse, or their disappearing act, or whatever we're going to call it."

"But the disappearance does produce beneficiaries," Jackson said. "Many species—including the insects themselves—are probably lost simply on account of having evolved into new species. Speciation should occur much more rapidly at the edge of extinction, where your numbers are very small and new traits are not likely to be diluted by an all-enveloping, massively successful gene pool. Large populations lock you into a status quo, right?"

"Right," Richard conceded. "If this picture makes sense, then nature won't always act as you'd expect a blind force should, selecting and eliminating individual genes. But insect species dropping off the face of the Earth so new species can evolve? Does that make sense?"

Richard was shaking his head. "No. I can't believe in self-destruct genes. It just can't be!" There was no denying that flood tides of mites, bacteria, black fungi, and bats could be traced back to vanishing insect populations; but it was frustrating to have it all figured out and yet not understand it. Evolution was supposed to be a game of dice, a game of chance. What Jackson and Bill were suggesting meant that God had not merely stopped playing dice with the universe; he had tossed the dice where they could no longer be seen—down biology's black hole.

"DNA working in its own best interests?" Richard continued. "Time bomb genes? No. This picture is wrong. Something else is causing the insect die-off."

The President said to Richard, "Maybe living systems are more complex than you have imagined. Perhaps even more complex than you *can* imagine."

"I don't think so. Sure, there's complexity. Sure, there's variety and intricate detail; but when I look at genes, when I look at wings and claws and adaptive coloration, I also see a beauty and a simplicity to the whole scheme. The basic rules of variation, selection, and adaptation are simple, just as the basic rules in a chess game—including the moves that the pieces can make—are simple; but the game itself provides infinite variations, infinite possibilities."

"Then what could cause the insects to fade out all at

once; or, if your fossil record is telling the truth, to do this repeatedly?''

"Not self-destruct genes," Richard said. "I doubt DNA cooperates with itself that way, across species lines and worldwide. If anything, DNA is always in an arms race with itself. Maybe every few thousand years or so, a new virus pops up, nature's equivalent of a secret weapon: able to kill a whole genus of animals, maybe even a whole *insect* genus. You randomly wipe out a genus, and usually it's unimportant—the world doesn't notice it's gone. Maybe every once in a while you hit a genus that a lot of other plants and animals depend on, so it takes some of them down with it. And if one of the new casualties happens to be even more important than the first victim . . . hmmmm . . . you might start a chain reaction. . . .

"I guess if we imagine thousands of viruses emerging, killing, and then dying with their victims, then if you throw the dice for long enough—say, over the course of millions of years—then sooner or later you're going to come up snake eyes. Either you hit the center of a web which spreads out to a whole class of animals, or a whole bunch of viruses come up snake eyes all at once, and a whole class becomes overloaded and dies. It gets even worse, I suppose, if you throw in one or two other stressors: a long-term warming or cooling of the climate, recession of the seas from the coastlines, or the odd asteroid impact . . . or even us. So maybe the mass destruction of life-forms is little more than an unfortunate convergence of several independent, normally noninteracting events. Maybe even some of these events—like periodic bombardments—come in cycles, amplifying the others. When too many stressors combine at once, they resonate as a single—and deadly—chord. In this sense, the pulse of extinction becomes a kind of crystallization event. . . ." He fell silent, his thoughts shooting along a new tangent, in which mass extinction became not an example of failure and descent into chaos but rather an example of life's capacity to organize itself.

"Crystallization . . . crystallization . . ."

"Yes!" Bill said. "I think I see it! A pulse only appears chaotic, but what it really represents is order. True chaos is achieved only when the heart seems to become stable—that is, when it goes flat line, and we call this death. So a surge of extinction and speciation, like crystallization, might appear to arise spontaneously and then to replicate itself with terrifying rapidity—which means that what the extinction pulse truly reveals about Earth is . . . it's alive . . . each heartbeat contains destiny within it. . . . One minute you have dinosaurs roaming the planet from pole to pole—uncountable hundreds of millions of them. In the next layer of rocks, a wave of extinction passes over the Earth, and new species of birds and mammals appear. And flowering plants appear. And the insects surge forth again, spreading among the new species of birds and mammals and plants, settling into new niches, until they become new species themselves. Crystallization exhibits the same pattern: One minute you have a liquid with all the molecules drifting randomly about. The next minute, a crystal forms, and on each one of its facets molecules are arranged in identical fashion and begin transmitting a pattern of molecular recoil throughout the entire solution, locking it into a new status quo."

"Bullshit," Leslie said.

"Pardon?"

"I said, this is bullshit. You're dragging us miles and miles away from what should be the real focus of all our attention. I care rather little for the specifics of why the insects have bowed out on us. What I do care about is, now that we know they're gone, what will happen to us and what are we going to do about it?"

"Yes," the President said. "Trigger-point viruses. Insect dormancy. All of this is very fascinating. But I'm afraid causes aren't half as important as effects right now."

"We may not have the luxury of figuring out why this is happening," Leslie added. "Put simply, we may not have enough time."

The President flinched. "If I may indulge my vice of trying to be hopeful, please tell me that the mites are the worst of it."

"I wish we could," Richard croaked. "But when we designed the carbon filaments that bind the *Bluepeace* together, Jackson and I were forced to learn more than we ever wanted to know about spiders, silkworms, and their relatives; and along the way we developed a unique appreciation for the services that the insect world provides for us.''

Leslie broke in: ''And the removal of those services, as Richard has pointed out, could be very much like the removal of Earth's immune system.''

''How, specifically?'' asked the President.

''Death of insectivores and fruit eaters, for a start,'' said Bill. ''Remove the insect and plant ecologies that so many animals depend on and—bang!—they're dead. And the removal of so many birds and mammals causes still more ripples in the ecosystem—''

''And as we're beginning to see,'' said Leslie, ''without nature's undertakers, the accumulating dead just accumulate, polluting water supplies and contributing to a chain reaction of dislocations.''

''Even the trees won't rot, as they fall over in the forest or drop their dying limbs onto the ground,'' said Richard. ''Ants and termites, wood roaches and wood-boring beetles—they're like the macrophages in your bloodstream. They consume and recycle everything nature discards.''

''There's going to be trash piling up all over the world,'' Jackson said. ''Breeding grounds for disease.''

''With nothing except fungi and bacteria to break it down,'' Richard continued.

''And that won't do it. That won't make it,'' said Jackson.

''Hmmm . . .'' Richard was frowning. ''Unless . . . we end up knee-deep in fungi . . . which may be the case if we've lost the fungus gnats.''

''Ohh . . .'' Bill said absently; and then, after a pause, blurted, ''Oh!'' followed by laughter and exclamations of, ''Oh, my God!''

The President's nose wrinkled. ''What, I'm afraid to ask, will happen if we take out the fungus gnats? What do we lose with them?''

''Quite a bit,'' said Bill. ''Fungus gnats have always been good indicators of the general health of forests and cash crops. Because some of them are tied to specific fungi, we can use them much the same way we use the presence of certain antibodies in human blood to track the footprints of specific viruses. When the fungus gnats are present, it means they're actively invading a wood- or crop-destroying fungus. And if the gnats aren't there anymore, then from the fungus's point of view it's all a matter of: *While the cat's away, the mice will play.* The living wood of the forests—and the corn, the wheat, the rice—''

''They'll be defenseless,'' the President said.

''Absolutely. And the loss of just the honeybees means fruit production is down drastically. The loss of other pollinators has probably driven it down even lower, which is why the fruit-eating bats are starving. And many of *them* pollinate the plants and disperse their seeds. Any plant that depends on the insects or the bats for pollination is going to change its ways, very quickly; or it's going to go extinct, very quickly.''

''What plants *don't* require insect pollination?'' the President asked.

''Wind pollinators,'' Richard said. ''Grasses, mostly. Wheat. Corn. Rice. Barley. Bamboo—''

''All the ones that evolved during the last extinction,'' Leslie observed.

''Yes,'' said Richard. ''Except that during the past century they've been so overbred that their seeds no longer drop naturally from the stalk to the ground. Without humans to warehouse and plant them, corn and wheat would be extinct in a year.''

Leslie shook her head. ''It gets worse: For years Wilson and the geneticists were warning us that all the wheat in America had been bred down to one highly desirable strain without any discernible genetic diversity at all. The corn, too. And the barley. Wilson worried that the emergence of a single, highly resistant fungus, against which one of those overbred plant strains would have no natural immunity, was an inevitability that could wipe out the entire American bread basket in a fortnight. And now you're telling me that we may be facing a worldwide explosion of fungi?''

''It certainly looks that way,'' Bill said. ''The world

could become a wall-to-wall disaster area if we took just the fungus gnats away.''

"Or just the ants," Jackson said.

"Or just the termites," Richard said.

"Termites?" asked the President. "I thought losing them would be one of the few silver linings to this cloud."

"Not at all," said Richard. "What we humans regard as the destruction of a house is really nature's way of breaking down dead wood and putting it back into the ground as nutrients. In addition to being recycling machines, the termites are food for a lot of animals that just don't feed on anything else. Did you know that the so-called anteaters really eat termites and nothing else?"

"No."

"It's a sure bet they're plunging toward extinction, now. Mr. President, it's such a deeply interconnected picture that every time I think of one insect group disappearing, I'm watching a diverging regress of other disappearances. It's really com—''

In Washington, the President held up a hand, cutting Richard off in New York, and swiveled his chair away from the view screen. When he reappeared, less than a minute later, he patched in video of a wrought-iron gate crested with batlike gargoyles. Neither the gate nor the gargoyles had presented an obstacle to the intruders—the billions of them.

"Bangor, Maine," the President said, and bit hard into his lower lip. "You . . . you say these . . . *motes*—aren't the worst of it?"

The scientists nodded.

"Look . . . I need to do some work here, okay?"

"Understood," Leslie said.

The white line went dead.

"Cool!" Tam and Georgiana had said; and their little spying operation really had been cool . . . right up to the moment the President showed his video of monsters in Bangor. It looked too much like Long Beach and brought back to Tam the heartbreaking reality of how Mommy had died. They switched off the notepad and stared at the blank screen, saying nothing.

Of all that they had witnessed and heard, the "motes" were the most easily understood topic, and therefore the most frightening. The rest of the scientists' words were mostly incomprehensible and, though impressive, failed to convey to either of them that mite outbreaks were but the tiny pinnacle of a very substantial iceberg. What, for example, did "resetting the tempo of evolution" or "genetic time bomb" really mean? Georgiana pondered that for a moment. And for another. And another. But she had no answer. She envied the grown-ups. She wondered if one day she would be able to speak as they had about DNA, crystallization, and chaos theory, and to *understand* it.

The door to the cafeteria popped open, and a petite, red-haired woman stepped inside. It was Georgiana's friend, Sharon; one of the *Bluepeace*'s pilot engineers. She was carrying a large box of leaves and dirt with a microscope propped on top of it.

"Hi!" Georgiana said. "What's that?"

"Work to do." Sharon put the box on the table. "Wanna help?"

"Sure!" said Georgiana.

"That depends," said Tam.

"On what?"

"On what you want us to do."

"Well . . ." Sharon frowned, but Tam thought she detected the hint of a smile. "While Georgie's parents are out filling more boxes with dirt, a whole bunch of us are going to be spending the better part of the afternoon picking through this stuff looking for insect eggs. Do you know why?"

"Because all of a sudden insects are getting very hard to find," said Georgiana.

"You know about this?"

Georgiana nodded her head. "Yes," she whispered. "We heard people talking." *We heard the whole thing when we hacked into the President's conference call*, she left unsaid.

Sharon turned to Tam and narrowed her eyes, as if to say, *What have you been up to?* Tam stared back at her, as if to say, *Who? Me?*—and the pilot knew immediately that the girls had indeed been up to no good. *No matter,* she thought. Would that a year from now, or even a week from now, the mischief of two schoolgirls would still be important enough for any of us to worry our little heads about.

"What I'd like you to do," Sharon said, "is start picking through the leaves and overturning the rocks and pathway slates outside this building. I'll give you magnifying glasses, and if you find any bugs—any bugs at all—bring them back to me."

Tam frowned. "Daddy really doesn't want me going outside. Not without him."

Sharon nodded and waved a hand toward the box. "Then, let's hope my pile of dirt has some live eggs in it."

Tam stood on the tips of her toes and looked inside the box. "What's so important about bugs?"

"Many things," Sharon said. "Most people don't know this: We *need* the insects. But they don't need us. The insects survived a very long time without us."

"So, we're not that important," Georgiana said.

Sharon grinned. "Not nearly as important as we like to believe. Do you want to know how important we really are?"

Georgiana nodded; but she wasn't really sure she wanted the answer.

"Okay. Try this thought experiment: There's over six billion of us on planet Earth today. Now, imagine that I could take all those people and put them in a big box, allowing for each person about six feet of height and a few inches of breathing space so they don't kill one another. We build this box as a perfect cube, equal on all sides. How many miles high do you think the box will be?"

After a moment's thought, Georgiana turned to the computer, ready to map out the foundation of the cube and command the machine to construct all the necessary equations and drawings. But Sharon stopped her.

"No," she said. "I want you to think this out for yourself. Make your best guess. There's a lesson in this," she said mischievously—"and a surprise."

"A thousand miles!" Tam guessed.

"Nope."

"Two thousand?"

"Guess again." And Sharon's grin widened. Georgiana understood, then, that Tam was headed in the wrong direction; and that therein lay the lesson, and the surprise. Georgiana thought it a pity that Sharon had not become a teacher, or that she did not have children of her own. She was really good with kids. "But I'll have *plenty* of time for children," she had once said, "if we ever get Project Biotime working."

Georgiana did not know much about deep-ocean bacteria or radiation resistant segments of the cockroach genome. She could not even pronounce the titles of Sharon's papers. What she did know was that in this city of dreams, some of the scientists had been talking about extending human lifetimes hundreds of years, and that the research had been moving along quite nicely until Sharon's cockroaches—whose natural resistance to DNA damage was said to be a key to the fountain of youth—began dying.

Sharon's long tenure at Brookhaven had in fact begun with the lowly cockroach. Armed with a grant for the study of roach migrations in large buildings, she had painted names on their backs before releasing them into the public areas of the city's museum. In time, she ran out of names and was forced to resort to numbers. By then, the story of the visiting senator who wanted to know why a cockroach he had seen in an elevator displayed the name "Alice" on its wings had become legendary, as had Sharon's habit of gleefully emptying boxes of roaches within eyesight of museum visitors. No wonder that the chairman had transferred her to Biotime and *Bluepeace*.

"Two hundred miles?" Georgiana guessed.

"You're getting warmer."

Tam frowned. "But it can't be much smaller than that!"
Sharon smiled. "Oh, yes it can."

"One hundred miles," Georgiana said.

"Keep going," Sharon said.

"Twenty miles?"

Sharon made a downward motion with her hand, as if flattening a large box.

"Smaller?" Georgiana stared off into space, trying to

visualize the shrinking cube of human flesh. "I don't believe it."

"Believe it," Sharon said. "I've done the calculation myself. Your notepad will verify this: It's only two miles on a side. And it's even smaller than that if you squeeze them head to head, shoulder to shoulder. Then your cube will be only about four times as high as the World Trade Center Twin Towers."

"All the people in the world?" Tam asked, with a sigh.

"All the people in the world. Now, suppose we pushed that cube off the edge of Manhattan Island and submerged it in the Atlantic Ocean. Do you know how much it would raise the level of the world's oceans?"

Tam nodded. "Not very much, I'm guessing."

"You're guessing right. Not very much at all. Not even the width of a human eyelash. So, the next time you meet someone who thinks he's really big, tell him what I've just told you, and then ask him who in the world he thinks he is."

"Wow," Tam said.

"Yes. The first thing everyone should learn is that we are not the center of the universe."

"The world, either," Georgiana added.

"Not by a long shot." Sharon laughed, noticing how eager children were to grasp concepts that filled most adults—even the President—with frustration and dismay.

"Until very recently," she continued, "there was probably an ant living on Earth for every second that had passed since the Big Bang—and *that* happened more than eight billion years ago. At any one time, there must have been more than fifty million insects for every human being alive, and if you squeezed them all together in one place, they would form a cube more than twenty times as massive as ours. All those insects—and let me tell you something: There is no known species of plant, other than seaweed, that was not in some way both attacked and helped by them."

"Then if they're gone," Georgiana said, "and if plants are hurt *and* helped by the insects . . . then if you take away both the hurt and the help—"

"Then what?" Sharon encouraged.

"Then shouldn't everything balance out?"

"Oh, if only nature were that simple."

"But it's not simple?" Tam asked.

"Oh, someone's always trying to come up with simple explanations," said Sharon. "But nature is far, far from simple. Especially in the insect world. Take, for example, the cockroach's cousin, New Zealand's giant weta. It's the heaviest insect in the world, but it is barely larger than a mouse. After so many tens of millions of years of experimentation, you'd expect nature to produce a more efficient insect breathing technique—something like a lung—that would allow them to grow larger without suffocating themselves to death. A simple test. But nature failed. So, a few insect species managed to get around this limitation of size by bunching themselves together into colonies. The most amazing, most complex colonies of all are the ones that live in South American caves: We call them army ants."

Georgiana glanced over at Tam. She was hanging on Sharon's every word.

"While they nest," Sharon said, making spidery shapes with her hands and bringing them together to form a basket, "the ants cling to one another, using their legs and bodies to form tunnels and egg chambers. The walls of those chambers are made of living ant flesh; and when the flesh gets hungry, it breaks apart and moves out into the jungle, like a great, black army. Each ant behaves so like one of the cells in your body that it is easy to think of the army as a single animal, weighing as much as all three of us put together, but having a half million mouths spread out over several acres."

And now the "motes" had taken over the army ant's niche, she left unsaid.

12

Crisis Redefined

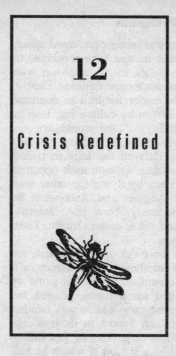

DAY 3, 8:40 A.M.

Jake understood, as he waited in a river of stalled traffic, that he had been too preoccupied by a succession of thwarted travel plans to be paying much attention to current events, but even he knew what another mote outbreak meant—especially this outbreak.

Bangor.

Had he really heard it correctly?

There was an unreality to the name. Bangor. Home. The newscasts and internet reports were vague and sometimes conflicting, except on one detail—casualties. There had been heavy casualties. Bangor was Newbern and Long Beach writ large.

Sheila would not be coming after Jake and their two

girls. No doubt of it. His plan was being overturned again, but the reality had not yet sunk in, and Jake continued to behave as if Sheila and the police might catch up with him at any moment. He was no longer thinking clearly. He discovered that it was far easier for him to continue fleeing the authorities, to be driven by culture lag, than to give up and accept the possibility . . . the probability . . . the near certainty—that Sheila no longer existed. So, *still* he cursed himself for having delayed too long in taking the children west, for not realizing, as soon as it occurred to him that he might reach Paris by flying the other way around the world—via Los Angeles and Asia—that he should have rebooked immediately. Now L.A. International Airport was closing itself off to eastern traffic. Train routes, too, were closing down.

Finally, he had decided to *drive* out of Long Island; for his money would not last if he stayed much longer in a place where price gouging continued to be the game of the day. He had been gouged for a room, gouged for breakfast, gouged for the rental car—which was handed over to him with little more than vapors in its tank. He had been gouged even for the five gallons of gasoline— the maximum amount alloted by a station at which he had waited in line more than an hour.

Gas lines. Who would have believed it?

Now he waited in rush-hour traffic, hoping that by the time he reached the Triborough Bridge he would still have enough gas to carry him into rural Connecticut, where he would not have to wait half the morning for a fill-up.

Half the morning . . . Jake looked at his watch and frowned. It was not even 9:00 A.M., yet already the sun was hot on his face. Today was going to be another scorcher on Long Island, but he did not dare turn on the air conditioner. It used too much gas. So he rolled the windows all the way down and thanked his lucky stars that Wynne and Michelle were still sleeping peacefully in the backseat. He wanted to avoid another stop in the local gas lines. He wanted to be on open road, with the wind blowing through his hair, before the noon sun turned Queens Boulevard into hell warmed up. Unfortunately, Jake's luck had taken such turns lately that what he wanted to happen and what would happen always seemed miles apart. It was like one of nature's laws, one of its unbreakable laws.

What the media would soon be calling "the New York City gas riot" did not occur in New York City proper but rather, on Jake's side of the East River, in Queens. There was, as yet, no real shortage of supplies, just a general feeling that the men and women who trucked fuel into the region would either stop coming or would charge extortionist prices to do so. The psychology behind the riot was simple, as were the causes of all chain reactions: Anticipating shortages, people who ordinarily did not think twice about driving around with their gas tanks only a quarter full decided—thousands of them all at once—to top off their tanks in an effort to guard against the coming shortage. Thus did they create the very shortage they had hoped to avoid. With demand suddenly threatening to exceed supply, it became a seller's market. Gas prices doubled in a single night. Five-gallon limits were imposed, and lines of cars built up outside gas stations, clogging lanes ordinarily reserved for the flow of traffic.

Somewhere up ahead at least two such lines had slowed Jake's progress to a crawl. Other drivers had rolled down their windows, too; and conversations could be overheard, some of them rising to a hysterical pitch.

"It's all right," Jake heard a man call into his notepad. "You start the meeting without me and I'll be there in a while." The man wiped sweat from his forehead as he closed the lid on his pad.

"Quiet! Quiet!" a mother demanded of an unruly child. "God! How I wish you were never born!" The words stung Jake. He could never imagine himself saying that to Wynne or Michelle.

"Felix, you must wait for me," begged a green-eyed Chinese woman with an Australian accent.

"No," replied a voice from her pad. "I've had enough of this."

Suddenly, Jake was aware of a dull, thudding noise. A cloud of dark smoke appeared some dozen car lengths ahead, thickening as he watched, then driving straight up into the still air. The chain reaction had begun. One frustrated commuter, after waiting nearly an hour and a half in a gas line—his second line that morning—had just heard the station owner announce that fill-up would henceforth be reserved for neighborhood customers only. This cost the man the last ounce of his self-control. He threw a crowbar at the station owner, then pumped gasoline over his own Corvette and set it afire.

Jake was unable to see what happened next. He heard glass breaking and metal being pounded, and a chorus of screams as if a score more of tempers had suddenly surged and flared. It was a shocking sound, and the people in the cars on either side of Jake stopped speaking to their pads and their children and started to listen. In seconds, it became a roar. He perceived it coming toward him as a shock wave of moving bodies. In the lane ahead, they threw open car doors and climbed over the doors and one another to get away from the center of the riot. For a moment Jake was too astonished to stir—and his moment of hesitation spared him from grabbing his two little girls and stepping into the path of the storm.

The men bounding over the hood of his car jolted Wynne and Michelle awake; and then the stampede, the greater mass of it, passed them by with such bewildering swiftness that still Jake sat in the front seat, motionless, dumbstruck. Had one of the rioters possessed an Uzi, and swept it in his direction (and he believed, but could not be certain, that he had heard gunshots crackling amid the breaking glass) the barrage would surely have slain him in his seat.

With the pressure from the people trying to run away from the outburst slackening, Jake waited not a moment longer; he scooped up his two girls from the backseat and fled—holding one child under each arm—into the tail end of the stampede, looking back with panicky eyes and then turning to rush into the lobby of the Mutual Insurance Building.

The room was crowded to the stairways and the halls. For twelve long seconds the shouts and thuds in the direction of the gas station grew louder and the street sounded like a battlefield, yet the people in the lobby seemed curiously silent and calm. They simply huddled toward the stairs, trying to keep as far as possible from the front windows.

There was a wall screen on one side of the lobby, tuned to CNN. Jake watched the screen, waiting for a forecast of when the chaos outside might end and when it might be safe for him to leave New York. He expected to see skycam views of the street he had just fled, and there were indeed aerial views on the screen, but the caption had nothing to do with Queens. Another place was dominating the nation's news—Bangor.

DAY 3, 9:15 A.M.

The sun had been up too many hours to permit a clear infrared scan of the town, but the two pilots and the CDC observer were confident that in spite of the warming asphalt and sod, their equipment would gather enough information to tell the story. The copilot watched two of the lead tankers, up ahead, in the sunlight. They trailed veils of white mist from their underbellies; and the sudden whir of hydraulics told the observer that his plane, too, had commenced "bug-bombing." He carefully checked the infeeds to his notepad, identifying, from rows of rectangular, infrared "blackouts" (meaning cold windows), dead buildings whose air conditioners were still active. There, he thought, lay the realization of the CDC motto: *Hell has our number.*

The copilot tapped his shoulder. "Coming up on Mote Central," he said. "You see it?"

He leaned forward in his cramped, fold-down seat until his nose was practically against the notepad screen. The Bangor baseball diamond passed below in a blur of red, yellow, and computer-enhanced blue. By the time the Victorian homes of Broadway swept underfoot, the plane was skimming two hundred feet lower and the terrain was shooting by even faster; but the observer swiveled his wing-mounted cameras to account for the motion, and the resolution improved dramatically.

His jaw slackened. He saw nearly two dozen amoeboid

splotches on Broadway, spreading body heat over the road, the sidewalks, across doorsteps and cars.

"Oh, my God," said the copilot. Looking out the cockpit window, his view was not filtered by scanners and screens. He saw the bodies themselves, splayed across sidewalks and doorsteps.

"I'm counting twenty-one infrareds on Broadway," the CDC observer announced. "The scanners won't let us see through glass and plasterboard, but"—he noticed faint heat signatures flowing along mite paths near open doors and windows—"but it's going to be a repeat of Long Beach, guys. We'll find most of the bodies indoors."

The copilot cleared his throat. "God! You mean, it's worse than it looks?"

"Yes, sir. Worse than you imagine."

"I can imagine quite a lot," the copilot insisted. "How can it possibly get any worse than this?"

The observer frowned and tapped the screen. "Is this a multiple-choice question?"

DAY 3, 3:40 P.M.

"This is an incredible situation," Leslie announced over the com-link. "We must have sifted through a ton of dirt and leaves, and we've failed to find a single live egg or pupa."

"Not even one?" the President asked.

"One of the *Bluepeace* pilots found a cockroach in the cafeteria. That's the sum of it: one miraculous little survivor. Under the circumstances, you'd think a cockroach would be cause for celebration—and for a moment it was—except that where you find one, you're normally supposed to find hundreds of them."

The President recalled a mural he once saw at the American Museum of Natural History. The painting showed pterosaurs clambering over a cliff overlooking a Jurassic sea. He remembered now, that when he had looked closely, he'd noticed that the artist had shown cockroaches clambering among the pterosaurs. It was an odd detail, odd enough to have stuck in his memory, and it illustrated that the lowly cockroach must indeed have ridden through a great many cycles of extinction, outliving even the mighty saurians. As for how and why, theories abounded. Richard, Jackson, and Bill seemed to produce a new one every ten minutes; but the ones they kept returning to were rife with the words *chaos, crystallization,* and *statistical certainty.*

Is that what it all comes down to? the President wondered. *A recurring M set? Are we to become victims of mere mathematics?* No. He was not prepared to accept this, even in theory.

"It can't be very likely that you happened upon the only living cockroach in all the world," the President said.

"It does give us some hope that the insects will come back; but I doubt we'll see them in large enough numbers, or in enough variety, or soon enough to do us any good."

"Haven't you found any other insect traces? Anything at all?"

"After the roach, I think we all soared through bouts of wishful thinking, Mr. President. That's when I noticed the hibiscus plants. They're flourishing. Well, and why not? They're self-pollinating. I literally began tearing them apart, looking for aphids. We know the ants are gone. Ants feed on aphids and aphids just love hibiscus buds, so it followed that I might find a live aphid or two. Even if they're not the most efficient pollinators in the world, just one living female would have been cause for more celebration, because aphids can rebuild their populations really fast. They're literally born pregnant; in some cases grandchildren have begun to grow in the mother's body even before she is born. If all those grandchildren happen to live, Grandma could produce six hundred billion aphids in a year. But no such luck. I didn't find a single aphid. Just spider mites. Lots of spider mites."

"Anything else?"

"That's all we've got from this end. So far you're one of maybe a dozen people on Earth who have all the pieces of the puzzle, but very soon our problem will be as obvious as a mile-high billboard. I'm afraid we're looking at a world ecology that's shriveling literally from the roots up. Did you know that ants, not worms, are the most prominent maintainers of the planet's soil?''

The President shook his head.

"Well, they are. And without them we're going to see desertification on a grand scale, all over the world, even where it rains, until worms, or spiders, or something else takes over for the ants. And that could take fifty thousand years. Or a million. Who really knows?''

"All right," the President said. "So we have the mites to deal with. They're frightening; but we can soap-bomb them as soon as they show up. I'll also grant you that agriculture is going to be hit hard. So, we're facing rationing at the very least. And forests will start to die. That raises questions about greenhouse gases—but even so, doesn't most of the oxygen we breathe come from the oceans?''

"That's true, but—"

"But in your opinion, is it possible that America and the world can survive this crisis, economically speaking?''

"Economically?"

"Yes."

The insect pathologist returned an expression of incredulity mixed with worry. It seemed to her a rather frivolous concern, and while there was a certain logic to getting opinions from as many different sources as possible, it seemed odd on the verge of crazy to be asking an entomologist about the economy.

"You needn't look so jolted," the President said. "It's a very important issue, not nearly so irrelevant as it may sound on first hearing. You know what the insects are worth to us. I know the economy. If insect death is truly dragging down the world ecology, and if the ecology can in turn drag down the economy, then our civilization really is hanging by a thread.''

"Our civilization? I'm beginning to worry more about our species.''

The President looked at her with an expression that said *You've got to be kidding*, and she returned one that said *No, I'm not*.

"Economically speaking, Mr. President, it looks like

real estate is going to be a very crummy investment by this time next year.''

"How so?''

"There's going to be a real glut of vacant homes on the market. A lot fewer of us.''

"So that's it, you think? It goes all the way up the food chain?''

Leslie nodded.

"You're all agreed on this?''

"It's the conclusion we're coming to.''

"Is there anything we can do?'' asked the President, hopefully. "How about cloning insects from preserved tissue? Releasing them into the environment? Mass-producing them somehow?''

The insect pathologist shook her head. "Richard and Jackson are discussing those possibilities. One problem I see is that whatever in our environment is killing the insects, or whatever is programmed into their genes to cause the die-off, will just keep on working against the clones. Another problem is that I don't think we have enough time. My best guess is that when you take the insects away, you can expect people to start dying about six weeks later. We're there now. Things could start unraveling very fast.''

"Then . . .'' The President tried to keep a wave of depression from constricting his throat. "What gets through this alive? Does anything survive?''

"Survival of the scavengers, initially. Seagulls will eat almost anything. I imagine they'll actually experience a population boom for a while . . . until the supply of unburied bodies runs out.''

"So this *is* the genuine article,'' the President muttered.

"Pardon?''

"Nothing,'' said the President. "I can't thank you too much for your frankness,'' and his chin constricted, and he tried to choke back tears, not wanting the scientist to see him this way. "Just keep me informed,'' he said quickly, and killed the line.

In the next moment the surge of sorrow disappeared under an upwelling of anger, as denial had been swallowed by sorrow. The anger surprised him, directed as it was against—of all things—seagulls!

"Blessed be the scavengers," he whispered to the empty room. So, the seagulls and the jackals and the vultures are going to inherit the Earth. The thought dismayed him; made him think that if there was a God behind any of this, he had to be a psychotic; made him think of a strange story he once heard about seagulls being unable to burp—which meant that if you fed them Alka-Seltzer they would fill up with gas and explode. It made him think actually of putting that experiment to the test; but the anger suddenly abated and was replaced by something even stranger, something like acceptance mingled with numbing disbelief. With this strange mixture came a clarity of thought, a clarity born of horrors.

There had been many predictions of when and how civilization might be destroyed, and whence the destruction would come. As Reverend Jim Jones, David Koresh, and a thousand other false priests had proved through the ages, man does not bear with sanity a belief that his world will end. Time and again, in only slightly more superstitious ages, self-appointed prophets had announced that the reappearance of Halley's comet, or the end of a century, or some hidden truth in the Book of Daniel or the Revelation of Saint John foretold the time of Tribulation. Witches were sought out, crushed under rocks, burned at stakes, or tried by water in efforts to appease God and forestall the catastrophe. Unbaptized babies were catapulted from slings against the bows of newly built ships to atone for sins and forestall the catastrophe—a practice that lived on, in sanitized form, as the custom of christening ships by smashing bottles of champagne against their prows. Cats, which the mobs decided were evil by association with witches, were hunted throughout Europe and slaughtered— whole bonfires of cats, in efforts to forestall the catastrophe. Vain efforts. Without the services of the cats, rat populations swelled, the better to bring on a catastrophe by spreading the Black Plague.

The President knew enough about human nature not to expect the modern mobs (and there would be mobs, he was certain) to act any better. The only difference was that this time it was not the prophet or the priest or even the New Age seer who had foretold the fall of civilization. This time, the doomsaying was coming from the very group of people he had learned to regard as coldly rational, not given to hysteria, and guided by civilization rather than by instinct. It was coming from the scientists; and to the President, that was enough to say it really was coming. There seemed no point in trying to keep it secret. As Leslie had suggested, the reality was looming as large as a billboard. There was already enough information circulating on CNN, and enough evidence in everyone's backyard, for anyone to put the pieces together and figure it out. *Sweet Jesus,* the President thought—*a sixteen year old should be able to figure it out!*

The President knew more, of course—much of it from his scientific and economic advisors. For weeks, a little-known epidemic of asthma and skin rashes had been sending residents of Brooklyn and Queens to hospital emergency rooms in droves. It was said that the subways themselves sounded like roving TB wards. The culprits were now identified: mites—the same varieties involved in the so-called mote outbreaks. Apparently they had been feeding, in the walls of apartments and in the air passages of office buildings and subways, on the bodies of dead insects. Then, as the mite populations expanded on the sudden bounty, the supply of insect bodies abruptly ran out and, in most neighborhoods, the mites began to starve. Air ducts suddenly became filled with disintegrating mite corpses—tons of them. Fans and trains spread them through the air, and the people inhaled fungus- and bacteria-covered mite legs until at last their immune systems became overwhelmed, producing shortness of breath in people who had never experienced symptoms of asthma before, raising strange boils on people whose skin had always been healthy, and producing lethargy in people who had always been energetic.

Citywide plagues of "sick-building syndrome" did not concern the President. *That*, America could easily have learned to live with. But the mites had not starved off everywhere; and the President began to appreciate how life often had a way . . . of finding a way, as the disasters in Long Beach, Newbern, and Bangor had proved. But even these, America could easily have dealt with. What had changed, really? Cars were still being built. Crops were still being harvested. Brad's ale and Coors beer were still being brewed. Factories in Puerto Rico were still drawing carbon dioxide out of the air and turning it into plastic. The Andrew Lloyd Webber/Stephen King musical, *Survivor Type,* was still sold out until next spring. The cornfields of Kansas and Nebraska were still producing Tholian silk. The businesses of the nation were intact, and the economy should have remained similarly intact. Logically, it should have; but people's fears and behavior had a way of undermining logic, until what "should be" and what "would be" no longer knew each other.

The stock market had tumbled nearly 5 percent, meaning that billions of dollars simply disappeared from the nation's economy. With the Bangor outbreak, transportation breakdowns continued apace. Now truckers, in addition to pilots and train operators, were refusing in ever-increasing multitudes to carry passengers or goods to what they perceived as an entire coast turned deadly. The panic among the truckers was bound to further the panic on Wall Street. Already, interest rates were starting upward, meaning that people might stop taking out loans and making major purchases (assuming that by this time next week there would be any goods available for purchase on the East Coast). Soon, Cleveland and Detroit would be shipping fewer ceramic and carbon composites, Kansas would be shipping fewer orders of high-tensile silk, and the businesses of the nation would no longer stand intact.

But even a major recession could be dealt with. The worst a recession could do was erode national confidence and render him a one-termer, and that wasn't so bad, not so bad as—*as what?* If the scientists were right, the famine striking at the heart of India was really a preview of much of the world during the next twelve months, and the Great Depression of the 1930s—which triggered a global war and heralded the first atomic bomb—might seem utterly nostalgic by comparison.

A cheery thought.

Add to this, military reports that India was certain to

move troops into Pakistan and Sri Lanka, that Pakistan might retaliate with nuclear force, and that no fewer than two submarines, presumably Indian, were shadowing the *Nimitz*.

Add to this a sudden escalation of the Cold War between Tokyo and Beijing.

Add to this reports that more people had been killed by *Desmodus* than were originally believed, and that the front line might be moving north, coming slowly and surely this way. According to the latest Brookhaven report, the Schutts had been digging up half the island of Tobago, assisting the New York team in its search for signs of insect dormancy, but with no success. As yet, there were no real clues pointing to how cockroaches and other ancient insect groups had survived these evolutionary resettings (if that's what was really going on!).

The President looked at his watch.

4:00 P.M.

Tobago was a thousand miles farther east than Washington—which meant 5:00 P.M. The President knew that darkness in the lesser Antilles fell like the shutting off of a lamp, with almost no twilight. He made some quick mental calculations: The line of shadow that now bisected the Atlantic was almost twelve hundred miles east of Tobago, and approaching the island at 1,040 miles per hour.

Another long night of *Desmodus* was about to begin.

13

Into the Belly of the Beast

Not a bird could be heard to sing nor an animal to move, as Bill and Janet left an array of mist nets, and their car, on the roadside and made their way toward an abandoned church. The only sounds were those of their own feet on the dirt road, the ticking of the car radiator behind them, and the Caribbean lapping at the base of a mini-lighthouse barely forty yards beyond the church.

Having spent most of the day overturning logs and digging holes in the forest—looking in vain for insect eggs and larvae—they now broadened their search to include bat roosts under bridges and under the eaves of buildings. This broader search, too, had proved unsuccessful. Yet as they traveled the island, the true extent of the night's bloodletting was becoming horribly apparent: as if a huge, phantom cloud had passed over Tobago, entering this home or that, leaving a home next door untouched. Most of the victims seemed to have died in their beds without ever waking up. This was at least marginally in character for *Desmodus*. They were known to be sneaky creatures, meaning that if you happened to be sleeping out in the open and they came upon you, you usually did not know about it until you woke up bleeding from unclotted wounds. But Bill had never heard of vampire bats attacking in large enough numbers to kill, or attacking people who were wide awake and putting up a lively resistance; and yet there were reports, unsubstantiated thus far, that at least two of the island's residents—an old innkeeper and his wife—had put up a terrific struggle before they died. In his own bedroom, the innkeeper had supposedly fired several rounds from a shotgun, and then used the weapon to swat at his tormentors. The gun was still lying at his side, broken in two. Beside his wife lay a broken umbrella.

None of this made any sense to Bill. Giant flocks of vampire bats swarming into houses and slaughtering whole families? If he had not seen it himself, he would have dismissed the story as tabloid bullshit. Since when did animals built for nipping blood in stealth suddenly become so aggressive? It was as if the bats had undergone one of Richard Sinclair's crystallization events—all of *Desmodus* at once—forming a new behavioral pattern. Nature provided very few examples of such change—but examples did exist, one of them, perhaps, right under Bill's nose; and in the natural world it was the exceptions that best probed the rules.

Probing nature's rules always produced a sense of fear and wonder.

This was part of the attraction.

This was the way of it: Bill understood that if he could not bear the darkness, if pushing half blind into new frontiers became not a longing for the mysterious so much as a dislike of shadows leering from odd corners, then he should go back to the sunshine and never make exploring his profession. The frontiers of the night were never meant to be inhabited by the meek.

Prey switching. Bill wondered. Definitely not a subject

for the timid. There was little doubt that it had been witnessed in Long Beach two days ago, and that here, on Tobago, *Desmodus* was right now switching its attention from cows to humans. Add to this latest development, evidence that prions had leaped to bats, probably from some recently vanished insect species . . . and the picture just kept getting crazier . . . and crazier. . . . Bill hoped to inject some small measure of sanity into the mix by finding one of *Desmodus*'s resting places before nightfall. Then, with a little luck, he could snare four or five of the sleeping bats and express mail them to Atlanta for a prion search. He decided that the old church looked like a good prospect for a roost: all rot and splitting timbers and peeled paint. It dated back to Tobago's plantation days, when large numbers of workers formed a local congregation; but with the breakup of this part of the island into little ma-and-pop farms, the congregation had shifted elsewhere, leaving behind this brooding structure whose spire and roof were beginning to sag under their own weight.

Right, Bill told himself. Get a fresh sample of live bats. Camp in the car, near the mist nets—and if there's any trouble, shelter in the car with the windows rolled up real tight. That was the plan; but the plan was—

"Nuts," Janet said. "This is nuts. We should be back at the house and sealing ourselves in by now."

"Don't worry," Bill said, his eyes taking in every large wooden splinter, and shadow, and paint flake under the eaves. "I think we're both smart enough not to get caught outside in the dark."

"Yeah, but this can wait."

Bill's eyes stopped at a shape in the shadows, globular and dark brown. His heartbeat and respiration cranked up, until he realized that it was only a paper wasp nest— empty, presumably.

"No, *someone* has to find out if these bats are full of prions," he said. "Someone has to find out where they're hiding," and then, thinking aloud, "I mean, they've got to be roosting somewhere big enough to house a whole shitload of bats. Although, then again . . . they're so damned opportunistic, they could be roosting in *hundreds* of different places—almost anywhere."

"But if they were sleeping everywhere, we'd have found some of them by now," Janet said.

"I would think so . . . so, let's check this one last place."

Now Janet's pulse and blood pressure shot upward, impelled by the twin-engine exhaust of her adrenals, which were being called into action by a funny, internal voice that shouted *Danger! Danger, Will Robinson!* "Look," she said. "We can do this tomorrow. We can do this in midday or better yet mid-morning. We don't have to be here now. We're putting ourselves at a disadvantage. We're not dealing from strength if we're working at sunset with the possibility of a large swarm of unpredictable animals."

Bill shook his head. He did not have a useful answer. The events unfolding on at least two continents were so monstrously out of place that he'd be the first to admit they overshadowed his thinking, making him take chances that he normally would not. "Look," he said. "*We're here*. We'll be in and out of there real fast. It'll take ten minutes, and then we won't have to drag our asses back here tomorrow."

Great, Janet thought. *We're setting ourselves up*. If Craven or Limardo had tried writing a scene like this into a movie, the audience would never have bought into it. Certainly Limardo would never have tried. It just looked too stupid, too contrived: two people who should know better, walking, eyes wide open, into the vampire's den. In Hollywood, of course, ten thousand hungry mouths would be waiting behind those church doors. Janet really did not believe this to be the case; but she did know that what they were doing was dumb even by Hollywood standards. Yet here they were, doing it for real. As they reached the church steps, Janet glanced toward the lighthouse at the end of the road. It stood barely fifteen feet high, and was hardly worthy of being called a "light*house*," for the building was little more than a hollow, concrete pedestal with an automatic lamp and a tiny glass enclosure on top. The keeper, who had been whitewashing the pedestal, paused and waved to the Schutts, a friendly "hello" wave. Bill returned the greeting; but Janet got the distinct impres-

sion that the man's wave was just an act. Something in
the way he moved bothered her, but she could not say
what, or why.

"So, let's say the insects do stop reproducing and go
dormant," Bill said, the thought seeming to have come
out of nowhere. "Now, here's a scary thought: Let's say
the comets only *used* to bombard us every thirty-three
million years. And let's say insects and perhaps a few
other ancient organisms *did* adapt to the periodic bombardments—adapted to the point that their dormancy itself
causes extinctions and resets the Earth's biological clock.
And what if by now the comets have simply stopped coming? Does the adaptive response live on? Do we get the
extinction anyway? Does the cycle continue even in the
absence of the trigger for the cycle?"

"Sometimes I think your brain is just going to explode," Janet said. "Sometimes I think it already has."

He tried the church door; it was tight, but still movable
with a hardy shoulder shove. Its rust-clotted hinges
groaned hellishly, and the Schutts stepped into the hot,
shadowy interior.

In Plainview, Long Island, at the Saint Pius X House
of Prayer, an unknown artist had carved one of the world's
most original, and most haunting, altar crucifixes. The
wooden Jesus, life-size, looked out directly at his congregation, and was posed in such a manner as to suggest he
was about to step off the cross into open air. The artist
had carved two duplicates. One simply disappeared into
history. The other ended up on the isle of Tobago, in the
now-abandoned plantation church. The wide-open eyes
had a strange, piercing quality—which was why the members of the Tobago congregation, when they moved on,
left the statue behind.

(—behind, but not alone)

A new congregation had come to the wooden Jesus.

(—of it, not above it)

They crowded over his body, locked leathery arm over
leathery arm, and knitted themselves together with an embrace of claw and sinew into a living membrane of muscle
and bone and fur. They were a nightmare of flesh-and-

blood engineering: a human shape made entirely of *Desmodus*. Its face seethed and swarmed. Its cheeks clicked with the hungry, hollow rhythm of self-honing incisors, and from each of its eye sockets, three heads stared. All around, countless pairs of ears perked, suddenly made awake and aware, with all their attention drawn in unison toward voices at the church door—

"Sometimes I think your brain is just going to explode—"

And in the caverns of Jesus' eyes, six pairs of bat eyes glittered and blinked, then turned as two toward the Schutts. On either side of the crucifix, ten thousand little bat hearts beat faster. Ten thousand bodies squirmed, and stretched, and smeared anticoagulants over their teeth.

As soon as they stepped through the door, the Schutts understood the smell; it was a thick, breath-stopping smell. There was a moment's hesitation, no more than a moment's, when Janet suppressed a gag reflex and went rigid with disbelief. The smell was stronger than at the Colberts' house, much stronger. There must have been thou—

And then she grabbed Bill's arm and began tugging him toward the door; but he yanked his arm away and, unbelievably, stepped deeper into *Desmodus*'s den.

"Are you crazy?" she whispered.

"Shhhh!" came the reply.

The sun still shone on the horizon, and though it was dark and sheltered in the church, shafts of sunlight still slanted through broken windows, slanted almost horizontal. Motes of dust flickered in the shafts. As his eyes became accustomed to the shadows, Bill began to see details. Horrible details. Something shivered and writhed above the altar, giving the impression that someone was up there on the crucifix; but he realized that—

(that was impossible—)

"Jesus . . . Christ . . . almighty," he whispered. The tall fixtures on either side of the altar were alive. The entire wall was alive.

Bill strode twenty feet down the center aisle.

"What are you doing?" Janet said. "Let's get the fuck out of here!"

"Whoa! Whoa! Wait a second. I've got to see this.

They're not going to attack us if we're standing and moving.''

The words were barely out of his mouth when one bat flapped its wings and dropped from Jesus' jaw, sending forth a shower of chaos that spread with astonishing speed from the cross to the towering structures on its flanks. The altar spilled bats like a slashed throat spilling blood. Whole clouds of bats swirled round the floor at the front of the church, hopping, crawling, climbing over pews as Bill began to back off and as a tiny voice inside him screamed, *Vampire bats don't do this!*

"You were saying?" asked Janet.

"Never mind—*RUN!*"

And they did; Bill could hear the living mass of *Desmodus* scrabbling over pews, over the floor and in hidden corners—forming two wave fronts that were beginning to crest on either side of him, like walls, like the Red Sea in the time of Moses. *So many of them!* that voice inside of him said. *Vampire bats don't congregate in such large swarms!*

Yet there they were, twenty feet ahead of him . . . already on Janet's legs! She was almost out the door, almost in the daylight and the open air, but not—

A motion immediately to his right, more felt than seen, told him that the precursor wave was pacing him, and would burst out the door with him if he ran after her. A thousand screeching voices told him they were rising to eye level, rising like summoned spirits, to become an unholy halo around his head. He could see only one option—

"*Run!*" he yelled again, then slammed his full weight against the door, sealing the exit behind her.

"*Bill?*"

Eerie, surely imaginary silence—the connection to him broken, for all time.

"BILL!"

She was standing on the church steps, swatting bats off her legs, catching glimpses of the late-afternoon light as it grew dimmer, turning the street as shadowy as the world on the other side of the church door.

"BILL!"

Curses and shouts of "*RUN . . . RUN . . .*" Muffled. Fading.

And the sun was setting behind the rim of Earth. And her legs were covered with blood. And the tips of her fingers were slashed from swatting at defiant claws and fangs. And as the blinding rays retreated across the surface of the Caribbean, the first wave of *Desmodus* scouts rippled through breaks in slats and windows.

"This way!" a voice called. "Hurry! It's safe here!"

Unreality and numbness settled over her, and she ran across the dirt road toward the keeper, swatting at herself as she ran, raising a blood-spattered hand to shield her eyes.

And within a span of seconds that seemed to stretch immeasurably she had reached the lighthouse and the keeper had pulled back the door and she leaned against the steel ladder in the center of the tower as he bent over to pluck bats off her body and smash them beneath his feet—and then she felt a hand close suddenly on her arm and saw tiny batwings flittering noiselessly on top of the polished glass panes ten feet overhead—

Bill's goddamned genetic time bomb, that funny internal voice shouted.

Bill! she wanted to cry out.

We must get Bill!—

but her lips would not move and her eyes refused to stay open and she felt consciousness slipping away even as the keeper's grip tightened alarmingly. Numbness. Sweet numbness. And darkness. Numbness. Darkness. The sun had set below the horizon. The swarm had risen above.

14

Darwin's Warm Little Pond

The writer of the Ninetieth Psalm proclaimed: "To you, a thousand years are but a single day. Before the mountains were born, before the earth and the world came to birth, you were God. You can turn man back to dust by saying, 'Back to what you were!' "

As the biblical scribes viewed the history of life, from dust man came and to dust man would return. Dust to dust. The imagery was haunting and poetic; and to those who spent their lives poking about in the cellars of time and occasionally pulling skeletons out of the earth—to men like Richard Sinclair—the inevitability of dissolution was both immediately apparent and mythologically consistent. But it was impossible, during the last days of the old world, for most people to believe that cockroaches and dinosaurs, and the blood that ran in their own veins, had risen from the dust of Earth. Unless they happened to believe in miracles. Or unless they happened to be scientists.

Charles Darwin saw, at the cradle of life, a warm little pond. "It is often said," he wrote to a friend in 1871, "that all the conditions for the first production of a living organism are now present, which could ever have been present. But if (and oh what a big if) we could conceive in some warm little pond, with all sorts of ammonia and phosphoric salts, light, heat, electricity, etc., present, that a protein compound was chemically formed ready to undergo still more complex changes, at the present day such matter would be instantly devoured, or absorbed, which would not have been the case before living creatures were formed."

About a century after Darwin wrote his letter, scientists began finding remnants of warm, underground streams that had flowed through and perhaps even burst forth as geysers from certain crumbly, claylike meteorites. The meteorites themselves were made mostly of interstellar dust, carbonaceous soot, and ice. They were little splinters from once-larger bodies, and subtle clues offered by aluminum 26 and other radioactive decay products placed the warm, wet interiors of the asteroid parent bodies all the way back at 4.6 billion B.C. Some of Darwin's warm little ponds, it seemed, had formed far away from Earth—and, by 4 billion years ago, had frozen solid. But much had occurred, during that half billion years of warmth: Alongside meteoritic salt veins and microgeodes full of pyrrhotite crystals were found ethanol, purines, globs of protein, and *porphyrin molecules*—actual precursors of chlorophyll and hemoglobin. There went carbon, hydrogen, nitrogen, and oxygen, teaching humanity not only—*as above, so below*—not only how life's building blocks might have originated on Earth—but showing beyond serious dispute that biology, the production of order from chaos, was the product of some of the most likely chemical reactions undergone by some of the most common elements in this part of the universe.

About the same time, oceanographers came upon environments very similar to those that once existed inside the asteroids: deep ocean geysers spewing sulfide-laden mineral grains and salts—including pyrrhotite crystals—to which primitive bacteria and proteins clung. The biochemist Cyril Ponnamperuma saw immediately that the volcanic springs were yet another source of Darwin's warm little ponds.

"Life must have evolved in such places," he once wrote to Richard Sinclair, "must have originated through a process of natural selection that began with the exhalations and regurgitations of the planet itself, with volcanically heated water and the dust of the Earth." He was saying, in effect, that if humanity insisted on tracking its ancestry all the way back to the beginning, it had better be prepared to think a little more kindly of dust and clay. Richard, for his part, began to see that sometimes the process of scientific discovery was the disquieting feeling of climbing a mountain, only to find rabbis and priests, Buddhists and Islamic scholars sitting at the top and saying, "See! We knew all along!"

The Protocell Era, from which simple organic compounds emerged as living cells complete with genetic machinery, began when the Earth was practically new, a mere three hundred million years old, give or take a few tens of millions of years. The first "useful" proteins, those that by sheer chance appeared on or inside preliving bubbles of organic sludge and were able to induce reactions that added to their bulk, invariably prolonged the survival of individual protocells. The life span of a protocell was thus directly related to the complexity and effectiveness of its metabolism; and time, the destroyer, saw to it that most protocells and their descendants ran down and eventually fell apart, dispersing their contents for future absorption by other protocells. Those bubbles graced with the ability to absorb molecules from their surroundings—and to capture energy and direct it toward the knitting together of absorbed molecules into substances that could promote the survival not only of the bubbles but of their daughter bubbles—became ancestors of the first true life-forms to populate the seas. What they required, if such compounds as hemoglobin and brain proteins were to be evolved, was something akin to a team of carpenters and a set of blueprints to be passed on to each daughter protocell, guaranteeing that it was able to construct the same enzymes needed for all the reactions important to the parent's survival. What they required was Bill Schutt's ultimate parasite. What they required was DNA.

There were many possible routes to the construction of genetic machinery capable of bridging protein and nucleic acids; and at one time or another nature must have experimented with all of them. In some cases, the genetic blueprints had evolved from back to front, with the strongest, most resilient proteins becoming templates against which the first nucleic acid codes were assembled. Life from nonlife: More than four billion years later, vestiges of this process still existed, and were spreading out of South America and across the isle of Tobago with all the murderous speed of a wildfire. Under a sufficiently powerful microscope, the "mad cow" prion looked more like a collection of carefully machined parts than a creation of carbon chemistry. Proteins had been spun into helices and hollow sheets held together by tubes. The infectious protein lacked all trace of a genetic code, and was thus able to infiltrate the body of its prey without attracting the attentions of the ever-vigilant white blood cells, or triggering a fever, or calling any other of the body's immune defenses into action. Lacking both DNA and RNA, it crept through layers of tissue as if invisible, perceived by the immune system as nonliving, noninfectious matter; and yet it came alive the moment it made contact with a surprisingly abundant protein built from an almost identical sequence of amino acids and exhibiting an only slightly different shape. The intruded-upon protein, affectionately nicknamed "Stanley," after its discoverer, resided mostly in the neurons of the brain and, though churned out by the neurons' own DNA, served no known function, except perhaps to provide a means of reproduction for the intruding prion.

From its outpost in the brain, a single prion molecule, once brought into contact with a normal Stanley protein, could induce it to refold, or recrystallize, until it matched the shape of the intruder. What happened next was a miracle of molecular evolution, a spreading domino effect in which the intruder and its recrystallized twin transformed other Stanley proteins, which in turn transformed others, and so on, until brain fluids, spinal fluids, and the blood itself became filled with prions.

For most of man's tenure upon the Earth, prion diseases had dwelled in obscurity. They were little more than footnotes in medical journals, grim curiosities to be brought up only at in-laws' dinner tables, such as the New Guinea laughing sickness, which was believed to be spread by the habit, among headhunter tribes, of eating uncooked human brains. The afflicted usually died in fits of laughter, and the only cure recommended by native witch doctors was a blow to the neck with a very sharp axe blade; but even this did not always work. By the time the patient became symptomatic, the brain was usually so far gone that the severed head (especially if it landed with the neck pointed skyward, so that blood still pooled around the cerebral cortex) continued, for a half minute or more, to roll its eyes and move its lips in lungless, silent laughter.

Just ahead of the end days, a variant of the New Guinea laughing sickness had taken up residence in Great Britain's cows, where it became known erroneously as "mad cow disease." In an effort to prevent the infectious proteins from spreading, there had been bonfires of cows. Futile effort. Even as the cows were shot and piled like cordwood for burning, horseflies ingested their infected flesh; and before most of the world's insects ceased reproducing, and before a great many of their three-month life spans ran out, another human activity—rapid global transport—had brought one of the flies to Guyana, where it happened (not surprisingly) to bite a cow.

Faced now with new environmental pressures, and no insect transportation to new sources of Stanley proteins, the prions, like every virus, like every tree, like every lizard and every mammal that was to filter through the coming extinction, would not filter through unchanged. By the time the first Guyanese *Desmodus* took blood from an infected cow, the prions were already shifting—shifting like wax, shifting like clay—into multiple new shapes. The sheer, spreading numbers of them guaranteed diversity: folded one way, they made *Desmodus* drowsy; folded another, they made it hyperactive; folded another, they had no effect at all. Folded one way, they converted *Desmodus*'s normal Stanley proteins to the intrusive prion form slowly, giving rise to long incubation periods; folded another, they worked more efficiently and could cause disease quickly.

Before anyone knew that the new prion strains even existed, a single infected bat had shuttled back and forth from cow herd to cow herd. Being a gregarious animal, he returned to his roost every night and shared blood meals with his roost mates, and in so doing passed the silent death to twenty other bats. How many those twenty passed it to was open mostly to guesswork. If one were to use, as a guide, the standard network marketing strategy, whereby each new distributor (theoretically) builds a business by recruiting at least five new distributors, then one found at least a hundred second-level prion distributors beneath the first infected bat. Using the same formula, on the third level those hundred had gone on to produce five hundred new distributors, and two levels farther down, the five hundred had infected thirteen thousand. The thirteen thousand, meanwhile, spread the infection to at least ten times as many cows, before sickened cows became distasteful to them and they turned their attention to human hosts. It threatened to become a pattern of spread any Amway executive would have appreciated and envied. On the fringes of the rain forests, nature had forged a multi-level marketing plan that could not possibly fail.

The chief difference between how the newly emerging prions affected their carriers (the bats) and their hosts (cows and humans) was that they tended to act slowly against the bats and to do only so much damage; whereas once inside a cow's brain, or a man's, they acted quickly and did not know when to stop. Mortality approached 100 percent. The prions flunked as parasites.

The headaches began about a month after a migrant bat, finding the sickened cows distasteful, switched to a new prey species and bit a sleeping shore worker on the leg. He became aware of a persistent throbbing behind the eyeballs that circled slowly, over the course of days, to his left temple and around the back of his neck. Aspirin was of no help; there was no fever in need of lowering and, far from alleviating the galloping in his head, the pain was soon joined by a maddening itch that made him want to scratch the skin off his genitals.

He was not a wealthy man, so he lived by a work ethic that compelled him to show up and carry on with his duties no matter how sick he happened to be feeling. He had never missed a day's work, not from the time he was a teen, and he was not about to start slipping now. Meanwhile, a life-form so strange that most biologists refused to acknowledge it as "living" was hijacking his body. Spreading from neuron to neuron, it converted normal Stanley proteins into dangerous ones by an ever-widening pattern of molecular recoil that induced the benign molecules to change their shape. The Stanley proteins themselves could trace their genesis back to a Permeo-Triassic swamp, to a prion that had infiltrated sperm or ovum of some ancestral protomammal and succeeded in making a snippet of viral RNA, then cellular DNA, in its own image—with the result that the Stanley gene lived on, in one form or another, in all mammals, awaiting only the intrusion of the prions.

Arguments about whether the prions were alive, like viruses, or dead, like crystals, or somewhere in between, were moot. They were multiplying inside the man's brain cells, multiplying at rates that would send shivers through a CDC biohazards specialist. On the day the Schutts began their fatal search of the island, prions were accumulating in the cellular organelles known as lysosomes—which under normal conditions were filled with enzymes capable of digesting even the most resilient components of an offending bacterium or an aberrant speck of tissue, reducing even the structural supports of cell membranes and chromosomes to a structureless fluid. Throughout his brain, under extremely abnormal conditions, prion-saturated lysosomes were losing their powers of containment. They burst open and spilled forth their contents, and the cells themselves, in response, were lysed. As the diseased cells died and leaked corrosive enzymes, creating microscopic holes in the brain—first tens of millions, then hundreds of millions of holes—their prions were released to attack other cells. The very seat of the man's consciousness was possessed by a chain reaction—which, limited only by the available supply of Stanley proteins, was transforming its small corner of the universe into prions and liquefying brain tissue.

The pain he felt radiated mostly from the swollen tissues surrounding the brain—for, mercifully, the brain itself possessed no pain receptors. What he noticed most, aside from the throbbing in his left temple, was a loss of coordination and a frightening droop in his left eyelid. He was largely unaware, however, that his personality was changing. He became alternately euphoric and depressed, and between bouts of depression, his euphoria was sometimes buoyed up by delusions of godly power. As capillaries corroded and ruptured, squirting clots in every direction and triggering a half million ministrokes, he found his loss of emotional control increasingly amplified by psychotic episodes, modulated only by a brain damage–induced lethargy. The shore worker tried to counter his mounting fatigue and increasingly muddled thinking with huge doses of coffee, which raised his blood pressure and caused his lysed capillaries to bleed out even faster. But the caffeine did have the desired effect: It ratcheted up the rate at which his dying nerves fired. His short-term memory returned, ebbed again, returned; and between sudden onsets of beastial fantasies, the like of which he had never known before, he sometimes failed to understand where and who he was.

He felt as if he were awakening from a million years of strange dreams—someone else's. Blundering into the oncoming night, and trying to know himself, he could not comprehend why there were smashed bats at his feet, and why the sight of the unconscious woman provoked him to laughter. Crying out to her his joy and agony, the word *keeper* bubbled up from somewhere deep in his brain, and with the punch of a switch the rotary lamp blazed to life overhead, and began sweeping the lighthouse panes with the glare of day.

And when he looked up—

Madness.

Utter madness.

A thousand faces were illuminated by the lamp; and his mind, too, was suddenly illuminated. As the army ants had been known to do, the nest of bats had reared up as a single, unified being. It swallowed the lighthouse whole.

Clinging to one another, linking their legs and bodies to enclose the structure in a velvety brown carpet of bats, they became as the lining of an artificial stomach built on a cyclopean scale; and the stomach's eyes flashed wild and red in the sweep of the lighthouse beam; and the keeper could see nothing beyond those eyes. No moon. No stars. Nothing except that undulating curtain of wings and fangs and fur.

The stomach knew itself, he understood. Knowing itself, and hungry, it squeezed and convulsed. It wanted to smash the glass and the wood and the concrete. It wanted to get in at him, and at the woman.

"Go away," he growled, and laughed, realizing that the giant would not go away, would not excrete the lighthouse until it had digested the meat inside, until nothing remained except shattered glass and a concrete shell.

And suddenly the thought of being digested alive, of becoming part of the monster, did not repel him. The giant was, in that moment, a miracle to him, and he ascended the steel ladder, humming to himself a childhood hymn once sung in the abandoned church—

> *Gather round the table of the Lord—*
> *Eat his body, drink his blood,*
> *and we'll sing a song of love—*

He could not remember the rest; but no matter—no pain, no remorse; nothing except a longing for the swarm's embrace.

Snatching a harsh breath out of the dark, Amy came almost awake—almost. One hand had drifted instinctively down along her right hip and across her belly, then toward the wetness that was now sending a subdued electrical pulse up through her nipples; the pulse brushed onward through the skin of her neck, along the fringes of her ears, and through her entire body.

Jerry . . .

She did not know what it all meant; but no matter—no logic, no chain of cause and effect; nothing except a longing for Jerry Sigmond's embrace.

She realized that it was dark outside and the alarm clock would soon be chiming and that she must get ready for work; but she shut her mind off from any thoughts except the fact that in two hours she would see him again, and she imagined that one day soon his lips would be brushing over her ears and her neck, kissing and nibbling very, very gently. One hand traveled up, closed over a breast and trapped a nipple between two wet fingers. She felt Jerry caressing the pink tip with featherlike lips, moistening it with his tongue, and she let out a faint moan.

Jerry came awake slowly from his nap, and as always, he awoke with a hardness between his thighs. He did not exactly yearn for Amy's embrace; but this was *survival* and, as the old cliché weavers had said: "Any port in a storm."

He possessed Amy, now; far more than 90 percent of her. He knew it. He could feel it. Soon, very soon, he would own her completely—life, blood, and soul—and that particular thought did arouse him; although in a well-lighted cell with cameras and recorders peering in, it was best to keep thoughts of self-arousal beneath the covers. If he gave in to fantasy urges, one of his jailers would be hawking the video to tabloid television within the hour; no doubt of it. Becoming a one-man porno show was no way to plan a comeback.

But the daydream nagged him nevertheless, and he slid beneath the sheet onto his right side, facing the concrete wall, keeping his fingers far away from the part of him that was so ready, so desperate to receive them.

He saw himself biting and sucking hard at her nipples, moving urgently from one to another—biting not yet hard enough to break the skin . . . not yet . . . not yet hard enough . . .

She raised her knees, grabbed his hair, and gasped—

"Would you like me to be part of you?" he imagined himself saying.

He bit harder, feeling Amy's muscles tense and quiver. "Will you obey your man? Your *man!* Will you give all your power to him?"

He heard her whimper, "Yes." He felt the girl surrendering herself to him, her will, her soul; and the thought of it increased his pleasure until it became unbearable and without even the touch of a hand his body tensed and loosened and made every nerve tremble with an all-enveloping tickle and release that was at once like the aftermath of a good sneeze, and yet very unlike a sneeze. And he saw in her a subservient bore; he saw her unleashing him upon the airwaves; and he saw himself in his natural element again, manipulating whole crowds of people, whole churches, whole cities; and he heard himself whispering to her, "Welcome to prime time—bitch!"

Snatching a harsh breath out of the dark, Janet came almost awake—almost. One hand drifted instinctively down along her right hip, reaching for the imagined security of the notepad, only to find the pad's strap broken.

Bill . . .

Farther down, her hand crossed more than a dozen little holes bleeding into the fabric of her jeans. The anticoagulants saw to it that the wounds—more than a hundred in all—remained fresh. The floor of the lighthouse smelled vaguely of iron and copper, like the floor of a slaughterhouse, sending a wave of shock and revulsion through her.

Janet's fingers began to shake.

How much? her internal voice asked. *Ten percent? Fifteen?*

Her right palm dropped to the floor with a hollow splash. Fully 20 percent of her blood volume lay pooled about her.

The other Jesus is looking for you, remarked the voice that Janet heard but did not hear.

You're losing your mind, she told herself. *It's the price you pay for losing so much blood—*

"Bill . . ."

The other Jesus is looking for you, the voice repeated. *He seeks the brown dwarf. He wants you to know that this time he does not come as a lamb led to the slaughter.*

This time he comes with a sword in one hand and a dagger in his teeth.

Yes. Yes, Janet thought, trying to bring herself more fully awake. *Jesus and the brown dwarf seek red giant for trinary relationship. Very good. So this is what people feel like when they bleed to death . . .*

This is survival! the voice said; and that finally got through to her frontal lobes, and to her adrenals, jump-starting Janet to full wakefulness. Her eyes widened; and she suddenly wished they had not.

Something deep-rooted and instinctive made Amy suddenly wish she had not let herself yearn for the warm, gentle touch of Jerry Sigmond. Her eyes glistened with what could have been tears, but she moved her fingers between her bare legs anyway, moved them more quickly, more urgently until at last she could hold it back no longer and cried both joy and anxiety to God and her absent lover. Teeth clenching, spine stiffening, a black serpent of despair slithered through her from the moment the delightful and all too short-lived quaking abated beneath her palms. Love. Pain. Mutual parasitism. Pain.

He's using you, she tried to tell herself.

And I'm using him, she answered for herself. *Isn't that what it's all about? People feeding off each other?*

She tried again to sidestep any thoughts of what she was getting herself into. It did not matter. Jerry Sigmond (*the* Jerry Sigmond) thought she mattered. Nothing else was important.

But a bad time is coming, a tiny part of her subconscious was trying to tell her. Amy finally had to admit that events far larger than her own concerns were trying to break loose upon the world. In the East there were wars and threats of wars. In the West, the Californians were turning paranoid against people from the East. In South America, crops were failing. Everything in Brazil was rumored to be dying. At home there was fear of motes, and stock exchanges were getting jittery, and disagreements over gasoline were starting to turn ugly.

She tried to deny that the crisis criers could be right this time. They had been wrong so many times before.

Yet if a worldwide rationing of food and fuel, or a depression, or something even worse was coming, wasn't a survivor type like Jerry Sigmond exactly the kind of man she wanted to stay close to?

Sure, she told herself. *People would follow him even through a universal deluge. He'd be standing right in the middle of it—Jerry Sigmond: the eye of the storm.*

And would I really be safe there? a part of her asked. *Was I really going to be safe in the eye of a storm?*

"Jesus," she said, and laughed. "Was anybody, anywhere?"

The madman atop the ladder was scratching furiously with one hand, scratching at his genitals, scratching until he bled. Janet had seen prion-infected cows driven by an intense itch to scrape off their hair and skin, and hence the common name for mad cow disease: "scrapie." It was probably in her veins, too, she realized. She could see that the bats' kidneys were working overtime on the panes above. They had excreted an ooze of digested blood. Her blood. Bill's blood.

"And we'll sing a song of love," the madman warbled. "Ale-looo, ale-loo, ale-loooo-oooh—"

The finger of rotating lamplight stabbed at the bats, agitated them, made their eyes flame like dazzling red diamonds—diamonds from hell; and there, atop the rusted ladder, hung the keeper with one hand in his unzipped pants. His lips and nose were pressed flat against a pane. He had discovered, to his apparent glee, that rubbing his face against the glass and imitating the bats' high-pitched squeals drove the swarm mad. They scrambled and scratched, trying to get at his eyes—scrambled until they bunched together into thick, heavy clots that eventually sagged and peeled away under their own weight, then dispersed in flurries of wings.

Janet thought of commanding him to stop, but then gave it a second thought. Trapped, as she was, with nothing except one-eighth inch of glass separating her from the belly of the beast, was no place to be irritating a madman. She watched a new clot of bats forming near the keeper's face. They clawed and bit at the wooden frames between the panes—

Can enough of them, working together, pull the wood apart? Janet wondered, and then felt herself dozing—but an upsurge of adrenaline stopped her after only a moment . . . or an hour . . . or three hours . . . when she became suddenly conscious of a new sound.

The keeper was still up there, but the hand that had been in his pants now wielded a large iron spanner. The sound that had triggered the adrenaline surge was the spanner tapping against the glass, tapping harder as the seconds passed, but not yet hard enough to break it . . . not yet . . . not yet hard enough. . . .

Janet grabbed the ladder and tried to stand, but her knees buckled beneath her—

"Noooo!"

"The beginning and the end," he declared, and tapped a little louder. "I am alpha and omega. The heavens and the Earth will obey this Messiah."

She tried again to stand, but her knees would not obey. Her feet just flopped and slipped uselessly in a lake of her own blood.

"You would like me to be part of you?" the keeper said.

TAP—

"Would you like to come in and have a little drink of me?"

TAP—

"All power in heaven and on Earth has been given to me."

TAP—

"The power of life and death."

TAP—

On the other side of the pane, *Desmodus* watched.

Desmodus waited.

The vampires were a patient lot, ancient beyond humanity; they could afford to wait.

Immunogenetic therapy . . . antibiotics—they won't work on prions anyway, that voice within Janet remarked, and as she listened to the taps and squeals, her blood-starved brain became peculiarly calm, yet active—a self-contradictory sourness and sweetness, like strawberry syrup and sour cream poured over buttermilk pancakes—sourness and sweetness, pleasure and pain: She wondered how many millions of years ago the evolutionary time bomb had been planted in the bodies of insects and in the minds of bats, giving them, as if in anticipation of humanity's arrival, a blueprint for humanity's removal.

"Just a little harder!"

TAP—

Janet saw *Desmodus*'s eyes burning fiercely, hundreds of eyes. She watched them huddle, watched them pull together into a solid ball against a bright, hairline fracture in one of the panes. She watched the fracture widen under six successive hammer blows; she watched the pane shake loose in its wooden frame; she watched it break.

15

Marching to Valhalla

A day later, Adam Handelsman, known variously as "Scanner" and "Klaus" to his friends, as Captain Handelsman to his subordinates, drove his white Mustang west on U.S. 70, through the very heart of the Kansas wheatfields. He was running nearly thirty miles over the speed limit, with the air-conditioning and the radio up full. The sun glared viciously off the hood—*and let it glare,* the captain thought; the windshield darkened automatically to keep him from squinting, and the temperature inside the car was a heavenly sixty-five. It could be roaring hellfire out there, for all Scanner cared, and he would *still* be happy. He and his wife had just spent three gloriously romantic weeks at their favorite reef-side villa on the isle of Martinique. Morning hikes in the forests of Pelée. Lunch in the seaside village of St. Pierre. Night dives on

the wreck of the *Roráima*. Midnight feasts of spiny lobster
and wine on the beach.

Twice-yearly stays at the villa were one of a half dozen
paybacks for a job that kept him away from home, and in
virtual confinement, for six months out of every year. Most
marriages could not handle such strains, but Scanner had
discovered that, in his case, absence really did make the
heart grow fonder. Their time together was always like a
whirlwind romance leading through a honeymoon to the
pleasure and pain of departure, and to the bitterness of
long separation and the bittersweet feeling that they were
finally beginning to grate on each other's nerves, mixed
with sweet anticipation of the next honeymoon.

This last honeymoon had been the best so far. Even the
mosquitoes had left him alone.

"Paradise sans pests," he said to himself, and smiled.
He did not know how the French had managed the feat,
but paradise without mosquitoes was paradise *sans pareil*.

What will they think of next? he wondered, as a Green
Day oldie faded into a top-of-the-hour news segment. In
keeping with the long tradition of crisis crying, none of
the news was good. The captain of an Iranian oil tanker
was refusing to dock at New York's Staten Island. The
Mutual Surety Insurance Company was trying to back out
of paying Long Beach and Bangor policyholders by declaring the mote outbreaks "acts of God," and the Cold War
between Japan and China was said to be heating up again.
Scanner switched away, searched the other channels, and
stopped at a *real* oldie—

"Thoomp! Thoomp! Thoomp! Another one bites the
dust!"

—by a group whose name he could not remember. The
DJ had dedicated the song to *Dermatophagoides pteronys-
sinus* and *Sarcoptes scabei*. Scanner could not figure out
why. Must be an inside joke, he decided . . . *very* inside,
and pressed the accelerator a tad harder.

Something bothered Scanner remotely. Something was
missing. Driving at this speed, through this part of the
country at this time of the year, he should have by now
spattered his entire windshield with the bodies of flying
insects. This was, after all, the state in which the Grass-

hopper Act had been passed in 1877. Still on the books, the law granted the governor authority to draft every able-bodied male between the ages of twelve and forty to collect and kill "locusts" in time of plague.

He could not understand why the clean windshield made him nervous. The state's five-dollar bounty on a bushel of severed grasshopper heads—now *that* should have given him the creeps. A windshield not needing to be scraped clean of dried, smashed bug parts—that was a blessing, not a curse. Scanner had, after all, waged (and lost) enough household wars with cockroaches, and termites, and flies to make him question the survival value of human intelligence—indeed, to suspect that the phrase "human intelligence" might be the ultimate oxymoron. He once rendered the air in his home so toxic with supermarket bug bombs that he actually made himself sick; yet the cockroaches remained fruitful and multiplied, and he could not avoid, with some embarrassment, asking himself if cockroaches could laugh. Refusing to admit defeat, he then summoned a professional exterminator, who explained that he could use the inexpensive legal stuff, which would not solve his problem, or he could use the expensive illegal stuff . . . very clever species indeed, the only one in all the world known to spend a month's salary turning its home into a bug-proofed, air-polluted, air-conditioned cocoon, and then to fire up the barbecue pit and eat in the yard.

He wished someone would invent a bug bomb that could wipe every cockroach and no-see-um in the world immediately out of existence. He hated them that much. But no matter; at least his workplace was guaranteed free of pests. The government had spared no expense on that measure. Even the remotest possibility of a pharaoh ant or the infamous "TV roach" nibbling on a wire or accidentally bridging a circuit with its body and causing a random short was an intolerable risk. And if three or four such improbable events were to line up at once, and in the wrong sequence (a possibility whose probability was multiplied in proportion to the size of the infestation) . . . intolerable. Utterly intolerable.

So, in what was to become the ultimate realization of his mother's oft-repeated warning, "Be careful what you

wish for; you may get it," Scanner blazed westward on
the two-lane blacktop, passing, on either side, horizon-
spanning fields of wheat and corn in which no fungus
gnats or no-see-ums stirred, and in which the first black
speckles of crop-rotting fungi had begun to take hold.

The sun was setting when the guards ushered Scanner's
car through the gate and past a system of motion sensors
that surrounded a nondescript, one-story support building,
two squat, barely visible electromagnetic pulse sensors,
and two hardened antennae which, according to government specifications, would remain functional even in the
event of a fifty-kiloton nuclear blast originating at a distance of one half mile.

A half hour later, he had descended the access shaft
from the support building and taken a seat beside Mark
Luftig—"Widow-maker," to his friends. The two men sat
in the center of a capsule whose hull was steel-reinforced
concrete six feet thick. The capsule was mounted on, and
ringed by, giant springs in a shock-isolated room that was
itself suspended within a blast-proof outer structure. The
blast room was titanium and permaglass and was suspended like a pendulum by means of four hydraulic- and
computer-controlled shock isolators.

The capsule was brightly lit to keep the crew's serotonin
output—and hence their moods—at optimal levels during
long periods of isolation underground. Being brightly lit,
with a well-stocked library of films and books, the capsule
was also a place built for one of Scanner's favorite pas-
times: reading. Fortunately, some Washington bureaucrat
had decided that shielded launch capsules might be the
only places on Earth in which the accumulated wisdom of
the ages would likely survive an asteroid impact or some
localized nuclear war that happened to go global. Unfortunately, on account of the limited availability of space,
other bureaucrats decided that the library would have to
be computerized—shrunk down to a volume smaller than
a beer can. Scanner wondered if anyone, thousands of
years in the future, trying to rebuild civilization anew,
would ever figure out how to retrieve records from the
software, assuming an electromagnetic pulse from a nearby
detonation did not erase it completely.

The only real book in the capsule, and thus the only one guaranteed to be readable by future archaeologists, historians, and empire-builders, was a thick black manual stamped with the words:

UPDATE No. 45
WEAPON SYSTEM OPERATION INSTRUCTIONS—WING III
USAF SERIES LGM30G MISSILE

Scanner was reading a stack of blue sheets to be added to the manual. The top sheet was stamped, FILE IN ACCORDANCE WITH T.O. 00-5-2. In typical military fashion, it proclaimed:

THIS IS TOCFN INDEX SHEET 1 OF 26

PROJECT: SORESPORT.
AUTHORITY: USAF/NORTHROP-GRUMMAN.
CLASSIFICATION: NTK STATUS.
SUBJECT: REASSIGNMENT OF FIVE (5) ADDITIONAL MISSILES TO CAPSULE COMMAND POST REQUIRING MODIFICATION OF MAINTENANCE DUTIES AND DEPLOYMENT INSTRUCTIONS.
SYSTEMS AFFECTED: TARGETING, CREW SAFETY.

THE INFORMATION CONTAINED IN THIS MANUAL IS APPLICABLE TO THE THOR WEAPON SYSTEM AT WING III AFTER INCORPORATION OF FIVE ADDITIONAL GUIDANCE PROGRAMS AND THE GUIDANCE IMPROVEMENT PROGRAM, WHICH PROVIDES NEW COMPUTER PROGRAMS AT THE LCC AND LF. FOR APPLICABLE ECPs SEE PAGE C.
EACH MISSILE COMBAT CREW MEMBER WILL BE ISSUED A PERSONAL COPY OF UPDATE SHEETS FOR THE OPERATIONS MANUAL. IT IS THE CREW MEMBER'S PERSONAL RESPONSIBILITY TO POST AND MAINTAIN THE MANUAL IN ACCORDANCE WITH T.O.00-5-1. EVERY EFFORT IS MADE TO KEEP THE OPERATIONS MANUAL UP TO DATE. HOWEVER, IF AN ERROR OR DEFICIENCY IS DISCOVERED, PROMPTLY SUBMIT AN AFTO

FORM 22 (TECHNICAL ORDER SYSTEM IMPROVE-
MENT REPORT) IN ACCORDANCE WITH T.O.00-5-
1 AND COMMAND DIRECTIVES. THIS MANUAL IS
INTENDED TO TELL HOW TO OPERATE THE
WEAPON SYSTEM SAFELY AND EFFICIENTLY—
HOW TO DO THE JOB—SO, TO BE A PROFES-
SIONAL, THE CREW MEMBER SHALL READ AND
FULLY UNDERSTAND THIS DOCUMENT.

COUNT YOUR PAGES.
REPORT ANY MISSING PAGES TO TOCFN AT
   ONCE.
INSERT LATEST CHANGED PAGES.
DESTROY SUPERSEDED PAGES.
COUNT YOUR PAGES.

Scanner pulled out the first superseded page. "Well,
one thing we can say for sure," he said with an ironic
smile. "This job offers a lot more responsibility than we
could have found in the private sector."

"I'll buy that for a dollar," Mark said, and then, after
a pause, "Am I reading too much between the lines on
these new sheets, or does this read like they're getting a
bit nervous about something?"

"I don't know. What's the latest on our news-com?"

"It's getting kind of flaky out there, Cap. When I got
down here, the old change-out crew had the whole tail
end of a disk red-lined for us. They say the Indians and
the Chinese have filed complaints about the *Nimitz*. Looks
like we're just gonna let Sri Lanka and Pakistan twist in
the wind, now. Turkey and Japan are up in arms about
that action—or, rather, inaction. On top of that, the Turks
and the Greeks are rattling sabres at each other again.
Something to do with fishing rights. Meanwhile, we've
lost Trinidad."

"Trinidad?" Scanner said. "What do you mean, we've
lost Trinidad?"

"It's Trinidad and Tobago, actually," Mark explained.
"As of eight hundred hours, they've been radio silent. No
more news is coming out of that area."

"Nice."

ALTHOUGH THE MANUAL CONTAINS PROCE-
DURES FOR PEACETIME OPERATIONS, IT IS TAC-
ITLY ORIENTED TOWARD ON-ALERT STATUS AND
TACTICAL LAUNCH PROCEDURES. MODIFICA-
TION OF WEAPON SYSTEM OPERATING PROCE-
DURES, BOTH NORMAL AND EMERGENCY, IS
HEREWITH MANDATED BY A FACILITY CHANGE
INITIATION REQUEST (FCIR) WHICH IS ASSIGNED
A MASTER CHANGE LOG (MCL) NUMBER DURING
COORDINATION. TIME COMPLIANCE TECHNICAL
ORDERS (TCTO) AUTHORIZE AND GIVE INSTRUC-
TIONS FOR INSPECTION AND MODIFICATION. AN
MCL DOES NOT RESULT IN A TCTO AND THERE-
FORE ALL REFERENCES TO MSLs IN THIS MAN-
UAL WILL BE NOTED SIMPLY AS "BEFORE
INCORPORATION OF MCLs" OR "AFTER INCORPO-
RATION OF MCLs." AFTER ALL EQUIPMENT HAS
BEEN MODIFIED, THE OBSOLETE INFORMATION
AND ALL REFERENCES TO THE MCLs SHALL BE
REMOVED FROM THE MANUAL.

"Has anyone said why Trinidad is out?" asked Scanner.

"Just that no nukes were involved. No military action.
Beyond that, it's NTK only; and I guess somebody upstairs
has decided we don't need to know."

"I wouldn't worry," Scanner said, leafing through his
blue sheets. "The media will be on top of it soon enough."

"Believe it," Widow-maker said. "If left up to Command, they'd probably tell us sometime next week. But
with CNN on it, we'll probably have film by lunchtime
tomorrow. With *Current Affair*, maybe by dinnertime
tonight."

"Too right. If the President has an irregular bowel
movement, somebody will post it on the evening news."

"I guess George Orwell got it all backward. It's not
Big Brother who is watching us. It's us watching him."

Scanner snickered and continued to read.

BECAUSE THE EFFECTIVITY OF THE THOR
WEAPON SYSTEM DEPENDS ON A SECOND

STRIKE CAPABILITY, THE SYSTEM MUST BE ABLE TO PERFORM ITS CRITICAL FUNCTIONS (RE: THE SORESPORT MANEUVER) EVEN AFTER EXPOSURE TO A HOSTILE NUCLEAR ENVIRONMENT.

WEAPON SYSTEM HARDNESS IS A MEASURE OF THE ABILITY OF THE THOR WEAPON SYSTEM TO WITHSTAND EXPOSURE TO VARIOUS EFFECTS OF A NUCLEAR ATTACK: SHOCK, VIBRATION, AIR BLAST, ACOUSTICS, ELECTROMAGNETIC PULSE, RADIATION, THERMAL, AND DEBRIS. THE CAPA-BILITY TO WITHSTAND THOSE EFFECTS CAN ONLY BE ACHIEVED IF THE SYSTEM RETAINS ITS DESIGNED-IN HARDNESS. THIS REQUIRES THAT THE COMBAT CREW BE THOROUGHLY FAMILIAR WITH THE CAUSE AND EFFECT RELATIONSHIP ASSOCIATED WITH MAINTENANCE ACTIVITIES. BEING AWARE OF THE IMPORTANCE OF NORMAL MAINTENANCE ACTIVITIES, AND THEIR POTEN-TIAL EFFECT ON WEAPON SYSTEM VULNERABIL-ITY, IS A PRIMARY STEP IN PRESERVING HARDNESS. WHAT APPEARS TO BE A ROUTINE TASK MAY REQUIRE MANY EXTRA PRECAU-TIONS.

WARNING: LAUNCH CONTROL CENTER IS VUL-NERABLE TO EFFECTS OF UNEXPECTED ENER-GETIC DISASSEMBLY OVERPRESSURE WHEN BLAST DOOR IS OPEN. CLOSE BLAST DOOR AS SOON AS POSSIBLE AFTER ENTRY OR EXIT. STAND CLEAR OF BLAST DOOR WHEN IT IS OPENED OR CLOSED.

THE OPERATIONS MANUAL TAKES A POSITIVE APPROACH AND NORMALLY STATES ONLY WHAT CAN BE DONE. UNUSUAL OPERATIONS OR CON-FIGURATIONS ARE PROHIBITED UNLESS SPECIFI-CALLY COVERED HEREIN. MISSILE COMBAT CREWS ARE FORBIDDEN FROM TAKING ANY UN-AUTHORIZED ACTIONS WHICH COULD DEACTI-VATE ANY LAUNCH CONTROL CENTER EQUIPMENT.

WHEN NECESSARY TO DISTINGUISH BETWEEN

MISSILE COMBAT CREW MEMBERS, THE FOL-
LOWING CODE LETTERS WILL BE USED:

MCCC—MISSILE COMBAT CREW COMMANDER

DMCCC—DEPUTY MISSILE COMBAT CREW
COMMANDER

PERSONNEL CODING WILL HENCEFORTH BE
USED TO INDICATE WHICH INDIVIDUAL STEPS OF
A PROCEDURE ARE PECULIAR TO A SINGLE MIS-
SILE COMBAT CREW MEMBER. REASSIGNMENT
OF CODED TASKS MAY BE ACCOMPLISHED AT
THE DISCRETION OF THE MCCC.

CODE 26 M33-NYC 6-8-86B CHANGES/REVISIONS:
ADD JULIAN DAY TO IPD PROCESSOR UNIT.

COUNT YOUR PAGES

THIS IS TOCFN INDEX SHEET 12 OF 26

WARNING: TWO-PERSON RESPONSE IS REQUIRED
FOR ALL ALARMS IN LCEB AND TUNNEL JUNC-
TION. ENSURE THAT WEIGHT OF PERSONS AND
EQUIPMENT IS EVENLY DISTRIBUTED AT ALL
TIMES AND DO NOT ALLOW EQUIPMENT AND/OR
PERSONS EQUIVALENT TO THE WEIGHT OF FOUR
PERSONS TO CONGREGATE IN THE IMMEDIATE
VICINITY OF ANY ONE SHOCK ISOLATOR.

WARNING: POLYCHLORINATED BIPHENAL (PCB)
BEARING EQUIPMENT NOT YET CHANGED OUT.
USE CAUTION WHEN WORKING AROUND ENCLO-
SURES WHERE PCBs MAY BE PRESENT. AVOID
SKIN CONTACT IF SUBSTANCE IS NOTED, ESPE-
CIALLY IN EVENT OF POST-ENERGETIC DISAS-
SEMBLY LOSS OF CONTAINMENT. DO NOT
INHALE FUMES. DO NOT WEAR CONTACT LENSES
WITH RESPIRATOR IN CONTAMINATED AREA. IM-
MEDIATELY NOTIFY BIOENVIRONMENTAL ENGI-
NEERING (IF EXISTENT). EXPOSURE CAN RESULT
IN SKIN RASH AND POSSIBLE INTERNAL HEALTH
COMPLICATIONS. CAPSULE IS CAPABLE OF SUR-
VIVING OVERBURST AND RADIATION EFFECTS,
BUT LEAKAGE OF INTERNAL FLUIDS, IF NOT

CONTAINED, MAY PRODUCE INHALATION EF-
FECTS AND COMPROMISE CREW SAFETY/MISSION
OBJECTIVES. ONCE RELEASED, PCBs WILL NOT
BREAK DOWN INTO NEW CHEMICAL ARRANGE-
MENTS. INSTEAD, THEY MAY BIOACCUMULATE
IN FOOD AND CREW. THE EFFECTS ON CREW ARE,
BUT NOT LIMITED TO: JAUNDICE, DIGESTIVE DIS-
TURBANCES, THROAT AND RESPIRATORY DIS-
TURBANCE, CHROMOSOMAL DISLOCATIONS,
HAIR LOSS, SEVERE HEADACHES, AND IMPO-
TENCE.

WARNING: DISREGARD ABNORMAL STATUS INDI-
CATIONS THAT MAY RESULT WHEN INTERROGA-
TIONS WITH OTHER LAUNCH FACILITIES ARE
INTERRUPTED. IF ALCC ASSISTANCE IS RE-
QUIRED FOR SOLE SURVIVOR CONDITIONS, FOR
ELECTRICALLY ISOLATED LAUNCH FACILITY(s),
OR LF(s) WITH UNKNOWN STATUS, ACCOMPLISH
STEPS 37 THRU 41 AS APPLICABLE. OTHERWISE
PROCEED TO STEP 42. UNDER SOLE SURVIVOR
CONDITION, IF OTHER LFs HAVE NOT REPORTED,
DELETE ALL SQUADRON TIME SLOTS. MISSILES
WILL ACCEPT ALCC COMMANDS SIX MINUTES
AFTER ALL TIME SLOTS DELETED. WHEN *DE-
LETED* PRINTOUT OCCURS, ENSURE *PROGRAM SE-
LECT* SWITCH IS IN *OFF* POSITION; THEN MCCC
AND DMCCC SIMULTANEOUSLY ROTATE BOTH
LAUNCH KEYS CLOCKWISE AND HOLD FOR AT
LEAST 5 SECONDS. NOTE *MISSILE AWAY* INDICA-
TION(s) FOR PARENT FLIGHT TIME OF OCCUR-
RENCE AND ADVISE ALCC. IN ACCORDANCE
WITH NEW SSC DIRECTIVES, LOG THE FOLLOW-
ING CODE:

H7 A7 T7 R7 E7 D7

THIS IS TOCFN INDEX SHEET 18 OF 26

REVISED ESCAPE PROCEDURE: CONTINUING POST-
COMBAT ESCAPE WITHIN UNVENTILATED TUN-
NEL REQUIRES CONSIDERABLE EFFORT. AIR IN

THE TUNNEL WILL TEND TO BECOME HIGH IN
CARBON DIOXIDE CONTENT. TO ALLEVIATE THIS
CONDITION MISSILE COMBAT CREW SHOULD AL-
TERNATE WORKING PERIODS IN TUNNEL. IN AD-
DITION, CREW SHOULD WEAR SELF-CONTAINED
BREATHING APPARATUS OR PURGE TUNNEL AT-
MOSPHERE WITH AIR FROM SHOCK ISOLATOR
SYSTEM. REMOVE SAND UNTIL UPPER END OF
TUNNEL BECOMES ACCESSIBLE. REMOVE FOUR
RETAINER PINS, LIFT STEEL CROSSBAR, DISCARD
PINS AND CROSSBAR, AND PULL AWAY 2 BY 4s
FROM INSULATION. BREAK UP RIGID INSULA-
TION AND EXPOSE EARTH. DIG TOWARD
GROUND SURFACE, IN FIVE MINUTE SHIFTS,
UNTIL BREAKTHROUGH.

Scanner frowned at the page. *Breakthrough into what?*
he wondered. The eight-ton blast door, the subsurface
"lightning shunts," and the twenty-four blast valves designed to close so quickly, upon sensing an overpressure,
that even as, in the world above, Scanner's Mustang was
deep-hammered onto a quarter-inch bed of molten glass,
Scanner's ears would barely begin to pop. The valves
guaranteed that he would be walking about and taking in
air at least long enough to turn the right keys and push
the right buttons. He was smart enough to know that he
was fooling himself if he believed anyone in charge had
really intended this place to keep him alive beyond the
accomplishment of his mission objectives. The fact that
Cold War–era transformers were still being soaked in Cold
War–era PCBs (it was cheaper to keep the antiques than
to replace them), even if to do so in the confines of an
underground enclosure might expose peacetime crews to
DNA scrambling, made very clear where the powers that
be thought he stood. Crystal clear.

He was leafing through the rest of the update sheets,
looking for any new maintenance procedures that were
chemically or physically hazardous, when he came upon
a page that more precisely defined his standing.

THIS IS TOCFN INDEX SHEET 26 OF 26

THIS MANUAL PROVIDES THE BEST POSSIBLE OP-
ERATING INSTRUCTIONS UNDER MOST CIRCUM-
STANCES, BUT CANNOT BE USED WITHOUT
SOUND JUDGMENT. MULTIPLE EMERGENCIES, AS
AN EXAMPLE, REQUIRE CLOSE SCRUTINY BY THE
CREW PRIOR TO INITIATING A GIVEN EMER-
GENCY PROCEDURE. CREWS SHALL BE FULLY
KNOWLEDGEABLE OF COMMAND POLICIES RE-
GARDING THE WEAPON SYSTEM. COMMAND DI-
SASTER   CONTROL   PROCEDURES   MAY   BE
REQUIRED IN CONJUNCTION WITH TECHNICAL
PROCEDURES CONTAINED HEREIN. SOUND JUDG-
MENT SHALL BE EXERCISED AT ALL TIMES.

Yes, Scanner reminded himself, and laughed. Always
exercise sound judgment during a nuclear holocaust. This
was, after all, the only country in all the world so optimistic about the outcome of such a battle that its Congress had
invested more than a hundred million tax dollars trying to
figure out how to collect taxes and deliver the mail after
the Apocalypse.

Someone must have walked away with a fortune in con-
sulting fees, Scanner guessed. A whole lot of someones.
A whole lot of political favorite someones. But when it
all came down to bottom, Scanner was troubled by neither
congressional optimists nor the consequences of their optimism. The most absurd optimists of all, the ones who *did*
trouble him, were those who still believed that arms reduction should lead logically to total disarmament and who
argued that there was no longer a need for places such as
this, no need for America to sustain a balance of terror.

Scanner knew that as long as uranium existed, someone,
somewhere would always have at least one atomic bomb;
and he knew that once upon a time there had been only
three atomic bombs in all the world. They tested one to
see if it would work. Then they dropped the other two.

So here he sat, like a grub within the earth, ready to let
fly, at a nanosecond's notice, the thermonuclear inverse to
the Golden Rule.

It was not a bad life, all things considered. Scanner was optimistic that the notice would never come. And he was, after all, a reader. And life in the capsule gave him plenty of time to read; all the time in the world. And he truly enjoyed the separations from his wife. And the reunions. And the twice yearly honeymoons on the isle of Martinique. And the last honeymoon had indeed been the most perfect yet.

He smiled, and changed out the last page—

SOUND JUDGMENT SHALL BE EXERCISED AT ALL TIMES.

COUNT YOUR PAGES.

REPORT ANY MISSING PAGES TO TOCFN AT ONCE.

COUNT YOUR PAGES.

—and then he loosened the laces on his right boot. He ran a hand down the inside of his sock, and his pulse quickened a beat as his fingers passed over two round swellings and found them larger than they had been the day before. They itched, and he hoped the wounds had not become in any way infected. They were the only fly in the ointment of what promised to become the memory of an utterly flawless vacation.

Something on the isle of Martinique had crept under the bedsheets and bitten him during the night, leaving twin punctures that, by the time he awoke, had stained the sheets with red. In a moment of uncharacteristic panic, Scanner wondered if he somehow had become a hemophiliac overnight; but by late morning the bite had begun to scab over, and except for the swelling and the itching and the unpleasant memory, it was by now mostly forgotten. Meanwhile, an ancient protein that was a life-form and yet not a life-form had acquired a source of Stanley proteins and was slowly—very slowly at first—making copies of itself inside Scanner's head.

II
PENETRATION

Ignorance is itself a map.
—George Zebrowski

To recognize knowledge as ignorance is
*   noble;*
but to regard ignorance as knowledge is
*   evil.*
—Buddha

16

Clasp the Monkey, Saturn

Late Holocene Cycle
Phase II

Every child learns sooner or later that she is not the center of the universe. At age seven, the distance across the Atlantic Ocean from New York to London seems utterly huge. That's nearly four thousand miles, but it can be traversed by a beam of light in just under one forty-sixth of a second. The ocean, for all its frightful majesty, is ultimately reduced by the knowledge that it happens to be wrapped around the surface of a planet—wrapped only partway, for the Atlantic reaches barely one-sixth of the way around the Earth's almost 25,000 mile circumference. And then the child learns that the distance from the Atlantic Ocean to the Sea of Tranquillity on the moon is nearly ten times the circumference of the Earth, about a quarter million miles, or almost one and a half seconds away at the speed of light.

Beyond that, as the child grows and learns more, the distances never cease to provoke a sense of wonder. Mars and its carbonaceous moons Phobos and Diemos, on their closest approach to Earth, turn out to be almost 50 million miles away—nearly five light minutes, or two hundred times the distance to the moon. The distance to the nearest star, the Sun, is fully eight light minutes, and beyond that are the other stars of the galaxy, six hundred billion of them, dozens of stars for every man, woman and child on Earth. The nearest of those stars is the Alpha Centauri trinary: twenty-five trillion miles away—about four and a half light-years, or a half million times the distance to Mars. And that is the *nearest* star.

By the time the last day of the old world had arrived, the children of Earth knew that their world was not unique, for nearly every star in the sky was being orbited by planets. Even if almost all of those planets were as lifeless as the sands of the moon and Mercury, then across the span of a galaxy twenty-five thousand times as wide as the distance from Earth to Alpha Centauri, the existence of other Earths was, given so many throws of the cosmic dice, statistically inevitable; and beyond Earth's galaxy, at a distance only twenty times the diameter of the Milky Way, lay the Andromeda galaxy—another island of six hundred billion stars—and beyond Andromeda, for more than eight billion light-years, upwards of three hundred billion galaxies filled the visible universe.

The continued survival of prion diseases, and the existence of ancient, self-assembled porphyrins and proteins in carbonaceous meteorites, hinted that life itself could emerge spontaneously, like a crystal, through nothing more (or less) improbable than the versatility and self-organizing properties of the carbon atom. Self-organized complexity invariably radiated outward over planetary surfaces, like ripples in a pond, and all ripple effects (including random variation) produced their own rebound, or feedback effects (including natural selection filters). Thus was biology reducible to the production of order from chaos, and evolution to chaos with feedback. With the odds against the formation of life so drastically shortened, it was possible to believe that at least as near as the Andromeda galaxy, other masses of carbon (that is, other somebodys) were asking the same questions human beings had been asking for more than eight thousand years: Where did we come from? How does our universe work? How did it get here? Will it last forever—or die? And where in it do we belong?

On a blue-white planet orbiting a rather average and insignificant yellow star, carbon, the great organizer, had come to know fire and uranium, titanium and silicon; and most important, it knew itself. Knowing itself, and lonely, it had detached pieces of its own planet and hurled them into orbit on contraptions of flying fire. One day the largest orbiting pieces were gathered together under the flags of many nations, whose leaders christened the detached Earth *Space Station Alpha*.

On the day Scanner crawled into a man-made cave under the Kansas farmscape, a dozen people were orbiting Earth. They were carbon and phosphorus, iron and sulfur, trying to understand themselves. On the planet below, a network of phone lines, satellite relays, notepads, and fax machines had enveloped the world, from pole to pole, in a single living membrane of human thought. *Alphatown,* as the space station had come to be called, was an extension of the membrane's sensory organs; and some months earlier, *Alphatown* had itself grown artificial eyes, and thermosensors, and motile ganglia, and cast them into the frontiers of the night.

Viewed from the distance of the *Darwin II* spacecraft, more than seventy light-minutes from Earth, the Saturnian system was the entire solar system writ small. At its center was Saturn itself, a brown dwarf star that, in spite of being nearly a hundred times as massive as Earth and measuring nearly a half light-second across, had failed to accumulate enough mass to burn brightly as a second sun. Its ring system, measuring two light-seconds in diameter, was a miniature version of the asteroid belt, enclosed by a suite of miniature planets, among them an ice world called Enceladus.

At about the time Scanner relieved Widow-maker for his first sleep shift, the *Darwin II* probe—built in Japan, tested and launched from *Alphatown*—was descending toward Enceladus through trillions of twinkling ice crystals that occupied the worldlet's orbit, forming Saturn's outermost ring.

Enceladus's center was molten glass and iron. Its outer core was a carbonaceous asteroid covered with water and ice. Unlike other carbonaceous asteroids, it had not frozen through to its center some four billion years ago. The production of order from chaos, and chaos with feedback, had not died there, for Enceladus was a world caught in the middle of a gravitational tug-of-war. On one side, no farther away than Earth was from its moon, but a hundred times more massive than Earth, was Saturn. On the other side were Dione (a seven hundred mile-wide satellite that approached within one half the distance separating the Earth from the moon) and Tethys (a six hundred and sixty mile-wide moon that swept past Enceladus at a hair-raising, near-collision radius only twice as large as Earth's circumference). The alternating gravitational jolts dumped enormous amounts of frictional heat into Enceladus's interior; and despite the fact that the world was small enough to fit comfortably within the eastern and western borders of Kansas, it was one of the most geologically active, and strangest, bodies in the solar system.

Because the world had no atmosphere, and because surface temperatures never exceeded a noontime high of –300 degrees F, water erupting through fissures and vents emerged directly into cold vacuum, flashing to vapor and freezing instantly to needles and flakes. As *Darwin II* closed the distance, its cameras focused their attention on what appeared to be a snowstorm in space, rising a hundred miles above the crescent moon.

Avoiding the snow geyser, the robot settled into an orbit only twenty miles above Enceladus, and sprouted twenty yard-long whiskers—radar antennae, with which it began to probe beneath the Enceladan crust to a depth of three hundred yards. Meanwhile, its telescopic cameras mapped the entire surface, revealing details only six inches across. Two weeks later, as fighting broke out across Pakistan, and as China annexed a half dozen islands from Japan, *Darwin II* climbed down from orbit and landed on a field of fresh-fallen snow. After erecting a relay station and sending panoramic views of the horizon earthward, a horizon on which the rings of Saturn, seen vertically and edge-on, reached all the way up the sky, the robot powered up its nuclear reactor to full steam, pressed the reactor head against Enceladus's surface, and used the snow and ice as coolant. Sheets of mist flashed out pallid yellow; and after a dozen minutes the robot sank from view, leaving behind only its communications antennae and a flag bearing the emblem of the Planetary Society. After an hour, it lay at the bottom of a twenty-foot-deep pit that jetted a column of crystallizing steam heavenward. If allowed to continue venting in this manner, the artificial volcano would eventually have buried *Darwin II*'s antennae under a glaze of snow and ice, and if the robot ever did break through to a new ocean within Enceladus, the hapless explorer would be immediately erupted up through a real volcano of its own creation, a volcano whose lava was water and whose ash was ice. So, after descending twenty-five feet, the robot unfurled a Mylar umbrella behind itself. Most of the ascending steam froze against the umbrella's underside, froze three inches thick during the first ten minutes, another nine inches during the second ten, until at last almost no steam at all escaped, and instead of vaporizing and jetting out through the tunnel, the reactor-warmed ice merely liquefied and formed a pool. After deploying two more umbrellas, and descending another twenty yards, *Darwin II* shut down its reactor just long enough for the upper layers of the pool to freeze, forming a plug within a plug.

Then, depositing signal relays behind itself, somewhat like the trail of bread crumbs in the Hansel and Gretel fairy tale, the probe heated up again and continued its journey to the center of Enceladus, carrying on its back two robot submarines named *Nemo* and *Lindenbrook*, neither of them more than a tenth as long as *Darwin II*, neither of them larger than a mouse.

And so it was that the last days of the old world were the beginning and the end of a small corner of the universe coming to understand itself. Triumph. And defeat. Triumph. Years earlier, a bulkier, more expensive probe had dispatched two seismic sensors to the Enceladan snow-fields before firing two grapefruit-sized capsules containing robot helicopters at Titan's cloud tops. The probe itself had been a magnetic rail gun and, having carried its cargo to Saturn and accomplished its mission objectives, it used the recoil from the Titan heliprobes to give it a final nudge toward Enceladus. When it hit the Plain of Sagan, the worldlet rang like a bell; and the noise that came up through the ground was music, for it revealed a whole new ocean to be explored. Water completely enclosed a rocky core only ninety-five miles across. The core—the actual surface of Enceladus—was literally a world within a world, a planet so small that *Nemo* and *Lindenbrook* could travel all the way around its three hundred mile circumference in a single day. But circumnavigating the core was not their job. Their builders had more important concerns in mind: Darwin's warm little ponds.

The men and women who had planned the mission knew from the robot *Galileo*'s asteroid flybys, and from its spectroscopic analysis of volcanic fountains on Jupiter's moon Io, that sulfur was ubiquitous in the solar system. They knew that sediments on Enceladus's sea floor must therefore be laced with sulfides. And they knew from exploration of Earth's own abyssal plains that whole ecosystems were possible in worlds without suns, so long as sulfides were available for the manufacture of food, and carbon for the manufacture of life.

Seventy light-minutes away, in humanity's cradle, the possibility that even a humble, sulfide-eating bacterium might be living inside Enceladus had divided the Roman Catholic church in two. On one side were Jesuit radicals who saw the discovery of the universe as the ultimate triumph of human reason, and who saw within the infinite wilderness an opportunity to truly know the mind of God. On the other side, equally and oppositely radical, were the traditionalists, who saw the very idea that life might emerge naturally, throughout the cosmos, as a disruption of man's special relationship with the Creator, and who saw, in such possibilities, questions too disquieting—even heretical—to ask: Did God make alien flesh in his image, too? Was the Jesus of the Gospels the savior of humanity alone, or did he visit, in one form or another, all intelligent beings across all the universe?

After a month, *Darwin II* had descended three thousand yards; but still, it had miles to go. A week later, and seven hundred yards deeper, the probe passed through an ancient, icy fissure that had filled with upwelling water and clotted solid, probably while dinosaurs still roamed across Montana. The ice clot had a brownish-blue hue, and it was there that *Darwin II*'s chemosensors detected the first faint traces of porphyrin molecules. That was the day the motes, after six weeks of quiescence, broke out across a four block area of Queens; the day the newer, surprisingly lower projections on the midwestern wheat harvest were released; the day the bottom fell out of the commodities market.

DAY 67

The news from *Darwin II*'s chemosensors went back through Space Station *Alpha*, shot through a nerve system of satellite relays into news centers and notepads around the entire circumference of the planet, and brought almost no response at all.

On an ordinary day, hints of life on (or, rather, in) Enceladus would have been profoundly inspiring to some, simply profane to others; but today it was merely an irrelevant oddity, matched as it was against the dawning realization that the crisis criers might have been right after all and that all accomplishment, all discovery—the labor of centuries—would, in the end, count for nothing if the discoverers and the laborers were themselves doomed.

A kind of shock state, or numbness, was settling upon humanity's nerve endings, on Enceladus, and humanity itself, on Earth. The sensory pleasures of discovery were suddenly no more relevant to the world than fine dining was to the violently ill. Enceladus became a footnote on the internet. Nothing more. It was dwarfed by video footage of oil tankers, heavy with cargo, lying low in the water

off Manhattan and Long Island. The captains claimed that
fear of mite contamination prevented them from docking;
but as dwindling gas supplies reduced traffic on the Long
Island Expressway to, mercifully, one third its normal volume, and as cars formed lines more than two blocks long
at every gas station, the net and the airwaves came alive
with speculation that if the captains were truly afraid, they
would simply have turned their ships around. They were,
in the opinions of most observers, waiting for diminishing
supply and increasing demand to drive the wholesale price
of their cargo up high enough, wherever that magic figure—"high enough"—might be.

Though no one had officially closed the borders of Long
Island, ship and truck traffic, and hence delivery of fuel
and food, was becoming increasingly sporadic. The traffic
on the Robert Moses Bridge, spanning Long Island Sound,
was light and unusually orderly, limited almost exclusively
to cars and minivans. Most of the vehicles were heading
away from the island, and a few were loaded down with
camping equipment. As the 81st Airborne soap-bombed
Queens County and the price of milk, when it could be
found, soared to pornographic heights, Long Islanders—a
growing number of them—were beginning to suspect the
real scope of the breakdown, and by the hundreds, by the
thousands, they were now hauling up stakes and seeking
the imagined sanctuary of the New England woods, where
they could go fishing and camping until the crisis blew
over and life returned to normal. Their car radios and
notepads told of riots and communications blackouts in
India, Thailand, and parts of Africa. In Japan, where every
hour of every day, billions of dollars flowed through businesses and banks, a major food shortage had wiped clean,
as if it never existed, 26 percent of the nation's gross
national product. For the recovery effort, a huge glut of
cash was drawn back into Tokyo, halting Japanese investment elsewhere in the global marketplace. Interest rates
worldwide were now soaring, and businesses from Australia to Long Island were reeling. Many of the Connecticut-
bound Long Islanders were among the newly unemployed,
the dispossessed. Following the old Ann Landers/Adelle
Sigmond philosophy of "When life hands you lemons,

make lemonade,'' they tried to view all the bad happenings as an opportunity to get away from it all and take a much-needed vacation in the country. Those who had already reached the overcrowded campgrounds were beginning to discover, too late, that the streams were being fouled by rotting game, that the fish were dead, and that the very soil had gone sour.

As they crossed the bridge, the Long Islanders passed another lane of traffic marching in from the opposite direction, equally orderly, and deceptively peaceful. The drivers could not have behaved more orderly if gathered in a funeral procession. Some of them were curiosity seekers, hoping to witness a mote-bombing up close; but most were country people, hoping to find better conditions in the large towns. As they passed one another, the people exchanged puzzled glances that said, *Fools! You're going in the wrong direction!*

But that was the way of it at a time like this: The grass always seemed greener on the other side . . . not at all unlike the other great lie that a thousand parents in a thousand cars were telling their children: ''Shhhh! It'll be all right.''

CNN was visiting the City of Dreams, interviewing the Einsteins, leaving Jerry Sigmond unnoticed and unheard in his cell, in the uncommon position of being on the outside looking in.

They should be interviewing me, he seethed. *I could tell them what this is really all about, what's going to happen next.*

Stock footage of the Bangor and Long Beach mote outbreaks appeared on the TV screen outside Jerry's cell.

''Except for the Queens incident,'' Jackson Roykirk said, ''the outbreaks seem to have stopped with the approach of autumn. But this is not a time for complacency.''

''You mean, they'll be back next summer?'' the interviewer asked.

''Probably.''

Jerry wondered how this aging, gape-jawed pygmy of

an interviewer—and his little eggheads—had come to cast such large shadows.

"So, what you're saying," the interviewer continued, in what Jerry saw as a penchant for asking soft questions and fawning over his guests, "is that the mote attacks and the fungus outbreaks on our crops and the red tides and the bat problems in the south—that all this apparent rebellion of nature against us is the result of an insect die-off?"

"That's exactly what we're saying," said Jackson, and Richard nodded agreement.

"And how did *that* happen?"

"Right now I'm trying to keep an open mind on possible causes," said Richard. "There's the Fantasia theory, the genetic time bomb theory, the crystallization theory—"

"Keeping an open mind?" Jerry sneered at the screen. "An open mind is one thing, Richard. A hole in the head is something else. I think you've always displayed something else."

"Crystallization?" The interviewer leaned forward and seemed to be loosening one of his suspenders.

"Yes, crystallization," Richard said. "It's a way of visualizing how a pattern of change can start small, perhaps in only one place in one part of a forest, and grow into a chain reaction of mass extinction that eventually covers the entire globe.

"Here's a good example: ordinary glycerin. For nearly two hundred years after chemists first extracted the substance from animal fat, no one could get it to crystallize. As a matter of fact, until about 1910 all the standard chemistry books proclaimed that glycerin had no solid form. Then, one day, by a one-in-a-trillion chance, a specific combination of jostling motions in a barrel of glycerin being shipped out of Vienna crystallized a single molecule. By the time it reached London, all the glycerin in the barrel had crystallized. The chemists and the physicists said it was impossible; but when they sampled glycerin from the barrel, they discovered that after the snowflake-sized needles had seeded further crystallization in their own jars of glycerin, all the other glycerin in all the other laboratories in the world began to crystallize, and no one has been able to stop it since. So perhaps origins and crises in the history of life are just chemical and mathematical certainties—perhaps all the apparent order and disorder in our world arises from nothing more exotic than crystallization events.''

Footage of blackened crops and of a mite-blackened helicopter sitting motionless on a beach became a backdrop for Richard's voice-over. Jackson put a hand to his head and played devil's advocate to the crystallization theory for a moment. And then for another. He imagined sulfur and pyrrhotite crystals forming near a volcanic vent . . . amethyst in a cave . . . salt in a Triassic pond . . . the crystals were never the same size or shape, of course; and if a solution was sufficiently saturated, the result was a random process in which rival crystals competed for a dwindling supply of salt or sulfur, sometimes engulfing or parasitizing their neighbors to produce what rock collectors called ''phantoms,'' with only the fittest ones triumphing, to produce the largest crystals. But the analogy between crystallization and life worked only so far, Jackson realized. Though it could be said that a salt crystal forming on the edge of Israel's Dead Sea was, like a living system, capable of exchanging material with its environment—even reproducing itself by seeding daughter crystals—it ''lived'' without benefit of the infinite variety offered by a genetic code and was therefore no different from the salt that once crunched under the toes of the dinosaurs.

''Crystallization events cannot be the whole picture,'' Jackson said. ''If they were, then I'd have to wrap up this conversation by saying that man's greatest evolutionary step was the one taken by a woman: by Lot's wife, the day she turned into a pillar of salt.''

''False analogy,'' Richard said, and laughed. ''Crystals themselves are nothing more or less than molecular viruses; but they do provide very good examples of how new patterns might arise and shoot through entire populations. The crystallization of the first glycerin molecule was an improbable event; but given trillions of glycerin molecules, and enough time, improbable events become inevitable. Thus, glycerin crystallizes because it has to. The insects die because they have to.''

Jackson was not so sure and, as pictures of New Jersey's Dinosaur Creek excavation appeared on the screen, he began to speak in favor of Bill Schutt's genetic time bomb theory.

Jerry Sigmond laughed. The world is going to hell in a hand basket and they give us genetic time bomb theories! Not believable, Jerry decided. At best, Richard and Jackson were afraid to tell the world, in plain English, that they just did not know what the fuck was going on. At worst, they did know and were covering for someone. Time bombs, indeed! Crystallization events, indeed! Richard and Jackson belonged on the scientific sidelines, along with those nut cases who talked about palladium reactors, extraterrestrials, and the lost kingdom of Atlantis.

In a head-to-head debate, Jerry thought he could easily paint Richard and Jackson as a pair of fools. But it made no difference now. A great change was coming, and he, not the Einsteins, would be its compass. Of that he had no doubt.

''The rat cage is coming,'' Jerry had warned. ''When you crowd a whole bunch of rats together and you trim down their food supply, they behave just like people. What you end up with is rage. Unfettered rage.''

Amy had tried to force Jerry's vision of humanity out of her thoughts. It was too dark; but she could not close her eyes to it any longer, not after she saw a disagreement over pizza and a glass of water turn into a riot that nearly killed her.

She had found a pizza shop on Twenty-eighth Street, still in business, still crowded, still stocked full with ice cold sodas and beer and fresh-brewed coffee. The small, family-owned shop was part of a growing, and thriving, underground economy. Cash was not accepted, only gold ''coin'' and barter.

After trading a handful of multivitamins for a corner piece of Sicilian and a can of Coors, Amy watched a Chinese family pay for a whole pie with a panda-engraved sliver of gold. Then the wife asked the shop owner for a glass of water, and that's when the trouble began.

The shop owner, a man in his fifties, demanded another sliver of gold. When the woman protested that water should be free, he explained in great detail how expensive it was, these days, for him to wash a used glass with soap and hot water. With an expression on her face that said Here—take it, you cheap bastard, she shoved a shiny, five-dollar sliver in his direction.

Ordinarily, it might have ended there; but the shop owner's wife had been looking on from behind the counter, looking on and seething, until at last it seemed a flashbulb had gone off inside her head. She wasn't about to let the Chinese eat in peace—not after the affront.

"You!" she shouted across the crowded parlor. "You people come here to this country, and you think you *own* it. You take our food. You take our jobs. And you think we owe it to you!"

The shop owner stood beside her and said nothing. The shop owner's son stepped in from a back room and said nothing. The Chinese woman's husband said, "Please stop," and her child said, "Can you just let us eat?"

But the shop owner's wife took this as an invitation to shout even louder, and to start calling the woman an animal, and to call her husband an animal, provoking him to stand up and holler, "Shut up!" and, as patrons began lifting their pizzas and beers and heading for the door, the shop owner's son shouted, "Don't you tell my mother to shut up!" and the earth seemed to move, suddenly, as shouts of anger reached a crescendo. Cups and trays and slabs of pizza flew. A chair crashed somewhere near Amy's shoulder, and there was the unmistakable sound of breaking plate glass. Amy bolted in the direction of the sound and followed a dozen other customers through an opening that only moments before had been a wall of glass. She glimpsed two customers off to her left, snatching up beers, vitamins, and gold on their way out, taking full advantage of the distracted shop owners.

As she slowed from a run to a walk and turned at the nearest intersection, Amy realized that her head hurt. There was a long, thin cut in her scalp—either from a thrown plate that had grazed her skull or from having run too near a blade of glass jutting from the broken window frame. She traced the cut lightly with two fingers, afraid to rub too hard and squeeze out more blood. It had already spattered onto her jeans, and when she looked down she saw that they were torn and that her blouse was in ruins.

As a guard in a high-security prison, Amy thought she had already seen people at their most troubled. She thought she had become accustomed to seeing it, even become bored by it. Yet to her, the pizza brawl was totally horrifying and totally disorienting.

The rat cage . . .

Perhaps Jerry had a true sense of human nature after all. Sugar, gas, and almost everything else of value was being rationed, and there were hints that it was going to get a lot worse before it got better. A survivor of Bangladesh had uttered terrifying phrases to the Senate: "Plagues . . . and a great famine . . . turning first this way, and then that way . . . until finally it blanketed my whole country."

People were scared, and Amy understood that scared people rioted, scared people killed. Jerry had cautioned her that if a famine really was coming, the least dangerous time (from a rat-cage point of view) was when the masses, weakened by hunger, eventually lost their fighting edge and resigned themselves to follow anyone who promised a way out. The most dangerous hour, he had reckoned, was only now approaching. People were still reasonably well fed, and the rationing made them irritable; and the irritated, frightened crowds still possessed enough energy to fight.

"At first, you'll see only sporadic outbursts of rage," Jerry had said. "But if the rationing continues to worsen, the politics of the rat cage will prevail. Then you can look around and take your pick from the rogues of death row. Most of them are rank amateurs, compared to what the average, wage-earning family man is capable of when he loses himself in an angry mob."

The cage . . . Amy thought about that long and hard as she tore a rag from her blouse and mopped blood from her scalp. She was, at this point, Jerry's gatekeeper. He

depended on her more than his "average, wage-earning
family man" depended on the government's constantly
expanding list of rationed foods. Today, he depended on
her far more than she depended on him, but she knew that
this would have to change, if a storm was coming. The
bloodstains on her clothes and the sounds that could still
be heard behind her in the direction of Twenty-eighth
Street—ugly sounds—told Amy that the storm really was
coming and that it really was time for a change.

"This is your house," said Richard, and Tam knew that
he was talking about the lab, and that there would be no
going home to Long Beach. Ever again.

He stroked her left cheek with the back of his hand and
that was when Tam pulled away and began to cry.

Richard put an arm around her shoulder and tried to
pull her close, but she pulled away with a sharp jerk.

"Tam, Tam, don't. Please don't cry," he murmured.
"Everything will be all right."

"Will it?" she said, steely eyed. There was always a
hint of panic in Daddy's voice, in what little she heard of
Daddy's voice these days. He was out the door early every
morning, and he returned later and later every night. The
spying operations with Georgiana had shed little light on
what was obsessing him and the other grown-ups. The
words they overheard were always too big—except for
cockroaches. What, Tam wondered, made her less important than trying to clone a stinking cockroach? And why
were Daddy's eyes getting redder every day for lack of
sleep? And why did he look so scared?

"I love you," he said.

"That's not what I asked!"

"It'll all work out, somehow," he said, and cursed himself for living in this time, and for having brought a child
into it. More and more of his waking hours were being
spent away from her, in the lab and at round table discussions over notepads, in the hope that if he and the other
scientists worked very hard and were very resourceful,
they might come up with the equivalent of a miracle vac-
cine or they might manage at least to preserve some small

part of civilization or, failing that, he might be able to buy a little more time for Tam.

Buy more time for what? Richard asked himself. *So you can spend more time away from her? What new scar will that put in her?* he wondered. The scars had already settled too deep. In all his life, Richard had never known a sight so torturous as the bewildered, searching expression he'd seen in Tam's eyes the morning a set of footsteps only vaguely similar to Dawn's approached the cafeteria door. That look was always present, to one degree or another: Tam was searching for Mommy; and to know that hopeful and hopeless expression was to know heartbreak.

He noticed also that she was trying to eat every scrap of food in sight; and he guessed that a weight problem lay in her immediate future, if not for the fact that the local food supply was dwindling and ration coupons were becoming part of their daily existence. Richard did not have to be a rocket scientist to see that his little girl was lonely beyond words. Or that she was scared. He was scared, too—scared to let her know that sometimes even daddies get scared.

"Everything will be all right," he said again.

"You promise?"

He thought long and hard, and then he said, truthfully, "I'll do my very best. I'll do everything I can. Is that good enough?"

"Will everything *really* be all right? Can you promise that?"

His troubled silence was answer enough.

The days were getting shorter and cooler, but at noon the sun was still strong enough to soften the asphalt on some of the National Laboratory's older parking fields. In an energy-economy move, the offices and the guest quarters had been allowed to grow stifling hot, giving Richard first-hand experience of what summers must have been like in his grandparents' time, before air-conditioning became so commonplace as to be considered a necessity. He found it difficult to imagine how people once worked and slept in the heat and humidity; but surely they had managed, so surely it was manageable. Only the main labora-

tories and parts of the museum were cooled by the hum
of squat, rooftop air conditioners—not for the benefit of
the scientists inside but for their machines. Some rooms
were in fact so cold that people wore sweaters—which,
by providing contrast, only intensified the unbearable heat
of the living quarters. Richard's days were spent with Leslie, in one of the more cramped labs, flashing through
hundreds of micro-MRI scans on his notepad. On one wall,
a hand-scrawled sign under the thermostat warned, DO NOT
RAISE TEMPERATURE ABOVE 55 DEGREES F! THE MACHINES
LIKE IT THAT WAY.

The City of Dreams could afford to keep its machines
"happy" for a year or more, if requisite, with no additional support from the outside world. Equipped with its
own generators, the city was not subject to the increasingly
frequent brownouts being experienced by the rest of Long
Island. The machines would have power, Leslie supposed,
long after the food ran out.

The micro-MRI lab, and its notepad connections to research teams all over the world, was the first major step
in the scientific investigation of the insect die-off, and the
last slim hope of finding a treatment, if not a cure. If one
went by the book, the CDC protocol for even the worst
imaginable biological emergency consisted of three se-
quential stages: isolation and identification of the problem,
characterization, and treatment. But the death of all the
world's insects—which on first hearing always sounded
more desirable than dangerous—was proving to be a rather
larger emergency than even the CDC's board of directors
had imagined. Under time-critical circumstances, sometimes the rule books had to be read backward.

First, possible treatments—the cloning and release of
crisis-immune insects was one—had to be proposed. Then
the treatments had to be tested against whatever process
was killing the insects off, to find out whether or not the
characteristics of the disease process precluded all treatments. If one of the proposed treatments worked, then and
only then could science afford the luxury of finding out
how and why the process got started.

The micro-MRI, designed to dissect, at the molecular

level, the cause of a disease, was now set up to design a cure.

Leslie and Richard sat side by side at a cluttered table. Amid the clutter: three large jars of centipedes—food for the spiders. A lone bonsai spruce stood in the center of the table, surrounded, at treetop level, by a detrital filing system of books, journals, and hard-copy notes. The oldest notes lay at the bottoms of the piles, mostly forgotten and awaiting future refiling; the youngest (and most relevant) lay at the top. They included a column of handwritten figures on yellow paper:

Retrieved 47 viable cell nuclei (roach) from leg muscle.

5 actively mitotic (cryo-preserved Tuesday).

6 tested and reserved for scanning.

Implanted contents 36 nuclei (roach) in eggs (spider) Wednesday.

10:30 A.M. Thurs.: 28 embryos viable.

1:30 P.M. Thurs.: 26 embryos viable.

4:30 P.M. Thurs.: 26 embryos viable.

7:30 P.M. Thurs.: 26 embryos still viable!

10:30 P.M. Thurs.: 26 embryos viable.

1:30 A.M. Fri.: 25 embryos viable.

4:30 A.M. Fri.: 23 embryos viable.

7:30 A.M. Fri.: 23 embryos viable.

10:30 A.M. Fri.: 23 embryos viable.

1:30 P.M. Fri.: 21 embryos viable.

4:30 P.M. Fri.: 4 embryos viable.

7:30 P.M. Fri.: All embryos lost. No mitotic figures.

The idea of cloning cockroaches had seemed hopeless from the start, but Richard insisted that it was their first best hope. If the laboratory's one surviving cockroach was somehow immune to whatever had killed its brethren, and if they could successfully implant its DNA into the nucleus of a spider's egg, and if they could successfully modify the spider's egg to provide all the nutrients the developing roach embryo needed—then what? There were too many what-ifs in Richard's cockroach-cloning plan for Leslie's tastes. To begin, even if it worked, all the clones would be male, like their gene donor. What if a surviving female

could never be found? How, Leslie asked herself, would
we then repopulate the world with scavenging roaches?
By modifying spider eggs, one at a time, forever? No, that
would not do. In order for the treatment to succeed, billions of egg-laying cockroaches were necessary. Without
a mother, there could be no egg. Without the egg, there
could be no mother. And without at least—at the very,
very least—a score of other insect species leaving behind
clonable survivors, the treatment would not work, could
not work, for cockroaches constituted only one small portion of the world's insect ecology. The image of poor
Noah, commanded by his God to find two cockroaches for
the Ark—male and female—came quickly to mind and
made her chuckle inwardly. And two dung beetles, she
told herself, male and female. Two gnats, male and female.
Two hornets, male and female. Two fleas, male and
female . . .

Richard was tense, tired, and in no mood for laughter.
Memories of Long Beach still haunted him. He studied
the series of DNA scans already recorded on his pad, while
Leslie manipulated the magnetic fields with her notepad,
and recorded a new set of scans.

All the embryonic cells appeared simply to have stopped
dividing. They were the direct descendants of muscle cells
retrieved from the severed leg of the roach known throughout the facility as "Sole Survivor." By inducing hydrogen
atoms to resonate, or "light up," the micro-MRI revealed
differences in the hydrogen halos of adenine and guanine,
uracil and cytosine, ribose and phosphates, allowing Richard and Leslie, with lightning speed, to scan and record
huge segments of DNA. Information was collected so
quickly that it was impossible to analyze and compare the
segments (and all the structural proteins and repair systems
that were attached to them) without the aid of terabyte
notepads.

Naturally, in terms of sheer memory power, the notepads themselves were not big enough. Leslie had downloaded DNA scans of the dead embryos, one at a time,
into the lab's Nomad and Cyberdyne mainframes. They
were being compared, gene for gene, against DNA from
Sole Survivor's leg muscles and DNA from a specimen

collected way back in 1973—courtesy of the Vanderbilt Museum in Northport. The three-way comparison had taken two days to set up, and had been running for an hour. Nomad and Cyberdyne saw nothing obvious: no genetic differences inconsistent with normal population diversity, no hint of the DNA equivalent of a shut-off valve or an aberrant oncogene unique to the embryos and/or their gene donor, no peculiar DNA knots or loops, nothing that looked like a good explanation for the embryos' failure to thrive.

Not that Leslie and Richard really knew what they should be searching for. If they were scanning human DNA, the task would have been more easily accomplished, in spite of the fact that the field to be scanned was more than a dozen times larger. Cyberdyne's files already contained multiple copies of the human genome representing every race and race mixture on Earth. But no one had foreseen a situation in which files of the cockroach genome would be needed, until it was too late. Without a baseline for quick comparison, they might never learn what had gone wrong with their first attempt at finding a treatment. They were learning, now, that there was something far more disturbing than failing to find answers; there was the very real fear that they were failing to ask the right questions, that they had no measure of the scope of their ignorance. But no one could blame them: After all, no one had ever before been called upon to perform an autopsy on a nest of cloned cockroach embryos.

"Nature isn't giving us any breaks," Leslie said. But Richard wasn't so sure. While there were no great differences jumping out at them from a comparison of the chromosomes' actual DNA skeletons—from the actual genetic coding sequences—as Richard watched the computer move automatically along a length of scanned, reconstructed, and artificially animated insect genome, he began to notice breaks and dislocations in the structural proteins that enclosed Sole Survivor's DNA.

"Take a look there," Richard said, pointing, and displayed three identical chromosomal segments on Leslie's pad. "It looks like Sole Survivor's structural proteins have fared even worse than an insect's that's been lying all dried up in a specimen tray since the 1970s. You'd expect it to be the other way around.''

''So, you think Sole Survivor's embryos simply burned out?'' Leslie asked.

''From old age?'' Richard suggested.

''From advanced old age,'' said Leslie.

''Let's go look at some other segments,'' Richard said. Leslie wrote several commands on her pad and sat back. Eight seconds later, the first of five, side-by-side sets of regulator genes began scrolling down their pads, with dislocations and breaks in the DNA's structural supports highlighted. The two youngest strands (from Sole Survivor's embryos and leg muscles) displayed more hot spots than the oldest one (from the Vanderbilt specimen). Then the second set produced the same result. And the third. And the fourth. The fifth series showed hot spots not only outside the DNA skeleton but revealed two breaks appearing to descend from the faulty structural supports into the DNA itself.

Leslie said, ''I suppose, with one gene affecting so many others, and without a normal roach for baseline comparison, it could take us the better part of a year to figure out if these two cracks are a cause of the damage we're seeing or an effect.''

''I'm tempted to say it's an effect.''

''I agree.''

''I'm also tempted to say we should settle the question.''

''Normally, I'd agree with that, too. But we don't have a year.''

''Too right.''

''Okay,'' Leslie said. ''So what are we looking at? Senescence? If that's the case, then Sole Survivor is a straggler, aged about a hundred and twenty in cockroach years. *Someone* had to be among the last to die, just as someone had to be among the first. They're not robots, you know. They may all be dropping from the same cause, at about the same time, but we shouldn't expect them all to drop on the same day.''

Richard's thoughts were racing, but all he could bring himself to say was, ''Interesting.''

"What, specifically?"

"That we might have failed because we were trying to clone a roach that was running down into old age. This gives us two clues we didn't have before, and they both stink. *A*: The cells of a very old insect are going to be different, as a matter of sheer definition, from those of a young one preserved in a museum display; so any attempt to concoct a treatment for the insect die-off based on what few survivors we might find is more likely than not doomed to failure. *B*: The only treatment I can think of right now is cloning survivable insects; which means insects preserved in museum displays; which means cloning the dead."

Leslie grinned. This was the same Richard Sinclair who had thwarted her attempts to clone a saurian virus. Other scientists, and many theologians, had become her declared enemies over this same issue, over whether or not it was dangerous to disturb the sleep of the extinct. But now—

"I guess I was a woman ahead of my time," she said.

"No one is born ahead of her time," Richard shot back. "There are visionaries and there are circumstances. Everything else is hindsight."

"The circumstances have changed."

"Yes."

And she took this, and ran with it, as the closest Richard would ever come to giving her a compliment. "However, the question of the hour is, Where do we start? Bug boxes from the museum? Or . . ."

"Amber?"

"Maybe," Leslie said. "If Bill's genetic time bomb theory turns out to be correct, then the older the better."

"We should run scans on the other 1973 roaches," Richard said, and Leslie nodded agreement. Better to eliminate, right now, even the smallest possibility that the single 1973 specimen already examined might be the exception to the rule, and Sole Survivor the rule, against which the exception had been compared and assumed to be the rule. Common sense predicted that this was probably not the case—almost definitely not the case—and that the examination of the other 1973 specimens would waste the better part of the next twelve hours; but to do otherwise would be to risk pursuing, based on a false conclusion, a course of investigation and treatment for hundreds of hours, or hundreds of days, only to find that it led to nothing except an even greater stretch of wasted time, at a time when time itself was more precious than gold, more precious than all the gold in the world.

Two hours later, the first sample was ready for scanning, and two more were, in MRI parlance, "waiting on the runway." Richard scribbled a set of instructions on his pad, loaded them into the scanner's computer, then poured himself some coffee. He looked down at the steaming cup, nearly the last of a dwindling supply.

They watched the notepads—which displayed a countdown to the first readout of a DNA segment: T minus 3:21 minutes.

"What do we do if they all come up looking like Sole Survivor?" Richard said.

"Don't ask that question."

T minus 2:15 minutes.

Leslie frowned, and crossed her fingers.

Jackson was on the pad-link with a fellow polymath named Doc Coher. He had begun his career as an entomologist working for the United Nations, and he was the only man known to Jackson old enough to have encountered a live leopard in the Indian rain forest. To judge from the accounts trickling into his pad from Xian, Vancouver, Rio, and Seoul, Jackson was beginning to understand Leslie Wells's fear that his own species might be as extinct as the leopards one day. There was plenty to be afraid of, every time he gazed south and reminded himself that somewhere out there, according to the latest reports, was an island called Tobago that had no populace—or, as the case may be, no human populace.

"Of course, people should, by now, have stopped dying from insect-borne diseases," Coher said. "Whereas, in many of the poorer countries, you used to have a couple of million people a year dying from malaria, now they're going to die from starvation. Take your choice. Personally speaking, I'd rather have malaria."

"So, with the crops beginning to fail," Jackson said,

"why don't we just enlarge the fishing fleets? Or harvest plankton? That ought to supplement the food supply."

Coher shook his head. "Won't work. A very high percentage of those microscopic plankton, even during normal biological times, are poisonous. There's simply no way of separating all the poisonous varieties from the edible ones, especially if you're talking about processing hundreds of millions of pounds of plankton—which is what's required to just barely supplement diets in this country alone.

"As for the fish, when you get right down to it, for thousands of years we've basically been hunter-gatherers at sea. Nothing has changed, really, except we've gotten more efficient at it. Now we sweep the seas with giant, roving canneries, dragging behind themselves nets large enough to swallow the great pyramid at Giza. The truth of the matter is we've already hunter-gathered the seas to the breaking point. The cod have all but disappeared from the North Atlantic, the shrimp from the South China Sea. Even without this crisis, which is bound to accelerate the overfishing problem, we were getting perilously close to killing the goose that lays the golden egg. We can't hope to feed this country's population on even half the ocean harvest of ten years ago; and in most places, we've already fished it down to far less than half."

Jackson seemed on the verge of tears. "And the bacterial blooms are killing off all the freshwater fish?"

"I wouldn't worry about that," Coher said. "I think the freshwater fish were dead long before the bacterial blooms got anywhere near them."

"How?"

"Starvation; that's absolutely mandatory."

"I don't understand."

"Just look at this bunch over here." Coher pointed to the right side of his screen, and displayed a long string of Latin names accompanied by illustrations. "Recognize any of them?"

"Sure. Mayflies and their larval forms. Damselflies. Caddis flies. Water boatmen . . . the rest, I'm not so sure of."

"Diptera, mostly. And all of the above—even the mosquito larvae—are essentially the only source of food our freshwater fish and their developing fry have. It's the same for the salamanders and for the frogs. All those fish that migrate from the ocean to spawn—the salmon, the trout—they're gone. They're just gone.''

"And there goes a major source of food in the forest," Jackson added. "When you lose all the freshwater fish, next you lose all the animals that feed on them—''

"The mink, the otters, the bears—''

"Oh, it just goes on and on; all the birds at the river's edge and on the marshes—that alone will have a tremendous impact on the whole world." Jackson shook his head. "I hadn't thought about this," he said. "I thought our biggest worries were pollination and the soil—and prey switching; but if I keep thinking along *these* lines—''

"It keeps getting worse and worse, doesn't it?''

"Yeah." He shrugged. "So the salmon—even those that may be alive right now, out at sea—there's nothing for them to come back to and feed on in the lakes and rivers. No place for them to spawn.''

Coher said, "You also have to take into account that whatever tuna, cod, and redfish stocks are still out there will be depleted very quickly because the young salmon and trout, when they normally go out from the rivers, go out to sea in tremendous numbers. Suddenly they're not out there for the cod and tuna to feed on anymore. So your alternative food sources are going to disappear very quickly for more than one reason, not just because of an inevitable, panic-driven surge of overfishing, but because they're simply not being fed.''

"Amazing," Jackson said. "You don't even *find* insects out at sea, do you?''

"Not really. Just two or three minor species that I know of.''

"What kind?''

"Oh, just the occasional water strider that skates along the surface and nibbles on whatever's dead and floating.''

"Amazing," Jackson said again.

"What is?''

"That insects never even got a serious foothold in the oceans, much less conquered them, and yet their death will reach on to the high seas and deep under them.''

A smirk passed across his lips. One did not have to know Jackson for very long to notice that he possessed an unusual, if not downright perverse appreciation for grim irony. Jackson suspected that it had something to do with his family history, being, as he was, descended from Charles Drew, who in 1940 had perfected blood preservation techniques and organized America's first blood banks, then bled to death after a car accident because no one would let him into a "whites only" hospital.

Jackson sighed. "They were here first," he continued. "And they helped to prepare the way for humans to get here."

Coher nodded.

"And now," Jackson said, "they're going to prepare the way for humans to leave."

Scan after scan came back with the same answer. None of the other 1973 specimens were anywhere near as degraded as Sole Survivor. Leslie looked down at her pad with relief. The living roach was the anomaly, not its ancestors. The last scan had registered on her pad at 1600 hours; she and Richard had been working for nine hours without so much as a ten-minute lunch break.

At 1630 hours, the next 1973 batch was ready for scanning. That was when Sharon patched her report through to Richard's pad, announcing two more pieces of the extinction puzzle. First: The latest and the last truckload of dirt they would be allowed time enough to sift had yielded not a single live insect egg (indicating that if insects did disappear periodically, and if they did survive the resulting upheavals via the dormancy of their eggs, then their dormant eggs were exceedingly rare). Second: Sole Survivor had died—indicating that Leslie's old age theory and perhaps Bill Schutt's genetic time bomb theory were alive and well.

"So there you have it," Leslie said. "Evolution's time bomb."

"I hope that's not what it is."

"We can't spare the time to find out if Bill's theory is wrong," Leslie said. "All we can do is weigh the consequences of right or wrong against the possible treatments.

Now, if we clone, say, 1973 insects and there is no genetic time bomb, we won't suffer any consequences at all. But, on the other hand, if there *is*—''

''Then it catches up with their descendants a few decades later, and unless we've identified the problem, and fixed it by that time, we'll end by going through this all over again.''

Leslie said, ''But if we clone fossil insects from amber—amber from the Dominican Republic—then even if there is a genetic time bomb, it will take at least twenty-three million years to catch up with us.''

''And by then it will be someone else's problem.''

Leslie hefted a piece of amber about the size of a child's fist in her palm. In its center, its wings spread out in perfect symmetry, lay a brush-footed butterfly, an ancestor of the now-extinct red admiral butterfly. Richard had once called this ''the Mona Lisa of all fossils,'' flawed only by a crack that once divided the organic gemstone in two and exposed the whole interior of the insect's head capsule and thorax. After enduring megayears without harm, a museum curator had brought the stone home for study, whereupon his three-year-old son used it for a hockey puck. Richard was, at that time, a graduate student on an internship at the museum, and when the curator asked him to repair the fossil—to reseal the broken pieces with resin and to give its surface a fresh, jewel-like polish—the young intern was startled to see, in the exposed head capsule and thorax, almost all the butterfly's internal organs—mummified, perfectly. Those tissues not mummified had been so deeply penetrated by the ancient pool of tree sap that they were indistinguishable from cell samples placed on a microscope slide and smeared with Canadian balsam—which, like amber, was merely a form of tree sap. Richard recalled how the butterfly had seemed to him as if it were caught in tree sap only yesterday, and he would have believed that indeed it had, that someone gave a counterfeit to the museum, if not for the fact that the same piece of amber also contained the remains of a pollen-collecting bee known only from fossils. Intact internal organs and cell nuclei, and perhaps intact DNA too . . . it started a train of thought in Richard . . . all those years ago . . .

and it proved to him that sometimes the seeds of exotic discovery came disguised as a catastrophe (as in the case of a priceless nugget of amber converted to a child's hockey puck).

Neither Richard nor Leslie had ever lost that special, childhood ability to feel—to actually feel—the weight of time in the heft of a rock. To people such as this, the Cretaceous Period and the Eocene Epoch were not graveyards of discarded species but thriving worlds with ostrich dinosaurs and egg-laying mammals on their shores, ancestral otters playing in the streams, and the first bees taking wing. To them, as they picked through trays of fossils and layers of rock, the past was still alive. They were, in a very real sense, low-budget time travelers, and they came from a long tradition of paleontologists and archaeologists who had seen (sometimes with dying eyes) that time travel could be very addictive. The first fossil seashell or crinoid stem given to the wrong child often began a quest no less obsessive than that resulting from the first sip of whiskey given to an alcoholic. This, if nothing else, Leslie and Richard had learned from each other: She once tried to put a stop to one of Richard's projects, and he to hers; but the only force that could truly have stopped either of them was a well-placed bullet. Currently, they were both mainlining a past so distant that the last daylight to glance off the butterfly's wings had already left the Andromeda galaxy far, far behind.

Leslie's thoughts were with the butterfly's DNA. Even if she could get a complete genetic blueprint out of the amber, and reproduce it in a spider's egg, in order for this treatment to work, and for ''Mona's'' descendants to go out into the world and begin pollinating what few flowering plants might still remain alive, she needed a male counterpart. The only male specimen of Mona's kind consisted of a severed abdomen and a wing fragment embedded in a thumbnail-size chip of amber; but these would have to serve.

And so it was that the last great hope of civilization came to rest on a butterfly and a handful of her brethren who had blundered into rivulets of tree sap and struck death poses lasting almost forever. Sealed in transparent coffins of hardening resin, they had remained intact while the trees that created their tombs grew old, fell, and were devoured by termites, carpenter ants, and wood roaches, who left only the amber behind. In time, the whole forest ceased to be. The Atlantic Ocean doubled its width, the moon increased its distance from the Earth by more than three thousand miles, and the general temperature of the universe fell by nearly a half degree yet, unbelievably, a butterfly came down through the megayears unchanged in appearance—flash frozen in amber—with every facet in her eyes, every spur on her legs, all the pigment on her wings, intact.

It was a true wonder of nature; but if the scientists were to preserve even a small corner of their civilization, even bigger wonders, bigger miracles, were required.

Leslie laughed. "I remember when I was about nine years old," she said. "I broke my mother's favorite vase and tried to hide the pieces. I was a wreck—afraid of the hurt I would see in her face. She found out, of course, and I cried, and cried, and cried. But all she said was, 'Shhh! It'll be all right. It can be glued back together. Shhhh! It's not as if you've raised the dead.' And now"— she laughed again—"and now we're being called upon to do precisely that."

"We're gonna have to do it a hundred times over," said Richard. "Bees. Butterflies. A whole bunch of other pollinators. Termites. Springtails. Dung beetles. Ants. Did I say a hundred? Make that hundreds. We're gonna have to do it *hundreds* of times."

"I know. And if we just start with one male and one female of each amberized species—a brush-footed Adam and Eve, as it were—their descendants will have even less genetic diversity than the Siberian tiger and the mountain gorilla."

"Well, for insects, that doesn't seem to matter a great deal. The whole of New Zealand was infested by tens of millions of yellow jackets, all of them descended from only two wasps that disembarked from a crate of spare plane parts flown in from Europe. Up till the extinction, the wasps were doing just fine, thank you very much."

"Good," Leslie said. "It may be a long shot getting

that first pair of butterflies cloned, or producing that first pregnant queen ant; but if we succeed, that first brood should spread out all over the world.''

"Like a chain reaction, if we're lucky. The biological equivalent of fission.''

Leslie agreed. To date, she had wondered if there was little that might actually be accomplished, beyond making guest appearances on local television and radio stations, advising Long Islanders how to hand-pollinate their tomato gardens and how to build homemade greenhouses for the coming winter. On the grounds of the lab itself, greenhouse construction had become a major industry, and the growing crowds of visitors were given instructions for the improvement of their own gardens, along with seeds and produce, and camel hair artist brushes for artificial pollination. The people Leslie met struck her as being eager to learn, not because farm produce was becoming frighteningly scarce, but because it was becoming expensive enough to hit forcefully in the wallet. It occurred to Leslie that the cloning treatment had better work quickly or, some few months down the line, the lab's expanding network of greenhouses would become a prime target for mobs.

Already, it was starting. For the third day in a row, Long Island's *Newsday* reported that a home owner—this time a man in Freeport—had shot a teenager who raided his vegetable garden. To Leslie, the shootings were the first twitches of something horrible trying to be born. The shockwave of insect death was bearing down on her civilization like the approach of a freight train. At first, it had appeared only as a dark shape on the horizon, and if one happened to be walking on the tracks, that was the time to step out of the way. If one waited too long, by the time the danger was obvious and you could clearly distinguish its features, it was usually too late to move.

Little left to do, Leslie told herself, *if all the world becomes a mob. Little left except . . . to get out of the way?*

Yes. Perhaps. But where to? Actual shooting wars were breaking out across Asia, from the Ganges River to the Mekong Delta and the Sea of Japan. Even in the peaceful Aegean, the Greek and Turkish navies were firing on each other in a fight over—of all things—fishing rights. If the laboratories of the world did not come up with a treatment very soon, and make it work, the world would continue to spiral down into a widening spasm of country versus country, with no spoils remaining for the winners. Locally, it would eventually get down to neighbor versus neighbor, gutting each other's homes and greenhouses for food. Leslie supposed most of the Long Islanders would just stay here—behind their loaded guns—in their homes, with their corn and potatoes and their freeze-dried coffee and Hershey bars and beer and their pets, and smaller armed gangs joining with larger armed gangs. . . . She imagined they would eat their pets, at last, and then—

(Where? Where can we run to? How can we get out of the way?)

The new 1973 batch began to scan out on her pads; same as the old batch. "Time bomb," she whispered to herself, and shook her head, trying to dismiss thoughts of mob rule.

Leslie said, "This will take a while to check. I can take over from here, for the next hour or so. You go take a break."

"I don't mind staying," said Richard. "If you want to hatch Mona from a spider's egg, you'll sure as hell run into some rough edges that need ironing out. I might as well get started on them now."

Leslie looked up, brushing her bangs back from her forehead. Her eyes were tired but concerned, Richard noticed with surprise.

"When was the last time, Richard? When was the last time you had lunch or dinner with your daughter? Or took her for a walk? Or played a game of Monopoly with her?"

"Monopoly? Who the hell has time for Monopoly?"

"Will two hours—even three or four hours—make all that much difference?" She looked at him somberly. "I'd start spending more time with my kid, if I were you."

"What bothers you?"

"Time," Leslie said. "It's getting down to months, now. Soon it'll be weeks. Then days. And then you'll be looking back to this afternoon, and wishing you could take back just one of these precious hours that slip by when you're not watching." She returned her attention to the pads and made a brushing-away motion with her left hand. "Go play with your kid, Richard."

But Richard did not move.

"You're burning yourself out, pal. You know that, don't you?"

"Good," said Richard. "It keeps me warm."

Now that a real crisis—the genuine article—was upon the world, the media's weekly hit parade of crises was slamming into reverse, that is, into denial. To judge from the morning news alone, Sharon guessed that it was possible to believe, ignoring certain facts, that the world's yellowing and blackening fields might even produce a bumper crop next season. Sharon knew better, as she dumped Richard's latest version of the cloning recipe, and Leslie's latest scan results, onto the global internet, hoping that some research group, somewhere in the world, would find them useful.

The info dump had been on the net barely six minutes when the first respondents chimed in: Drs. Evelyn Merrick and Donald Craig, reporting from New Zealand, noted that crops there were reasonably free of fungal growth and that fish and oyster stocks had (so far) survived largely intact. Nevertheless, Evelyn was crash-mobilizing her own scientific team and wanted to pass along a few small modifications in Richard's cloning methods.

Sharon downloaded the advice, read it, and answered, "Welcome aboard, Dr. Merrick. Any friend of Richard Sinclair and Jason Bradley is a friend of mine."

Just then, Jason Bradley chimed in from the Pasteur Institute, noting that the French team had reached a consensus on Bill Schutt's genetic time bomb theory. They were supporting it, which meant that amberized insects seemed the most likely route to survivable clones.

Sharon recorded the message and relayed to Bradley the New Zealand team's advice.

The next message came from closer to home, from Dr. Sandra Shumway, of Southampton's Marine Science Center. It was a census of all the bacterial species now using up the oxygen in Long Island's waters and of toxic plankton blooms that were turning Long Island Sound and the

Chesapeake Bay into biological deserts. "The fact is," the report concluded, "there are more varieties of blooms taking place, and there are simply more toxic species in our waters than ever before."

Sharon shut off the pad, rubbed her eyes, and looked at the wall clock across the room. She had been working for twelve straight hours. Taped under the clock was a printout e-mailed from a group of paleontologists at Chicago's Field Museum. The wall chart showed, in excruciating detail, the periodic extinction record described by Richard and Bill. The lines spiked at the end of the Cretaceous, smoothed out again during the Paleocene and Eocene, spiked again at the terminal Eocene, smoothed again, then—right on schedule—spiked in the here and now.

She looked at the line that intersected her century with a mixture of sorrow and hate. If only it had come a hundred years later, or even fifty, there would probably have been people living on other worlds who could have survived this and preserved some vibrant remnant of civilization. But now—

"Why here?" she said to the impassive lines. "In all the unthinkable immensity of time, why did you have to come here?"

She had some ideas about that—some metaphysical, others not so metaphysical. She wondered if, perhaps, as the disappearance of each insect species seemed to ripple outward and undermine a hundred other species, might not the entire insect disappearance be traced, in reverse, to a cascade effect begun by the loss of just a few key insect species? Maybe Bill's genetic time bomb was really nothing more than a firecracker. If so, everything that was happening today was but the aftermath of a stupendous explosion that had begun as a very small flare—much like . . . Richard's crystallization event. She imagined the lowly aphid dying out, or simply ceasing to reproduce; and all the ant species that shepherded aphids, and depended upon them as humans depend upon sheep, began to die. And all the lacewings that fed upon the aphids died out. And in their turn, all the species that depended on the ants and the lacewings died out. And the shock wave just kept on expanding. And expanding. And expanding.

If this theory bore currency, it could all have begun slowly and entirely without notice, like the first aberrant cell of the tumor yet to be born. In the numbers game of evolution, it was possible for Sharon to believe that the cascade began decades ago, as a barely perceptible tremor, before mushrooming inevitably out of control. Perhaps *Melanoplus spretus*, the Rocky mountain grasshopper, had manifested as one of the cascade's first casualties. During the 1870s, from the high plains of Colorado and Montana east to Nebraska, *Melanoplus* had chewed every shred of plant life down to bare earth and pebbles. The grasshoppers formed living black clouds that blotted out the sun for hours as they passed overhead. In Kansas, the 1877 Grasshopper Act was passed, still on the books today—still offering bounties on dead grasshoppers—but the Rocky Mountain grasshopper had disappeared into history, and since the latter part of the nineteenth century could be seen only in museum display cases. The last living specimen was captured in 1902.

How? Sharon wondered. How could they just disappear? Had the billions of them—the trillion of them—eaten their entire food supply and then starved to death? *No,* she told herself. Some of them would have survived, and it only took two. Something else had happened to them, something no one quite understood yet.

Is that where it all began? she asked herself again. And she regretted that she would probably never know.

Tam and Georgiana found more and more opportunities for spying as the adults got busier and busier—so many opportunities, in fact, that most of the sneaking, and hence most of the fun, was going out of the game.

Most of the fun was going out of everything, these days. Even school would have been a welcome change of pace; but there was not going to be any school this season—at least, not normal school. Their parents had explained that other families, with other children, would soon be moving into the lab's guest houses, converting them into Army-style barracks. During whatever time they could spare, the scientists and their assistants would do the teaching.

"What fun is that?" Georgiana had asked. What could

be worse than having your parents and their friends for
teachers? Pass one little note in class, or make a little joke
and—no good. No good at all.

For Tam, it was all part of an increasingly bad and
unsteady world in which it was no longer a good idea to
get too close to anybody, because tomorrow morning they
might be "hurt" or "missing." First there had been
Mommy. Then Georgiana's friend the ant doctor. Then
Uncle Bill and Aunt Janet "went missing." Now, according to gleanings from the pad, whole places—places
with names like Saint Pierre and Port de France—had
"dropped off the face of the Earth," or gone "radio silent." Even the President was getting difficult to find. For
more than a week, now, Tam and Georgiana had been
unable to tap into the lab's white line, because it lay
mostly unused. Apparently, the President had stopped calling, distracted, perhaps, by more important concerns.

The pads gave very few clues as to what those more
important concerns might be, and what few clues could be
gleaned from the grown-ups' web-site chats were mostly
unintelligible. What, for example, was this Sandra Shumway person talking about when she referred to "blooms
of toxic species?"

"We've discovered the dinoflagellate from hell,"
Shumway had said. "It's living in North Carolina waters.
It must have been very rare, until recently. Now the mud
is full of them. Most of the time they hide in a cyst stage
in the sediment, until the fish swim over. Then they come
out of the sediment, attack the fish, kill them, then go
back to the cyst stage."

"What's a cyst?" Tam asked. "What's a dino . . .
dinofla—?"

"Dino-fla-jelly?"

"Yeah."

"I don't know. Let's ask the dictionary."

Georgiana circled the word with her touch pen, wrote
"define," and a quarter second later had an answer that
answered nothing, yet answered far too much:

Dinoflagellate: *Chiefly marine flagellate protozoans
of the order* Dinoflagellata, *which are important ele-*

ments of the planktonic biomass. These single-celled organisms can multiply explosively, creating the infamous "red tides," or poisonous tides. Dinoflagellate toxins are similar to those released by the anaerobic gas-forming bacterium Clostridium botulinum, which grows in sealed or canned foods (causing botulism). The toxins have a special affinity for the nervous system, interfering with production of the neurotransmitter acetylcholine, which is released at the nerve terminals and triggers contraction of muscle fibers. Dinoflagellate poisoning in humans occurs after ingestion of contaminated fish, shellfish, or heavily infested water, and generally manifests as muscular weakness, double vision, difficulty swallowing and speaking, progressing in a few hours to nausea, vomiting, and respiratory paralysis. Explosive growth or "blooms" of dinoflagellate populations may become self-sustaining biological chain reactions, in which the "toxic tide" kills fish; decaying fish increase the supply of dinoflagellate-supporting nutrients in the water; the nutrients trigger further dinoflagellate growth; more dinoflagellates generate more poison, killing more fish, and so on. Toxic red tides have been recorded for centuries and it is believed by some scholars that a seventeenth century B.C. injection of volcanic ash-derived nutrients into the eastern Mediterranean and the Nile triggered a red tide referred to in Exodus 7:20–21, "and all the water that was in the River was turned to blood; and the fish that were in the River died; and the River stank, and Egypt could not drink the water of the River."

"What is this?" Georgiana's brow furrowed. She wrote "define," and began highlighting words in the text—*marine, protozoans, planktonic, biomass, anaerobic*—and was just beginning to suspect that the computer was leading her into an infinite diverging chain of confusing words, when Tam's father walked into the room.

"Hi, kids," Richard said. He put two Cokes on the table—the first sodas Tam and Georgiana had seen in days—and asked, "Who's for a late snack and Monopoly?"

After a chorus of "Me!" and "Me, too!" the girls decided on Chinese checkers instead, and proceeded to beat Richard in six out of six rounds. Then, after a minor feeding frenzy, the three of them went outside for a late afternoon walk. From everywhere came the sweet smell of freshly mowed grass, mulch for the greenhouses— which would (hopefully) keep the vegetable harvest going through the winter. And there was the sound of machinery, also from every direction; "the refurbishing of the lab's Cold War–era security fences," Daddy had explained, "just in case."

They walked past the *Bluepeace* blimp and followed a path to a squat, glass and brick building with a large, corrugated steel garage attached to one side. The garage looked like a small airplane hangar and appeared to have been added rather hastily, almost as an afterthought.

The two hangar doors were open.

"What's in there?" asked Georgiana.

"Faded elegance," Richard said.

"Huh?"

"You'll see," Richard said, frowning. "It's a long story." He cleared his throat and led them through the hangar doors. Inside, the local electronics wizard, known to Richard and Tam as "The Don Peterson," was descending from the cockpit of the . . .

"Rocket ship!" said Tam.

"Not half the ship it could have been," The Don corrected. "It's just a prototype."

"Pro—?"

The Don laughed and made a squashing motion with his hands. "It's just a one-third scale model."

"Where's the big one?" Georgiana asked.

Richard shook his head. "There isn't one. Budget cuts. Around the time you were born, some guys in Washington got all lathered up against the particle-bed reactor."

The children gave him a questioning look.

"It's what powers the rocket," The Don answered. "A particle bed. It gets very, very hot, and when you pump cold hydrogen through it—pow!—big puff of smoke, and six thousand pounds per square inch roars out of the tail.''

The Don stood just over five feet tall. He dressed like a biker, and he talked about the great engine as if it were the last of the Harleys. He was descended from pirates, and horse thieves, and various unmentionables (but he was always proud to mention them, and hence the nickname, ''The Don''). His ship stood barely seventeen feet tall, on four landing legs, and was shaped like a sugar cone set on its head. The bottom of the heat shield had doors in it; they were swung open, exposing the landing gear and the engine bay. On the floor beside the rocket lay a smaller, squatter cone. Georgiana walked over to it and bent down for a closer look, adhering to the ''hands behind your back'' pose her father had taught her to use whenever in a museum or a laboratory.

''That's how we get back down,'' The Don explained. ''Every time it goes up, you have to bring one of those with you. It goes right there,'' he said, pointing to the rocket's nose. ''There's a little parachute inside, so you come down somewhat like an old *Apollo* space capsule. Once the ship's down to about a hundred and fifty miles per hour, the engine bay door opens, the parachute package is tossed away, and the whole thing just lands on its feet.

''When you're finished, just screw on another parachute cone package, gas her up with a little more compressed hydrogen, and you're ready for your next flight.''

''Can it go to the moon?'' Tam asked.

''It could. You'd have to stop at the space station first, once you got up to Earth orbit, so you could give it a fresh shot of hydrogen. From there, getting to the moon would be pretty easy. You could probably coast at a speed that would put you there in two days. Then you'd spend an afternoon collecting rocks. Then two days back.''

''Days?'' Tam was looking up at the cockpit, rather unpleasantly. ''It looks cramped up there,'' she said. ''Where do you keep the toilet?''

''We don't have one,'' said The Don.

''Yuck!''

"Yeah, gross," said Georgiana, and laughed. "So, you just do it in your pants?"

"Not exactly," The Don explained. "But it's really not much better than that. You have to put on a plastic glove"—affectionately called a shit mitt, he declined to mention—"and catch all the little turds as they come out. And in the weightlessness of space, they don't just drop free, as they would on a toilet on Earth; they actually hang there, and you have to reach back with your glove and *pull* them free." He noticed that he had the girls hooked, hanging on his every disgusting word. The Don laughed inwardly. The ship's nuclear reactor was far too removed from most people's experience, and was difficult for anyone except its builders or its operators to see as anything other than boring—or distant and unknown, and perhaps even dangerous because it was unknown. But the creature comforts of space—or even the occasional lack of comforts—*that*, people could immediately relate to.

"And you really have to make sure you get them all," he continued. "*All* of them. Because if one or two turds are still floating around, you may breathe them in while you're sleeping."

The girls got the giggles.

"Then, after you've got them all, you turn the glove inside out, put a bleach pill inside, and spend the next twenty minutes mashing the bag of poo in your hands until the bleach kills all the germs."

"Oooh, you couldn't get me to do that," said Tam.

"Yeah," The Don said. "I guess not. Back during the old *Apollo* days, most of the astronauts tried to hold it in for three days or more; and there was one who held it in all the way to the moon and back."

Tam tried to imagine it, and her face expressed pain.

"Can we look inside?" Georgiana asked, wanting to get a closer look at the cramped cockpit, so she could feel, vicariously, the primitive living conditions of the first astronauts.

"You can go up there and *peek* inside," said Richard, "but only if you're very careful and promise not to reach in and touch *anything*. Promise?"

"Promise."

After they had ushered the girls up the ladder, Richard turned to The Don and said quietly, "Do you think you could reach *Alphatown* in this thing?"

"Sure, why not?" came the reply.

"And," Richard said, after a pause, "if you removed the seat, and steadied yourself with lightweight harnesses instead and if you removed a few other pieces of nonessential equipment, and food, and water, and perhaps even if you went on a crash diet, do you suppose you could reduce payload mass enough to take, say"—he paused again—"two children?"

The Don looked at him strangely. "What the hell are you thinking," he said. "That this is planet Krypton, about to blow, and you're going to play Jor-El?"

Richard shot him an even stranger look, and said, "How did you know?"

Leslie outlined a new DNA program for the Nomad mainframe, and it notified her that twenty-two minutes would be required to complete the reprogramming and to test it. While the computer worked, she poured herself a very dilute cup of coffee and went outside for some fresh air.

She found Vinnie, one of *Bluepeace*'s pilot-engineers, pumping a fresh dose of helium into his ship's cells. The other three pilots, Vinnie explained, had been drafted for greenhouse duty.

"Airships just aren't a priority anymore," he lamented. "If I left it up to Administration, I swear to you, they'd pull this ship down, and break it apart, and cannibalize it for greenhouse pieces."

"Well, don't get too mad at me," Leslie said, "but I'm thinking of tearing a few pieces out of her myself."

"Et tu, Brute?" Vinnie frowned.

"No. It's not what you think. I'm talking about the dining tables, the chairs—and certainly we don't need paintings or carpets in there. The more we lighten her, the more people she can carry, and perhaps even a few chickens and goats."

Vinnie looked at her in frank astonishment. "What do you have in mind—a modern-day version of Noah's ark?"

He let out a burst of nervous laughter, and now it was Leslie who was frowning, disappointed that the pilot had guessed so easily.

Until this September, this awful September, Sharon had still held out hope of eventually starting a family, with or without a husband.

Precious little time for that now, she reminded herself. She had not worked so hard since her "farm girl days," back in college, picking potatoes for pocket money. Greenhouse construction did not pay as well—in fact, it did not pay at all—and the workday was longer.

The sun was falling behind the dormitories and the pine forest, making the whole underside of an anvil cloud glow canary yellow and sapphire orange. The breeze that riffled Sharon's hair carried a distinct underpinning of early chill. *Autumn will be here soon, and in full force,* she told herself. *We must work fast, if we're going to trap some small piece of summer indoors.*

Unfortunately, building materials were now in short supply, so the newer greenhouses became a patchwork of cannibalized parts. Furnishings and even beams from an old office building were being cut with sledgehammers and saws. Then the pieces were assembled into frames and covered with sheets of fabric and remelted plastic. They were not built to be pretty. They were there to ward off disaster.

Being surrounded by disaster, and surviving it, was nothing new to Sharon. Ever since a summer vacation pitched her into the Second Gulf War, her friends had always shared a little joke about her. They called it "the Sharon effect." Having walked away from, not one, but two plane crashes, and switched booking off a ship that went down, even Richard had decided that she was the passenger everyone wanted to be sitting next to when havoc struck.

Jackson did not think so. He had reckoned that of the billions of people who had lived upon this planet, it was statistically inevitable that a few (among them the seven who survived Hiroshima, then fled to Nagasaki and survived that too) would live through far more than the average share of close calls. He simply explained Sharon away as "a statistical anomaly."

Yet the joke persisted: "Sharon always lives at the edge of chaos, and always she will escape unharmed, by the skin of her teeth." Indeed, since the plane crashes, she had added to her credit a major car wreck, the Shanghai typhoon, the Auckland earthquake, and two tornadoes. "I've had every disaster," she once boasted, "except bubonic plague and a husband."

And she preferred to keep it that way.

Sharon had known only one or two marriages that could actually be described as happy. Most of her friends seemed to have chosen spouses with even less scrutiny than they had devoted to choosing their cars. The message was best driven home by a favorite aunt who, upon celebrating her twenty-fifth wedding anniversary, remarked: "You know, Sharon, if I'd killed the bastard twenty-five years ago, they would have let me out of prison fourteen years ago on good behavior."

Still . . . she wished she'd had a child. Then she thought of Tam and Georgiana, and the tribulation that loomed ahead; and she was suddenly glad she had not.

DAY 68

Jerry Sigmond's sudden departure from the airwaves had left behind a vacant niche; and talk radio, like most of civilization's pandoras, like nature itself, simply abhorred a vacuum. Now, an aging hothead named Puck had come east from California, ostensibly "to be here with y'all in the mote zone," but actually to occupy Jerry's niche.

On the morning after Leslie convinced Richard that he should spend some peaceful afternoons with his daughter—while there were still a few peaceful afternoons remaining—Jerry listened to his replacement's hype from the backseat of a police car, while his guard and his two arresting officers drove him to the city courthouse.

Jerry smiled. Puck presented himself as a former hot dog vendor from the streets of San Francisco. He represented the average working Joe, so he said, and in one

particularly interesting bit of monologue defined those who
went out and worked for a living as anyone being paid
less than a doctor or a lawyer; the clear implication being
that doctors, lawyers, politicians, and their ilk must be
raking in the megabucks and the megarations and were
therefore a nameless, faceless "them" who deserved to
be looked down upon and despised by ordinary decent
people. But even worse were the scientists.

"We are the inner circle," Puck said. "And those idle
rich, those Einsteins, those *parasites*, are all orbiting out
there, picking . . . picking . . . picking . . ."

His would-be replacement sounded as if he were beginning to believe in the craziness of his own press, Jerry
observed—to embrace it; and in time he would be swallowed whole by it.

"It is this Godless, intellectual elite—these so-called
secular humanists—who have handed us Godless
evolution."

A bit of a nonsequitur, Jerry thought; but it did not
matter. He could tell from the expression on Officer Guzman's face that this guy had style—style over substance,
but plenty of style nonetheless.

"Those secular humanists!" Puck shouted. "Those doctors, those anthropologist types, would tell us that instead
of moral men and women, we're nothing more than self-
conscious, self-centered piles of molecules. They tell us
that there is no God, just atoms and empty space. They
tell us that the Ten Commandments are therefore mere
suggestions, and that ethics are a matter of opinion.

"Well, I'm telling you that it is the teaching of Godless
evolution that has brought moral decay to America, that
has made even genetic experimentation seem perfectly
right and normal. And I'm telling you that this new layer
of decay—the motes, these crop-killing plagues we see all
around us—are a result of something that got out of the
laboratory. How can you possibly look at all this havoc,
and not begin to suspect that it is an artificial situation?"

Amy shot Jerry a worried and incredulous look. "You
said something like that yourself—not very long ago."

"About the scientists, yes," Jerry said, and he noticed
that Guzman and Cardillo were wearing the same expres-

sion as Amy, as if someone had walked over their graves. It wasn't just a matter of hearing Jerry's idea shored up by another; it was the fact that they were all coming to the thought themselves, or were on the verge of doing so. By echoing what was already at or near the surface, by thinking it for them, Puck was reinforcing his audience's trust of him, and sowing the seeds of distrust toward the nameless, faceless "them."

An ancient Lennon and McCartney tune came over the air—

They sang about revolution and evolution and wanting to change the world—

And Puck voiced over it: "The evolutionists. The gene splitters. The atom splitters. The Godless ones. I think we must include them, along with child molesters and drug dealers, as enemies of America."

Oh, that's a good one, Jerry told himself. *This Puck has all the personality and potential of a viper in America's bosom. I like him. I think I can use him.*

To anyone who was not living in denial, or in a mineshaft—or in a jailhouse, for that matter—the downslide was obvious. To Jerry Sigmond, it became suddenly apparent that his three escorts were living in denial, when they arrived at the hearing chamber and discovered that Jerry's lawyer had not shown up. Nor had the stenographer. Nor had the assistant D.A. Nor had the judge.

There were only security guards, a few reporters, fans, and curiosity seekers occupying the spectators' seats, and out in the halls the din of lawyers, clients, and court officials arguing about unannounced postponements and cancellations. Jerry checked his watch. They had arrived ten minutes early; but in such matters they should have been relative latecomers. It seemed to him that at least 20 percent of the workforce was showing up late today, or not showing up at all; the conversation between the two security guards, standing behind him, told Jerry all he needed to know.

One of them spoke a slightly broken English with clear inflections of Mandarin; the other spoke a more musical accent characteristic of Barbados or Jamaica.

"I'm worried," the islander said to his Mandarin friend. "I've got my kid's college fund all tied up in U.S. Treasuries and suddenly they ain't worth shit."

"I'm worried, too," said the other. "I did well to dump my citrus futures when they were high—"

Good move, Jerry thought.

"—but then I plowed it all into high-tech stocks and now, with no computer parts shipping in from India or Thailand, I'm getting wiped. My broker says her phones are ringing with all sells this morning, no buys; and she says there's almost nothing to buy anyway because people are afraid everything from overseas is contaminated with fungus, or prions, or something."

"My broker said yesterday that I should cut my losses and invest in something safe, like gold—but this morning no one was answering his phone."

Guzman looked at his watch and shook his head in agitation and bewilderment. "Fucking carnival," he said, then stood up, announced that he was going to find out what was keeping those horses asses behind schedule, and stormed out through the swinging doors at the back of the chamber.

Jerry tried to restrain a smirk. His case was never going to get anywhere near a jury trial. The world was breaking apart around him. And that was fine by Jerry. He overheard a spectator telling a friend that he had thought of taking his family to Seattle, only to learn from an aunt that rationings and shortages and unemployment were just as bad out there; and in the midst of this downward spiral that no one wanted to believe could get any worse, his guards fretted about rebuilding college funds and finding the judge. Jerry guessed that they must be among the last people on Earth still certain that in the colleges and the courthouses, life would go on, business as usual.

Snatches of overheard conversation told Jerry that vitamin C and multivitamin packs were getting almost as hard to find as fresh fruit and vegetables. Someone—lots of someones—were accusing lots of other someones of hoarding the stuff. Jerry guessed that it was only a matter of time before scurvy and a whole raft of other old, forgotten diseases began making comebacks. He decided that the guard who was so worried about his kid's college fund would do well to invest in vitamin C stocks. They would be worth more than gold . . . until the stock market ceased to exist.

Jerry supposed that if he could get out of jail before the world unraveled beyond recognition, his smartest first move would be to somehow corner the regional market in vitamin C. Not a difficult task, he decided, with the hoarders bound to run through their supplies sooner or later, and with the citrus crop gone to hell. Rose gardens, being only slightly less dependent on insect pollination than oranges, were only five steps behind them on the road to extinction. Rose hips were second only to lemons as a major source of vitamin C, and while it might be possible to implant rose genes into bacteria and trick them into producing the life-saving nutrient, Jerry supposed that it would be far easier to build a chemistry lab and churn out cheap rations of ascorbic acid. He began to envision a world in which items he normally took for granted would form the very basis of the new economy. But Jerry was not worried; he knew how to turn a good profit on other peoples' misery—and all the better for him if the legal system was beginning to crumble around his ears.

Looking around, it was possible for him to believe that this part of the country, and everything beyond, would soon be joining the Third World.

So be it, Jerry told himself: *If we're all going to be living in the Third World, then I'm going to pursue every means necessary to make sure I'm living at the top of the Third World.*

He leaned back in his chair and began to relax, humming to himself inwardly, silently. His secret inner voice hummed, *"Happy days are here again . . ."*

III
EVOCATION

Everything in the universe is hitched to everything else in the universe.

—ANON.

All philosophy ultimately dovetails with religion—which is ultimately reducible to history. All history is ultimately reducible to biology. Biology is ultimately reducible to chemistry. Chemistry is ultimately reducible to physics. Physics is ultimately reducible to mathematics. And mathematics is ultimately reducible to philosophy.

—ED BISHOP'S AND
RICHARD SINCLAIR'S FIRST LAW

God is in the details.

—FREEMAN DYSON

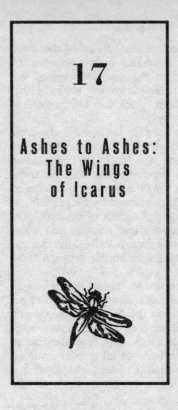

17

Ashes to Ashes: The Wings of Icarus

Late Holocene Cycle
Phase III

Darwin II was gaining speed. Since the discovery of the porphyrins, the spacecraft had sunk more than ten miles beneath the icefields of Enceladus. It still had miles to go before it broke through into the subsurface ocean, but whenever *Darwin II* stopped burrowing and quieted down for a look around, the world within the world was detectable by subtle groanings and creakings within the ice and by the distant roar of hydrothermal vents.

Each passing day, the reactor was forced to burn a little hotter, owing to scraps of meteoritic dust that fell out of the ice melt and accumulated on the bottom of the shaft, forming an ever-thickening, insulating barrier between the reactor and the ice itself. But the machine pressed on, clearing the debris as best it could, leaving behind clathrates of methane and ammonia, black ice, and yesterday. Weeks and weeks of yesterdays.

Nearly a billion miles sunward, in Earth orbit, the crew of Space Station *Alpha* had stopped paying attention to *Darwin II*'s dispatches. There was too much chaos down below. The ribbon of green vegetation that had, for thousands of years, snaked with the Nile through white desert sands, was now tinged yellowish brown by fungal infestations; and the river itself flowed the color of drying blood. Cairo and Thebes had descended into anarchy and widespread fires, as had much of the Jordan Valley, the suburbs of Athens and Rome, and the entire border between India and Pakistan.

Every hour and a half, the station passed through night and day—darkness, light, darkness, light. The fields of Sri Lanka had at last succumbed to the fungal onslaught and at night they blazed through veils of smoke, giving testimony to a desperate effort to slash, burn, and sterilize an infective agent that had been freed of all natural controls. Daylight revealed the Australian, Chinese, and American farm belts to be growing just as brown as India and its imprisoned island.

I'm sure I'd be able to see the color change from the surface of the moon without the aid of binoculars, Commander Harlan noted on his pad. Even the waters at the edges of the continents were changing, and though he was afraid to speak it to the rest of the crew—but perhaps they were also thinking it, and were afraid to speak it—the American knew that getting inside his shuttle craft and returning home was probably a bad idea.

Most governments, including Washington, had shut down what they called "nonessential services." This included the entire space program. Suddenly there was no money left for the ground crews necessary to support incoming shuttle craft. Not that money counted for very much. America's harvest was disappearing, and it seemed now that all the cash in the Philadelphia mint could not buy food from overseas. The night lights of Athens and Calcutta, either obscured by the smoke of food riots or simply gone out forever, were proof that civilization was sinking fast on the planet below. Harlan tried to convince himself that the people would hit bottom soon, and then they would pull themselves together; but he was beginning to suspect that being pampered, as he was, amid the loftiest of technology's achievements, he had failed to comprehend just how low bottom could be. In quick succession, all the farms had failed, the fish markets failed, the treasuries failed. CDs defaulted. Money was worthless. There was no tourism. No exports. There was little except spreading waves of refugees, outbursts of warfare, and threats of warfare. The fighting was bound to weaken any organized effort to find a cure for the world's ills, making nations and local warlords even more inclined toward fighting. The process was becoming cyclic and self-sustaining, like a serpent chasing its own tail. But this chase would not last forever. Nothing could last forever, least of all this horrible spasm. It would end when the serpent starved.

Harlan's vision blurred as California came sweeping up ahead, again. In microgravity, tears did not run into the lower eyelids, nor could they simply be blinked away. They gathered themselves into watery mounds over the pupils, and in this manner they behaved like badly cut lenses. One had to *rub* them away. Harlan closed his eyes tightly and rubbed, and when he opened them again, he saw.

America was in full daylight, covering half the sky. Sheets of smoke, in shades of yellow, white, and gray, were spreading now from the distant suburbs of L.A.

Why the fires? Why are they doing this? Harlan wondered.

He picked out the general vicinity of his own neighborhood.

Damn, I was short! Just another week and I would have been home with her.

—and home was a sea of smoke. Home. Could she have driven away in time, escaped ahead of the mobs? But there were fires in Oakland and outside Edwards. The whole state of California was going turtle. No, she was, as he watched, either being swept up in the horrors, or she was dead.

DAY 130, 10:40 A.M., KANSAS TIME

Thirteen hundred miles east of Los Angeles, in a spring-mounted cocoon buried deep within the earth, Scanner was finding it impossible to sleep. The headaches had started nearly two weeks ago, just after the first change-out rotation with the upstairs crew. The change-out was to have been a time of relaxation and sanity, up there in the Launch Control Support Building, with its spacious bunk rooms, windows, and a recreation room complete with pool tables and a sauna. They were even given two passes for a drive into town, Scanner and Widow-maker, so they could take in the latest movie and do some shopping.

Scanner guessed they were the last two passes the Air Force would ever issue. They had produced little cause for relaxation or sanity—just reasons for high blood pressure, headaches, and nightmares. The two men rode into town hoping to stock up on potato chips and Swiss chocolates, but they soon discovered that the base supply of government-issue Hershey bars had become, as near as either of them could tell, all the chocolate in the world. By the time they emerged from the third store, with nothing to show for their travels except a small bag of crushed and astronomically priced Cheez Doodles, someone had siphoned most of the gas from Scanner's car, leaving barely enough for the return to base. When he tried to buy a couple of gallons more—just a little added insurance for the trip home—Scanner found that there was no gas to be bought at any price. There was nothing, in fact, except the unnerving stench of rotting crops; and there was a look in the townspeople's eyes, a look such as Scanner had seen mirrored in pictures of the Dust Bowl era and the Great Depression, and he had a sense that these people looked upon him with fear and suspicion, and were hoarding anything of value from him, and from any other outsider.

During the two week change-out, he had watched the

wheat fields outside the electric fences shift from brown-spotted gold, to black-spotted brown, to black. He watched corporate wheat growers slash and burn the fields in an attempt to kill the infection. It was hopeless, Scanner observed.

He truly wished he had not seen the world above; and if not for the fact that his wife and his parents were out there somewhere, in that outburst of evil, he would have been truly thankful for the electrified fence and for a supply of food, fuel, and medicines that could, with a little rationing, last more than a year.

Scanner had plenty of reasons for migraine, but this headache never knew when to quit, and it seemed to throb harder every day, until at last it began to produce a mild but ever-present nausea. His favorite activity, reading, was becoming increasingly painful to his eyes, and his concentration seemed to be slipping. He wondered if he might be growing a brain tumor, and the thought sent a surge of adrenaline through him like lightning through salt water; for he understood, from his brief foraging expedition on the surface, that first-rate medical care was going to be very difficult to come by.

And sleep? How could Scanner sleep today, even without the migraine? Too much was happening too fast. The Chinese were annexing Australia and New Zealand. Calling China's behavior "reckless," the President was diverting a U.S. Navy battle group, led by the aircraft carriers *Independence* and *George Washington*, into the Coral Sea. A second battle group, led by the *Nimitz*, was finally responding to Sri Lanka's pleas for help and had taken position a hundred miles west of Colombo. Both China and India accused the United States of conniving with "separatist enemies" who might draw encouragement from the approach of U.S. warships.

"These wrongful acts constitute an important element of volatility in Chinese-U.S. relations," the foreign minister told CNN.

"We will by no means provoke warfare," added an Indian Foreign Ministry spokeswoman, "but if we are provoked and attacked, we must relentlessly destroy our enemy."

"The U.S. fleet is there to observe and to be helpful," General Andrews had announced. He then insisted that the regions were not on the brink of war; but it was Andrews himself who had called to put the war capsule on "yellow alert."

"Christ on a pony," Widow-maker had said. "Cap . . . are they really going to do it?"

"No way," Scanner answered, and then he'd gone on to explain that they would never begin throwing nukes at each other—which wasn't, Widow-maker thought, very reassuring. If history served him correctly, every military strategist of any renown had agreed, during the 1970s, that if two oil-producing nations ever went to war with each other, bombing each other's oil fields was "the last thing in the world they would ever do." And yet, when Iran and Iraq went to war, what was the first thing they did?

Presently, the pain was stabbing at Scanner's temples and circling around to the place where the neck met the back of his skull.

"Hey, Cap . . ." Widow-maker called from his console.

"Yeah?"

"Give yourself a break and try to get some sleep. We need you alert."

"I *am* alert. Everything's going to be okay. Just wait and see."

Scanner did not believe a word of what he'd just said. His body was slowly breaking down. He could feel it. The whole world was breaking down. He could see it, and hear it. One of the change-out crew, upstairs, had simply packed up his belongings and gone AWOL—presumably to be with his family.

"I wouldn't want to be standing in his boots," Widow-maker had said, "when they finally get around to court-martialing him." Scanner laughed. If America and the world broke down much further, taking leave without papers would soon have all the overmastering relevance of next season's World Series—none at all, presumably.

To Scanner, sleep was the most relevant concern of the moment. How else to perform the job he was trained for? Certainly not when he found it impossible to stay alert and he lacked the energy even to shave in the morning

and his skin felt prickly and cold and he began to feel
like a snail with a beard and some distant corner of his
brain began to *like* the feel of it and sleep continued to
elude him because of the headaches . . . the neck aches . . .
and the headaches made worse by Widow-maker's endless
replaying of the computer's Sinatra collection.

Sinatra . . . Sinatra . . . oh, how he was growing to
hate that voice grating on his ears and his neck, and on
the back of his skull. How he wished he could tear it out
of the computer's memory, how he wished he possessed
the power of a thousand suns, so he could strike out across
the world and erase every trace of Sinatra's existence.

But he *did* have the power, his subconscious realized,
with a start. And if the chain of command ever disintegrated, as ultimately it must, then in time the Thor missiles
would be his. All his, if only he played his cards right. If
only . . . he could possess his birds.

If only . . .

DAY 130, 1:40 P.M, WASHINGTON TIME

Fifteen hundred miles east of the Kansas wheat fields, the
President's pad showed a helicopter view of a Los Angeles
intersection filled with people. They were, to judge from
their clothing, ordinary shop owners and business people
and, in some cases, even quite wealthy. But there was
nothing ordinary in their behavior, or in the rage on their
faces, as they pulled a man from a truck and broke glass
over his head and dislocated his shoulders and kicked in
his ribs until he vomited blood. From the nucleus of the
mob, puffs of gunsmoke burst toward the helicopter, and
the camera pitched left in a dizzying blur before the
ground rushed up and cut the scene off with a wash of
static.

It was different in every city. L.A. and Chicago were
rioting, while Detroit, Cleveland, and Miami had pulled
together. Washington had surprised the President. Most of
those elected to positions of leadership had simply abandoned the city, and in their absence, it was the cab drivers,
the Nurse's Association, and the firefighters who had orga-

nized the mass construction of greenhouses on the Great Mall, who were now, with a team of curators from the Air and Space Museum, building excrement-fed, hand-pollinated hydroponic gardens along the avenues of sky-lit shopping malls, and who had come up with the idea of converting every basement into a mushroom cellar.

We just might be able to weasel our way out of this mess, the President thought, *if only we can hold it together just long enough for someone to find a cure.*

He looked out the bullet-resistant windows of the Oval Office and what he saw was a city whose people were going to make it through the coming winter, so long as they did not rebel against a diet of tomatoes, potatoes, and mushrooms—which were among the only crops known to possess a natural resistance to the black fungus. But there were worse choices on the menu: at the CDC, they had tried to cultivate the rapidly growing black fungus itself as a food source, by impregnating it with vitamin-producing genes from the very plants on which it preyed. The first patties delivered to the White House looked like and were shaped like hamburgers; but they tasted like rubber and left an aftertaste like gasoline.

I'd rather starve to death than eat that stuff, the President thought; and then thought he should be more careful about what he wished for.

The lawn below depressed him, because the array of soldiers and helicopters made this place look more like a maximum security prison than a presidential compound. The scene beyond looked a little better: the plastic-lined greenhouses running the entire length of Pennsylvania Avenue, and beyond the greenhouses a skyline that was brighter and more sharp-edged than he'd ever seen it before—owing to the gradual extinction of smog-producing traffic.

But beyond the skyline, the news was far from bright. At last count, more than ten thousand had died eating fish, clams, and lobsters hauled from the spreading red tides, and tens of thousands more who had survived the fatal harvest would suffer permanent damage to their nervous systems.

On one of the pads, behind him, CNN reported that,

incredibly, one small corner of the New York Stock Exchange was still functioning. Ascorbic acid and other local trade goods were being bartered; and gold, apparently, was still considered to be worth something. The President smiled. Culture lag was proving to be powerful medicine. He imagined that for those few Wall Street executives who had shown up for work, it had more numbing power than Novocain, maybe even morphine.

Another item reported that India would respond if U.S. ships remained in the Palk Strait dividing Sri Lanka from the mainland. In Washington, Andrews was quoted as saying the United States retained its right to move through international waters.

The sun had descended just low enough to tint the Washington Monument with crisp autumn gold, and to drive home the message that out there, in the east, the *Nimitz* was in darkness, when Amber Murdoch knocked on the door behind him.

"The door's open," he said, without turning.

Amber stepped into the room alone. "The Brookhaven group sends you glad tidings," she said.

At the words, he felt the familiar urge to be hopeful again, to believe that his country could be pieced together again, if only the insects could be resurrected. When he turned to face her, he was smiling. "The embryos? They're still alive?"

"Better news than that. They tell me two of them are actually hatching. We've got caterpillars, Mr. President. Twenty-four-million-year-old caterpillars."

"Then we *are* going to get through this after all. So, my crazy Long Islanders came through—cleared all the hurdles."

"Except for the Puck problem, sir."

The President flinched. "You mean, he's still on the air?"

"We've had five Marine helicopters searching for him almost around the clock," the chief of staff said. "And we've been unable to find him, or to pinpoint where he's relaying his broadcasts from. Yet somehow, he and Jerry Sigmond managed to find each other."

Amber scrawled something on her notepad, and theme music from the movie *Patton* came over the speaker.

"We picked this up at seven this morning," she explained.

As the theme music faded out, Jerry Sigmond announced, "Hello, New York. This is Sigmond and Puck for Radio Free America, and this morning there's only one thing to talk about, isn't there?"

"Yeah," said Puck. "Like what's the government done for *you* lately, besides wasting tons of fuel sending these black helicopters looking for yours truly?"

"You can call it the Great Famine, or the Great Bugout, or you can just call it the Plagues; but we all know that it boils down to the same thing: an unnatural, manmade situation. Nature just doesn't work this way—to its own destruction and across so many species lines."

"What he means," Puck said, "is that all this trouble comes to you courtesy of the same people who brought you the atomic bomb and held back all the cancer cures. You can call them the eggheads, or the nerds, or the Einsteins, but it all boils down to the same thing: Something got out of somebody's lab."

"I've heard some horror stories lately, about how American scientists developed a virus meant to weaken the economies of Africa and Asia by killing off all their honeybees; but the geniuses forgot Rule Number One of bio-warfare mechanics: viruses mutate. And while we pay the price for their foolishness, where are those scientists now?"

"Jesus," Puck said. "Sweet bleeding Jesus, you better know where they are."

"Yes. You would think they'd be out here, helping to clean up the mess they created. But, no. Out east on Long Island, at a place they call the City of Dreams, they've fenced themselves in and are living high off the hog— while the rest of us live like animals."

"Hunted like animals," Puck said.

"You bet. Black helicopters! What are they so afraid of? Are they afraid we're telling the truth?"

"You have a right to remain silent, so shut up!"

Jerry Sigmond laughed, his warm endearing laugh. And

then he turned serious again. "I have a little piece of paper around here somewhere that says something about the right to free speech. It's called the United States Constitution. Perhaps they ought to read it sometime. This was still a free country, the last time I checked, or at least it used to be until the likes of Richard Sinclair and Jackson Roykirk got involved."

"Birds of a feather . . ." the President said, and shut off the playback. "How do we stop this, before they get the whole lab trashed? Can we assign more helicopters to Brookhaven? Dispatch more patrols?"

"I don't think it will make any difference," the chief of staff said. "They're very clever. The last transmitter we found was hidden in an old pay phone, and the signal was being patched through by a phone call routed all the way around the world, at least four times. And it gets worse: We think it's all prerecorded."

"I hate this hacker bullshit!" said the President, and then he turned his back on Murdoch and went to the window. Thoughtfully, he hoped the miracle of amber-derived clones might just be enough to pull the nation out of this nosedive and he wondered how he could possibly protect the scientists and their caterpillars from Sigmond and Puck and their mobs.

DAY 130, 1:45 P.M., WASHINGTON TIME

The most useful butterfly tissues were those in which the cell nuclei had been thoroughly saturated by very fluid, sun-warmed tree sap. In such cases, the genetic blueprints contained within were so perfectly intact that even when the ravages of time had cracked a chromosome or torn holes in it, the adjacent pieces were held in place by the surrounding resin, as if by glue.

The trick lay in microsurgery, in the ability to extract an individual cell nucleus from the amber in ten cone-shaped pieces. The cones could then be scanned under a micro-MRI, as easily as one scanned a laser-engraved compact disk. In this manner, revealed by nothing more exotic than the telltale patterns of hydrogen atoms arrayed on hydrocarbon skeletons, entire chromosomes and their supporting structures could be distinguished from the tree sap, and could be reproduced within a computer's memory. The rest of the trick was not so easy. Even among the best preserved fossils, a single cell could not possibly retain the entire genome of its owner.

In Mona's case, six cells had to be sampled. From her male counterpart in time travel, whose DNA was even more degraded, eighteen cells were required. To obtain a complete genetic code, Richard Sinclair had invented a "match-and-patch" technique, in which all eighteen damaged sequences were lined up on the computer screen. Then, using whatever genetic markers they had in common, somewhat like the markers on a spectrum, the sequences were superimposed on top of each other. Though each DNA strand was peppered with gaps—the result of potassium-40 and carbon-14 decay, and the occasional cosmic ray track—Richard had decided to approach this problem in much the same manner as the archaeologists who had found multiple copies of the Book of Isaiah among the Dead Sea Scrolls, every one of them crumbled to pieces and mostly missing. In both cases, a program for matching and patching missing segments—for building a single composite "text" from partly damaged copies—had solved the problem.

Once everyone knew what the butterfly code looked like, the next step was reproducing it in a living creature. This proved to be a little trickier. The task involved comparing the butterfly code, gene for gene, against a spider's, and tricking the spider's genome into playing a game of "genetic piggyback." The game became possible only because all organisms possessed genes, DNA repair systems, and structural proteins in common with all other organisms. That the game was possible at all supported Bill and Jackson's idea that DNA really did not care wherein it dwelled, as it moved like an ancient parasite from body to body, from generation to generation, leaving behind an immortal trail. By understanding the trail—by truly understanding the footprints of genetic change—it was possible to build the embryo of an australopithecine man-ape by altering just under 1 percent of the DNA contained in the human genome. A mouse could be turned into a man by re-editing it only 50 percent. Even cockroaches and spiders, it seemed, shared nearly 15 percent of their primary regulator genes with humans.

Spiders and butterflies were, genetically speaking, relatively close to each other; and while surgically editing a man's DNA into a man-ape's was (given even the aid of computer-assisted "snip," "transport," and "paste-up" enzymes) a dauntingly tedious and time-consuming task, it was, nevertheless, at least three times as easy to change a spider into a butterfly, because arachnids and insects possessed fewer than a third the number of chromosomes found in primates.

From spider embryo to butterfly, Mona, the traveler from 24 million B.C., had become the world's first biologically morphed life-form.

"A biomorph," Richard called her.

There was a time when the morphing of mere computer-animated images on a movie screen had seemed fantastic. Now the age of biomorphing had arrived, brought about by necessity, brought about by catastrophe. Jackson Roykirk appreciated the irony. While Mona slept within the earth, preserving her DNA, the brutal aftershocks of the last mass extinction must have force-fed the development of intelligent life. Now, forced by another world-encircling wave of extinction, beings Mona had never lived to see were bringing her back to life.

But she still had a long way to go, Jackson knew. Resurrection was not yet assured. The first hatchlings were only now emerging, and there was the matter of finding the right food plants, and hoping that no genetic sequences had been misread, and accidentally stitched in, to produce a latent but fatal defect. Months might pass before he knew whether or not her progeny could repopulate the world. But Mona was patient beyond measure, he had observed. Mona could wait. Not so, humanity. Much as Jackson would have liked to think of his kind as masters of the world, he was forced to accept what the fossil record had been trying to tell him: it was the insects, by their presence and even by their absence, that had been ruling the Earth all along.

Termites and stink bugs and bombardier beetles, Jackson thought, *I bow before thee.* And then he decided that Voltaire had gotten it right after all: God is a comedian playing to an audience that is afraid to laugh.

"Daddy? Now that we have caterpillars, when can we go home?"

"It'll be a couple of years, hon—if ever."

"But that's . . . that's . . ."

That's a very long time, Richard noted, a sizable percentage of her life. But the operative words were, "if ever." He knew that the truth was, "probably never." The world seemed to be changing at a geometrically accelerating rate. The Marines had landed at Brookhaven, in their black helicopters, and more would soon be assigned. The place was now an armed encampment. Richard guessed that the soldiers must have laughed out loud when they received their orders: protect the baby butterflies, at all costs.

Before the military sealed the perimeter, dozens of workers had moved in permanently with their families, becoming just one more reason why Tam wanted to go home; the barracks were now as crowded as submarine staterooms. But by comparison to what the pads showed of the world outside, this was luxury.

There were reports of "road warriors," gangs of thieves on motorcycles who were exceeded only by gas shortages and fear of motes as causes for the stranglehold on the nation's traffic. In Suffolk County, the entire fishing industry had been wiped out by toxic tides. In central Nassau County, a power struggle that had begun as political infighting over the equitable distribution of food and vitamins was said to have deteriorated into a "police action," now on the verge of erupting into open warfare.

Richard sensed that biomorphing was becoming, increasingly, a race against time; and he was afraid that time had one leg up on him. He was, as yet, unable to answer the big question: How many biomorphs would be needed? Fungus gnats, just for a start; at least three or four species of fungus gnats. And dung beetles. *Ants—how many species?* Richard wondered. *And which ants were the right ants? And if we can't find a queen, is it possible to tweak a few regulator genes and biomorph one? And the bees: same problems, same questions. Ditto for the termites. And then there were the aquatic insects—absolutely essential if the fish were going to come back to the rivers.*

If we had another year, Richard told himself, *we might be able to resurrect enough of them to turn the trick.*

But he would not get another year. Other laboratories were beginning to drop off the net, as if they were somehow falling off the edge of the Earth, one by one. For the better part of a week, no one had been able to reach Jim Powell at the Vancouver research station, and now the entire city of Vancouver, without any warning, without even a cry of alarm, seemed simply to have winked out. And add to these developments the Puck and Jerry Show—which painted him, and Jackson, and the others as both destroyers of and parasites upon humanity. They were accused of hiding, now, behind electric fences, where, guarded by black helicopters, they lived among luxuries an emperor would have envied.

Richard did not know very much about Jerry Sigmond's newest sidekick, but he knew all about Jerry Sigmond. Desperate times always brought men who had charisma and could mesmerize to the fore—the Hitlers and Lincolns of the world. Mr. Sigmond was no Abraham Lincoln. In a world that had lost its natural immune defenses, he was an aberrant cell on the loose. Richard had seen this cell up close and in action; the monster worked very hard at making people like him, and the pattern of his life was simply this: The minute some poor soul began to trust him and let him get too close, Sigmond began crawling around in his mind and working him over. He usually got that person into something.

In more civilized times, Richard had survived attacks by Sigmond and his fans, just barely; and he knew that in a world descending toward chaos, the insufferable Jerry Sigmond would lead all his listeners into something. Most of them were hungry and frightened, and getting hungrier. Most of them probably believed that in a just universe, bad things did not happen to good people unless someone had done something bad. They needed someone to blame for their hunger and their fear, and Sigmond was willing to provide the scapegoat. He would send the hungry and the frightened crashing right through the gates, convinced that there was something evil in here worthy of murdering and burning, and of course, robbing. The greenhouses would be smashed. The laboratories would be smashed. The mainframes . . . the biomorphs . . . and this is how their last hope would end. Richard guessed that in the aftermath a few among the hungrier and even more frightened would realize, too late, that they did not have minds of their own. Whenever men succumbed to the rule of the mob, even a goat could lead them around; and Richard knew, better than most, that in this case they were about to be led by the devil.

DAY 130, 1:50 P.M., WASHINGTON TIME

"What in the hell are we doing here?" Ronni wondered aloud. According to the latest news reports, it seemed to her that if the *Nimitz* was supposed to be displaying and projecting power anywhere on Earth tonight, it belonged back home, offshore of Washington, D.C., or New York, not here in the Palk Strait, poised between India and Sri Lanka, two countries that were, in essence, going Code Blue.

"Ours is not to reason why," advised her copilot. "Ours is to respect the chain of command."

And so, here they were, Ronni and Al, cruising the strait at patrol altitude, under a full moon, in an antiquated F-14. Their Tomcat was, in fact, the last Grumman aircraft ever built, having rolled out of the Calverton plant, and onto old George Skurla's runway, in the spring of 1995. There were only a dozen of these planes left aboard the *Nimitz*; and while it was true that they took up less space below-decks than the Stealths, they were very loud in the infrared wavelength and they displayed, for the Indians, radar cross sections as wide as barn doors. But that was the whole point: The admiral wanted the patrols to be seen. Their mission was not to engage Indian ships and planes in battle, but rather to intimidate them into withdrawal from

Pakistan and the isle of Sri Lanka. For their part, the
Indians had no designs on engaging the United States
Navy—

(Did they?)

No, that defied logic; but Ronni remembered Dettweiler's warning that a wounded or desperate adversary often
struck out in ways that defied logic.

The logical assumption was that both sides were on a
mission of bluff. New Delhi had declared Sri Lanka and
Pakistan were part of India and not protectorates of the
United States. The secretary of state had said India would
face grave consequences if it continued to resolve its differences with Sri Lanka and Pakistan by force. Ronni's
squadron commander had declared that this would end
without untoward incident, but there was too much confusion for anyone to be making declarations. Dettweiler's
drones were picking up infrared hot spots all along the
India-Pakistan border. The fighting was fierce, and Pakistan was clearly the loser; yet news reports from home
suggested that Pakistan was repelling the occupation. The
reports also said India's foreign minister, who declared the
Nimitz's actions hostile, had lodged a protest with Washington. Amber Murdoch, however, said India had not
protested.

This was not a time to be playing games of chicken,
by everything Ronni knew.

Ahead of her, twenty miles away in the night, lay the
roving island runway—huge to the ground support crew
who lived upon her, as small as a postage stamp to a pilot.
Al called in the Tomcat's remaining fuel weight, to which
the ground crew would add the known weight of the fliers
and the empty weight of their aircraft as they fine-tuned
the tension on the deck's arrestor wires. Coming through
a patch of dense air, the Tomcat's nose dipped slightly.
Ronni compensated for it without a thought, and was concentrating on the red point of light in her heads-up display,
keeping the homing beacon nicely centered, when a flash
on the port side startled her.

"What the hell was that?" Al called over the com-link.
It was far away to the left of their flight path, three hundred miles or more, and it had left an afterglow that

streaked the clouds in that direction with brilliant yellow light. As they watched, the clouds faded to champagne orange and sapphire pink; and then the hull of the sun rose on the western horizon. A sunrise in the west . . . then Al understood. "Oh."

"This is Scorp," called a voice from the control van. "What did you see? Over."

"I think three million people just died," Ronni replied.

18

A Chronicle in Amber

The frustrating part was not knowing what had happened; the worst part was not knowing what was going to happen. The computer links to Los Angeles, Vancouver, and a number of other cities had been snapping off at a fairly steady rate, so there was plenty of cause for disquiet even before, half a world away, the city of Madurai exploded.

Wing III's communications systems were designed to operate even after nuclear weapons detonated somewhere nearby.

Captain Adam ''Scanner'' Handelsman listened to the increasingly stress-driven voices coming over the capsule's speaker system, and his headache worsened. The majority of the messages were not intended for his ears, but they came through anyway. The black book said that in time of national or even planetwide disaster, if General Andrews and the other commanders ever stopped transmitting, he and Widow-maker would own their capsule and, after a period of waiting specified by the book, could either keep their birds locked down, "in the nest," or allow them to fly off in accordance with Project Soresport's Sole Survivor protocol. The capsule's designers had dictated that even if the information getting through was confused or incomplete, in such times it was better that missile combat crews receive too much rather than too little news.

"This is Harlan calling from *Alphatown*. Multiple bursts over India and Pakistan. I say again, we are seeing a massive nuclear exchange on both sides of the India-Pakistan border."

The capsule's own seismic sensor array, one of the new ones that could hear the foundations of a skyscraper being dug in Manhattan, confirmed the observation. Parts of northern India were beginning to sound like an anvil chorus.

"Good God," Widow-maker said. "What do we do now?"

"What we're paid to do," Scanner replied. "We sit tight, and we see if this war spreads."

"*Soresport*, this is *Looking Glass*. *Soresport, Soresport*, this is *Looking Glass*. Exchange is confirmed. Situation is defense condition two, repeat: defcon two . . . no report from the van. . . ."

"Jesus wept," Scanner muttered to himself, and he wondered about his wife, up there on the surface. If the spasm tearing across India should ripple through all of Asia and leap across the Pacific—

"Correction, *Looking Glass*. This is *Blackstar*. Have received message from the van. *Alphatown* gives visual confirmation that the van is afloat. No Indian attack on U.S. Nav—* * *—plume nuclides eastbound—Tropic of Cancer east longitude eigh—* * twenty knots—gold and U 238 casings indicated—"

"Condition remains Strategic Alert; say again, *Blackstar*. Status is defcon two. *Tacamo PAC* out."

Scanner and Widow-maker looked at each other. Simultaneously they reached for and felt the keys dangling from their necks. Then they looked at the red key panels on their consoles.

"*Looking Glass*, this is *Blackstar*. Repeat, *Looking Glass*—the van has chimed in. *Alphatown* confirms exchange is limited to India and Pakistan only . . . no confirmation of—* *—"

"All Wing III commanders, this is *Looking Glass*. No India attack on U.S. naval forces. I repeat, attack involves India and Pakistan only, no launches against United States forces."

Scanner poured himself a large cup of coffee, and washed down four aspirin. He wondered if maybe the guy who went AWOL had the right idea after all. The thought of going topside, fueling up his Mustang, and racing off to find his wife did more than merely cross his mind; but he squashed the thought dead. There was duty; and so long as his junior officer laid off the Sinatra, and refrained from quoting T. S. Eliot or the Revelation of Saint John—

This is the way the world ends
This is the way the world ends . . .
I saw a pale horse, and a pale rider upon it.
And the name of the horse was Pestilence.
And the name of the rider was Death.

—Scanner felt he might be able to handle even the Apocalypse. He'd have to. *Have to*. There was no hope of going up to the surface for a change-out with the back-up crew, not with ESA—emergency strategic alert—in effect. Nor was there any chance of seeing his wife anytime soon, for he and Widow-maker were likely to be down here for a very long time.

He looked toward the center of the capsule, toward the living and sleeping area, where the floor was layer upon layer of vacuum-sealed rations. There were the basic—and notorious—K rations, with their tins of salted and virtually indestructible Spam, compressed bread, essence of malt, barley, wheat, and oatmeal; there were cans of sauerkraut, peanut butter, Campbell's chunky Manhattan clam chow-

der (they'd be fighting over those, soon enough), and condensed orange juice. They would remove the floor, a layer
at a time, slowly expanding their living space as they
burrowed into their food supply, like weevils.

Historically, the Germans had a habit of associating the
names of objects with the sounds they made. After bell
makers-turned-cannon makers learned that by closing off
the mouth of the cannon before lighting the fuse, the entire
cannon could be made to explode, the device they invented
became known as the *bum* (for *boom!*). In keeping with
this tradition, the first one-thousand-pound bomb was
dubbed *ein laussen bum* (meaning, ''a loud boom''). After
the first atomic bomb was dropped on Hiroshima, they
called the fission device *ein grossen laussen bum* (or, ''a
big loud boom''). The next obvious step was the fusion,
or H-bomb, which was pronounced *ein grossen laussen
bum all ist kaput!*

It was H-bombs, that day—the whole exchange, between India and Pakistan. They were not tactical weapons;
they were designed to vaporize towns and cities. They
were weapons of terror. Nothing less. And nothing more.

As news of the bombings raced around the world, fear
raced with it. In Singapore, where the last reasonably functional stock exchange continued to hang on, sustained by
what amounted essentially to betting against falling stocks,
clever investors were raking in fortunes . . . until the final,
bomb-induced panic rendered their money worthless. The
value of stock certificates, cash, even diamonds and gold:
gone, wiped away. They weren't important anymore.

On Long Island, infrared satellites revealed people moving in great amoebic masses toward the Robert Moses
Bridge. They knew the world was going mad. They knew
that the India-Pakistan war might escalate at any moment,
especially with the U.S. aircraft carrier *Nimitz*, its escort
ships, and at least two nuclear submarines sitting stupidly
in the crossfire. They knew that if it spread, the great
population centers were the last places on Earth in which
anyone with even a demented logic wanted to be caught.
So, on foot and by cart and on bicycle, the exodus began:
more than a half million people, trying to reach the wilder-

ness of upstate New York, Connecticut, and Massachusetts.

When a Skycam reporter landed near the Connecticut side of the span across Long Island Sound, he found what he estimated to be a quarter of Nassau County's population proceeding in a strangely orderly procession, with blank expressions on their faces. When he asked them whence they had come, they pointed toward the towns and said, "That way." When he asked them where they were going, they pointed away from the towns and said, "That way."

From that moment, the withering of the world's cities quickened its pace, as if in the final stages of a disease. Like the termite hives before them, the huge superbodies of social organization—and roads, and websites—were collapsing. Few were able to keep a grip on logic or sanity, after the first bomb fell on Madurai.

Jake decided that he must have been mad to linger so many weeks on Long Island, making his way only slowly eastward, and ultimately trading escape to the mainland for the comfort of a recently abandoned house. The whole second floor was a sunny living room whose huge, slanting windows were fitted with thin-film solar collectors. This meant that even during the frequent brownouts and blackouts, it was possible for him to operate notepads and television sets, and to receive news from the outside world. He could not be certain which would be worse for his two little girls: bringing them into the wave of human chaos that was said to be roaring on the other side of Long Island Sound or subjecting them to slow starvation, if not warfare, on the island.

The owners of the house had left behind a very expensive video system and great works of art, yet taken every scrap of food with them. Jake had thought he might be able to hunt squirrels and birds, but other Long Islanders thought of it first and, at least locally, had hunted them to depletion; and even traces of cats and dogs—there were none. He had sought out work in exchange for food; but no one was hiring. Now he and the girls were down to eating toothpaste, wild scallions, and tulip bulbs; and there seemed to be no options left to him except to join the exodus across the sound or to choose between Jerry Sigmond and the Marines.

He had tried not to fall in with Sigmond's gangs. He was not fooled by clever rhetoric. Jake Hoffman knew an abomination when he heard one. He also knew (hoped) that some small fraction of the rhetoric could be true. According to Sigmond and Puck, the Marines and the scientists they guarded were living like kings, out east in Brookhaven. Local rumor had it that they were even passing plant seeds and small amounts of food out through the gates. If *that* was true, Jake guessed that the gates must now be swamped with people and he would have no hope of getting near—but the possibility seemed worth investigating. He was alert for *any* possibility of feeding Wynne and Michelle, even if, as a last resort, that required him to mortgage his soul, or the souls of his children, to Sigmond's army.

And it might come down to that, he feared. Little else seemed to be working. The government's food distribution center in Freeport had proved to be a particularly bad bet—nothing except more chaos, threats, and sights which made him doubt that there was very much in humanity worth saving. The announcements of organized distribution centers had turned out to be fairy tales. The officers who might have become heroes seemed too well fed, and seemed to be giving packages mostly to their equally well-fed friends. Disenchantment, that's what they gave.

Jake had received one morsel of bread and, pretending not to be hungry, had given both halves to his girls. He then observed a young man sitting on a bench, savoring his own half morsel and clearly hungering for more. The man's child, a little blond boy of about three, glanced away toward a sudden commotion near one of the bread lines, leaving his own morsel unguarded on his lap. The father snatched it while the child was looking away and swallowed it in a single gulp. Jake thought he had never seen a sight so heartrending as the boy looking down at his lap and wondering where his piece of bread had gone, then looking up to Daddy in bewilderment, and Daddy looking back at him, trying to feign innocence, looking at him with an expression that said, *What's wrong?*

He learned something, then. He really did. No government, either local or national, was ever going to pull this wounded Earth back together. No prince was going to ride in on a white horse and save his two little girls. Sleeping Beauty was dead, and Snow White, and Rose Red.

He had, for a while, hoped to stay in the house indefinitely, or at least until the situation improved, but hunger was forcing the inevitable choice upon him; he could not bear to watch his girls sliding slowly and surely toward starvation. So, he filled a pillowcase with the few useful provisions he could find—a fully charged notepad, flashlights, knives, a BB gun—and decided that he would strike out toward the east with his daughters, eastward toward the City of Dreams, where, in addition to having a supply of plant seeds and food, they were rumored to have the airship *Bluepeace*. It occurred to Jake that if what was now a very bad situation sank to fucking horrible, the scientists, who must even now be picking out the safest places on Earth, might take his children with them.

"I need to tell you something," he said to five-year-old Michelle, as he stuffed a little panda into the pillowcase. "I need to tell you this, and I want you to remember it forever and forever."

"What, Daddy?"

"It's your mother," he said, and seemed to choke. "I loved her very, very much."

At first glance, more than a hundred days ago, when Jake Hoffman and Jerry Sigmond crossed paths at Kennedy Airport, Jake had been a doting father, taking a brief arcade and hot dog break between connecting flights. At second glance, it was easy to see that he was not what he appeared to be at first glance. He became a disturbed and disturbing creature, sneaking away under a false name, abducting his two little girls from their mother.

The second glance, like the first glance, scarcely provided a clue to what was actually happening, and why. Jake had been an electrician in Bangor. He was very good at his craft, very successful; and he believed that he would have had a happy life with Sheila, if only she possessed a will of her own. Her father was a cruel, pitiless man, who never tired of telling her that she had married below her station. His efforts to drive a wedge into the marriage did not cease even after Jake, in an attempt to hold out the olive branch, took up the slack on his father-in-law's debts. Jake noticed that Sheila was moving away from him, becoming more aloof, until at last the rift seemed irreparable.

About the time the crops began failing in India, Jake decided to take drastic action. He began hacking into his Social Security and DMV records, altering his identity, and the identities of his two girls. No one would ever find them until and unless he decided otherwise—and the fact of the matter was simply this: He did want Sheila to find them. He had planned to send for her at the proper time, via her notepad; and he had cleaned out the bank accounts in such a manner as to leave only enough money for Sheila to follow—alone.

Jake's escape to France was, at bottom, a last-ditch effort to save his marriage. The insects, of course, had intervened.

*　　*　　*

Sender: Sarzeb@sri.lanka.net,
To: wildhog.NOM OHM, 7737 -70
Regret no communications are now possible with Dr. Edward Bishop, or with anyone else at Lucent Technologies, New Jersey.

Leslie nodded, pounded the Save button, selected a type size that could not be read without aid of a magnifying glass, and ordered a hard copy from the printer. The entire message, after she trimmed off any excess paper, was barely half as wide as the nail on her index finger. With a tweezer, she immersed it in a little capsule of homemade resin: amber, a vault for the ages.

Leslie supposed that in central Nassau, those who had not fled across the water, and who were turning—probably more and more of them, now—to Jerry Sigmond as their Moses, must be . . . well, she would learn soon enough. There were preparations to be made first.

Presently, *Cyberdyne* was working on an Oligocene carpenter ant, while Jackson and *Nomad* smoothed the rough edges out of a newer, quicker scanning procedure recommended by Dr. Merrick's group in New Zealand. This gave Leslie the time to continue the project she had conceived when she began to realize that, although the caterpillars would soon be pupating, although they now had dung beetle embryos, and fungus gnat eggs, and the first ants might soon be on their way, none of the scientists were going to have time to do all that they planned to do. But that was not going to discourage them from doing everything they could until they couldn't.

In this interlude between biomorphs, Leslie was getting busy with a project for future historians, preparing what she was certain would be a record of the last days in the City of Dreams—

> *It's getting kind of close. We've got reports of a resistance movement in Connecticut, forming against refugees from Long Island. Also reports of fires in northern New Jersey, following armed attacks on oil refineries. I expect much of America is about to become a very special hell reserved for the living who wish they were dead (our only consolation being that everyplace else is beginning to look even worse).*

She had no idea who the future historians might be, no guarantee that they would even be able to read English. So she had included, also shrunk down to microscopic type, the pages of a dictionary with all the words cross-referenced in multiple languages. It was Leslie's modern-day, computer-generated version of the Rosetta Stone.

It occurred to her that the record might not be found for another thirty-three million years and that by then the historians (if such existed) might not even be the descendants of humans but, rather, animals. For a moment she considered providing a detailed pictionary, in which a word like *dog* would be followed by a picture of a dog; but she wondered if dogs, which would surely have disappeared by then if for no other reason than that they would have evolved into something else, would mean anything to, say, a few highly evolved vampire bats. For that matter, it was probably hubris to expect that the troubles of a few humans living their last days in a small corner of a sinking world would, after the passage of millions of years, have any meaning at all to another species.

So she decided against anything larger than a "bare bones" pictionary. Unlike a multilanguage dictionary, she could not just tell the computer to punch it out automatically. It required work—tedious work—and more than a thousand pages. It would have left no time, or room, to place anything else in the amber—

So here we sit, more than a little frightened, as all around us the world's biological clock resets itself. How strange it is to sip what may be the last clean drinking water we will ever have, and to think that blooms of putrefactive bacteria in the waterways, and the mites, and the black fungi, and the rest of the plagues have always been waiting on the ecological sidelines, counterbalanced by insects. And strange, too, it is to believe that the lowly and wretched fungus rot will inherit the landscape, feeding first on dead or dying farms and forests, then creeping as great wood-devouring mats into the graves of our cities. Nature resetting itself. It should strike you as a marvel: How chance operating over vast periods of time begins to look like design, giving the illusion that there is a malign intelligence about evolutionary change—which is at once exhilarating and frightening.

She had considered preserving some of the great works of literature: *Claudius the God, Dante's Inferno, The Tempest, The Fountains of Paradise*—but in recent decades millions of copies had gone out to the world, and somehow, somewhere, she expected at least a few of them to survive. But history? For all Leslie knew, no one else in all the world was compiling a history of these days. There was only room enough in the amber, and time enough at the lab, to snatch little vignettes—

This is a series of three frames downloaded from the Alpha *Space Station* (Alphatown) *and photore-*

*duced for amber embedding. It shows a bright flash
erupting in northern India, apparently over the city
of Calcutta.*

And she decided, almost as an afterthought, that the
children should be involved in the project. Most of them
drew stick-figure parents smiling and waving from the
front door of the barracks. Or they drew pictures of zuc-
chini flowers and pumpkins growing in the greenhouses.
These she reduced, and embedded. Only a handful of the
children wrote actual messages to the archaeologists:

*Dear people in the future, I hope you don't have
hunger and bombs there . . . or motes . . .*

On the table before her, she had produced three piles
of amber capsules filled with little strips of paper. She
merged the three piles into one, tossed them into a bucket
of freshly melted resin, and stirred. After it hardened, she
would bury it in the laboratory's landfill. Richard had told
her that in 1938 and 1964, time capsules had been buried
in the Flushing World's Fair grounds, with artifacts and
messages to future generations. But when historians tried
to determine, in 1992, exactly where the capsules lay, they
realized that no one knew any longer, and that no one was
ever likely to find out, because there was really nothing
in the city park that would bring archaeologists to dig
there. Richard had suggested that if she wanted her time
capsule to be found, she should bury it in a garbage pile.
Leslie laughed, upon first hearing this, but Richard cut her
laughter short. He had spent years in the deserts, descending with spade and toothbrush into the cellars of time,
peeking in on the lost worlds of the Minoans and the
Babylonians, and he reminded her that one of the first
places he went to, whenever he broke through earth into
a dead city, was its landfills.

"The refuse that ancient people left behind," he had
explained, "includes broken pieces of pottery and other
discarded implements of everyday life. Because they were
garbage, they were left undisturbed by later civilizations,
and because they were left undisturbed, layer upon layer,

garbage dumps always have been, and always will be, highly prized time portals to archaeologists. If it were up to me, Leslie, we'd have built our landfills even higher, and made pyramids out of them.''

Pyramids . . . tombs . . . She resumed work, preparing a new strip of paper for a new amber nugget. A progress summary and a strip of queries from a lab in the Azores came off the printer and was embedded. A report from New Zealand began, ''We all agree here that biomorphing is the best hope for a cure,'' then lamented that while the North Island's resin deposits were, as a rule, more than ten thousand years old, they were also depressingly free of insect fossils. Leslie embedded the report. She preserved another from Oman. And notations of a desert of silence from Vancouver . . . stop.

She sipped tea that was still warm but very diluted, owing to a tea bag which had already been used four times. No sugar, of course—every grain of sugar was reserved for the biomorphs. No lemon, either. She wondered how much longer the lab's generator would keep the lights and the mainframes going. *This won't last,* she told herself, and began to record the latest historical revelation:

> *I think Jackson, and Sharon, and almost everybody else around here makes too much of our successes. We have biomorphed no more than a half dozen insect species, and we have no guarantee that any of them will survive the winter. Richard has pointed out that we may have to do this hundreds of times, and I'm afraid I have no choice but to agree with him. If this is how the age of dinosaurs ended, with a whimper, and not with a bang—No! Why couldn't it have been an asteroid or a comet falling upon our civilization? We would have been able to beat that. But this? Death of insects? And then the soil—the very skin of Earth—rotting? You can't defend yourself against this sort of thing. You can't destroy it. You can't reason with it. And now this struggle to make a handful of insects? Meaningless! Richard knows it. I know it. We're like corks swept up in a tidal wave. But Jackson! He keeps telling me that*

what happened to the dinosaurs will not happen to us, because we're a lot smarter than the dinosaurs, and a lot more adaptable. Denial. But sooner or later he'll come around to seeing that the only way out of this mess is to load up the Bluepeace *blimp and call, "All aboard for Ararat!" Yet for now, denial holds most of our little clan together, and keeps the biomorph project going, and I guess when it all comes down to the very bottom, at least we'll be able to say, in good conscience, that we did not sink without firing a shot. So I held my tongue today, for a change. I did not remind Jackson Roykirk that seventy million years ago the dinosaurs were a lot smarter, much more widely adapted, and a hell of a lot faster than snails and slugs. The lowly slug is doing very well, thank you. Ditto for fungi and mites. Maybe nature is telling us that size and smarts, grace and speed don't count for very much.*

And there you have it, she told herself, feeling ever more the historian. It was her best lesson of the day, and she decided she should drink to that, if only there were something left to drink.

19

Return to Babylon

DAY 131

Historically, the Americans had a habit of wrecking their own language with political correctness and doublespeak. Somewhere between the 1960s and the 1990s, "plane crashes" evolved into "downed aircraft," then into "in-flight anomalies"; the final evolution suggesting that nothing particularly bad had happened. Denial: it was a very powerful potion. People fired or laid off from their jobs became "downsized," then "experienced a sudden expansion of career opportunities." Again, it was difficult to tell, from the phrase alone, whether this was a good thing or a bad thing.

By the time the motes emerged, plane crashes were being called "unscheduled disassemblies of aircraft," so

304

it came as no surprise to Tom Dettweiler when the horrors north and west of the *Nimitz* were officially termed "multiple unscheduled energetic disassemblies of thermonuclear devices."

His screens showed a clear, starry night; but in the direction of the cities the stars were blotted out by towers of clouds drifting east. They did not reflect the moonlight, like rain clouds; but, rather, they absorbed the light, as if someone had sprayed black ink across the sky. Tom guessed that tomorrow afternoon, black rain and radioactive acid would be falling upon Burma's rice fields—what was left of them. He wished he could send his drones in for a closer look, but whatever they saw of the fires would be of interest only to historians; and sending drones into the war zone was forbidden, now; and it made for crummy history, anyway, Tom judged.

(Sour grapes?)

According to the latest orders, he wasn't even allowed to go out on deck, much less launch a robot. No one except essential personnel—ground crew for the planes—was allowed outside. So far, the fleet had managed to stay out of the line of fallout and crossfire, but the situation could change at any moment. All flood doors and watertight compartments were sealed. In its present state of emergency strategic alert preparedness, the *Nimitz* could be blown into a dozen pieces and, according to the guys who had designed the compartments and the seals, most of those pieces would remain afloat.

Tom hoped the carrier would not be called upon to put that theory to the test. There was little reassurance in the knowledge that none of those oh-so-clever designers had ever come aboard for a cruise.

"Still clear ahead and below," Scorp announced.

All the ship's radar and sonar systems were on. The Tomcats were up, very radar visible, a full squadron of twelve; and even the two escort subs had cranked up their speed screws, making themselves very noisy. The *Nimitz*'s new sensors were very good at what they did, even with the screws blaring (indeed, with proper filtration, cavitation from the ship's own propellers could actually be used to enhance sonar resolution). Washington was ordering the entire fleet home. Suddenly the rules had changed; the first rule of order: Get out of harm's way. The current catch-phrase in the military for such orders was "strategic with-drawal," a polite expression for what the officers sometimes called "the Monty Python Maneuver," mean-ing, "Run away! Run away!"

The task force was both advertising its retreat and, with radar and sonar shouts, projecting a hemispherical shell more than twenty miles in radius, into which not even a seagull or a school of minnows could enter without being noticed. The force was steering a hundred miles clear of the continental shelf, where the bottom was shallow enough to be within cruising depth of Indian submarines, and might offer hiding places for them. In the strait, with fully two miles of water below, any so-called lurkers would be forced to hover within the water column, well above crush depth, where they could easily be illuminated by sonar.

Scorp's screens continued to show *all clear.* "They don't even seem to be looking for us," she said.

"Unless the Indians have a few Stealths left," the recon man added. "Or unless they're flying a little covert, just outside our range."

"I suppose they're too busy right now to be thinking about us."

"I wouldn't suppose very much at a time like this," Tom said. "For instance, everyone's concerns seem to be focused on India. They're the ones who have been making all the noise about our so-called 'hostile actions' in the strait, so if anything else goes wrong, they become the obvious suspect. But they're also the bigger, better armed of two warring nations, and almost certain to win. If any-one were going to try drawing the United States into this war, I'd be more worried about the side that's losing."

"Pakistan?" the recon man asked.

"And it would look like India," Scorp said.

"Again, there's no telling at a time like this," said Tom, and he hoped that he, Scorp, and the recon man weren't the only ones who realized this.

"God!" Scorp growled. "What a tangled web we weave."

Presently, the entire formation was moving south at twenty-two knots, two hundred miles southwest of Colombo, and more than a hundred miles southeast of India's perimeter of land-based air cover. The last trace of Indian naval activity, called in by an F-14 scout, had been in the north, just beyond range of the *Nimitz*'s air cover. The clearest exit was south into the open spaces of the Indian Ocean.

Minute by minute, mile by mile, the computer-generated maps showed the way to be clear of all except a pair of whale carcasses in the deep scattering layer, and near them a school of sonar shadows, barely denser than the water itself, each about the size of a New York City bus. "Squid," Scorp announced. The beauty of the system was that it showed what your sensors could detect in exquisite detail. The problem lay in what it could not show, such as the sub that had passed through these very same waters, directly across the *Nimitz*'s path, two days earlier. It had left no sign of its passage, save for three hydrophone arrays and a handful of rubber-coated, sonar absorbent mines, each measuring only two feet in diameter. The arrays and the mines had plunged two miles to the bottom, where they blended undetectably with mud dunes and giant sea cucumbers.

A third of a mile away on the *Nimitz*'s port side, the escort submarine *Argus* had just passed within a quarter mile of a mine emplacement. Far below the horizon, the one man and two women listening to the hydrophones realized they had just scored a lucky shot; for in the world of tactical nuclear weaponry, a miss was as good as the next mile.

In the depths, a weight was cut loose, and the mine began to rise, slowly at first; but within fifteen seconds it had reached an upward terminal velocity of twenty-two knots. Left on its own, it would break surface in six minutes. In two minutes it would be vulnerable to submarine and carrier-based countermeasures.

The business end of an atomic bomb was heavy, neutron-emitting metals, cut and arranged into a very specific geometry, so the easiest way of defusing it was to knock that geometry out of alignment. One did not even

have to take a high school physics class to know how to
disarm a nuclear weapon: you simply gave it a hard
whack.

But this bomb was not going to get anywhere near being
vulnerable to a whacking. A little sensor on its underside
kept track of its upward velocity. Twenty-five seconds into
ascent, it was just over three hundred feet above the bed
of the ocean and at least a minute and a half from the
window of vulnerability. Three hundred feet of height was
all it needed. Now, rather than absorb a major portion of
the blast, the seabed would reflect it at the surface. *Argus*
and *Nimitz* might just as well have been two fleas blundering into the barrel of a shotgun.

At precisely that moment, halfway across the world, the
President had just turned down a demand from General
Andrews and Amber Murdoch to clear out of Washington
and relocate to Camp David.

"We have to work by example," he protested. "I'm
not about to leave this city, not so long as its people are
pulling together. Leaving now would be taken for exactly
what it is: elitism, abandonment."

The President closed the pad-line on Andrews and Murdoch, and reviewed the latest CNN footage of Los
Angeles, and the *Alphatown* shots of India, as he waited
for the Brookhaven group to get back to him on the white
line. There was loud hammering outside. Against Andrews's advice, he had ordered the Marines to pull down
the rose garden, to withdraw their security perimeter nearer
the White House steps, and to give most of the White
House lawn over to greenhouse builders.

They used to call this place Babylon on the Potomac,
the President reminded himself. *And yet the city holds up
so well*. He wished he could say the same for California,
Connecticut, and northern New Jersey. His pads showed
twisted bodies still lying in front of L.A.'s Beverly Hills
Hilton after many days, and there was footage of a lethal
resistance by one Connecticut town against refugees who
had swarmed across the Long Island Sound bridge. The
townspeople had actually sent a helicopter to dump sulfu-
ric acid on women and children. And then a self-

proclaimed militia came after the fleeing wounded. A CNN cameraman recorded an infant being shot out of its mother's arms with such force that his little shoes flew off. The next scene was too much for the President to bear, as the woman, with an expression on her face that he had never before seen, gathered up pieces of skull and pinkish-white matter and tried to push them back together again. The man who had fired the shot crept up behind her, and was about to fire another round when he suddenly clutched his throat and toppled. The reporter had apparently crossed the journalistic barrier between the observer and the observed, and become a participant in the story he was reporting.

Watching from the safety of his office, the President's world tilted irrationally, like a dish, and he felt as if he were standing on its edge. Every new frame of video showed streets of broken glass, overturned trucks, and debris that included smashed LTV sets. Everywhere the cameras turned he saw scars: office buildings in Los Angeles still smoldering, their former executives, with a look of madness in their eyes, offering for barter powdered milk looted from hospitals.

A couple of hundred miles north, these same images were being relayed directly to Brookhaven. Richard's world, too, was tilting. There was a sick, twisted sense of déjà vu about the whole mess. He'd seen this before, all of it. He had spent a fair portion of his career digging in ruins, often finding civilizations stacked on top of each other like the layers of a giant cake; the oldest, most romantic, and mysterious of them always lying at the bottom of the mound, naturally. But now, for the first time, he saw the youngest, uppermost layer of ruins still gleaming in the daylight—the beginning, perhaps, of the next Atlantis legend. Coming to terms with the destruction of ancient settlements—with the loss of the Minoans and the Babylonians, and behind them the dinosaurs—had always been exciting to him, even rip-roaring fun, but this was too immediate. This time it was his own home in Long Beach, and the homes of friends as far away as Tucson and Paris, that were becoming the substance of archaeology. It was a painful and belittling picture to behold. There was no romance in it. No dignity either.

He came to the scene of the mother and child in Connecticut.

"I wonder if Leslie will put *that* in the amber," he said to no one in particular, and shut it off. He then wrote the appropriate numbers on his pad and returned the President's call.

"Leslie Wells tells me you want an archaeological view on all of this?"

"It might help."

"I don't think so," said Richard. "I . . . I hear people have begun moving back into Long Beach. They're cutting up the boardwalk for firewood?"

"It won't do them much good. Outdoor wood is usually soaked in all sorts of preservatives, isn't it? You wouldn't want those chemicals burning in your house."

"It won't matter, in the end." Richard breathed. "Look . . . I don't want to wax too pessimistic, but even if we already had all the different species of biomorphs, it would take years to repopulate Earth with insects. That's why I keep thinking about the crash of civilization in ancient Babylon—the droughts, the crop failures, the city people becoming nomads. Do you know it's the fall of Ur you're actually reading about in the Bible, when Abraham begins his wanderings?"

"Yes . . . I've heard that."

"So, what do you suppose the populations of Long Island and Connecticut a year from now are going to look like in comparison to what they were before the insects died? I'll bet you'll find that there are a couple of million people missing."

The President shook his head slowly. "Even without the mites and dinoflagellates, we'll be facing scurvy, cholera epidemics. . . ." Already, power outages were spreading across the country, which meant no clean drinking water. And the river water was polluted with rotting animals, and in most places the people did not even have fuel with which to boil the water. In some of the towns the only fuel was whatever the citizens could scavenge by cutting up furniture and trees. The President expected they would exhaust these sources by spring, and then—what would they do *next* winter?

"Suddenly, Mr. President, you're going to see a real decline in population. It happened many times in ancient Babylon, and because those people were always writing the details of private life down on clay tablets, we have a very clear record of the early stages of collapse."

"Yes, it was usually economic collapse, wasn't it?"

"Exactly. It's after the economy went that people started charging the city gates, tearing down the monuments, murdering their leaders. And each time, their economy crashed because of nothing more dramatic than the gradual buildup of salt in their irrigation ditches. Scariest thing I've ever seen: How easy it is to bring on a cascade of economic failures at the very first stages of environmental degradation."

"Leslie Wells seemed to think me a little dumb to have expressed those concerns a while back."

"Well, I'd say your concerns were right on the mark," the scientist observed confidently. "In Babylon, it always started with warehouse scribes recording diminishing returns and wildly inflated food prices. Property values declined. And then trade collapsed, and you'd get records of warring city-states and rebellion, and then the record invariably broke off . . . except for one case I know of in which a lone scribe wrote, 'Ur is destroyed. Bitter is its lament. Evil has descended upon our land. Bodies dissolve like fat in the sun. The gods have abandoned us like migrating birds. Smoke lies over our city like a shroud.' "

"So it's environmental degradation first," the President summarized, "then collapse of the economy. Well, we've already run through those two phases. Next it's the collapse of authority."

"We're in that phase now, I'd say."

"What happens next? What happens between the first rebellions and the scribe who sees smoke lying over Ur like a shroud?"

"It seems to go quite quickly at the end, as near as I've been able to tell. Archaeologically, it looks like a universal disappearance. And the difficult question, when a civilization falls, is whether the people die or whether a lot of them wind up practicing lifestyles that are archaeologically invisible, which would be tribal nomadism . . . as I say, your biblical wanderings of Abraham and Lot."

"Or, in modern times, Mad Max syndrome," the President said quietly.

"Gee . . . could be," Richard said. "It's hard to pick out very many details from a culture's last days, because when more than half the population is starving and, among the remainder, those who have any energy left at all are busy venting their anger and tearing down the monuments, people usually stop keeping historical records; and then it's almost impossible to see what's happening. So we don't really know how it all plunges down in the end."

"That's probably just as well," the President said. "We'll find out soon enough, unless you get those insects out. I don't suppose—" He stopped in mid-sentence. The red notepad—the bad phone—was chiming again.

The universe was full of such intriguing, seemingly impossible scales of time and space. The part of a second during which an atomic bomb compressed its innards was so infinitesimally small that from the bomb's perspective the world of man ceased even to move. During that chip of time, the actual, reactive heart of the bomb was barely larger than a golf ball, yet it produced a light so powerful that it could be glimpsed through the bomb casing (if one possessed cameras fast enough, and camera boxes hard enough), as if the casing itself were of no more substance than a plastic sandwich bag. Indeed, it would have shone through a slab of steel, two feet thick, as if it were a sheet of glass a quarter inch thick, before the steel dissolved into a scatter of electron-stripped nuclei, all in that instant. And the rest was aftershocks.

"Circling around for final, with one thousand pounds of fuel remaining," Ronni announced to flight control. She banked slightly east, and then, more than a mile below her in the night, a light appeared—a light of such intensity that Ronni believed she could distinguish details of typography on the floor of the Indian Ocean, though she understood the water to be more than two miles deep. And she knew—*knew*—that she was seeing the backlit shadow of

Argus down there, and lightning bolts, underwater lightning bolts snaking for miles and miles in every direction.

In the first part of a second, long before she could breathe a startled *What?* into her com-link, the light under the sea faded from a dazzling white pinprick to a large yellow disk, then swelled to a greenish-yellow sphere. She felt, at that same instant, an electronic buzzing in her ears. It had reached her faster than sound, as fast as light itself, as if she were flying through a giant electron gun—which, in fact, she was.

By the time she pulled back on the stick, jerking the Tomcat up and—hope against hope—away from the nuclear storm, the very waters had snapped back from the place where the mine had been; they retreated a quarter mile in every direction and formed a low-density bubble whose walls, shining brighter than a thousand suns, were a compressed plasma in which every element ever assembled in the universe had been re-created. By that time, the bubble's lower hemisphere was already impacting the seabed, and back-blast effects were already rendering the bubble unstable.

Looking aft and directly below, Al saw what seemed to be cubic miles of seething hell bursting up toward the cigar-shaped silhouette of *Argus*. The silhouette shattered before his eyes, shattered into ten thousand pieces, shattered to dust; and then the shock bubble touched the ocean surface and yawned open, and its mouth was a steam catapult aimed at the stars.

Ronni punched the afterburners on full and used the thrust-vector capability of the Tomcat to scoot horizontally as the storm's boundary shot vertically and astern. She would have thrown back her head in triumph, if the G forces had not already done so for her. She was going to live, at least for a little while, thanks to a bit of flying skill combined with the great good fortune of being located just outside the edge of an atomic geyser whose plume was now shooting miles overhead. If only the wings would hold together through the coming shock wave, the stories she would have to tell. No one had ever flown through an atomic blast before . . . but she had been slowing to approach when the explosion occurred, and her plane was

still subsonic. Afterburners were just not designed to kick
her away fast enough—not because Tomcats would not
withstand the acceleration, but because human bodies
could not—and the compression wave was spreading horizontally now, faster than Ronni's plane.

The screens in the *Nimitz*'s van had shown a glow in
the east, a glow that came from near and far, from the
water itself.

"What the—" someone called in a tinny voice over
Scorp's receiver. The tinny voice, as much felt as heard,
barely preceded the glow—yes, Scorp was sure it came
first, *sure of it,* and its tinny quality meant the caller was
speaking through sonar. Radio waves did not travel very
well through water. The sonar call meant someone aboard
Argus was crying out to anyone who might be in a position
to help.

"Countermeasures!" the voice shouted. "Contact bearing—" The com-link went dead.

For a second, perhaps for two, Scorp tried to snatch at
the possibility that the call had been ended by an equipment failure. This was true, but it was not the sort of
equipment failure she had in mind. Her hope was dashed
when the shock wave burst her sono-speakers and cut
across the sky like a mighty wing. After it had passed, the
view screens displayed a column of steam and brilliant
blue lightning spreading up, and up, and up; and an infrared spark cometing down: one of the F-14s.

"Damn if we're not gonna make it!" Ronni breathed
with relief after the compression wave passed and the air
cleared. Then she saw her runway, down there, floating
near the very rim of the geyser. And she saw the tidal
wave, huge and wedge-shaped with a thousand white fingers arching toward the flight deck and the island stack.
It must have started out at about five hundred feet, and it
was losing height rapidly, to judge from the glimpse she
had of it—

"EMP," Al called. "Hardness systems worked. We've
got most of our electronics intact."

"Good."

Ronni shut down the afterburners and leveled out, thinking herself lucky to still be taking in air and flying a plane that seemed to be operating—at reduced power but operating nonetheless . . . until she made the mistake of banking the Tomcat to starboard for a better look at the plume. That's when the . . . *things* overtook her—just things—coming up with the plume and filling the sky: water mixed with deep sea ooze and rolled into black drops as large as ping-pong balls. A whole stream of them pounded against her windshield, and with them came the dust of *Argus*. A piece of someone's coffee mug went into the left air duct. A piece of metal plating struck the left wing like a bullet. A shoe lodged in the Tomcat's nose. Something black and fleshy thudded against the engine casing. Ronni banked away instantly and, miraculously, the plane continued to fly reasonably unscathed, until, after a span of only three seconds, she made the additional error of trying to throttle up.

That's when her bird took the pewter mug handle that was lodged in the air duct, where it had lain in wait like a blood clot in a lung, and sucked it into the turbine— into the Tomcat's heart—where it could do the most harm. Suddenly the turbine sounded like an old vacuum cleaner trying to pick up rocks, and the plane died in Ronni's hands, and there was little left to do except point the corpse's nose gently in one direction and prepare for punch-out.

But punch-out to where?

Her last glimpse of the *Nimitz*—lit up by at least a half dozen lightning strobes—had shown the wave stumbling and collapsing; but she knew that it still had to be two hundred feet high when it reached the flight deck.

By the time they saw the aftershocks on their screens, mere seconds had passed. By the time they heard the high-pitched rumble rolling toward the van, there was hardly time to dive for the false safety of the opposite wall. Someone had told Tom Dettweiler that the approach of a tidal wave sounded something like a freight train. But a freight train wasn't even in it. This wasn't a roar: it was a squeal—like a hundred million pigs stampeding.

Too bad we're facing broadside, the recon man thought, and there followed a rapid-fire sequence of pictures in his head, of what might have been, if only the carrier had been facing tail-first into the wave. He saw that the *Nimitz* might actually have surfed the monster, so long as the nose managed not to go under. But facing broadside? Inertia. All was inertia.

During the first second and a half after impact, the deck hardly moved. All the shell plates on the port side—both layers of them—rippled and dished inward, many to a depth of twelve feet, sending forth a compression wave that shot through the solid frame of the carrier from port to starboard, in scarcely one thousandth of a second. As it traveled, far ahead of the water wave, it slammed watertight doors and compartment seals out of line, shredded pipes and passageways and storage tanks, and softened everything in its path for the water wave that followed.

When finally the water wave crossed over to starboard, when finally inertia did give way to acceleration, the port side was hoisted eighty feet into the air. On the hangar deck, equipment lockers bolted to the ceiling broke loose or burst open and spilled their contents, while beneath them, on a floor that slanted more than thirty-five degrees, planes broke their moorings and plummeted toward the starboard bulkhead. Caught amid the tumbling debris, those flight crews who survived more than two seconds could hardly believe their eyes. Landing gear and engine casings and permaglass and tail sections mashed down upon the starboard wall as though they were, collectively, a mighty steel hammer and the wall an anvil.

On the flight deck, most of the *Nimitz*'s island stack was uprooted and pitched overboard. Near its base, Scorp saw the van's port side bulkhead explode inward. It struck the screen behind her with such force that the most substantial surviving piece of it was no wider than a grain of sand.

According to the last bank of equipment still sending out telemetry from the *Nimitz*, the port side lifted, then dipped abruptly, signaling that the carrier fell into a trough behind the wave, before being lifted again by a second wave.

*　*　*

"I'd skip the punch-out," Al said quickly.

"Roger that," said Ronni, and nothing more needed to be said. They saw the base surge—a wall of droplet-and-debris-heavy air—spreading out from the collapsing stem of the column, and the downblast, the death cloud. And they knew what numbers lay within those roilings. From the looks of it, Ronni was guessing a tactical nuke packed to 335 kilotons. An underwater explosion was, in terms of radionuclide production, about as dirty as a bomb could get. Activation of seawater and mud meant sodium and a lot of other short-lived isotopes, which meant that if, by some special miracle, she could have stayed aloft for two more hours (and if her mud-spattered plane were not already too hot), her hourly dose would be down to a survivable five rems. But presently she would be averaging forty thousand rems per hour, down there, during the first ten minutes—a fatal dose within forty-five seconds, and two minutes later her DNA would be scrambled eggs. All protein synthesis in her body would simply come to a halt, which defined death; but a very special horror, reserved strictly for recipients of massive radiation doses, was that the body sometimes took a while—twenty minutes or more—to realize that it was dead.

To be still moving and thinking yet dead—interesting but definitely not high on Ronni's list of the most peaceful ways to end. Like every other good fighter pilot, she had planned for this possibility, for the day when she might go down in a bad place with no hope of recovery. And like most good pilots she had decided that on this day she would not punch-out. She would go the "Proud Mary" way: flaps up, nose down, and ride her bird in . . . and so she let the death cloud rush up and fill her entire field of vision—so fast—so close——she could alm————

20

Point of No Return

DAY 132, 9:15 A.M., WASHINGTON TIME

"*Looking Glass, Looking Glass,* this is *Blackstar.* The van is down. Repeat, the van is down. *Alphatown* also confirms attacks against Turkish naval forces near the island of Cyprus—"

"Has the whole world gone fucking mad?" cried Widow-maker.

"It's spreading," said Scanner. "You know what that means?"

"Yeah. It means we're cooked!" Widow-maker shouted. "It means they've suckered us into the tenth level of hell and that sooner or later, the heat will be coming right down our throats."

"You fools! You blew it all up!" Scanner said mockingly.

Widow-maker looked at him strangely.

Scanner looked back at him, more strangely. "It's *Planet of the Apes,* pal. Only this time it's for real. The *Holy Cost:* Glory be to the bomb, and to the holy fallout."

"Calm, Skipper." Widow-maker looked at the black book, then at the latest status report on the screens. The caps on their missiles were still sealed. Washington and *Looking Glass* were still in control. And so far, no one had ordered them to launch their birds . . . so far. "Look here, Cap, this isn't the scenario we were trained for. There's really no point in this anymore. What are they going to order us to do? Bomb India? Bomb a country that's already dead?"

"What are you saying?"

"I'm saying we should leave. Just shut all of this down and go home. Find our families, before it gets any worse."

"So that's your idea of duty: to leave a nest of birds lying around, just for the taking, maybe even by enemy hands?"

"We can disable them, of course," protested Widow-maker. "That's easy. There's lots of ways. Blow the covers, for a start. The maintenance crews are already going AWOL in droves, so after a few weeks of rain and snow getting inside the nests, the birds will literally be rotting. No one will be able to launch them even if they want to."

Anger flared in Scanner's eyes, a genuine, raw anger that came from somewhere deep inside. "You scared, twisted fuck!" the captain growled, raising a hand to the side of his head.

"Huh?"

"You mutinous dog! You Sinatra-loving sack of shit!" He swatted the black book off the console. The ring binder snapped open and papers flitted like dead leaves through the CO_2-scrubbed, dust-purified air, then landed in a random scatter at Widow-maker's feet. He was scared, so deeply scared that he dared not admit it to himself. It was the kind of fear that numbed and paralyzed, and converted a previously agnostic junior officer from denial to secret, hopeful bargainings with God: *Oh, please don't let it get*

*any worse, right now. Oh, please, if only you could let
the skipper calm down long enough for me to bring him
under control. Dear God, if only—if only he would come
under control just long enough for the birds to be crip-
pled—oh, God—oh God—I'll be good, I'll obey all your
covenants if only—*

The last thing Widow-maker saw was a sheet of paper
at his feet. Its final paragraphs warned:

> *COMMAND DISASTER CONTROL PROCEDURES
> MAY BE REQUIRED IN CONJUNCTION WITH
> TECHNICAL PROCEDURES CONTAINED HEREIN.
> SOUND JUDGMENT SHALL BE EXERCISED AT
> ALL TIMES.*

> *COUNT YOUR PAGES.
> COUNT YOUR PAGES.*

''Mr. President, I beg of you. We've got to move down
to EWO status. You've got to authorize me to let the
combat crews insert their keys. For all I know, we could
start losing capsules and silos at any moment.''

''I'm sorry, Andrews. There were *two* countries out
there in nuclear engagement, and we don't *really* know
which one of them fired on us. We haven't exactly seen
anyone stepping forth to claim credit, have we?''

''Then I suggest we hit every military installation in
India *and* Pakistan. Hit them hard. Teach them a lesson
which they and the world will never forget.''

The President frowned. A flashing yellow box in the
upper left corner of his pad announced that Seoul had just
dropped off the net. ''The world, General? It seems to me
there's not much left of it to carry on your lesson.''

''That's probably true. But we can't afford—especially
now—to be sending the wrong kind of message: that we're
willing to stand by and let any psycho on a violent crusade
nuke our carrier forces and get away with it.''

''But which psycho, General? You're asking me to au-
thorize the killing of thousands, maybe millions of people.
Which psycho are we talking about, here. India? *Maybe*.
But by rights we can only strike back at the country that

fired on us; and to determine that, we need forensic evidence, a piece of wire that can be traced to a specific manufacturer, a chemical trace, or—"

"What you require is impossible. About two millionths of a second after the bomb detonated, all of its parts simply ceased to exist."

"Well, that's the crux of your problem, then, isn't it?" said the President. "Atomic bombs don't leave forensic evidence."

"So that's your answer? We just sit still? Do nothing?"

"I'm afraid that's so, until and unless we have proof."

"This will change," the general said. "This will change."

In spite of the fact that she and her colleagues had spent more time than anyone on Earth tracing the chain of cause and effect back to the death of insects, Leslie Wells still wondered how the world had been brought so low. The answer always came up the same: The world today was like the *Nimitz,* a cork swept up in a tidal wave. Only one other team had come so far as the Long Island group: the Pasteur Institute. They reported their first biomorph success just three days prior to the Paris food riots. That was nearly two weeks ago. Leslie's latest entry in the amber read simply this: "Pasteur—all quiet now."

Brookhaven's biomorph team had fallen into a pattern of meeting in the cafeteria for a "coffee break" and a brief conference every afternoon at four. All agreed that this was a good way to save time, as the attendees could snack and get their "caffeine fix," while at the same time summarizing results and catching up on the latest happenings in world news. Despite the fact that the last of the coffee and batter-fried Mars Bars were long gone, and the last of the tea bags were so diluted from repeated use as to be hardly worth the effort of resoaking, the conferences continued on schedule.

Except for the news from the Indian Ocean, today's conference was no different from the day before's. As usual, when she glanced at the others, Leslie saw that no one in the room, including herself, had been getting enough sleep. And their faces were thinner; not enough food. Soon, very soon, even the children would come under strict rationing.

"Any new species?" Sharon asked.

"We've got a working bee genome," Richard said. "Stingless honeybees from the Dominican Republic. If only we could get them out in the spring, they'd be a tremendous help . . . might even save us."

Leslie's turn: "And beetle grubs. We're going to need those real bad. What few birds have survived will find nothing much to feed on next spring except worms. Earthworms are the only shot we have at keeping the soil at least marginally alive, so we'll need the grubs not only for soil maintenance, but also as a diversion-type food supply for the birds."

"That's assuming the birds, as they began starving off, didn't hunt the worm population down to extinction," said Jackson.

"We can hedge our bets a little better," added Sharon, "if only we can identify, in the amber, a beetle whose grubs were even more beneficial to the soil than earthworms."

"We need time, Sharon."

"Well, then we'd better hurry, because we don't *have* time." She did not need to elaborate.

"Our friends on the airwaves?" Richard asked.

"Sigmond and Puck!" Sharon replied. "They went quiet for a day or two, probably just relocating. I thought the Marines might have got them; but they're as loud as ever now. Tooling around with people's heads. They're blaming us for the bomb. They're blaming us for the plagues. They're blaming us for everything. It's only a matter of time. We've got a cure coming through, but it's only a matter of time before they put a stop to us."

Leslie nodded. "That's right. I'm all for freedom of speech, but these guys are shouting *'fire'* in a crowded theater. This operation has become too important to risk losing. We're going to have to move, if we're going to save anything."

"Bluepeace?"

"That's what I'd recommend," Leslie said. "I've given it a lot of thought; and it *still* seems our best option."

Richard looked up. "Great idea," he said, with a trace of sarcasm. "America is already becoming boat people with nowhere to go. Where do you propose we flee to? The high Rockies?"

"That's not far off the mark, Richard; if for no reason other than there has always been very little by way of a native insect population up there."

"Very little else up there, either."

"You're missing my point. Think, Richard. Think: life without insects."

"You mean, places where they won't be missed?"

"Yes, yes," Leslie said. "Places where yanking them out of the ecological mix won't make all that much difference, because they were never a very big influence to begin with."

"There's the Arctic tundra," Richard said.

"Antarctica," Sharon said.

"Lower your latitudes a little," Leslie instructed.

"Some of the more remote Pacific islands," Jackson ventured, "including New Zealand."

Richard slapped the top down on his pad. "Damn! How could we have missed that? How could I have been so stupid?"

Leslie smirked, and Richard returned an icy grin that said, *Don't dare say it.*

New Zealand had yielded an even more extensive amber record than the Dominican Republic, ranging from Coal Age forests to the present-day kauri trees living right on top of the amber beds they had created. But the New Zealand amber beds differed from the Dominican amber beds in one respect: an almost complete absence of insect fossils—which Richard, up to this moment, had dismissed as meaning "no data."

As a graduate student he once held, in blocks of kauri resin as large as footballs and as clean as citrine, pieces of a puzzle, and he drew from them a seemingly reasonable but perfectly wrong answer: "*no data.*"

He had failed to find, in New Zealand resins, even traces of the native beetle that drilled holes in household furnishings. In the absence of termites, beetles were, naturally, occupying the termite's niche, but they were not nearly as efficient as their hive-building brethren; and Richard now realized, with a start, that this might explain why New Zealand's trees tended to grow more slowly than their cousins on the continents and why they lived longer, toppling only rarely to the forest floor: They supplied only as much wood as the beetles could harvest, only as much tribute as the forest floor demanded.

No data, indeed!

Richard had been looking at the picture upside down. He had been taught to view forest ecology as a carefully balanced state of affairs: the so-called "balance of nature." But now he was forced—all of them were forced—to see the delicate interconnections among beetles, trees, fungi, and birds as an ongoing adaptive arms race witnessed only in the snapshot perspective afforded by human lifetimes. The first leaf-cutter ants to encounter a forest might easily have denuded the entire forest—and many probably did, to their ultimate ruin. First contacts between species were almost always antagonistic until, through generations of massive casualties on both sides, they eventually evolved what gave the appearance of being a carefully regulated immunity to each other . . . some of the leaf-cutter ants used once-ant-killing, ground-dwelling fungi to digest the leaves, while the ants themselves cut only as many leaves as they could take without killing the forest—for those hives that did kill the forest simply died. Meanwhile, some of the trees evolved defensive toxins against the ants (medicines for man), yet at the same time drew benefit from ant-fertilized and -aerated soil. Such balancing acts, viewed backward and across geologic timescales, had left millions, probably billions, of dead ants, fungi, and trees in their wake and, viewed forward over those same timescales, were going to leave billions more dead. Balance was an illusion, albeit a stubborn one.

Local ecosystems existed only by truce, a truce that persisted via unthinking, unfeeling geologic consent. Sometimes the mutual tolerance between species evolved into interdependence, even mutual addiction—the ant and the tree, the orchid and the bee—and after this had occurred, if you suddenly killed *all* ants and bees, you broke the truce; you undid the evolutionary labor of eons.

And now the Chinese had annexed and occupied—what country?

"New Zealand!" Richard said. "China! Do you think their scientists figured it out: that insects play only a minor role in New Zealand?"

"That's hard to say," said Leslie. "It's no secret that the Kiwis are faring better than the rest of us. And they've no navy worth factoring into invasion plans. No Air Force. And a small population; not much chance of developing a resistance movement. It was a smart move. It just might work for them, in the short run."

"Maybe in the long run, too," Richard said. "I think you're onto something. There are islands—far from the continents—where insects never really got a strong foothold. Oh, those places will still be hurt by the die-off, but you'll find that their ecologies have been shaped to a much lesser degree by the activity of insects. If you look at a place like New Zealand, you'll notice a few insects living on the forest floor, but you'll also see that the process of decay has been given over largely to pill bugs, millipedes, worms—and you'll probably find that the worms and pill bugs are still there, doing their job."

"Can the *Bluepeace* make it to New Zealand?" Jackson wondered aloud.

"I think so," Sharon said. "But then we'll have to depend upon being welcomed by a Chinese occupation force, and while that's a slim bet, it still makes more sense than staying here."

"There are, of course, other islands that were insect deficient long before the die-off," said Leslie.

"Optimism," Richard said, and reopened his pad. "If my notes are correct, Jackson, you said not so long ago that as insects had heralded our coming, they were now preparing the way for humans to leave. Leslie actually put that one in the amber."

Leslie cleared her throat. "Yeah—well, Richard, lately I've been thinking about your bamboo die-offs, the ones that threaten China's pandas every hundred and twenty years."

Richard smiled. "Bill Schutt's DNA time bomb theory."

"Yeah. One has to wonder. Those few pandas that lived through the biological upheavals eventually emerged into a world that had bamboo again. But those few people who live through the insect die-off are going to be living in a world that will still, for a very long time, be hostile."

"Which brings us back to what I've been saying all along about humans being infinitely more adaptable than dinosaurs," said Jackson. "No matter what you throw at humanity and the world, perhaps man, like a rapidly mutating line of cancer cells, has a great deal of staying power. I imagine that even if the India-Pakistan war went global—the Earthly equivalent of radiation therapy—small numbers of men and women might conceivably wait out the radioactive tides in a nuclear submarine parked beneath Sidney Harbor. Do you see what I mean? We've always said the cockroaches would be the last creatures alive after an asteroid impact or a nuclear holocaust—but a submarine has a harder shell, and is more radiation proof, than anything the cockroach was able to evolve over hundreds of millions of years. The sub is a superior adaptation, and we accomplished it in a geologic microsecond, without the complexity of a genetic overhaul. What I'm saying is that technological evolution has already exceeded organic evolution by orders of magnitude. What I'm saying is that while it's true that we may get knocked back into a Dark Age for a while, it's also true that from the moment this Earth sprouted intelligent life, it was here to stay."

Sharon shook her head. "Humanity as an Earthly cancer. That's a new one."

"I suppose so, but try to imagine looking down on Earth from on high, watching all the city lights going out during the next few months and whole nations becoming radio silent. We know that there will probably exist a few isolated places where civilization and street lighting will endure. Places like New Zealand."

"Little tumors that managed to survive," said Richard, and his mouth dropped open as he thought it over.

"And if you could take a grandstand view of the planet over the next two hundred years, Richard, what do you suppose you would see?"

"Looking down on Earth, I expect we'd see people

from New Zealand spreading up the east coast of Australia, draping streetlights over the nightscape, like glowing cobwebs. Eventually, the lights would spread through Indonesia into most of Asia.''

''And you would guess from this,'' Jackson said, ''that humanity was metastasizing again.''

''So the moral,'' Leslie explained, ''is that we must predict where those few isolated outposts of streetlighting are likely to be—identify the tumors of future civilization—and get ourselves inside one of those tumors.''

''The Azores were always insect deficient,'' said Richard. ''And Iceland might just make it, but agriculture and fishing should be easier in the Azores. My bet's with the Azores. I think they'll be one of your tumor sites.''

''Richard?'' Sharon asked, while trying to call up an atlas on her pad. ''Who owns the Azores? It's Portugal, isn't it?''

''Yes. And I expect that once the Portuguese figure out what we've just figured out, they'll begin wondering how many others might be coming to the same conclusion. They'll probably throw up a naval blockade against refugees.''

Leslie took that one. ''Trust me: They'll let the *Bluepeace* in, if for nothing else for the fact that she may be the only reconnaissance ship still functioning when this is all over. She can limp along on solar; and I don't think they can expect any oil shipments from Iran for a century or so. Add to this the fact that we have the cure, and the amber, and equipment to continue manufacturing the cure. Add to this the fact that if we stay here, we'll all be dying by spring—murdered, no doubt, and the cure with us. The Azores will let us in because we have something to sell them, and they'll be getting it cheap. Dirt cheap.''

''For our lives,'' Jackson said.

''Yes. A blimp and a few insects for our lives. Sort of gives new meaning to the expression 'life is cheap,' doesn't it?''

''Not really.'' Jackson shook his head, and chuckled to himself. ''The standards have changed, that's all. You could probably buy all of Colombia for a pair of fungus gnats or a nest of ants. And I'm not talking about the movie studio; I'm talking about the country.''

DAY 149

History would never record how the pagan fell in with the rabbi.

After a bitter lesson in the power of mob rule, Dr. Ed Bishop of Lucent Technologies retreated, for a while, on horseback as far as possible from human proximity. Now nature itself was teaching a bitter lesson: *Dracunculus*. Bishop suspected he had acquired the parasite even before the first tremors of insect death were felt on the stock market, during one of his hiking trips in Frost Valley, where he had carelessly sipped water from a stream whose insect-starved dead were feeding both bacterial blooms and population explosions of the microscopic, one-eyed crustaceans known as water lice.

He was sure he had been infected during the summer; no doubt of it. He was also sure that the organisms could never have taken command of his body, using him as a host in their reproductive cycle, if he had not been made vulnerable to them by malnutrition. And he was certain that with supplies of food and clean drinking water breaking down everywhere, the swelling in his legs was, like the first robin of spring, merely the harbinger of new life— or, in this case, a new plague.

Wheels within wheels, Bishop told himself. The tiny water lice, when he first ingested them, must have themselves been infected with the even tinier larvae of the guinea worm. A small voice in the left hemisphere of his brain began reciting crude conversion formulae for vitamin deficiencies, and his right side began running a little movie picture of worm larvae capitalizing on his weaknesses, piercing the lining of his intestines, and mating there. They weren't tiny, anymore. After the males died, the females had migrated throughout his body, settling finally near the surface of his skin, in his arms and in his legs. Some of the females were two feet long now, and they blistered his skin with masses of living larvae. The blisters burned, producing in him an urge to submerge himself in a river or a stream, to soothe the pain. In spite of the fact that the water was freezing cold at this time of year, the urge was irresistible. He also felt an urge to rub the blisters, to make them burst and drain, so that if and when he did bathe, a new generation of millions of water lice–seeking larvae would be released; and the life cycle would begin anew, fueled, Bishop knew, by billions more larvae released by thousands of other malnourished, worm-breeding hosts just like him.

He recalled a scene from the Book of Job, in which the hero of the tale was reduced by a whim of God to a man whose flesh, swollen and clothed with worms, hung down from bones burning with internal heat. He tried to stow that thought, to bury it; but when he ran a hand beneath his coat and touched the blister on his right arm, he felt one of the large females twitch beneath his fingers, as if trying to wiggle away from his touch. His breakfast would have come up, then, if there had been any breakfast in him. The last decent meal he had eaten was squirrel; and that was two days ago. Squirrels would eat anything—anything at all—so they thrived and multiplied, like seagulls, until their meat came into demand and everyone started hunting them down. This morning he had tried to fortify himself with grass roots, somewhat following the example of his two horses, who were becoming too exhausted to be used as transportation, yet were increasingly valued as a potential source of food. He was sorry for that. They had served him well, trudging faithfully along difficult backwoods paths after mobs had broken down the gates of Lucent and uniformed peacekeepers joined in the looting and left the offices and laboratories blackened and smoking.

He felt now as if he had been traveling for weeks, and perhaps he had. During his one and only attempt to ride back to the lab, still hoping that someone or something could be salvaged, he was forced into retreat by sniper fire. That was . . . how long ago? Before the India-Pakistan war began heating up and certainly before his pad began blacking out. The machine's batteries had been sucked so dry that it could only be used for occasional eavesdropping on the net. But that was enough. The pad told him that

Brookhaven was still up and functioning, and working toward a biomorph solution. "Might work," Bishop told himself, so he contrived to set out for the enclave, hoping he might be able to help.

The pad also told him that he must avoid Jersey City at all costs, and East Orange, and all the large northern towns. There were reports of gangs racing through the streets in stolen vehicles, brandishing assault rifles and grenade launchers. The fighting was only worsening the widespread food shortages. Workers for an emergency food distribution system, mobilized to feed nearly two million people throughout northern New Jersey, were threatening to abandon their posts unless military personnel intervened to stop the gangs. The United Nations had, in typical foot-dragging fashion, finally come around to declaring this "a serious humanitarian crisis" while, the last time he tuned in, he came across a posting from the deacon of the Kennedy Avenue church: "Lord, please help us out of this madness—your children are dying."

The so-called Garden State, for reasons that were unclear even to its inhabitants, was not holding up so well as other parts of the country. Only California and northern Connecticut sounded worse, and had Bishop heard Jackson's comment about Colombia, he would have laughed and wondered what made the scientist so sure that either the studio or the country still existed.

A mile-high lens of black smoke continued to build on the horizon, somewhere behind Manhattan. An outburst of evil was sweeping over the world; and one of its epicenters was the oil refinery district of New Jersey and the towns that surrounded it. In better times, the district would have been the most direct route to Long Island, but Bishop knew better than to go there. Not north. Not east. In those directions lay madness. So he proceeded, very carefully, very tediously west, staying off-road as much as possible, glancing over his shoulder, and listening continually for the crackle of distant gunfire.

He wished today that he had dressed more warmly, in spite of the burning worm wounds. In the northwest, a bank of dark, low-hanging clouds was threatening snow, or sleet, or both; and the only sensation more frustrating

than the cold was the emptiness in his stomach, made all
the more frustrating by the sudden, unmistakable scent of
roast rabbit in the air.

Bishop dismounted and hitched the horses to a tree. He
had no difficulty finding the source of the scent, for the
man had foolishly built his campfire far larger than was
necessary, and was sure to attract the attention of anyone
passing near the clearing. The cook was a man of about
sixty, wearing hiking boots, blue jeans . . . and a thick
sheepskin coat. *Foolish with the fire,* Bishop thought.
Smarter than I was with the clothing. He was sitting on a
rolled-up Mexican wool blanket, cooking his rabbit on a
stick. Without standing, or even turning his head, he said,
"I hope you intend no foul play with that sidearm, sir."

"None at all," said Bishop, and held his hands out to
his sides.

The man put the rabbit aside and stood up, slowly, with
his palms outstretched as if to say, *I bear no weapons.*
"No," he said. "You don't look like one of the crazies."

For long seconds Bishop said nothing, but stood at the
edge of the clearing sizing the man up, waiting for him
to make a sudden move for a gun that might or might not
be hidden under his sheepskin. Finally, he said, "No, you
don't look the type, either."

"But looks *can* be deceiving."

"I know," Bishop said with a smile, and the cook
walked toward him with his gun arm outstretched.

"Rabbi Zuscha Freedman at your service."

Bishop extended his own gun arm and shook hands.
"Edward Bishop. And don't worry—I'm not a gangster."

"Good. Have you eaten today?"

"A little."

"Do you like rabbit?"

"Love it."

"Well, there's more than enough for two, so you might
as well pull up a rock and stay for lunch. You're the first
person I've spoken to in over a week, except on the pad."

"My pad's just about dead," said Bishop.

"Mine's holding up a little better," said the rabbi. "I
managed to get a full charge at the Ryetown Hilton, just

before full-scale anarchy broke loose there. They burned the place to the ground, you know.''

"The hypercube Hilton? Gone?''

The rabbi nodded. ''That accent . . . you're from Long Island, aren't you?''

"Valley Stream, originally.''

"And lately?''

"Lucent Technologies, New Jersey.''

"So you're a scientist!'' The rabbi chuckled. ''You've come the wrong way. You're practically in the middle of Jerry Sigmond country. He's all but calling for egghead lynchings, these days.''

"Yeah. I've caught some of his broadcasts on my pad.''

"So, what were you thinking?'' Rabbi Freedman headed back to the campfire and split the rabbit open. Thunder rolled back and forth within the clouds as he handed Bishop a handful of meat. He bit into it eagerly.

"I was thinking of Brookhaven,'' the scientist said, between bites. ''From what little I've been able to pick up on my pad, they've made some progress toward a way out of this mess.''

"Don't believe it,'' Freedman said. ''At a time like this, government propaganda runs amok. They're probably just trying to calm everyone down. I really am beginning to wonder if all this mayhem is just too big to be solved by human meddling.''

Bishop stripped a piece of bone clean with his teeth and swallowed gently, savoring the meat. Nothing in memory had ever tasted so good. He thought of asking the rabbi if rabbit was kosher, but then thought better of it; and he saw that the man's gums were bleeding, and the scientist understood that while being more smartly dressed and better fed than he, the thought of scurvy had not yet occurred to Zuscha Freedman.

Bishop licked rabbit grease from his fingers, wiped his hand on a pants leg, and withdrew a half dozen cut roots from his pocket. ''Here,'' he said. ''You'd better chew on these.''

"What are they?''

"Dandelion roots. They'll taste a little bitter, but you look like you can really use the vitamin C.'' And none too soon, Bishop thought. An old scar on the rabbi's right hand was already opening up, beginning to bleed after twenty years or more. Bishop had seen this before, as a graduate student helping to program MRI scanners for a New York City hospital. One of the interns had invited him to have a look at "an interesting case." It seemed a Liberian sailor had forgotten all about the importance of vitamin C intake, and his body displayed scars just like the one on Rabbi Freedman's hand. In the absence of vitamin C, collagen began to break down, especially the fibrous bundles of connective tissue that held old wounds closed. When scars became undone, wounds opened up again, and one could easily bleed to death from dozens of different sites: the healed dog bite . . . childhood's scraped knee . . . the incision through which an appendix had been removed . . . the site where the appendix had been attached . . . the gum line through which teeth had erupted . . . the site of circumcision. In modern times, this simply did not happen, and it was plain to Bishop that the doctors and the interns had never before seen a real live case of scurvy, and after a week, it became apparent that they were more interested in studying the sailor than in curing him, or even telling him why he was ill. One day, Bishop hinted to the man that he should drink a quart of orange juice and "walk away fast."

"We're apt to see some widespread scurvy cropping up soon," Bishop said.

"And, I'd expect, a lot of other diseases we haven't seen since the Dark Ages," he added, after a swallow. "When you're weak from malnutrition, and then one disease sets in, your body becomes a breeding ground for other diseases. Right now, there must be hundreds of millions of people all around the world, getting sick from malnutrition. When people are hungry and sick, their bloodstreams become triggers for population explosions of viruses—Coxsackie, cytomegalo, Epstein-Barr—you name it. Increase the number of viruses and you increase their overall rate of variation. Increase variation, and a few of those variants are bound to be more dangerous than their ancestors. So in the numbers game of survival, whatever *your* blood breeds eventually gets back to *me*. And vice versa. So we really are our brothers' keepers.''

"My brother's keeper," Freedman said. "Sounds pretty spiritual for a scientist. Maybe the world could use a few more atheists like you."

"You've been listening to too much Sigmond; and he's got you jumping to wrong conclusions. I've known two paleontologists—evolutionists—who were also Jesuit priests. And me? I'm an old pagan; a Wiccan."

The rabbi laughed heartily and did not know what to say. The words Glinda spoke when she first met Dorothy in Oz came quickly to mind—"Are you a good witch or a bad witch?''—but, no. That wouldn't do. Instead, he said, "A warlock? Now that *is* interesting," and, as if on cue, thunder rolled again, closer this time.

"I'm not all that familiar with your faith," Freedman admitted. "But from what little I know, you guys have a reverence for nature—almost a worship of it."

"It *is* worship."

"And yet nature has turned against you, has turned against all of us. I'm just wondering: How does this fit in with your worldview? Isn't this a contradiction?"

"No. Nature may be doing evil things to us, but I don't believe senseless evil exists."

The rabbi looked astonished. "You don't?"

"No."

"Nor I."

Bishop bit a rabbit femur in half and sucked greedily at the marrow. "Now," he said, his voice muffled, "let me give you a God's-eye view of what's been happening. When they were inventing pottery, lamps, and ropes near Jericho, about twelve thousand B.C., there were fewer than eight million people in the world. But today we've spread ourselves from the Yukon to Antarctica; and if you try to imagine the biosphere as a living, deeply interconnected system, could not the ever-expanding billions of us be Earth's equivalent of a viral bloom?"

"Then New York City and this entire tristate area are reduced to a major infestation of *Homo sapiens,* right?"

"Sure. In which case, maybe the death of insects, and all these plagues—" Bishop broke off, reminded suddenly of his infected limbs, of twitching, pain-dealing worms as long as snakes—"maybe they're nothing more than Earth's immune system striking back at an infection."

"And the infection is us?"

"Yeah. Basically, we need to make a new pact, or covenant, with Earth. The old covenant has expired, and let's just say the bill is coming due. If we kept treading the old path, we might have ended by destroying all life. So maybe life is striking back."

"There was some talk on the net about time bomb genes. You don't believe that?"

Bishop shook his head. "I think my friends in the City of Dreams have got it wrong. Genetic time bombs aren't necessary. Maybe an irritant is all that's really necessary to trigger all this trouble. Maybe the dinosaurs got too successful, became an irritant, and the Earth responded as our bodies would respond to the flu. That covenant I just mentioned: I'm thinking we waited too long. The deal didn't get made. And now we're being foreclosed."

"Now you're the one," said Freedman, "who's beginning to sound like Sigmond. He says science and technology created this mess."

"No, all humanity did it. We've made it difficult for life on Earth, so now life is defending itself against humanity. And maybe not all humanity will be destroyed; but humanity will have to make a new and difficult pact if it's going to survive, because no matter where people go to hide, they cannot hide from nature."

"A pact, you say. A covenant in which human behavior will have to change dramatically?" The rabbi smiled.

"And part of that covenant could include re-creating or resurrecting the insects—a possibility you referred to as a government myth spread over the internet to calm everybody down. Propaganda or not, I think it has to be done. We have to repopulate the world with insects. We have no choice."

"You mean, we're being called upon to go out into the wilderness and become restorers. . . ."

"Exactly," said Bishop.

Thunder rolled again, more distant now. "I see . . . and do you suppose this will require a spiritual change?"

"I expect so," Bishop said dryly.

"Yes, I guess that's one possibility—one of at least two that seems likely right now. Spiritually and behaviorally, we will be forced to change."

"And if we don't, there is no place safe for us. Nature is just going to keep coming after us, hitting harder and harder, until our attitude shifts."

Freedman said, "And then, of course, there's the other possibility."

"What's that?"

"That we're, right now, finishing the job of destroying ourselves. Armageddon." *That's what the prophets had called it,* Freedman reminded himself. But for the India-Pakistan conflict to consume the whole world *would* be senseless evil, and the rabbi no more believed God allowed senseless evil than the Wiccan believed the universe to be senseless. It was as God had told Job: The reasons for evil might be hidden, beyond Job, beyond humankind. He also thought of Elijah, who journeyed into the wilderness of Mount Carmel to be a recluse and to find God. And there he saw an earthquake, and a wind that hurled boulders and smashed them to pieces, and fire raining down from the sky; and he came to believe that each instance of nature breaking loose with violence was an instance of God's revelation. But God said, "No. None of these are me," and He told Elijah that His presence could be found in the voice of human conscience. "So," the rabbi cautioned, "I think we believe very much the same thing, you and I: That when violence occurs, it's man's job to stop the violence, and to try, insofar as we can, to understand the reason why the violence occurred."

"Yes. We do appear to have arrived at similar conclusions; it's only the words we use that differ. Where I say 'nature,' you say 'God'—"

"And maybe we have slightly different views of what constitutes God—"

"But probably not so much a difference in His behavior."

Freedman laughed. "I think you're right," he said. "There probably are little outposts on Earth—your city of dreamers, perhaps—where a new covenant will be made and nature's violence can be stopped. From what little I've been able to receive on my pad, Washington, D.C.—of all places, *Washington*—is beginning to sound like another outpost of civilized existence. That's where I was heading.''

''Why not Long Island?''

''Already been there,'' Freedman said, and pulled a tin of tea bags soaked in hot water from the fire. ''I happened to be out of town when it all started. My family was in Long Beach.''

Was? Bishop almost asked, and then he recalled how it had all started. ''I'm sorry.''

Freedman poured some of his tea into a second tin and handed it to Bishop. ''I doubt there's much strength left in the bags, and I've nothing except Sweet 'n Low to go with it—''

''It'll go down just fine, like the freshest Earl Grey,'' Bishop said, and sipped. ''Thanks.''

''You know, the Flood must have been something like this: It brought civilization down, almost wiped the world clean. Noah didn't want to save himself. He wanted to just die with his neighbors. But God wouldn't let him. God said, 'No—the world will be cleansed, and you will be among the sole survivors, and you will become a new human race. Much better. Less evil.' Maybe that's God's plan in this catastrophe also: to produce a new human race.''

Bishop listened. He was becoming a very good listener, in his old age—what the rabbi might have called ''one of God's chosen.''

''In our tradition,'' Freedman explained, ''we believe that thirty-six 'saints,' or 'righteous ones,' keep the human race afloat. There must always be these thirty-six people in the world, and because of them, the world is never really destroyed. There's always some remnant.''

''For different reasons,'' Bishop said, and emptied his tin, ''that's what scientists and pagans believe: Someone will always survive. I'm pretty confident of that myself. Humans are pretty tough, not easily disposed of. We're a very sticky infection.''

''Well, in my view, it would have to work that way, because if it doesn't work, then you might as well drop atom bombs on the whole world. Finish it. Period. So,

from my traditional sense, there will have to be some
remnant from which God can develop a new world, if not
on this planet, then on some other planet."

Bishop looked at him quizzically. The rabbi poured him
more tea and he just held the tin in his hands, warming
his fingers.

Freedman said, "You find that surprising, coming from
the orthodoxy?"

"Yes."

"Let's face it: We live in a very large universe. I don't
think God is limited to Earth, as such."

Bishop nodded, and sipped. "I . . . have two horses,"
he said, and he guessed that Rabbi Freedman might tell
him that this circumstance, too, was part of God's plan,
although the reason he had taken two horses had more to
do with logic than with providence: He wanted to alternate
mounts as he rode, always giving one a restful walk, keeping it fresh, and thus making better time toward his destination. "If you really do believe that there must always
exist little gatherings of people who will make the world
survive, well—for what it's worth, I'm placing my bet on
the biomorphers. So why don't you come back to Long
Island with me? I expect, if we play our cards just right,
we'll be reasonably safe there."

"Oh . . . well and why not?" Freedman said. "I guess
I can always visit Washington another day."

"Then you accept?"

Freedman raised his tin and clicked it against Bishop's.
"Here's to a safe journey."

Bishop clicked back. "And here's to better days. To
good days."

"Every day above ground is a good day," said
Freedman.

"Amen to that." They clicked their tins together again,
and drank.

They rode southeast toward the Connecticut Turnpike,
mounting and dismounting as they went, so the horses
would remain as rested as possible. They kept to the
woods, and by late afternoon the cloud banks had drifted
east, depositing behind themselves neither snow nor sleet;

and that night there were stars in the sky. Dinner turned out to be far less appetizing than lunch: just some roots scrounged by Bishop and bits of rabbit liver and intestinal tract that Freedman had saved for just such an eventuality. Bishop built a fire—this time no larger than was absolutely necessary—and, using some spices the rabbi had been carrying, made a rather tasty soup out of rabbit tripe and roots. It was a satisfying if not filling brew. Both of them knew that tomorrow's pickings might be even slimmer, so they consumed only half of it, and packed the remainder for lunch.

As they sat around the fire—Bishop grateful for the extra woolen blanket—they saw a tiny meteor hurtling west to east without burning out.

"*Alphatown,*" Bishop announced, and they talked long into the night about what Rabbi Freedman had said about God's attention not being limited to Earth alone, and the odd coincidence of civilization being torn down at precisely the moment it was ascending into space—at precisely the moment it dreamed of colonizing the sands of the moon and Mars, at precisely the moment it became potentially infectious to other worlds.

Bishop thought about that for a long time, and slept fitfully, only at intervals—thinking about it, dreaming about it. Before they broke camp, shortly after daybreak, he activated his pad and, with the last expiring effort of its batteries, grabbed a satellite downlink and tuned in on the infection.

"And now it's atomic bombs," said Jerry Sigmond.

"What did those scientists do?" said his cohost. "Look around you! What did they do? The government, or the provisional government, or whatever is running this country now, doesn't want you to hear us. That's why they're sending out helicopters, looking for us. But this is America! And it takes more than helicopter gunships to keep a free people down."

"Ever since the Book of Exodus," said Sigmond, "history has been teaching us that there is no greater power in the world than the will to be free. Against that force gunships are meaningless in the long haul. Fucking fleets of ships are meaningless. The Einsteins, and the disinte-

grating government that coddles them, have declared war
on us. On all of us.

"People! I call upon—— * * *——" The pad's power
fluttered, washing away Sigmond's voice in a momentary
upsurge of static. When he returned, he was calling his listeners to join him in what appeared to be a prayer.

"Help us to conquer the apostles of arrogance, greed,
and cultural elitism. Let us drive them out of their lair and
into the sea—drive them out like the vermin they are, until
they reside in the darkest place in hell."

And with those words, Bishop's pad went dead. Freedman decided against wasting his own pad's energy on
more of the same and, looking restlessly to the south, he
came to the very edge of deciding that Washington was
the better destination after all.

"Long Island!" the rabbi cried. "Not for nothing, Doc,
but if I were you, I'd be steering a couple of hundred
miles south of Sigmond's clan."

"No. I can be of more use at the lab. Jerry Sigmond is
just words. Just charisma. The only scary part is that sometimes he seems to get it right—the old ploy of hiding lies
in the truth; it makes them much easier to swallow. But
I'm not worried. Sooner or later people will realize he's
a monster."

"That's what they said about Hitler. And too soon the
whole world was spinning out of control. And too late
they got smart."

"Remember?" Bishop asked. "Remember what I said
about playing our cards right?"

"Yes. You believed we'd be safe."

"That's part of *my* tradition, my faith: If I play my
cards exactly right, I will survive. Now, I'll grant you that
there are very few good cards left in the deck. But if
anyone's devising a way out of this . . . take my word
for it: Brookhaven's the best card in play." What Bishop
left unsaid was his own life lesson: that one could play
his best cards and yet fail to win. He remembered Richard
Sinclair's analogy of the best-adapted dinosaur in all the
world finding itself living on the Yucatán peninsula, right
under the hammer fall of an approaching comet. In any
kind of random game, it was possible to make all the right

moves and still lose. But the rabbi decided to play Bishop's card over the Washington card, and at lunchtime they gathered more roots and consumed the last of their soup. About midnight they arrived at the hill overlooking the Connecticut Turnpike and the Robert Moses Bridge.

The span was completely deserted. There was not a vehicle upon it, not even a stalled or abandoned car. Someone had doused all the lights; but across the sound, on Long Island, the power grid was still up and most of the North Shore villages still glowed.

Neither of them had ever known the turnpike and the bridge to be so quiet—had ever even imagined it. New York and the tristate area were said to be the loudest mouth on Earth. The silence was unsettling. As he rode, Bishop kept his hand poised near his pistol. On horseback they passed through vacant toll booths into the left, southbound lane, where a large moonlit sign warned:

THIS LANE FOR CARPOOL USE ONLY,
24 HRS, MONDAY THRU FRIDAY
PENALTY $200 FINE AND 2 POINTS ON LICENCE

Bishop kept to the HOV lane, laughing to himself inwardly until, as he reached the center of the bridge, searchlights blazed at him from the north and south entrances and red police lights came to life alongside the lamps. The two horsemen were bracketed in, trapped.

I told you we should have gone to Washington! Bishop expected Freedman to say, but instead the rabbi resorted to gallows humor:

"Toto, I don't think we're in Kansas anymore."

Bishop's brow furrowed; he did not quite get the joke.

Leslie Wells's chronicle in amber had been reproduced in triplicate, providing her an extra measure of guarantee that if future archaeologists dug up the entire landfill, even if some of the resin blocks did not survive, the excavators would still be likely to obtain a complete record of the city's last days. Her entries were abbreviated, by necessity, and though life for the dwellers in the gated community was mostly long periods of routine interspersed with short bursts of drama, the chronicle preserved only the most memorable events, naturally. Future historians who failed to consider this would be misled into believing that the days were filled with drama.

Tuesday: New York City is, by some accounts, "still the crime capital of the world." But at least it still has a mayor, and a police commissioner, and full electrical power. Suffolk County, by comparison, is in disarray. Here at the lab our power supplies are running steady, but outside the gates we have reports of frequent brownouts, the result of some sort of mob action. There are accounts of ongoing firefights, especially in the Hamptons, where well-armed and well-stocked neighbors are either defending their greenhouses and canned goods or trying to raid someone else's. Nassau County, insofar as can be ascertained by helicopter flybys and emergency-band broadcasts, is quieting down, aggregating into a loose coalition under Sigmond and Puck, who are beginning to resemble, more and more, local but frustratingly invisible warlords. In that case, I'm afraid what we're hearing is the quiet before the storm.

Wednesday: Alphatown has provided us with confirmation via telescopic downlink that Lucent is down. Burned to the ground. Total loss of mainframes and expertise we could have used to double our efforts here, to get out twice as many biomorphs twice as fast.

Thursday: The stripped-down Bluepeace should be able to carry our entire community to the Azores—plus all the tools necessary for continuation of the biomorph project. Our arrival has been cleared by the Portuguese government. Officially, the Bluepeace now belongs to Portugal. Not exactly legal, but if any Washington lawyers have a mind to stop us, they'll have to run their injunction past the

Marines . . . after they run through Sigmond's psychos.

Saturday: Today the first minute traces of radiation from the India-Pakistan death plume circled the globe and showed up on our detectors. Sharon had predicted the plume's arrival almost to the minute, and we awarded her a prize of absolutely worthless passes to next season's Rangers games, and fifty grand in hundred-dollar bills.

Sunday: One of the Marines brought two children through the gate tonight, together and alone. They are three and five years old—Wynne and Michelle. They have been calling for Daddy ever since. Heartbreak. The officer who took them in says that Daddy simply walked them to the front gate and told the sentries he had done all he could. He kissed them and then, without any warning or fuss, without asking anything for himself, he turned and darted off into the night. I have a feeling that the idea of Bluepeace as latter-day ark did not escape him . . . which means the idea is out there . . . which could be dangerous. Wynne, the younger of the two girls, asked me if I was "Mommy." Michelle tells me that Mommy went away—"to be with Grandma." Grandma, it seems, went to heaven a long time ago. We will take the girls with us on our flight to the Azores. It is agreed that we will take the father, too, if he shows up at the gate; but there is no chance, I think, that we will ever see him again. In a little more than two weeks we shall be ready for the flight, assuming that Sigmond's mobs will stay away that long, and assuming the war stays overseas.

As it turned out, Richard had been right when he told the President that the actual details of a civilization's final plunge always went unrecorded. This was no less true in the land of Lincoln than in the land of the biblical Abraham. On the same night Leslie took Michelle and Wynne into her arms, she embedded what was fated to become her last entry in the amber chronicle. It was a note from Tam to the future, and it was the last written record anyone would leave at the City of Dreams before all of its inhabitants became archaeologically invisible.

heaps of love and kisses to all from Tam X X X X X X X X X X X X X X X X X

21

Sole Survivor

DAY 152

The smell was awful. Even with the air-conditioning running up full, even with the body propped out there in the tunnel against the blast doors, Widow-maker was simultaneously sagging and bloating like a sack of rotten plums; and his dead man's burps, fueled by bacterial fermentation alone, without a single maggot to quicken his decay, were warm and humid, and permeated every cubic foot of air.

Scanner tried to wash the odor off himself; twelve times a day he scrubbed his arms and his hands, but the odor stayed, and stayed, and stayed. He could not get used to it. He could not just banish it, like background noise, from his mind—not when it was strengthening each passing hour. And worst of all, he realized he could not remember exactly how his friend had died. His memory was very clear up to the moment he drew his .38 on Widow-maker, but beyond that point, everything became vague, as vague as the news filtering in from above.

All contact with *Looking Glass* and *Blackstar* had dropped off, either because the planes were out of range or because they had gone down. All contact with the support crew upstairs, and with the four other capsules in the missile group, had also dropped off, either because the men had abandoned their posts or because their posts no longer existed. During moments of lucidity—and he had such moments, usually over cups of coffee—he tried to make contact with missiles under charge of the other four capsules, and was learning that none of them were any longer "talking" to his computers.

Insofar as his hobbled mind could ascertain from the conflicting data that came through, the other combat posts did indeed still exist. So the crews had either abandoned their posts or . . . or . . . or they were dead! Something had gotten to them, had gotten to all of them, had scrambled their brains, had even killed his friend. Some sort of sneak attack, Scanner guessed, like the one that had taken out the *Nimitz*—except that instead of atomic bombs, this attack had involved some sort of deep-penetrating nerve gas.

Suddenly, Scanner realized that he was going to die, and that he might be the only American missile combat commander still able to think and move—owing, perhaps, to an abnormally strong resistance against the toxin. The thought was sobering, and uncluttered his mind long enough for him to prepare a half dozen cups of coffee. He downed twenty aspirin with the coffee, hoping to kill his headache once and for all time; but the coffee only made it worse. It would have taken more than a headache and deteriorating health, however, to derail Scanner from his duty (or, at least, from what was becoming an increasingly personal interpretation of what constituted "duty"). He reactivated his pad and tried to re-establish contact with the still extant but uncooperative missiles. He would get the birds, sooner or later. He knew he could. He had always prided himself on being a can-do type of guy.

"Yes," he said to no one in particular, and yet at the same time to everyone in America, "trust me. Everything will be all right."

The Thor system had been built for a tactical-strategic exchange, based upon the assumption that its missile crews would be fully alert and in good health, and that the country would be intact at the onset of hostilities. There was even a strongbox containing several hundred thousand dollars in cash and gold, so that the mission support crew, sometimes called a "reconstitution force," could stock up on extra food and fuel in advance of the exchange. The possibility that civilization might disintegrate around them and that the crews themselves would flee had never been factored into the Soresport equation: a ring of five capsules, each in charge of ten missiles; three warheads in each missile; each warhead packing 335 kilotons, or twenty-five Hiroshimas.

Now four of the capsules were abandoned, and under the planned-for tactical-strategic exchange, this situation had been known as the "Sole Survivor equation." . . . Given: five launch control centers; four have ceased communicating with their missiles—the missiles' computers will then keep talking to, and will switch control to, the remaining capsule; should that capsule (the Sole Survivor) stop talking, the missiles, having lost contact with the last command and control center (a situation assumed, in pre-mite times, to be possible only under conditions of nuclear attack), would begin an automatic countdown to launch—going down from the Sole Survivor mode to Soresport. Combat crews did not like talking about the equation. In military circles, it was known as the Doomsday Machine.

On Earth above, a terrific cold front was driving snow across the Kansas plains. No one and nothing stirred within the unharvested fields, or around the forty missile silos whose protective caps had been shed and whose rockets were now being brutalized by snow and ice. The four combat crews, before they deserted, had thrown a wild card into the Sole Survivor equation by refusing to relinquish responsibility for their birds. Individually—each without the knowledge or consent of the other crews—the four deserting teams took steps to break their birds' wings.

They began by popping the caps and letting the blizzard into the silos. Then they drained lubricants from the capsules' generators and replaced them with pancake syrup, or condensed milk, or Pixie Stick sugar dissolved in water (and in one case, with all three). After the generators died, the crews instructed their capsules to continue sucking juice out of the batteries until they ran dry. Their last act of vandalism was aimed at the missiles' nerve centers: the SCN test. The onboard computers were commanded to run through a checklist of all systems and then to keep running the same test, back-to-back, back-to-back, until they became caught up in a Mobius Loop (or what, to a computer, was the equivalent of a nervous breakdown). Just in case any of the birds got wise to the ruse, and worked their way out of the loop, they would find the SCN test backed up by a second task: calculate *pi* to the very last digit. . . .

Scanner could not understand what had gone wrong, why forty missiles refused to assume the Sole Survivor posture, to flash their green lights on his screens, and respond to his computers. After a half dozen more cups of coffee—which intensified the galloping in his head and seemed to knock out some of the nerve connections to his left arm—he gave up on the dying birds. That left only the ten rockets wired to his own capsule: thirty warheads total, 750 Hiroshimas.

"I can still do a hell of a lot," he decided; but he reminded himself always to tread carefully in a burning house. He would wait here under the ground with his ten birds, listening to whatever news trickled in. If America burned to the ground, or if he died down here and could no longer communicate with his birds, they would go out into the world carrying in their talons the power of artificial suns—ten megatons worth of artificial suns.

During his training, someone had told him that the uranium 235 at the bomb's core was forged more than four billion years ago in the hearts of supernovae. An atomic bomb was simply the ash of stars that had lived and died when the solar system was dust. Refined to better than 90 percent purity, arranged in specific geometries, and tickled in just the right way, the primordial ash of Creation could be made to echo, billions of years later, the last shriek of an exploding star.

Is that what happened to the Nimitz? Scanner wondered. Was it really just that: the brief reincarnation of a distant sun? Sort of gives new meaning to the old expression "a blast from the past," doesn't it?

And then the coffee began to wear off and his thinking became more muddled. He felt that the time had come to stop worrying, and learn to love the bomb. Resurrecting dead suns; what he had just thought struck him as . . . beautiful, in its own way. Someone—he could not remember who—had said any sufficiently advanced technology was indistinguishable from magic . . . or from witchcraft.

Scanner laughed. Staring at his reflection in one of the screens, he laughed and laughed.

"Well," he asked himself. "Are you a good witch or a bad witch?"

Bishop supposed he would have found their guard— Amy was her name—Amy . . . and, yes, he would have found the woman interesting if not for that occasionally vacant look in her eyes, as if some of the life had recently been knocked out of her. It was a look such as spouses had when they were being abused, yet remained inexplicably loyal to their abusers.

It seemed that Jerry Sigmond was making all of Long Island his personal kingdom. That was, all except the oasis at the City of Dreams. To strengthen his grip, he had blockaded the Long Island side of the Robert Moses Bridge, and was pulling in anyone who came across, especially anyone who might be trying to reach the oasis.

After a brief, bridge-side inquisition and imprisonment, Amy and three of her fellow "officers" had confiscated the horses and driven the two "perps" to a temporary headquarters at the Nassau County Air and Space Museum. In handcuffs they were led down a long corridor with photographs of jet fighters and lunar modules hanging on the walls, through a door with an overhead sign reading MUSEUM EMPLOYEES ONLY BEYOND THIS POINT, and to a shuttered but well-lighted office filled with objects ranging from a hypergolic propellant tank to an ancient marble torso representing the minor god Prometheus.

Jerry Sigmond was seated behind a large desk, scrolling through blocks of data on his pad. To his right sat a puffy, somewhat punkish man of middle age: Puck.

Two seats had been placed before the desk. Amy and the three officers ushered Bishop and Freedman to the center of the room and left them standing. Their wallets, confiscated at the bridge and ransacked, lay one upon the other to the right of Jerry's pad. *Culture lag,* Bishop thought, and smiled. He should have tossed his wallet away a long time ago. His money was useless. His driver's licence was useless. And yet, spread out on the table, now, his licence, his Social Security number, his credit card numbers, and his Chase bank card became keys, providing his captor with all the confidential codes he needed to access TRW reports . . . college transcripts . . . a mortgage history . . . an FBI file . . . or even a complete record of video rentals. Bishop gulped nervously. He wished he could predict, and prepare his mind for reception, of what Sigmond would do to him. But that was impossible. Jerry Sigmond liked to keep people off balance. Why else had two plates, each holding a sandwich, been placed on the edge of the warlord's desk, within reaching distance from the chairs?

"The cuffs?" Bishop asked, wiggling his fingers.

Puck nodded to Amy. She recuffed Bishop's and Freedman's hands from behind to in front of them and motioned for them to sit down. "Is that better?" she asked.

"Much," said the rabbi.

Sigmond looked up from his pad and smiled. "I've been reviewing your employment histories," he said. "I don't see us having much use for the orthodoxy around here for quite a while—but *you,* Bishop, it says here you used to do some work for the military."

"Yes. Mostly satellite reconnaissance."

"Oh, come on, now. You're an R.P.I. man. And the old Bell Labs! I think we all know what sort of brainstorming sessions you've been involved in. I'll bet they've even given you access to Roswell technology. You're holding out on us, my friend."

Roswell—again! Bishop smiled inwardly. Anyone who thought scientists could keep a secret like that for more than half a century didn't know a damned thing about scientists.

"I have no idea what you're talking about," Bishop said.

"You don't?" Sigmond asked, calling a new block of paragraphs onto his pad, then turning the pad around to face Bishop. "Don't insult my intelligence," he said, and he motioned for Amy and the guards to leave. "I've got your resume."

"I'll be standing right outside," Amy interrupted. "Shout if you need me."

Sigmond's smile hardened, but he did not answer. Bishop noticed that Amy did not return his smile. She had known Sigmond long enough to start seeing through the cracks. His smiles had begun to frighten her, taking on the appearance of afterthoughts to real feelings too dark to be articulated.

When the door closed, he said, "Now, let me paint a picture for you. We've got a little problem out east: Marines, a nest of physicists, and biologists, and God only knows what else. They want me out of the picture. I want them out of the picture just as badly.

"Add to our side a little bit of hardware from the peace officers who joined my cause. This adds up to only a few grenade launchers and smart mortars. Enough to do the job? Maybe. But why rely on guesswork? Not when we can add a museum whose back rooms are crammed with all sorts of ground-to-air and ground-to-ground missiles— most of them, unfortunately, disarmed.

"Get the picture?"

He did get the picture: a hater of technology who needed rockets! Looking around, he saw all too clearly that he was sitting in what was already becoming the ruins of a lost civilization. All that was, was transitory; and he knew with grim certainty that Prometheus was destined for a second burial in the earth, and he knew with equal certainty that people would still be here, a thousand years hence, to ponder how a Bronze Age artifact came to be buried in the same stratum as an *Apollo* propellant tank.

Humanity will survive, Bishop told himself, and he realized with an even grimmer certainty that it was men such as Jerry Sigmond who were most likely to come through the extinction lottery. The meek were indeed about to inherit the Earth, and it was the strong who would put them there—in their graves.

Yes, the "very sticky infection" of humanity would persist; but it occurred to Bishop that if he were Freedman's God, he should pity the world.

"I take it," Bishop said at last, "that you've suddenly decided you *need* a few of us eggheads, in spite of what you say in your broadcasts. What's the problem? Can't get your rockets up?"

"Oh, I'll get them working soon enough. It's just that the more qualified people I have working for me, the faster my defenses will be ready. And after I'm through with that city of daydreamers, I'm sure we'll keep a few of its occupants alive, and put them to good use."

"You mean, slaves?" Freedman said.

"Oh, that's not quite so bad as it sounds," Sigmond said. "Here—" and he motioned toward the sandwiches, smiling that warm, all too friendly smile again. "Eat up. We've got fresh-baked bread here, for the more cooperative among us. Know it or not, you and your friend Bishop are slaves already."

The rabbi leaned forward and took a sandwich in his cuffed hands. He sniffed it, wondering if it might be poisoned, and then realized that it made no sense to kill them with poisoned food. Bullets and beatings were cheaper than bread. Food was too precious to waste on poisonings. So he bit in, and he discovered for the first time in his life that fresh bread tasted wonderful. After three quick swallows his stomach began to grumble—too much food, too fast—and he paused to say, "No ingratitude intended, but didn't anyone ever tell you that it might be a bad idea to have slaves as smart as or even smarter than yourself? That didn't work out very well for Pharaoh in Egypt."

Sigmond ignored the question. "You've had some experience with rockets, Bishop. The record shows it. Seems you were involved in some of the advanced preliminary design sessions on the Valkyrie Mark I, with my old friend Richard Sinclair.''

"But that's a robot probe—and it's *nuclear*. In its own way, it's a lot less clunky than a chemically propelled sidewinder or cruise missile. No hydraulics. Very few mechanical parts to worry about. What you expect of me is like asking a gunsmith to all at once know how to shape flint into a Clovis point.''

Sigmond smiled again, this time sarcastically. "Play the fool if you must," he said, "but don't play me for one.''

"Honest," Bishop replied. "This is totally out of my area of expertise. What you've got here are museum pieces—literally.'' The last syllables caught in his throat. He had played his cards wrong. He was going to be hanged or shot, he knew. Resignation and regret were welling up in him—especially regret: *Oh, if only I had listened to the rabbi . . . if only I'd gone to Washington.*

(if only . . .)

"You honestly don't believe that you could get a missile up and flying with a functioning guidance system?'' Sigmond asked. "Let's say I told you I want it up by next Tuesday?''

"Honestly," came the reply. "I'd need weeks to begin figuring out the old systems. Maybe months.''

"We don't have months," Puck injected. "We want an end to it now, this very week.''

"Then I'm afraid I can't help you. So what's going to happen to us now? Death?''

"Is that what you think I am?" Sigmond asked. "A murderer?''

Bishop and Freedman said nothing.

"Well, believe me—I'm not," he said with a sincerity that touched the scientist with horror. "Your friends have declared war on me, and all I'm doing is fighting back. You'll have to help me, of course. That's what I demand of you.''

Sigmond stood up, and walked over to a minifridge sitting on top of a table covered with schematics of old rockets. "Can I offer you drinks?" he said.

"Sure," said Bishop, wanting to believe Jerry Sigmond but half expecting him to turn around with a gun in his

hand instead of a drink. "A tequila sunrise, heavy on
the grenadine."

"We have no fresh orange juice," he said, in a matter-
of-fact way that left Bishop and Freedman dazed. "I'll
have to make do with the powdered stuff. Do you mind?"

Bishop shook his head. "And you, Rabbi Freedman?"

"Same," Freedman said.

"Same here, too," said Puck.

Bishop heard the clink of ice (*real* ice cubes) as he
leaned forward and placed the empty sandwich plate on
Sigmond's desk. When Sigmond turned around, his smile
had reappeared. He placed a cold glass in Bishop's hands,
and when he lifted it to his lips—oh, it tasted even better
than the bread.

"So," Sigmond said, as he put a glass in Freedman's
hands. "In return for a bunk and three square meals a
day, I expect you to do your best for me. The workdays
are long—fourteen hours, seven days a week; but that's
probably nothing compared to what you've already survived out in the woods. The way my guards tell it, you
traveled right along the fringes of mob activity, living off
roots and bark, mostly. Very resourceful. As you've said,
Bishop, I've decided I need a few clever men. Lucky
for you."

"Very unlucky for the Einsteins out east," Puck said.
"They're orbiting out there in Suffolk, but *we're* the
inner circle."

Sigmond looked at him patiently, and handed him a
drink. "There's work for you, Bishop, right here at the
museum."

"Rockets?" he said, looking into his glass.

"Yes. We've got about a fifth of them workable. I want
them *all* workable. You'll begin assisting my boys down-
stairs the moment you leave this room." He went back to
the minifridge. With his back to Freedman, he said, "I'm
sending *you* to Long Beach."

"Long Beach?" the rabbi said slowly.

"Why not? You don't have a problem with mixing concrete and moving heavy equipment, do you?"

"No . . ."

"Good. Because I'm getting rather tired of having to

stay on the move, of having to sleep in a different place every night just to keep our enemies from getting a bead on me. So, Long Beach is going to be my permanent headquarters after we hit Brookhaven. I intend to leave them with no airpower, and when that's accomplished, the same drawbridges that made the town so easy to quarantine will make it just as easy to defend. Looks like we're going back to the good old days of castles and moats.''

Enclaves, the rabbi thought. The whole country, and probably the world beyond, was fragmenting into little cocoonlike communities—into bunkered communities— led by local warlords like Sigmond and Puck . . . or the biomorphers. National and even global events were no longer of any concern. Only local survival conditions mattered. Freedman was witnessing the elusive last stage of Babylonian collapse: Humanity was withdrawing into itself, closing up like a hibiscus at midnight.

As Bishop drained his glass he noticed a wet spot on his shirtsleeve. There was pain beneath it. One of the worm blisters had broken, and the worm under the blister contracted suddenly, as if agitated by something. He wondered if the beasts would continue to grow inside him, and he thought: *Being shot, or hanged, or clubbed to death might be the least of your worries. . . .*

Bishop asked, ''Who, exactly, do you plan to keep out?''

''Anyone I can't use,'' said Sigmond.

''Yes, we are the inner circle,'' Puck said again. ''*I* am the inner circle.''

Weariness spread over Sigmond's face, a weariness that said: *as if . . .*

''And I'll keep out anyone who does not pledge his loyalty to me,'' Sigmond added. ''I've always been very good at reading people. It's a gift. I can sense a man who's going to betray me even before he thinks of betraying me. That's a very important tool, in time of war. Especially in this kind of war. We've got a lot of angry people here. Displaced people. They all want to strike out at somebody. What I've done is provide them with the requisite symbol of evil; I've pointed out a target for their anger. You'll be amazed to know how focused people can get when they have a clear target.''

Freedman's lower lip quivered.

Puck leaned forward, concerned. ''Jerry? You're being too generous with your mouth. Knowledge is power, and you're giving it away wholesale. What makes you think you can trust these guys not to make a break for Suffolk?''

''Generosity has nothing to do with it,'' Sigmond said. ''Believe me, I understand the score,'' he added, and thought: *I know I can trust these two men every bit as much as I trust you, Puck*—which was, in fact, the reason Jerry had poisoned their drinks. Bishop had signed his own death warrant the moment the warlord looked him in the eye and saw that even if he did know how to get the rockets flying, he was unwilling to help. Even with his rabbi friend as a hostage to ensure cooperation, Sigmond knew that he would have tried to subvert the rocket program from within. With Bishop out of the picture, the rabbi was of no value. And Puck? Puck was Puck. Reason enough.

Sigmond knew that the toxin was already settling deeply, irrevocably, into their cells. By midnight their dopamine receptors would begin failing. By noon, tomorrow, when Freedman was in Long Beach, and while Bishop was either wasting time with, or trying to misdirect the rocket team, and while Puck was scouting the Suffolk front, their muscles would begin to stiffen. Sudden onset of Parkinson's. Perfectly natural, in a world where new diseases weren't at all unnatural anymore. No one would suspect that Sigmond had killed his own men. By happy circumstance, though unbeknown to Sigmond, Bishop's infection would further camouflage his poisoning as a disease, when, after forty-eight hours, the worms attempted to flee his body. By that time, he would be catatonic. Two days later he, Freedman, and Puck would be dead.

And that's the way it ought to be, Sigmond reassured himself. *Four can keep my secrets, if three are dead.*

At the same time Jerry Sigmond was solving his security problems, Richard Sinclair led Tam and Georgiana, and a half dozen other Brookhaven children, to Leslie's greenhouse, where the very first biomorphed butterflies were emerging from two dozen chrysalides and spreading their wings. Richard found more than twenty children already gathered around Leslie, including Wynne and Michelle, known affectionately, throughout the enclave, as "the front-gate waifs."

"Now, don't touch," Leslie instructed, as she lifted Wynne up for a closer look. "They can be hurt very easily, so look only."

"Is that what's going to save the world?" Tam asked.

"They're going to help," said Richard.

A piece of golden hindwing unfurled as they watched.

"Oh . . ." Leslie said. "It's closer to a painted lady than to a red admiral."

"Is that good or bad?" asked Richard.

"Probably good. Painted ladies migrate in large swarms, like monarchs, but they're much more resilient. You'll find them even high up in the mountains. I expect they'll spread all over the place—pollinating. And because they don't mind cold weather—"

She broke off, not wanting to frighten the children; but Richard guessed which direction her worries were heading: If Sigmond's mobs came through the gates and broke down the greenhouses, the butterflies would survive the winter snows, and perhaps even make it far enough south to found new colonies.

"We've also got some very plump moth larvae and bee grubs," Leslie continued. "Right now we have to feed the baby bees hand-collected homemade nectar, and all that's left of our sugar, but if we can grow enough of them in the next generation, then once they're off and running and maintaining our crops, they'll be a good source of extra protein."

"Yuck!" said Tam, and even Richard winced a little.

"You may have to get used to that," Leslie said. "It's only in the west that people gag at the thought of eating insects. But in the east they have always been a major source of protein. In Thailand, I've seen bamboo shoots deliberately infested with grubs. When you chop the stems open, they're completely filled with shrimp-sized morsels—and they taste like shrimps, too."

"How do you know that?" asked Georgiana.

"Because I've eaten them."

"Uhhhh!" said Georgiana, and the other children joined her in a chorus of *oooohs* and over-dramatized vomiting noises. Leslie had captured their undivided attention, and Richard saw that they *loved* hearing this. Had any counselor telling ghost stories around a campfire ever been so popular as she was now? Richard doubted it.

Leslie said, "A year from now, when we have enough of them breeding, and before all the crops recover, we may all enjoy a meal of wasp grubs cooked in the comb."

"Yuck!" Tam said, and laughed.

"Or imagine this: a plump baked moth—"

Georgiana shook her head violently.

"Oh, come on, now! What can you possibly have against a winged shrimp fattened on sweet nectar? Shrimp. Crabs. Insects. What's the difference? They all evolved from worms, you know."

More *oooohs*, giggles, and pretenses at vomiting.

"And who here has ever tasted a lobster?" Leslie asked.

Fifteen hands went up.

"Did you like it?"

Twelve nods.

"So tell me: What is a lobster but a giant seagoing cockroach?"

That sparked the loudest chorus of *ooohs* and giggles yet. The Pied Piper of Brookhaven, Richard observed, and he wondered who would ever have believed it: that this insect pathologist had been hiding a soft spot for children.

DAY 155, 8:15 A.M., WASHINGTON TIME

"The fault, dear Brutus, is not in our stars, but in ourselves." So said an old Roman, according to Shakespeare.

"Sometimes the fault is not in ourselves, but underfoot." So said the President, to himself, at the hour of his death.

Such a little thing, he thought. Who would have believed it? And yet all around the world, economies had crashed, people were starving, buildings were being torn down in riot, power production and communication systems were breaking down. According to the latest reports, *Looking Glass* and *Blackstar* had dropped off the face of the Earth, and there was mention of an American submarine surfacing and firing cruise missiles into New Delhi and Multan, unleashing firestorms that danced themselves out over the graves of cities already devastated by nuclear strikes. The President was unable to confirm the story, or to determine if and when someone had broken the chain of command. But he did believe that a military coup was in the offing, if not already well under way.

"We've lost another sub, Mr. President." The new admiral stood in the doorway of the Oval Office.

"Is it true? Is it true that they fired on India and Pakistan, even after I ordered the fleet home?"

"Unconfirmed, sir. We still have communications with the *Alpha* Space Station. They tell us they saw two explosions: one in India, one in Pakistan. Kiloton range."

"Tell me what you think that means."

"It could have been India and Pakistan firing on each other again, or it could have been one of ours. I'm guessing it was one of the *Nimitz*'s escorts. Maybe it survived the blast, came up with its communications shot—came up angry—and popped off a couple of its missiles."

The President poured two cups of coffee and handed one to the admiral. There was no milk or sugar and the coffee itself offered at best a dash of flavoring for the water. Though the White House was known always to have been stocked with the most expensive beans and trimmings, the President had given almost all such frills to the Marines and the greenhouse builders, who had managed to keep the city above starvation and anarchy.

The President sipped, winced, and set down his cup. "You say you're guessing it was one of the *Nimitz*'s escorts? Can't you do any better than guess?"

The admiral set down his own cup without tasting. "We've lost contact with nearly four percent of the fleet— either because they were attacked or . . . or . . . it gets hard to tell."

"Or they became rogues with their own agendas," the President finished for him.

"As I said, it's difficult to tell."

Rogues? Nuclear-equipped rogues? There was a time when the President had been prepared to define the "motes" as a major disaster. And only a week ago, the crush of refugees into Washington had raised concerns about overcrowding and renewed food shortages; but overcrowding and mite swarms, when he added them up, were crises of trifling magnitude. Mites? When he looked back, the world during the first two or three days of the "motes" became nostalgic to him. Since that time, his very definition of the phrase "major disaster" had been rewritten.

"There's another problem," the admiral continued smoothly.

"Why am I not surprised?"

"Mr. President," the admiral tried to say softly, "it's the *Nimitz*. A number of my fellow officers are calling for retaliation."

"Retaliation against what?" demanded the President. "It'll be a miracle if anyone is left alive anywhere on or around the India-Pakistan border a month from now, whether or not we strike back. I'm not about to embrace that kind of madness. May God strike me d—"

Outside the windows, in the direction of the Washington Monument, the sky opened up. And the Monument was not. And the President was not. And a third part of the city was hurled into the Potomac. And the waters boiled, and turned to blood. And Washington was not.

22

My Way

"*Looking Glass*, are you receiving? *Looking Glass, Looking Glass,* this is *Alphatown*. Come in *Looking Glass*. We have visual confirmation of multikiloton burst at north latitude thirty———* *———Repeat, attack on United States at———"

Scanner checked his Smith & Wesson. Four bullets remained. That left ten rounds total, counting Widowmaker's gun. Regulations had called for six rounds per person. No extra ammunition. According to the book, the only time the weapons needed to be worn was if anyone except the wing commander and the two combat crew members happened to be in the capsule. He did not expect that anyone else would get down here now, not even the

security police. Topside, the AWOLs had probably taken
their M1s and grenade launchers with them, but even those
minimal defenses were not needed because the many feet
of reinforced concrete that made the control centers and
their missiles capable of withstanding nearby nuclear deto-
nations were protection enough.

In a ring of five capsules, in a sea of crises, each man
had decided how he was going to behave. Scanner's way
of coping was to stay at his post. He gulped coffee and
aspirin at a furious rate. He even tried masturbating—
anything to keep himself awake and aware. To an outside
observer the scene might have provoked nervous giggles—
but there was no cause for laughter: He was only doing
his best.

On his pad, the first helicopter downlinks of the Washington plume confirmed what the seismic sensors had already told him. The city was all smoke and dust; except
for glimpses, through clearings in the smoke, of buildings
whose outer walls had been hurled indoors, and a telescopic close-up of a woman, burned and blackened, wad-
ing into the Potomac and holding close to her breast
something the size of a large kitten, from which dangled
ribbons of curled flesh.

Scanner began to bleed behind his left eye. He leaned
back in his chair, raised a hand to his head, and suddenly collapsed.

Being immersed in death, Father Elton discovered,
could be as bad as being counted among the dead. At first
there had been a beautiful flash of colors—oranges, reds,
and yellows—and then smoke and twilight. No sound of
an explosion. Just colors. Dazed, he walked toward the
river, joining hundreds of other dazed, half-naked people
who formed lines and staggered in the same direction. The
skin of the man in front of him flapped like pieces of
tattered clothing from his back. He followed the walking
corpse aimlessly until it bumped headlong into the frame
of a smoldering bus filled with bodies. Its side was caved
in, all the windows were gone, and when the priest peered
inside he saw that the passengers' skin and clothing had

been stripped off. Only one of them stirred: a baby, still struggling inside its dead mother.

He stumbled away, leaving the man who had led him to the bus gaping and swallowing on the ground.

About a hundred feet from the bus stop, he paused, unknowingly, near the remnants of the bench on which Akihiro Takahashi had told Paul Tibbets how he spotted his airplane in the sky one sunny August morning. As the history books told it, the pilot had remarked, ''Yes, I could see all of Hiroshima below me.'' And then he grabbed Akihiro's right hand in both of his and said, ''We should never let war happen again.''

Behind the bench, the corner wall of a brick apartment house—all that remained of the building—towered three stories above Father Elton's head. Three children clung to the top of the tower, screaming. They were naked, and it registered somewhere in the back of the priest's mind that one of them appeared to be bleeding from his entire body.

At first grateful that he had been spared, as the unreality of the numb state succumbed to clarities born of atrocity, he began slowly, surely, to blame himself for having survived. As he reached the river and the first helicopters appeared overhead and as he waded through cold, upriver water descending upon hundreds of boiled corpses and as he watched a woman carrying her child toward him—pleading with the infant to open its eyes—barely noticing that as she stepped into the water the skin and musculature began to fall away from her bones, the merciful numb state started to crack. And he was touched by merciless guilt.

That's when he began wondering about the three children he had seen at the brick tower, and the ignored gasps of the man at the bus. As chance would have it, he was fated to live through the bombing, just long enough to know the special torment of never being able to find out what happened to those he left behind. History would never record the priest who waited for a quiet spring morning in the woods of North Carolina where, alone in a lean-to, he committed suicide. That's what it took to wipe away the memory of a cityscape at the edge of Dante's hell: the memory of black fire sizzling forth from a dead man whose body inflated until something yellow and ropy squeezed out and turned red; the memory of a woman who stumbled into him begging for water, her eyes gone, her lips formless, surrounding a blackened nub of charcoal that snapped off like a twig and turned out to be her tongue. All of this—the blackened things, the charcoal people, the dead and the still-moving dead—all of this had been wrought by only three kilotons.

Five hundred feet from the center of the explosion, the shadow of a vaporized window frame was burned into a concrete wall, and the angle of the shadow pointed like an accusing finger toward a ground-level explosion near the place where the Washington Monument had been— not the typical, high-altitude burst that would be delivered by a missile, but the ground-level signature of a car trunk bomb—which was also the signature of a terrorist attack. One hundred feet nearer the explosion center, more than half the people exposed to the blast received lethal gamma ray doses to their bone marrow. At a radius of 350 feet, *all* would have died within three weeks from damage to their marrow, to their gastrointestinal tracts, and their lungs. Fifty feet nearer, radiation death would ordinarily have occurred in three days from damage to the nervous system. But there were no radiation deaths in Washington. Anyone caught within the radius of gamma ray bombardment was reduced by heat and concussion into streamers of red mist that, after only one two-thousandth of a second, turned black.

And yet, for all the power it had unleashed, this bomb had misfired. Though one thousand times stronger than the bomb that had ravaged Oklahoma City in the spring of 1995, this bomb was a dud.

THIS IS TOCFN SHEET 24 OF 26

2-11. 10. TIME-ON-TARGET INTERROGATION. TIME-ON-TARGET INTERROGATION ELICITS A RESPONSE TO VERIFY THE CURRENT TAR- GET SLOT, EXECUTION PLAN, EXECUTION OPTION, AND REMAINING TIME-ON-TARGET DELAY TIME IN THE MISSILE(S). TOTI CAN BE COMMANDED AT ANY TIME FOR OP-

ERATING MISSILES, AT THE DISCRETION OF
THE COMBAT CREW OR WHENEVER MISSILE
WAR STATUS PLAN IS IN QUESTION.

COUNT YOUR PAGES.
REPORT ANY MISSING PAGES TO FCN AT
ONCE.
COUNT YOUR PAGES.

The blinking letters in the red sidebar gave latitude and
longitude of the strike, and the seismic sensors registered
three kilotons, just under one quarter of a Hiroshima.

Scanner could not tell how long he had been out. When
he looked in the mirror, he saw that the muscles on both
sides of his face were drooping and that one eye was
fully dilated. *The gas,* he guessed. *It's sizzling the nerve
connections in my head*—which was not far from the truth.
The prions were slowly dissolving his brain to a jelly.

One of the screens beeped at him, angering the little
core of mesosaur brain that dwelled near the base of his
skull. He did not want to answer the beeps. He did not
want to be called. He just wanted to lash out. He kicked
the screen, and then . . . and then . . .

"Latitude forty degrees . . . forty degrees north . . ."
He could not tell what time it had been when he passed
out, or name the day of the week, but latitude and longitude had stayed with him . . . and a sense of dedication
to . . . the task . . .

On another screen, ten rockets flashed red bars at him,
signaling that, having not heard from the last functioning
capsule, they were about to switch from Sole Survivor to
the Soresport mode.

That was . . . *bad,* Scanner realized, although he could
only remotely recall why. All he understood was that he
must talk to the rockets. That was part of the task.

He opened up his pad and scrawled his name with a
touch pen. The bars turned yellow with a flashing red
inside. He was supposed to write something else, he knew,
something important—but he could not remember what
it was.

Desperately, he started sifting through piles of TOCFN

papers, until at last he came across something familiar: Time-on-target interrogation. Yes, this *was* important.

The Thor system had been designed specifically to prevent an aberrant crew member from launching missiles. To begin with, *both* combat crew commanders had to agree on launch, and had to turn the launch keys simultaneously, in order to arm the bombs and fire up the engines. Every crew member knew there was a way around this obstacle (involving two forks, a broomstick, and duct tape), but even so, one had to first enter enable codes available only through Camp David, the White House, or *Looking Glass*. There were sixteen million possible combinations for the code. If someone tried to punch a code into a missile and it was wrong, the missile's computer would tell the other missiles, *Hey! Somebody just tried to enable me with a wrong code. Ignore him,* and all ten missiles would refuse to listen to the capsule for five minutes. Under this condition, a rogue commander could punch up combinations every five minutes and never find the right enable code, given even an entire human lifetime to do so.

What the designers did not anticipate—could not have anticipated—was the subsequent introduction of the Sole Survivor/Soresport equation. It created a staggering blind spot in a complex system whose primary function was to prevent accidental launch. That Soresport might ultimately subvert the very system it was intended to support was obvious from the start, as were all of history's great mistakes, when viewed with the power of twenty-twenty hindsight.

Because some strategic targets had a tendency to move, and because, especially in time of war, missiles might have to be retargeted at a moment's notice, enable codes were not required for latitudinal/longitudinal programming. Indeed, the missiles often asked crew commanders for targeting verification. This was among the first tasks the birds assigned to Scanner when he answered their interrogations as to whether or not anyone remained alive in his capsule. By answering them, he had delayed, by at least some hours, the Soresport countdown. The delay would continue, so long as he remained alive.

War plan? the missiles asked.

Scanner did not feel he possessed the energy to name individual targets for thirty warheads, so he wrote, "Primary launch command alpha," which instructed all ten birds to align on target #1. The rest was easy.

Primary launch command alpha installed. Select altitude slot # 1.

Scanner selected twenty thousand feet, and the rockets automatically dialed in their own launch delay times and altitudes, in accordance with prior programming, to guarantee that those reentry vehicles arriving behind slot # 1 would not enter, and burn up in, its fireball. The second strikes fell into slots of forty and fifty thousand feet.

Select latitude and longitude.

That was a hard one. He called a map of the world onto the screen, and by chance it was the Cook Strait that came up first. He guided a cursor with his finger, gliding over Auckland, Perth, and—

"How about Bangkok?" and then, after a pause, "Nope.

"Calcutta? Nah; been there, seen it, done it.

"Athens? Maybe next time.

"Toronto?

"Delmar?" He thought about it, but pointed his finger a little farther south . . . and then he saw it—

"Sinatra!"

For the first time since he could remember (and how far back was that?) he felt like laughing. Jokingly, and yet not so jokingly, he loaded the coordinates of a very special tormentor's birthplace into the lead missile, hoping, at least symbolically, to erase all trace of him. Within forty seconds all ten birds were flashing green on his pad, indicating that they all knew the same joke: 74 degrees, 1 minute, 3 seconds west longitude; 40 degrees, 45 minutes and 2 seconds north latitude.

Then, his strength failing again, he mumbled a very bad rendition of Sinatra's "Come Fly with Me," in the general direction of Widow-maker and the blast doors. Five minutes later his spine went rigid and, sitting bolt upright at his post, he sank into a coma.

The missiles tried in vain to contact him, and after a time, they switched quietly, irrevocably, from the Sole

Survivor mode to Soresport. Now the infective arc was nearly complete, having begun its journey as vector-switching prions, forced by the death of insects to take up residence in bats—that were, in their own turn, being swept up with many other of the die-off's survivors into a worldwide surge of opportunistic infection and prey switching. In bat blood, the prions had spread through Tobago and Martinique, to Adam "Scanner" Handelsman, whose brain was already crawling with death by the time he arrived in Kansas. There, the sickness bridged biology and cyberspace, taking new form in the programming of the Thor rockets, poised now to hurl themselves, as the clock ticked down, just a short ride south from the west apron of the George Washington Bridge. Three hundred thirty-five kilotons, thirty times over . . . the outrushing waves of heat and overpressure would resurrect, throughout Manhattan, the volcanic landscape that had existed sixty-five million years ago, and they would smash down walls in Long Beach and Freeport, as they surged on toward the *Bluepeace* and the City of Dreams.

23

All Aboard for Ararat

The same cold front that had spread snow and ice through forty missile silos in Kansas was bearing down on Long Island when news of the Washington disaster came. The blizzard was like none Tam and Georgiana had seen before.

With the further decay occasioned by war manifesting on American soil, and with no certainty who was president, or who was in charge of the Joint Chiefs of Staff, or if such roles even existed anymore, Leslie had called for a final, haphazard stripping down of the *Bluepeace*, so that it could be boarded at the earliest possible hour, while there was still a country from which to flee. Her motion was seconded unanimously, but six inches of snow that deepened to eight inches in an hour were hampering progress; and despite the strong winds, the snow formed an inch-deep layer atop the blimp's curved, dorsal surface, reducing its lift capacity and threatening to cut down on the number of people that could be evacuated.

"No way will we reduce ourselves to a lottery," Jackson said. "Either we all go, or we all stay and wait for the snow to melt." There were no takers for the slim hope that catastrophes even worse than Washington would not be showing up on their doorstep before the next sunny day. The people, every one of them, understood instinctively that Washington was indeed the end.

Vinnie, Sharon, and their two copilot engineers knew the *Bluepeace* in and out, the power and the beauty of her. They knew that, once airborne, they could rise above the clouds and use the ship's attitude control jets to roll her from side to side and shake some of the snow off. The problem was getting her airborne and keeping her that way in a blizzard.

Sacrifices would have to be made. Hard sacrifices. Hastily thought out sacrifices.

A crate of biomorphed eggs was loaded into the only stateroom whose walls were not being knocked down and tossed overboard, and a little electric heater was left in the room with them. The rest of the ship's heating systems were uprooted and discarded. Vinnie, Lenny, and Robyn had decided weeks earlier that in order to bring everybody out of the city, lift could be gained only by jettisoning all the *Bluepeace*'s air pressurization equipment and stripping out all the hull structures that had rendered the cabins airtight. The wide, double layer, pressure-proof dining saloon windows were now lightweight single sheets, and these transformations would have worked just fine for the evacuees, had they been allowed to wait for a sunny day and to sail over the Atlantic at treetop altitude. No one had anticipated a flight over the top of a blizzard, into rarefied air that was colder than the blizzard itself.

How long can adult human bodies survive in cold air? Vinnie wondered. There was no way to be sure whether or not some of them might die, and yet the decision was made: Only the children would be allowed to bring heavy overcoats. The adults would have to shed their coats at the foot of the ladder before boarding. During the two-day flight, they'd be obliged to huddle against one another for warmth. Suddenly, weight reduction and a speedy evacuation were the overmastering issues. Only the barest essentials—human lives, mostly—could be brought aboard.

Vinnie saw that copies of biomorph software were loaded into the insect stateroom, alongside the egg crate; but it had been decided even before the Washington emergency that substitutes for the Nomad and Cyberdyne mainframes would have to be built in the Azores. Leaving them behind was not merely a weight-saving measure. The scientists hoped that if the lab and the greenhouses survived, then whoever ended up running Long Island would, using the detailed instructions Richard and Jackson had prepared, be able to pick up the tools and continue the biomorph effort stateside.

More than two hundred butterflies, and a few handfuls of other biomorph hatchlings, were also to be left behind in the greenhouses. Almost all the plants in the greenhouses would remain behind, and only enough of the harvest was taken aboard to barely sustain the evacuees on a one-way trip to the Azores.

"I'm sorry," Richard told the children in the barracks, "but you'll have to leave your carry bags and everything in them behind."

"But why?" at least a half dozen voices whined. Tam's was one of them.

"Because the plan has changed," said The Don. He held his right thumb and index finger about two inches apart. "Every pound—almost every ounce we leave behind—is going to help us to get away. It's *that* important. We won't be able to leave unless we leave almost everything."

Tam was holding the little Figment dragon that had been riding with her in Mommy's Jeep ever since the big family trip to Disney World. Being the last tangible piece of Mommy she had left, Tam wanted it to ride with her still. She clasped the doll close to her chest with both arms, looking pleadingly at Daddy, and to know the thoughts behind that pleading look, yet to demand that she cast the doll aside, was, for Richard, to know sin; but there were

all those other lost parents and all those other children
with all those other dolls and toys—*pounds* and *pounds*
of dolls and toys.

"I'm sorry, hon—" He tried to sound firm, expressionless. "No exceptions."

"But Dadeee!"

"Now, listen! We're leaving all our goats and chickens
behind. We're leaving even—"

A siren stopped him. Loud and clear in the night, it
shrieked and wailed. Everyone, even Georgiana and Tam
and the front-gate waifs, knew the meaning of the wail
without being told: Something was wrong. Richard and
The Don knew more: The alert meant that motion detectors were registering ominous movements—troop movements, probably—at or near the perimeter.

"Okay," The Don said, lifting one of the waifs in each
arm. "We work this just the way we work the fire drills:
calm, quiet, and close together.

"Follow me to the blimp," he said, and nodded to Richard, Jackson, and the other adults. "You guys take up
the rear."

From high above the roof there came a sudden loud
hiss, deep and hollow, as if something were boring through
the air at high speed. Almost simultaneously, there came
a quick, guttural thud from the direction of the helicopters.
A second hiss and thud followed, then a third and a fourth,
then three more, and as the lights flickered and The Don
carried Wynne and Michelle through the door and everyone began following single file, Tam tore at one of Figment's furry orange ears with her fingers, then with her
teeth, until at last it came loose; and in the mounting
confusion she hid that last, little piece of Figment—that
last, little piece of Mommy—in her pants pocket.

At precisely that moment, some 1,700 miles away,
Soresport counted down to 00.00. Automatically, a gas-
fired ram catapulted the launch door off the first silo. The
fifteen-foot-wide, six-foot-thick slab of concrete skimmed
like a hundred-ton Frisbee over snow-covered fields, over-
flying a stalled pickup truck and a pack of wild dogs
fighting over a morsel of meat before landing a half mile
downrange on Mr. Robbins's barn. The rocket's engines

were sitting ninety feet below ground when they ignited, and by the time they came to the surface, they had already kicked the Thor to Mach 1. The sonic boom shattered every window in Mr. Robbins's farmhouse. In quick succession, nine more sonic booms started at ground level, accompanied by flying launch doors; and as they rose, the birds, every one of them, had but a single thought in its dim mind: 74 degrees, 1 minute, 3 seconds west longitude; 40 degrees, 45 minutes, 2 seconds north latitude . . . Hoboken, New Jersey.

Leslie Wells's first real indication that Jerry Sigmond had arrived was a peculiar push from behind, as if a giant's hand had slapped her headlong down the center aisle of the greenhouse, with such power that it burst her left eardrum. When she sat up, she saw that, miraculously, the lights were still burning, though with a fierce orange glow—and then she realized that it was not the lights at all but the glow of a fire that burned not quite eighty feet away, and in that direction the greenhouse—more than half of it—was gone. Overhead, the plastic skin of the building was a thousand tatters clinging to bent aluminum ribs. They blew frantically in the wind, and the snow was coming inside. Painted ladies fluttered within the swirls of snow, and Leslie saw that one of the carry crates, into which she had been stowing a selection of male and female hatchlings, was smashed in two on the floor. Its contents had been reduced mostly to yellow paste.

A second explosion followed, then a third, reaching her as soundless flashes and a rain of burning metal. A fuel-spattered chunk of helicopter blade—a twelve-foot-long guillotine—lanced straight out of the sky, like an arrow, and sliced through the planter table three feet to the left of Leslie's head. A piece of crankshaft big enough to have turned her brains into molasses pounded down near her right foot and carved out a crater. She was on her feet in an instant with only one thought in her mind: the barracks, where the children were. More explosions came, bringing with them a growing brightness that in its turn brought heat—and strangest of all: It seemed to her that there was actually time to pause and feel the warmth, to take notice of the objects revealed by the glare, and even to think how strange it seemed, to be seeing and feeling so much as she ran. Survival instincts had taken over, automatically shifting her brain into a state of maximum overdrive in which her senses swept over everything within sight, twenty-eight times each second, recording, as they had never recorded before, every detail, and crowding her mind with so much new information that each second was stretched to its outermost limits. She lived in a netherworld of slowed time. A new rip appeared to her left—just appeared out of nowhere—but her heightened senses and reflexes responded quickly enough to begin a slight, full-body ducking motion, which, in that part of a second, amounted to mere inches, but which also made all the difference in the world to her. A whizzing piece of titanium composite about the size of a dinner plate made a thin scrape across the back of her neck, then traveled on to slice through the sleeve of her upraised arm, nipping off a chip of bone as it went. She did not realize she had been hit. Her only sensation was being jerked sideways by her right arm, as if someone had tried to pull her out of harm's way, but there was no one there, by everything she knew. And then she was out the door and on the snow-covered path leading to the barracks.

Utter confusion. Too much was happening. Flashes of tracer fire up ahead. Then a burst of yellow-orange light, and half of someone's leg falling at her feet. She tripped over it, and hurried on.

Three hundred feet away, Sharon had left her post at the *Bluepeace* and was running in the same direction: toward the barracks. Three Marines ran with her. The pilot-engineer carried two pistols, one drawn and cocked in her right hand, the other tucked under her belt. She heard voices up ahead, shouting in the orange-white tumult: "Get 'em! Get the fuckers! Don't let 'em outta here!"

Beyond a radius of sixty feet, visibility was near zero. Bullets flew through the dark. The Marine on Sharon's right fell, his right leg hammered backward by a rifle shot. When Sharon turned in his direction she saw him rise, limping, raising his weapon—

"*Behind you!*" he yelled, firing off two bursts from his rifle.

Sharon turned, firing blindly in the same direction, making sure, during that chip of time, only that the other two Marines were nowhere near her line of fire. Shadows leaped at her and dropped prone to the ground, either from gunshot wounds or in an attempt to avoid being shot. Sharon was taking no chances. She emptied her revolver into the two figures nearest to her, drew her second gun and emptied it into a third, found a semiautomatic on one of the bodies and was about to empty it straight ahead when the soldier with the bullet in his thigh placed a hand firmly on her shoulder and cried, "Come on!"

She followed, and noticed that one of the corpses she passed was wearing a pair of safety glasses with an infrared scope fitted over the left lens.

Now why didn't I think of that? she thought, and paused just long enough to reach down, snatch the eyegear from the dead man's head, and put it over her own eyes. Now she could distinguish bright spots more than two hundred feet away, revealed by the heat they gave off. Some were intensely bright: buildings and machinery afire. Nearer, along the south wall of the barracks, fainter, cooler shapes moved busily to and fro: attackers and defenders. It was difficult to tell one from the other. Nor could Sharon make a reliable estimate of the attackers' numbers, nor did she try.

Inside the barracks, Richard could not understand how they had broken in so quickly, or what was going on beyond his—or anyone else's—sixty foot radius of reference. Though the battle seemed so clearly lost in the barracks, there was no way of knowing who was truly winning or losing on the larger battlefield outside, or how many of the enemy had broken through.

All the power seemed to have been knocked out, and the hallway was lit, now, only by red emergency lights mounted at intervals near the ceiling, astride heavy-duty battery packs. They made the blood that seeped from a bullet hole near Richard's right wrist, leaving large smears where he had touched the back of Tam's shirt, appear to be dark brown, almost black, like chocolate syrup. They lay on the floor, Richard and Jackson, shielding as many of the children as they could with their bodies. Jackson's chocolate stains were bigger than Richard's. Something had exploded near him when he tried to scout a back door exit, and his left leg was bleeding, and his left hand was gone, and he had bitten deep holes into his lower lip.

Only a handful of the children had gotten away before the rest were pinned down by heavy gunfire. The adults who led the escapees had been running in the right direction, as near as Richard could tell. They had bolted out the south exit, all of them, all toward the airship. All except The Don, who had gone out the wrong door, out the east door, toward the greenhouses and the particle bed, carrying one of the front-gate waifs under each arm. Richard expected never to see him again; and he was right.

In the dim red glow, two figures stood guard over Jackson, Richard, and the captive children while other figures, shadowy and night goggled, moved from room to room, smashing or shooting everything in sight. Yells and laughter celebrated the smashing and gunshots, and Richard knew that similar celebrations must now be occurring in the mainframe rooms, where biomorph samples, and instructions for their reproduction, had been prepared for anyone who entered.

The children flinched at the noises, but they did not scream or attempt to run, and Jackson began to worry that if an opportunity to flee presented itself, he would be unable to stir them to action. The silence of the children both startled and troubled him. People brought up on Hollywood versions of disaster were always surprised to discover how quiet human beings became at times such as this. Few men knew, really, that the cabin of a plane falling out of the sky could be quieter than a church . . . that a foxhole could be peculiarly active, yet silent . . . that people rarely spoke or screamed when their brains shifted into maximum overdrive and time, for them, became dilated.

And the children really were as quiet as if gathered in a church, all of them; but this was neither a plane crash nor a foxhole—and certainly it was not a church. It was a place of fear and unholy loathing—

"Get 'em! Get the fuckers!"

Jackson knew the voice. Richard knew it, too. Knew it too well. Yes, Sigmond had his act down just right: Always watch which way the parade is headed, and get in front of it. Same old game, played this time with guns and mortars.

Gifted abomination.

Jerry Sigmond had at last bound his audience together into an army, hiding hunger and fear in the smoke of hatred; and now that army was willingly—cheerfully—smashing and burning the very tools that might have saved it. In a month or two, Richard guessed, they'd be killing one another behind these gates, after they killed the scientists, after they ate or killed whatever still lived in the greenhouses.

He heard a sudden spurt of bullets drumming against the outer wall of the barracks, and he told himself: It's our Marines. Reinforcements. Maybe it will be all right. Maybe.

Fifty-three exits west on the Long Island Expressway, high above Van Dam Street, a silver star fell down from heaven. Across the Hudson, thousands of hungry, homeless people wandered the streets of Hoboken, searching for shelter and food while shelling and small arms fire threatened a flimsy, three-day-old truce between local warlords. They disappeared less than one two-thousandth of a second after the star reached its destination, some ten thousand feet above the blizzard's cloud tops. Instantaneous nonexistence. The edge of Ground Zero reached just two hundred feet short of the Van Dam Street exit. About midway between Hoboken and Van Dam, in a Manhattan bookstore called Science Fiction Mysteries and More, the asbestos edition of Ray Bradbury's *Fahrenheit 451* burst into flames. The airburst followed, ripping up mile after mile of the Long Island Expressway—which pointed like an arrow toward the City of Dreams.

"Don't move and no one gets hurt," Sigmond's chief of staff, Amy, shouted; whereupon Sigmond made her a liar by emptying two rounds into the back of Jackson's head. The three children beneath him seemed to whimper inaudibly, but otherwise dared not even squirm, knowing instinctively that this was not a time to be drawing attention to oneself.

"Why?" Amy hollered—and she found that she *had* to holler, in order to be heard; for although the sounds of gunfire had abated outside, the floor seemed to be emitting a high-pitched rumble, as if the Earth itself were beginning to scream.

"Why not?" Sigmond yelled. "Why not put every one of them out of our misery?" He swung his gun toward Richard, and thought he recognized the face, even though most of it was hidden against a child's head. "And who's next? Who do I have here? Is this really my old friend? Is this he with the sharp tongue?"

Richard said nothing.

"Get up off the floor! Show yourself!"

Richard pushed himself up, slowly, favoring his injured hand, trying not to glance down at Tam, fearing that if Sigmond realized who she was . . . Richard stowed the thought. Stowed it deep.

"Your tongue won't save you now. There's no more disciplinary committees! No lawyers! There's just—"

He never finished. The airburst shattered windows and broke walls and knocked Jerry Sigmond off his feet; and it spared Richard, by a margin of seconds, from summary execution.

"Run, kids!" Richard yelled. "*Run! Now!*"

They sprang and ran, Richard taking up the rear as more gunshots erupted. Marines, Richard guessed. Friendly fire.

"Heads down! Keep running!" Richard commanded. "Outta here! Everybody outta here!"

Something poked him hard in the calf, and on his very next step, his leg did not seem to be functioning quite right, as if one of the muscles had been partly severed— which, in fact, it had. Then something warm and slippery struck him in the face, and through the side of his eye he registered the image of a little boy's head opening up in a spray of teeth and bone.

OH GOD NO MY GOD NO HE'S SHOOTING THE KIDS—

"What are you doing?" Amy shouted.

"Nits grow into lice," Sigmond growled, and emptied two rounds into a child's back. The girl, about seven years old, dropped and did not move again. There immediately followed another spurt of gunfire, this time from Amy's weapon. Sigmond was knocked to the floor, not fully comprehending what had just occurred. He struggled to find his weapon. He'd dropped it, and he scrabbled around on the tiles, desperate to grab it before Richard and his nits got away.

Amy shot him again and again, shot him twice in the stomach—*No,* Sigmond realized, not *in* the stomach; that's where the bullets came out. Now his gun no longer mattered. Even the nits did not matter. Getting away was all that mattered. For some reason, his legs would not let him stand, so he crawled away from her, crawled away as fast as he could, feeling none of the intense pain that he was expecting, and he half wondered if he had really been shot after all. A viselike squeezing sensation—painless and even a little interesting, but not particularly pleasant—told him otherwise. Then Amy fired again, and he tried to quicken his crawl, but something seemed to be yanking him backward and there was a sound like a long, long sheet of calico ripping. He did not see, much less understand, that as he fled, his knees were snagging on his own intestines, and pulling them out.

Another airburst arrived, quickly following the first. In another second, the Marines were in. In another, Jerry Sigmond was dead, and Amy managed to outlive him by precisely six seconds. As she fell, Richard and the children burst through the exit, directly into the path of Leslie, Sharon, and three soldiers from the *Bluepeace.* Richard blinked. The whole western sky was aglow with a bright orange fire that shone even through the blizzard.

"How many megatons?" Richard wondered aloud.

"Does it matter?" Sharon said. "Come on! Move it! Everyone to the ship!"

But it did matter. At this distance from Ground Zero, 335 kilotons had been just powerful enough to crack walls and distract the enemy, but not powerful enough to maim. In the Goldilocks vernacular, "This little bomb was just

right.'' Jackson Roykirk would have appreciated the irony:
Scanner's madness had spared Richard, had ended the Sigmond horror almost as quickly as it began, and had allowed Richard to flee with his little girl—into the worst
horror of all.

Sigmond was gone, but the army he had brought crashing through the gates still lived—still carried through with
its spasm of shooting and smashing—proving once and
for all time that Sigmond no more led the parade than a
surfer leads the wave that uplifts him.

The sheets of wind-driven snow were still too thick to
see through, even under the strengthening light of the
bombs; but The Don could hear a horde of Sigmond's
soldiers yelling and firing and drawing near. The hangar
door was wide open, letting the snow gust in and giving
equally easy access to the soldiers. The horde would try
to shoot apart and tear down and scatter Don's cherished
''Delta Clipper,'' no doubt of it. The Don was counting
on it.

They huddled inside the clipper, The Don and the two
front-gate waifs, high above the rocket's particle bed. The
soldiers did not know this, could not know this, as they
reached the open door and stood for a moment wondering
what this strange machine standing before them might be,
as another shock wave rattled the building and unhinged
a side door. The men were getting used to the airbursts,
and were now only marginally distracted by them.

The Don watched a boy of about seventeen striding
toward the clipper, firing on it. One bullet glanced off the
permaglass window, leaving behind a white splash mark,
and The Don thanked all the gods of Serendip that loose
bolts, chips of spacecraft paint, and even Ed White's lost
glove—which, collectively, had so polluted Earth orbit that
Alphatown was struck almost daily by five-mile-per-second
''bullets''—The Don thanked whatever gods may be that
space pollution had done away with the paper-thin hulls
of the *Apollo* and *Columbia* era.

Below, the boy continued to advance, joined now by
twenty others who quickly surrounded the ship and began
concentrating their firepower on its tail section. Their bul-

lets drummed harmlessly off the reactor casing, and Don watched two of Sigmond's troops suddenly drop, either from ricochets or crossfire, he could not determine which—*and it won't matter,* he told himself.

The boy had paused to load a new clip, and had begun firing again—and a dozen more of his friends appeared at the hangar door—when The Don said, "Now!" and with a final tug at the straps to reassure himself that Michelle and Wynne were securely harnessed, he punched the ignition. The boy's face flashed out pallid white, and from the single, strobelike glimpse The Don got of his expression, he gathered that the soldier must have believed, in that part of a second, that one of his bullets had found its mark and destroyed the machine. The boy did not live long enough to realize otherwise. That smug, triumphant grin was still there when the blast of reactor coolant/thrust—pure, superheated hydrogen—converted him into gas and carbonaceous slush.

The clipper rose from the floor, its engine a frightful heat ray that swept first this way, then that way, killing at its slightest touch. More than thirty of Sigmond's army fell during the four seconds The Don took to guide his ship out the hangar door. Behind him, on floors that steamed like hot coffee on a winter night, were streaks of incandescent carbon and phosphorous that had, only moments before, been people.

The Don lifted the rocket to three hundred feet, and was about to throttle the burners up to Full Ahead, when his heads-up display revealed the infrared signature of the *Bluepeace,* just east of him, still tethered to the ground. Smaller, brighter infrared shapes were hurrying toward the airship—human shapes, most of them seeming to be represented in miniature—meaning children . . . and just a few hundred feet behind them, larger shapes, *adults,* were emitting the unmistakable infrared flares of tracer fire—meaning another horde of Sigmond's troops.

"Enough of this," The Don said, and then told the girls, "Hold on!" as he cut down the thrust and swooped tail first into a trajectory that would, when he throttled up again, stretch the harnesses to their maximum limit of G force protection, and would push the clipper near its maximum of ground-level thrust. He vectored his engine straight through the heart of the horde, and his target suddenly seemed to realize that something deadly was descending upon it, for as the particle bed blazed to life, two goggled figures attempted to lay a line of fire directly into the engine's nozzles.

"If they wing us," he said to the girls, "you needn't worry about me finding a smooth place to land—" and he grunted against the mounting G forces. "That's the great thing about this bird"—and he watched the exhaust plume play upon the ground, watched it erase the army upon the ground—"anyplace you pick; it's sure to be plenty flat when you get down!"

The G forces held, unchanging, and The Don's piloting made it impossible for Michelle to tell, as she lay in her harness, that instead of surging down and across the snowfield, the clipper was now rising above the Earth. Through the windows, Don watched the blizzard give way to starlight and false sunrises on the western horizon. Then the suns were far below him and his field of vision expanded with astonishing rapidity as the horizon, in every direction, receded. He thought he could make out city lights near Florida, and nearer to him, just south of the blizzard's lowermost fringe, Washington, D.C., glowed like embers in a campfire.

A half hour later, they were in daylight. The Don first spotted *Alphatown* through a sextant at a distance of 280 miles. By then, Harlan had gotten a radar fix on him, and as the gap closed to fifty miles, Don floated Wynne and Michelle up to the window and showed them the station glittering out there in the sunlight.

"Your new home," he said, as the clipper passed through sunset and into darkness. They did not see the station again until they were forty miles nearer. A single light flashed on and off, on and off in the night, and as the distance shrank to thirty feet, with the relative speed between the two orbiting bodies falling to zero, Don glanced earthward and noticed more embers shimmering on the border of China and across parts of Japan and as far south as Australia.

Robert Heinlein had been right, he told himself: *"The*

Earth is just too small and fragile a basket for humanity to keep all its eggs in.''

Tam did not quite understand what the tracer fire meant. Most of it seemed to cease after the passage of the glowing ball of light that swooped down out of nowhere, moving purposefully along the ground, beyond her field of vision, yet approaching close enough to warm her face and to momentarily convert the snowstorm into a rainstorm.

She remembered five or six men coming out of the shadows. Their clothes were smoking and they raised their weapons and actually got off a few shots before the Marines ''took them down.'' They were either trying to capture the *Bluepeace* or shoot it down—and Tam decided that they were trying to shoot it down because their guns had made little leak holes in the blimp's underside.

And as another ''airburst'' tore loose another ''mooring line,'' Daddy and the Marines and some of the other kids' parents shoved all the children into the blimp, shoved so hard that Tam's knee got bruised and her shoulder got pulled really, really hard.

And then the grown-ups climbed in and they were starting to remove their coats and throw them overboard when Sharon told them to stop. ''No need to save weight by throwing away your coats,'' she said, ''because there aren't so many of us anymore.''

Up to that moment, people had been shouting, ''We beat them!'' and ''We did it!'' and ''We're gonna make it!'' But the mood did not last. It evaporated even as the ship cut loose the last of its moorings and began following a radio beacon to a small group of parents and children who had lost their way in the blizzard. It vanished completely as the *Bluepeace* picked up the last of the stragglers and Tam and the rest began to realize how many were absent: Daddy's friend Jackson . . . the little boy with the Mets baseball cap who had so looked forward to his first blimp ride . . . Georgiana and her family . . . Tam guessed that some of them might still be fleeing down there, trying to get away from an army that, according to what she heard Leslie and the Marines saying to each other, no longer existed; or they might have broken their pads in the pursuit, leaving them with no means of communicating their whereabouts; or—and this seemed most likely—they were among the dead.

There was no hope of Tam ever finding out what had happened to her friend, and there was no time; every half minute or so, the air shook. "Atomic bombs," Daddy had said. Tam knew nothing about megatons, kilotons, or blast radii. She knew only that the grown-ups were speaking those words in hushed tones and that an initial moment of excitement, during which words like "victory" had been spoken loudly, had slipped away and left Daddy and everyone else who was old enough to know the meaning of the phrase "blast radius" looking more defeated than ever.

He probed at and bandaged his own hand, finding it swollen and painful but still workable. Funny, Richard thought, how you're not even quite aware you've been shot until the flight or fight response has passed and the adrenaline begins to wear off. He was sitting on the bare floor of the Grand Dining Saloon, with Tam sitting cross-legged before him, wrinkling her nose in sympathetic disgust as he mopped at the wound.

The floor was slanted down more than ten degrees astern. Sharon and Vinnie were evidently taking the *Bluepeace* up fast, hoping to avoid reflection effects from the ground if one of the bombs fell too near. Richard could feel the air thinning and cooling with the increasing altitude, but he knew, though the orange glow and the yellow flashes were increasing steadily in brightness, that the pilots would not take their ship too high; because the snowflakes, the billions upon billions of them, formed a natural shield against flash effects. At least, that *seemed* to be the plan, until Richard looked out the starboard windows and saw the blizzard suddenly dropping hundreds of feet below, and the world was starlight and back-lighted cloud tops.

"Ooooh!" said Tam.

She had never seen the like of it. No one, during all of man's tenure upon Earth, had ever seen the like of it. The ship was not, as Richard had first believed, bursting up through the roof of the blizzard, leaving the cloud tops below; but rather, the cloud tops had left the ship. The storm front existed as a vast, orange-white lake of mist; and from the west, spreading toward the *Bluepeace*, were concentric rings of undulating cloud tops—rings as wide as mountain ranges. The bombs were acting like giant stones tossed into a giant pond, and it was easy to see how the ripples unfolded: The airship had been ascending into the high point of one of those cyclopean sine waves, when the peak became a trough and, held in place by its own inertia, the ship was left dangling in open air.

"Look at it! Look at it!" Leslie said. And for a moment they all forgot exactly where they were, and exactly what they were looking at, and how foolish it was to be looking in that direction with unshielded eyes. On the horizon, near the splash zone from which the ripples emerged, a conical summit, higher than Everest, had come into being. It seemed to swell and spread even as they stared, absolute blackness against the ripples—except for the towering walls of fire that erupted through its foothills, actual hurricanes of flame.

"What's that?" Tam asked. "A new mountain? A volcano?"

"No," Leslie said, holding a compress to her neck— and Richard noticed that the back of her coat was covered with blood. "No, Tam. That's all smoke."

Leslie lowered her head, and found herself struggling to maintain balance as the floor suddenly dipped toward the bow and engine speed picked up. She guessed that the pilots must be trying to scoot back below cloud cover, back under the heat shield and—*Oh, no . . .* she thought, and shouted, "Turn away! Stop looking!"

But the warning came an instant too late. The false mountain became a dazzling diamond, its edges radiating a bluish-white corona streaked with fiery prominences. Tam blinked, and when she opened her eyes the air had shuddered again and the trough was a peak again and there was only swirling snow outside the windows; but the mountain's corona was still there, a brilliant green after-image shining against her retinas.

"My eyes!"

"I know," Leslie said. "It'll pass. But you'll never

believe how stupid we were—and how lucky: to have the bomb explode behind the smoke. Just a few miles east and it would have gone off this side of the cloud, flashing its full power into our eyes. Permanent blindness.''

''It was Manhattan, wasn't it?'' Richard asked.

Leslie nodded. ''I think so. Manhattan, or close to it.''

''I don't understand,'' Richard said, rubbing his eyes. ''Why are they all dropping on the same spot? And why so many of them?''

''It must be a mistake''—the ship dipped down another two degrees toward the bow—''or it's some kind of sick joke.''

Richard snorted a laugh, in the sickly manner that men sometimes laugh when they are close to hopelessness. ''Humanity,'' he said, as another detonation brightened the snow. ''And to think we used to dream of bringing this species to the stars.''

For thousands of years, humanity had been organizing itself into cities and governments—like ant colonies built one step higher. And now, Richard thought, some lingering residue of government, some small remnant of the disintegrating superorganism had, with its last trembling effort, decided it was perfectly all right to unleash one more hell upon the world.

''Wasn't it enough?'' Richard said in a near-whisper. ''Weren't the mites enough? Weren't crop failures enough? And bacterial tides? And plagues? And poisoned fish? Weren't these enough without some fuckwit throwing atomic bombs around?''

''Apparently not,'' said Vinnie, ending Richard's train of thought. Richard blinked at him, the glow of the corona still fresh in his eyes. He saw Sharon standing beside Vinnie. They were, both of them, supposed to be on the bridge with Lenny and Robyn. They were supposed to be either flying the ship or sleeping in their quarters just aft of the bridge, guaranteeing a continuous rotation of freshly rested pilots. For both of them to come aft had only one meaning:

''What's wrong?'' Richard asked.

''The ship's not steering properly,'' Vinnie said.

''Unusual drag forces,'' Sharon added. ''As if we've

got some breaches in the hull and the wind is just ripping through her.''

"Maybe it's just unusual wind conditions," Richard said hopefully. "Something stirred up by all these airbursts.''

"That's what we need to find out," Vinnie said.

Richard nodded, bent down to kiss Tam on the forehead, and, without saying so much as "good-bye" or "I'll be right back," motioned Vinnie and Sharon to follow. They headed briskly, and wordlessly, toward the aft companionway.

It is unlike Richard, Leslie thought, *to walk away without saying a word to his daughter.* But he had been right about one thing: that part about, "Wasn't it enough?"

"Jesus," Leslie said, putting a hand on Tam's shoulder. "What could happen next?" and then she wished she had not asked that question.

The deck lurched down another two degrees toward the bow and resisted Lenny's attempts to bring the ship level. There was also a list to starboard, equally stubborn.

Robyn noticed that the pressure in the ship's third helium cell was down slightly. She topped the sack off with gas from the reserve tanks, and was very grateful to have made (and won) her argument that Lenny's weight reduction program was becoming conservative to the point of paranoia, and to have kept all of the reserve tanks aboard.

Suddenly she bit her lower lip, and a slight quiver ran through her pen and yellowed a corner of her touch-screen as she watched the pressure in cell #3 dropping slowly but perceptibly, like the minute hand on a large clock.

"Okay, Lenny," she announced. "We've got some trouble here.''

"Say again?''

"Lenny, we have a problem," Robyn replied, and punched a copy of the readings onto his screen. "We're losing helium from cell three.''

"Okay, I see it. Right now the pressure is looking good.''

"That's only because I'm pumping in our reserve.''

"Do we have enough in the tanks to keep us aloft to the Azores?"

"We should," Robyn said, "except that—" and her lips jerked spasmodically.

Lenny noticed it, too: The far-left dial on his screen indicated a slow leak in the number one cell, directly overhead. "Okay," he said. "Let's stay calm. Tell Vinnie and Sharon to go have a look at it."

Outside the window, the snow was still being driven by powerful winds. The controls beneath Lenny's hands still resisted his commands, and the screens began to flash caution lights from the expansion joint that separated cell three from cell four. Within the joint, four of the tethers that ran from hull to hull, through the center of the ship, had snapped under the buffeting of the bombs; but *this should not have happened,* Lenny thought. The tethers were every bit as strong as strands from a spider's web, strong enough to be used in bulletproof vests. They should have held. But the tethers had broken anyway, and the ship was losing trim.

Up in cell three, Richard and the two pilot-engineers began their analysis of the leak. They crawled through a narrow, transparent companionway that ran from stem to stern through the heart of the cell. Sharon remotely controlled the searchlamps to illuminate the roof of the helium-filled cavern, while Richard and Vinnie inspected, telescopically, every square foot of the hull's curved underside for rips, tears, or punctures. They saw none. Only the floor of the cell showed any damage: three little bullet holes, far too small to account for the ominous leak Lenny was describing from the bridge, and they were located in the wrong place to be causing helium-venting, because, as helium saw the world, the bottom of a gas cell was really its roof. Helium always sloshed up, not down—which meant that the part of the cavern Richard regarded as the floor was where the up-sloshing helium pushed all the nitrogen, oxygen, and other "heavy gases." Therefore, any increase in helium pressure resulting from Robyn's attempt to stabilize the cell would only have forced these heavier gases down through the bullet holes and actually increased the ship's buoyancy.

Yet buoyancy continued to be compromised—which meant a sizable hole, or holes, in the roof; but search as they did, Richard and Vinnie saw nothing.

Sharon traded Richard's magnifier for her own, and she, too, saw nothing.

"So, what's your diagnosis?" Richard asked.

"It's not a big hole, or even a handful of moderately sized holes. So it must be a smattering of little holes."

"Too small for us to see?"

"Yes," Sharon said. "Maybe even microscopic."

"Yeah. Same conclusion I was coming to," said Richard. "That would mean *lots* of them. Lots and lots of them. For all we know, the whole ceiling could be riddled through, like a sponge."

"Dear God," Vinnie said. "How do we repair something like that?"

"We don't," Sharon said quickly. "So let's hope we're wrong."

Oh, there's that ugly word again, Richard thought. *Hope.* And what had the Greeks named the last demon to fly out of Pandora's box, the one Pandora almost managed to slam the lid on? They said it was the most horrible demon of all because it came disguised as an angel.

"Yes," Richard said. "Now I remember."

"Remember what?" said Sharon.

"How the last demon came out of Pandora's box. And hell came with her. And the name of the demon was Hope."

"Just what we need," Vinnie said. "Thoughts to get drowned by."

"Maybe we can turn back," Sharon suggested. "I'm sure we could reach Maine or the Massachusetts shore in one piece."

"And *then* what?" Vinnie was shaking his head violently. "No, that's no good. If we have to choose between the sea or famine and mobs, I think the sea will be more merciful."

"And don't forget the mite swarms," Richard added. "We haven't heard the last of them. They've been reporting outbreaks in Argentina. Chile, too. It's summer down there, now. The 'motes' like to bloom when the weather's warm, so even if a miracle occurred, and we managed to survive the New England winter, we'd only have to face those things again. It's like going from the frying pan into hell.''

"Richard's right," said Vinnie. "Turning back now adds up to committing suicide to avoid getting drowned.''

"Another cheery thought," said Sharon, and began threading her way aft along the corridor, toward the expansion joint. As she kicked open the hatch to the chamber separating the two cells, she realized, with a touch of shame, that in thinking of her own survival she had entirely forgotten about the biomorphs. The nearest laboratory still known to be functioning, still known to be capable of sustaining and multiplying the new insect species, was in the Azores. Against that goal, her own life was of no value. Against that goal, *Bluepeace,* and her crew, and her passengers, would be expendable.

"Okay," she said, as she ascended the ladder. "It's decided: We hold this hay wagon together as long as we can. And we drive it east as fast as we can.'' The last words came out high and squeaky, higher and squeakier the higher she climbed.

"Helium leak," she said, sounding like a refugee from the Oz Lollipop Guild. She would have worried about oxygen deprivation, if not for the ominous rip on the port side wall of the expansion joint, through which blasts of snow-filled air whipped into the chamber. There were no other holes in the room, none that she could see—which left the millions-of-little-holes theory intact.

She looked at the outer, aft wall of cell three thoughtfully and put her magnifier against it, bringing the dreaded theory to center stage.

"What do you see?" Richard called from below.

"Something like tooth decay," Sharon squeaked. "I think I'm seeing thousands of little cavities here. Microbial plaques. I've never *heard* of anything like this. It's—'' Just then, the ship made another lurching motion. Something nearby twanged like a broken guitar string, and Sharon felt a tickling sensation on her right cheek, as if a fly had alighted there. She tried instinctively to brush it away, but her hand closed on a thin strand of tether.

(What?)

The tether felt strangely brittle in her hand; and as she looked around the chamber, she noticed five other strands of the ship's webbing dangling free. She cut a sample from the fragment that had brushed against her cheek, surprised and horrified at how easily it cut. Then she climbed down the ladder and handed the strand to Richard.

"I'm afraid she's going down," Sharon said. "You can see for yourself."

The next twelve hours seemed to race by. Under the circumstances, Richard would have expected time to move slowly for him, as it had in the adrenaline pulse of the Sigmond attack. Perceptions of time, it seemed, had been arranged by a cosmic jokester. During the horrors of battle, a minute seemed longer than an hour. Now that every hour had become precious to him, now that he knew every minute aloft was a race against a sentence of death, an hour seemed barely a minute, and the transition from morning to midday came like a lightning bolt.

The microscope in the egg crate room revealed that the very structure of the *Bluepeace* had become diseased; and by the time Richard came up with the answer, Vinnie and Sharon reported that the number two cell was beginning to fail.

That was the death blow. Six helium-filled cells, tied together from stem to stern, were supposed to have made the *Bluepeace* the safest ship afloat or aloft. Even with all the reserve helium gone, and the number two and three cells deflating, the ship would have stayed in the air; albeit like a powerless balloon, without aerodynamic form, unable to move with grace, or beauty, or speed. Even this, Richard thought he might overcome by letting prevailing north Atlantic air currents push the *Bluepeace* eastward, toward the Azores. He was even drawing up a plan, in his head, for using the stern propeller, pulling in reverse, to drag his ship into north-south course corrections . . . until the final results came in. Richard had never imagined a wound such as this, with the first three cells venting and slowly sinking under their own weight. When they were empty, they would drag the aft cells down with them.

"Do we have enough helium in the tanks to keep the cells full?" Richard asked the bridge.

"Temporarily," Sharon replied. "But it won't matter."

"How long do we have?"

"At our current rate of loss, eight hours. Perhaps ten. We'll begin to lose aerodynamics an hour later."

Calmly, Richard asked, "How many hours to the Azores?"

"Twenty."

"Nooo . . . " The *Bluepeace* evacuation was degenerating into the best example Richard had ever seen of a good idea ruined by the failure of its designers to think their whole plan through. In the interest of giving the ship spacious staterooms, observation lounges, and dining saloons, Richard and Jackson had done away with the heavy metal frames of the ancestral dirigibles, replacing them with gossamer materials as light as silk, stronger than steel. The trick lay in making large quantities of spider silk, and they had accomplished this by editing spider silk genes into plant seeds. Overnight, a system which, for twenty-eight million years or more, had produced only corn silk, was recruited for the mass production of new materials. They had named the substance Tholian silk; but it was really biomorphed cornstarch, and as such it became the perfect substrate for the renegade fungi now making a clean sweep of the world.

"I did this," Richard told himself, and he realized that even the rubbery sealant lining each silken cell, even the walls of the Grand Dining Saloon, had been derived from corn.

The *Bluepeace* was dying, being eaten, as it flew, by the same disease that had blackened the world's cornfields. Sharon had likened the millions of microscopic cavities to tooth decay. The infection must have been working on the ship for weeks, unnoticed. One would have needed a microscope to find it, and during the weeks leading up to the blizzard and the bombs, Sharon and most of the *Bluepeace*'s other caretakers had been called away and reassigned to the greenhouses. The worst feature of microcavities, aside from their being difficult to detect, was that even if their rate of decay remained constant, as each cavity increased in depth, its surface area—through which life-sustaining helium was now being leaked—increased faster than its volume. Microbiology and mathematics conspired. Hidden weaknesses had been growing exponentially toward a critical breaking point, awaiting only the joining of physics to the conspiracy: the mechanical stresses of wind and snow and sine waves.

Richard looked longingly at the insect egg crate. He and Leslie had biomorphed two species of fungus-eating gnats, and many of the eggs were already hatching; but not enough of them . . . not enough. Richard thought: *If only we'd been given days instead of hours, and if only we possessed enough gnats, then I could set them free throughout the ship, and they just might be able to eat the infection and keep us flying a little longer.*

(If only . . .)

Nothing left to lose, he decided; nothing except that last, lingering shred of hope. He withdrew the gnat tray from the crate, swung open the door to the egg room, and shook the insects free. Twinges of pain shot through his swollen right hand as he rattled the tray; but it did not matter to him. It was the triumph of hope over reason, and Richard knew it. What use to send a few nibblers out against the infestation? What would be saved? Could they delay the downing of *Bluepeace* fifteen minutes—or even five?

"I did this," he said again. And he remembered how a failure to pay attention had left Dawn to the mites on that last day of the old world. First he had deprived Tam of her mother. Now, through yet another oversight, he was depriving her of life. . . .

God forgive me . . .

He closed the door behind him, climbed the spiral staircase to the *Bluepeace*'s B deck observation lounge, and found Tam and five other children sleeping in a warm, sunny spot on the floor. He was trembling.

Leslie had warned him, long ago in what seemed another world—at a time when there were still courthouses and stock markets and CNN—that eventually it would be getting down to days, then hours. Precious hours.

As he curled up next to Tam in the swath of sunlight, nudging her head onto his shoulder, Richard noticed that her fingers were clenched around a little fragment of stuffed fabric: an ear of Figment. And it entered his mind that he should have listened to Leslie Wells: that he should have taken more walks with his daughter, eaten more meals with her, played more games, while there had still been weeks . . . months. . . .

God forgive me . . . God forgive me . . .

The bridge was filled with a new sound—or, rather, a lack of sound, a lack of buffeting winds. For all their difficulty, they had outflown the blizzard and reached open daylight. Below, ahead of the storm, Lenny saw gently rolling ocean unbroken by a single whitecap, and he thought: *We just might get out of this after all.*

Sharon had the same thought, as she looked ahead and saw, about ten miles away in the east, the shadow of a still fully inflated *Bluepeace* printed on the ocean surface by the setting sun. Exhaustion allied itself with wishful thinking. Sharon's was an exhaustion born of attempts to obey Vinnie and Robyn's orders to get some sleep, and finding that she could only lie down and think about the ship.

Thoroughly exhausted and slightly hopeful, she rose from her chair and strode aft toward B deck, grabbing a box of fresh bandages and ointment as she went. Now that it was possible to believe everything might turn out all right, she had at last found a good reason to check up on Leslie, Richard, and any other wounded passengers.

Three minutes after she left, six of the green indicator lights on Robyn's screen flashed yellow, then red. The sound of an expansion joint breaking under the failure of its tether system came from somewhere very near. Hoping to reduce all aerodynamic stresses on the hull, Robyn cut off power to the stern propeller. Lenny and Vinnie worked frantically with the attitude control jets, trying to keep the airship level and in normal motion; yet it nosed up and down like a dolphin swimming. Robyn followed through with an order for full speed astern on her pad, in an effort to cut the ship's speed even faster; but there were ripping sounds astern, and the *Bluepeace* merely nosed down two degrees, then another two; and Robyn, in response, tilted her body four degrees closer to the aft bulkhead and began to pray.

"I'm afraid she's gone, Lenny," Vinnie said, with a curious tone of detachment. Lenny glanced at him as if to ask, *Are you scared?* He was not scared—only disappointed that all their work and planning had been for nothing; and there was a sickness in his stomach, a sickness that spoke of defeat; and there was anger and an odd sense of synchronicity.

Lenny felt only anger, an anger propelled to new heights by Robyn's pleas to God.

"Oh, yes. He's listening to you," Lenny said, and kept the rest of the thought to himself: *There really is a God out there. And He really is watching. And He really is listening. And He really does know everything that is happening here on Earth—all the horrors, all the pain, all the dying. And let me tell you something: He doesn't care.*

He awoke to sounds of shouting and the feel of the floor swaying along the ship's horizontal axis. Richard did not remember how or when he fell asleep on the floor of the observation lounge. He remembered telling himself not to doze off; he remembered that something had been wrong with the ship, but the details remained misty and vague, during those first waking moments; and suddenly the shouts grew louder and the creaking and snapping noises—which had seemed distant and barely noticeable when he awoke—came closer, leaving no time for remembering.

With a terrific groan, the entire bow was yanked down, as if in a kraken's grip. Apparently, exhaustion and sleepless disorientation did not bother Richard's equilibrium, for as almost everyone else in the room slid against the forward bulkhead, he managed both to grab Tam by the wrist and keep his balance. He caught hold of the starboard rail overlooking a row of observation windows, and the bow continued heaving nose down until at last he and

Tam were standing on one of the rail's vertical supports; and the forward wall, against which the other passengers had slid, actually became the floor. Richard envisioned the *Bluepeace* standing perpendicular in the sky, like a tall building levitating, but a glance out the windows—running, now, floor to ceiling instead of wall to wall—revealed *this* building to be falling out of the sky, not standing, and showed nothing except empty sea below.

"Tam! Richard!"

He looked down and saw Sharon, about thirty feet away, clinging to the forward quarter of the same railing. "Wait there," she said. "I'm coming up"; and as she began hauling herself through rows of vertical posts tipped horizontal, the rail snapped in the middle; then the whole room snapped in the middle; and Tam, calling out to Sharon, beheld a surreal vision in which the *Bluepeace*'s bow cast off and floated her friend away, as gently as a ship casting off from a pier.

And the world became a blur to Tam. For a moment she thought the room was righting itself. Unexpectedly—miraculously—the ladder on which she stood became a rail again, and the floor became a floor again; then, just as unexpectedly, the room pitched down toward the stern and the aft wall became the new floor. The rail and the observation windows disintegrated. Parts of a damaged helium cell and a spiral staircase and masses of flooring and plumbing formed a cloud of debris, pushed, pulled, rolled and mauled.

Leslie Wells was alone in the egg room, just aft of the observation lounge, when the breakup began. An extraordinarily violent shove lifted one end of the room until trays of amber, biomorph software, and scalpels broke loose from the cabinets aft and rained down around her. An electric engine dropped out of its mooring, and in only three seconds would have crashed through the wall above her, if the *Bluepeace* were not being racked by such convulsions of bursting seams and shifting masses as to yank the stern completely free of the bow. The engine was thus deflected from its appointed course. It plummeted harmlessly toward the Atlantic, making a barely heard swishing sound as it went through the ventral hull.

The insect pathologist lay in a room plunged suddenly into darkness, except for a diffused grayness seen through jagged cracks in the wall—or the floor, or the ceiling. She found it difficult to tell one from another. On what, for the moment, passed for the floor, she found the egg crate. Her fingers patted its surface, and at precisely the moment she satisfied herself that it was intact and whispered the sincerest "Thank God" of her life, one whole side of the room collapsed and she dropped two stories, came down hard on a silken wall, fell through it, screamed, bounced off a large fragment of flooring, slid past the wide opening made by the fallen engine, and fetched up against the aft expansion joint.

The biomorphs did not fare as well.

Through her one undamaged but still-ringing ear, Leslie heard the egg crate somewhere below: the heart-sickening sound of it sliding and thudding—the box that held nothing less than the hope of her entire civilization—about to sacrifice itself to gravity.

"Not if I can help it," she snarled, and lowered herself through a rip in the expansion joint, saw the crate resting on a ledge of rubble, dropped another story, shimmied down through a maze of torn rigging, and arrived at the ledge, just in time to watch the crate fall out of her grasp—again.

Richard tried to turn his body, tried to lower himself down to Tam, but his chest and back were pinned firmly between jaws of debris, and an even stronger set of jaws was sending jolts of pressure through his left thigh, as if muscle and bone were being compacted, as if the debris might actually bite through.

Tam was six feet below, clinging to a wall support that dangled in open air, with the cold Atlantic a mile below and, owing to the ship's sudden loss of weight, receding farther with each passing second.

"Don't look down!" Richard yelled, holding his hand out as far as he could stretch. "Just hold on tight and climb up."

She clung to the creaking support, sobbing.

"Pretend there's nothing down there! It'll be all right! Trust me!"

She hauled herself up a few inches, her legs and arms wrapped tightly around the support, her eyes gazing into his.

"That's right. Just keep looking at me. Come on. You can do it—" And rivulets of his own blood streamed round his neck and down his arm, and began pattering down on Tam's face. If it was possible, at a time like this, her expression grew even more horrified.

"It's just blood, honey. Don't worry about it. It looks a lot worse than it is—" And the *Bluepeace,* what was left of her, shifted uneasily. Something large broke loose above him and began thudding down, coming closer.

"Hurry!" Richard hollered. "You can do it! Trust me!"

The thudding and sliding sounds ceased, and Richard thanked God—*Thank God! Thank you, God*—that whatever was coming had stopped. Tam climbed a foot higher, then another two feet, and another two. Then, as if by divine intervention, the *Bluepeace* shifted again and the pressure on his leg and torso was released slightly. He fought his way down those last few inches and grabbed one of Tam's wrists in a vise grip, just as the wreck heaved to his right and a small mountain of debris broke away, falling just inches from Tam's head and taking with it the broken wall support that had, up to that moment, been her safety line.

She swung back and forth in Richard's grip, her shoulder dislocating, her lower jaw quivering—and nothing except a mile of air and the ocean below—and her wrist growing slippery in Daddy's blood-soaked fingers. He flexed his arm and tried to haul her in range of his other hand, and realized that he was flexing with the last of his strength. He could now feel the effect of blood loss, could see it through eyes that were beginning to blur.

Both hands. He needed both hands—

"*Dadeee!*" and Tam, looking up, saw it coming: Suddenly that large *something* was thudding toward him again, coming closer, much closer. It pounded hard against his shoulder and slid snugly between a wall fragment and

Richard's one free hand as he reached out for Tam's wrist. He felt the object shifting beside him, felt that it would fall away with but the slightest movement of his body, and wanted only to shake it loose and free his hand for Tam when he heard Leslie screaming in terror and frustration somewhere high above. He glanced sideways to see what the object was and—

No! Goddamn it, no!

The biomorphs.

"Dadeee!"

Both hands. He needed both hands.

"Dadeeeee!"

And his little girl's face, more terrified than ever—

(It'll be all right! Trust me!)

Did she sense it? Did she really know the decision he was about to make?

"Dadeeeee-eee!"

Both hands! He grabbed her wrist in both hands; and the biomorph egg crate slipped gently away, tumbling end over end and out of view. He pulled Tam aboard, his body trembling with the effort, his vision fogging as he found handholds and footholds for her.

A minute later, another hand reached down and pulled Tam to greater safety. Richard turned his head so that he was facing the insect pathologist, but he could not see her.

"Hello, Leslie," he said warily.

She said nothing, but went about the business of freeing his leg and torso. He lay there gasping, his body heaving with pain as she pulled something knifelike out of his thigh and bandaged him with shreds of silk.

When she finished, he said, "They're gone, Leslie," and his voice cracked dryly: "I lost the biomorphs."

There was no reply, no movement.

24

Testament

At last, *Darwin II* had completed its descent from deep space, emerging into a sea roofed over with a world-encircling mantle of ice. Automatically, the ship went into its preprogrammed search mode, dispatching its two robot submarines. The world shone cobalt blue under the flood-lamps, and the cameras recorded a million points of back-scattered light. The roof of Enceladus was chandeliers upon chandeliers of hexagons and spikes of ice. The crystals had been growing and dissolving and regrowing for millions, perhaps billions, of years—and it was among the chandeliers that one of the seekers photographed a ghostly white creature that looked like a crab, and yet at the same time looked very unlike a crab.

The ship "understood," in its programming, that this was precisely what the builders had most hoped to find: life. Multicellular life. *Mega*cellular life.

Within a microsecond, the pictures were relayed to the surface and beamed toward Earth, and within that same part of a second, *Darwin II* had decided to send one of the seekers speeding down from the chandeliers, to take close-up pictures of what appeared to be a flock of reddish-yellow sea slugs with manta wings.

It was the discovery of the century. New oceans. Other-worldly life.

And no one on Earth was watching.

On the morning *Darwin II*'s signal washed over the Earth, Leslie Wells was trying to power up a dying battery in a scratched and badly dented pad. Her fingers were freezing, and the top side of the *Bluepeace,* as more and more of its helium leaked out through infected cells, was becoming a shrinking island on the ocean surface.

She had managed to make radio contact with the Azores, notifying them of twenty survivors: two adults, eighteen children. Yet even this small number would be forfeit if the pad died and the Portuguese rescue ship was unable to home in on Leslie's beacon before the stern slipped under. She jerry-rigged the wires to tap into a thin-film solar grid stitched into what had been the *Bluepeace*'s dorsal surface. As the hull of the sun rose on the eastern horizon, a resurgence of life in Leslie's pad brought some small comfort: Richard and Jackson had built at least one system that worked—or would continue to work for a little while longer, until the corn rot dissolved it. They had simply dyed some of the silk threads black, and sunlight, as it struck the light-absorbing threads, was causing the dye to release electrons. These were absorbed by adjacent threads laced with microcrystals of titanium dioxide—which produced an electric current that sustained, for Leslie, a last vestige of civilization.

On her pad, a message appeared: "*Bluepeace.* Have received your updated coordinates. We are twenty-six miles away. We can be at your side in about an hour."

"Thank you," Leslie said, and she watched a bright

yellow flare go up over the northern horizon, marking the
position of the Portuguese cruiser. She wrote the exact
position of the flare on her pad and radioed it back, con-
firming, for the rescue ship, her GPS coordinates.

Just then, the French research vessel *Ocean Voyager*
chimed in, now officially part of the Portuguese/Icelandic
Navy: "The *Voyager* wishes to know if we can be of
assistance. We are ninety minutes northeast of your
position."

"Yes," Leslie replied. "The *Bluepeace* has broken up
and we have been unable to make contact with the bow
section. Please widen search for survivors." And then,
almost as an afterthought, she considered how much easier
it would be for her to restart the biomorph project using
insect DNA contained in the fallen egg crate, even if none
of the eggs or hatchlings had themselves survived.

"Please keep an eye out for any floating crates," she
added.

"Still hoping?" Richard asked. He and the children
were slowly freezing under sheets of silk. Salt spray and
increasingly choppy water were not helping, nor the darkness approaching from the west: the cold front they had
outraced the day before. The blizzard was catching up
with them.

It's at least three hours away, Leslie guessed. Everyone
would be rescued by then; but she imagined that there
would soon be no hope of finding either the bow section
or the egg crate. Yet it was miracle enough for her to be
alive, at least for the short term. She'd take whatever few
blessings were handed to her. That was the way of it these
days: Life itself was enough.

The severed stern should never have survived, by everything she knew. At first, she had believed herself, and
Richard, and Tam to be alone in the wreckage, as it ascended rapidly to a height of two miles, then to three.
Then, as she followed Richard's directions along the com-
panionways to the helium and ballast valves, she shouted
for help from anyone who might still be within the ship,
and was astonished to hear more than a dozen children
calling back.

They set up a relay between the valves and Richard,

and a new communications system was born: shouting down the companionway. Under Richard's guidance, they lowered the stern to three thousand feet and, through the night, operated it as a free-floating balloon, milking every mile they could out of it, toward the imagined safety of the Azores.

At precisely 2:20 A.M. the balloon had settled gently onto the Atlantic, the tail end leading.

At 8:30, the first rescue ship appeared on the horizon, and fired another flare.

That was when the full weight of what had been lost broke through fever and blood loss and chills, and began settling into Richard's thoughts. The biomorph project would have to be started again from square one. From *less* than square one: Something equivalent to the Nomad mainframes and Brookhaven's micro-MRI scanners would have to be built from scratch, and to the best of his knowledge there were no museum collections of amber in the Azores. It could take years to bring the project back to where it had stood only three days ago, and in the interim, how many millions more would die?

The falling egg crate replayed in his head, over and over—

(Dadeeeee!)

What would you decide if you could do it over? his inner voice taunted.

What would you do, Richard?

What would you do?

And every time—

(Dadeeeeee!)

—he reached out and grabbed his daughter's hand.

"What did I do?" he cried.

"What else could you do?" Leslie said, wondering if he would lose his mind, and not about to blame him if he did. "You call that a choice?"

He was feverish, on the verge of lapsing into unconsciousness again. Tam held his hand, and looked at Leslie pleadingly. Leslie closed the pad and inched toward them.

"Richard . . ."

"Have I killed our last hope?" he said.

Their eyes locked for a moment and her mouth opened

as if to speak. She put a hand on Tam's shoulder and said, "Shhh . . . It'll be all right."

The seething hell that had swallowed the *Nimitz* was cooling now. A man could actually camp out on the carrier's battered deck for a week without fear of radiation sickness. The ship had broken into three pieces, and there was not a compartment aboard whose seals did not crack that night, when the sea was still lethally hot. Yet it was testimony to her builders, and to the quick action of her crew, that one of those pieces still floated.

But she would not last forever. Nothing lasted forever, not even great machines. Collectively, slowly filling compartments were tugging her down. When finally a key bulkhead groaned and popped, the starboard side frothed a dozen geysers and the *Nimitz,* what remained of her, began dropping like an express elevator.

Then, where the ship had been, red depth charges shot to the surface and inflated automatically into a little fleet of bright orange life rafts, each equipped with food, water, sunshades, and two pads with satellite uplinks. But no sailors swam after the rafts. No one and nothing moved upon the waters. The orange armada was as silent as a grave—which, in fact, it was.

Hundreds of feet below, the carrier seemed to be picking up speed in its two and a half mile free fall toward the bed of the Indian Ocean. Throughout the ship, lightbulbs were imploding under the increasing water pressure. On the hangar deck, the tires of jet aircraft began to cave in, and by the time the ship descended its first mile, Styrofoam coffee cups in the cafeteria were compressing smaller than shot glasses.

The *Nimitz* struck bottom at forty-five miles per hour, within five minutes of losing its grip on the ocean surface. As inertia took over—as the continued downward motion of the ship, and the funnel of water that trailed behind it, punched down with all the force of a tidal wave—steel doors were kicked in, walls were bulldozed out, and an outcrop of girders (all that remained of the carrier's island stack) was uprooted and hurled over the starboard side. What remained of the *Nimitz* after the downblast more resembled a squashed insect than a warship. To a submersible pilot, the damage wrought by the downblast would have been indistinguishable from the scars of the atomic bomb.

The abyssal plain onto which the ship had fallen was darker than any mine shaft, and three times as cold; and for the denizens of that desert, the arrival of the *Nimitz* was like the fall of manna from heaven. Within hours, bacterial cysts began settling on the hull. Some of them had been drifting for more than four hundred years in the cold and the dark, in a state of suspended animation, waiting to wash up on a friendly shore. Within minutes of touching the hull plates, they activated, and began oxidizing the iron. Within months, they would become thick bacterial plaques, forming the basis of a food chain for uncounted species of ribbon worms, bristle worms, lamp snails, slugs, crabs, and eyeless shrimp—few of them any larger than an aspirin. The desert of the deep was a desert only at first glance. Wherever food fell out of the sky, it burst into life.

As the desert had bloomed on plesiosaur skeletons before the coming of the whales, on sea scorpions before the coming of the plesiosaurs, it would bloom now on the corpse of the *Nimitz*. It was a strange womb, this desert: The shrimps and crabs and worms of the abyss had remained unchanged in both appearance and habits, some of them, for more than a half billion years. Here, in the deepest reaches of the oceans, life seemed never to have noticed that on the continents above the Age of Amphibians had come and gone, the Age of Dinosaurs had come and gone, the Age of Mammals had come and now appeared to be going. In the world below, whenever the decks above were swept clean, the parade of life—uncaring, unaware—simply moved on. The *Nimitz*-eaters were nature's survivors.

Nothing less.

And nothing more.

Richard did not feel much like surviving. The ship's surgeon had patched his wounds, then assigned him a private bunk belowdeck, on *Ocean Voyager*'s starboard side, before finally asking the wrong question: "Is there anything else I can offer, by way of comfort?"

Richard said nothing. Nothing at all. He just stared at the physician with absolute emptiness in his eyes and in his soul. He simply closed the door of his narrow stateroom and lay awake for hours in the bunk as the blizzard caught up with him and began to roll the ship from side to side until his feet pointed alternately downward, at such a crazy angle that he sometimes seemed on the verge of standing up in his bed, then upward at an equally absurd angle, so that blood and bile gravitated toward his throat.

Comfort? he thought acidly. *Comfort?* the doctor had asked! *My God, I am in hell.*

He might actually get there yet, he feared. His rescuers had come with one of their twin engines broken, and the bilge pump just forward of his bunk had clicked on and seemed never to stop whirring—which meant it was being overburdened. If the second engine failed—*Well, let's just say it won't fail,* he told himself. But his imagination conjured the sick, twisted joke anyway: after all they had come through, it somehow seemed fitting that their journey end with the *Voyager* settling down beside the *Bluepeace*.

God's joke, Richard thought; and he decided to force "God's joke" out of his head and never picture the *Bluepeace* that way again, as if to do so might jinx everyone's hopes.

No trace of the airship's bow section had been seen. No floating crates, either; yet stories of Sharon's extraordinary luck kept all sorts of hope alive, at least among the children. They spoke of Sharon in hushed tones, as if she and the missing bow had, overnight, become the new *Flying Dutchman*. The French physician had spoken a different tale. As he probed Richard's wounds and tried to make sense of the famine, the plagues, the wars—to find a reason for them—he spoke of God's vengeance against an evil humanity. Richard realized that he was hearing the beginning of legend, the next Testament.

How much of that Testament would, a thousand years hence, be casually dismissed as fiction, he could not know. Most of it, probably—which was, he guessed, as it should be and would be . . . unless some damned fool dug up Leslie's amber.

Then they'd know that he really did exist, that a cure really had been found, and they'd guess rightly that the rest of the story was true: The scientist who was the Abraham of the tale, its would-be hero, really did confront the fate of Earth on one hand, the fate of a single child on the other, and in a moment of Darwinian revelation . . .

Disaster.

(If only . . .)

Why couldn't it have been life or death? My life for the biomorph tray? That would have been a fair choice. An easy choice.

And the legend weavers would have spoken of self-sacrifice, of Richard's heroism, his martyrdom.

(If only . . .)

He had come at last to zero, to a dark place where he had not only accomplished nothing; he had actually made matters worse. It was an awful truth, but a truth nonetheless, that coming to zero could deepen a person, could give one more to live for than one would ever have had otherwise—if it did not destroy him, if it did not devour hope beyond the spirit's capacity for recall.

In that cold, empty room, with nothing except the very real possibility that he could let himself die of minor wounds, let himself die of guilt and despair—

If you die, idiot—if you fold up and die like a wimp— who will watch after her?

Who will watch her grow up?

Suddenly Richard Sinclair was weeping, trying to find some last remnant of the demon Hope, weeping because he feared she was lost to him, and because there was nothing else to cling to.

The biomorph project might be just as dead with or without him. Even if it could be resurrected, Richard understood that from the time he reached for the first brick and started to rebuild, more than a decade would pass before he could undo the damage of his *Bluepeace* decision. The repairs would be slowed still further by the loss of Jackson and so many other great minds; and Richard also understood that if he died he would erase even more

hope—for Tam, for everybody. And so he firmed a resolve
to pick up the first brick, to stay alive, to hold on to Hope.

He used the next roll to starboard to help himself out
of bed, found the long wooden staff that the ship's surgeon
had loaned him, and staggered into the narrow corridor
that led past the galley. A minute later he entered the aft
meeting room. It was the ship's communications center:
banks of screens and two broad windows angling down
on the "garage," where the submersibles *Jules* and *Jim*
were strapped in their cradles. The famed Canadian microbiologist, Roy Cullimore, was seated at one of the satellite
uplinks. "*Ocean Voyager* to Brookhaven," the microbiologist said. "*Voyager* to Brookhaven—anybody, check in
now!"

"Roy, this is Don at *Alphatown*. We can see it, from
up here. It's all gone. Lots of smoke, now. It looks like
people are burning whatever they can't carry away."

"Richard! Over here!" Leslie said. The room lurched
to port and a volley of sleet and rain drummed against the
outer windows. Bile tried to creep up Richard's throat,
and Leslie did not look like she was faring much better;
but that had not stopped her from turning the conference
room and the microbiology laboratory into a new biomorph planning center.

Richard was not sure it would ever work again; but
right now he had this job . . . this job . . . always the job.
He had come back from the numb state of Dawn's death
not because he was forged from steel, not because he was
so tough, but because it was his job to come back. As
yesterday, so today: *you're a scientist,* he reminded himself. *You're here to work. People need you.* At bottom,
Richard was not the sort of man who walked away from
his job; and for Tam, if for no one else, he had to do it
the best way he could.

"We don't even have a spider genome to start with,"
Leslie announced. "Or a computer that can store it!"

"I know," Richard said. He hobbled over to Leslie's
table, took a seat beside her, and opened the flap on a
new notepad. When the screen flashed READY, he turned
to the insect pathologist and put his hand firmly over hers.

"Let us begin."

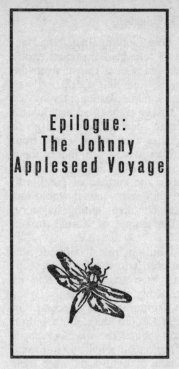

Epilogue: The Johnny Appleseed Voyage

*So I walk on uplands
    unbounded
and know that there is
    hope
for that which Thou
    didst mold out of dust
to have consort with
    things eternal.*

—DEAD SEA SCROLLS

*Late Holocene Cycle
Phase IV*

DAY 7,253

Viewed from the distance of the *Darwin II* space probe, from more than a light-hour above Earth, the single most breathtaking aspect of the Enceladus mission was that people had once been able to pluck titanium and silicon out of the ground and hurl it a billion miles. Miraculously, the machinery still functioned, both above and below the Enceladan surface, although the reactor's strength was slowly fading.

For nearly twenty years, now, nothing like it had ascended from Earth. *Darwin II* remained the most exotic assemblage of metals and ceramics ever drawn from the rocks and fashioned into tools; and like a 500,000 B.C. flint hand axe from the Nile, it qualified as an anthology of the people who had shaped it. Seen through archaeological eyes—either by a future human species that would go to the stars or by an alien species that would come from the other direction—the artifact would tell much about humanity's daring and genius, even its fallibility. In a far more benign environment than the surface of the Earth, free of the erosive forces of rain and wind, it would last almost forever. It would still be there, telling its story, long after the Sphinx and the temple of Karnak turned to lime.

The probe had traveled a billion miles; but that was nothing as compared to what the Earth itself was accomplishing—naturally, and of its own accord. The sun, its parent star, was tugging it, along with the entire solar system, five miles closer to Sagittarius every second. On Earth, the people had traveled more than three billion miles—nearly five light-hours—since the day *Darwin II* landed. They had journeyed more than a light-month since the building of the Sphinx, tens of light-years since their ancestors first carved flint hand axes near Karnak. Even if they never ventured again into the oceans of space, even if they chose to go nowhere, they would go far. Viewed from Enceladus, Earth was an eternal spaceship that grew its own passengers while en route.

At 4:20 P.M., Washington time, on day 7,253, *Darwin II* detected a slight change in the solar wind, in the hiss of ionized gas as it flowed from the sun's corona and brushed over Saturn's magnetic field envelope. Almost simultaneously, the crackling sounds, transmitted continuously through Enceladan ice, to *Darwin II*'s microphones, from thousands of micrometeorites striking the surface, strengthened perceptibly. Automatically, the probe's telescopes, infrared sensors, and photomultipliers began scanning the heavens, revealing that the solar system was sailing into one of the galaxy's dust lanes—again. The wind from the sun was burning a hole through the cloud, hurling vapor and veils of dust in every direction. At the edges of the hole, a glow of backscattered sunlight and excited electrons outshone even some of the stars, in certain infrared and radio frequencies. As seen by *Darwin II,* in those very long wavelengths, Earth and Enceladus appeared to be orbiting within a two-billion-mile-wide cave of light. Pebbles and boulders of ice were entering the cave, too massive to be nudged away by the solar wind; and a handful of darker, more ominous shapes would inevitably enter with them—masses of interstellar driftwood larger than office blocks and faster than rockets. They were rarer than red diamonds, these flying mountains. The vast majority were more than two thousand years away, the nearest more than two decades from Earth and Enceladus; but there were more of them moving into the path of sun space than had been seen for tens of millions of years . . . than had been seen since the terminal Eocene extinction . . . and the last days of the dinosaurs. . . .

Darwin II recorded the new images and numbers—more than any human mind could instantly absorb—and transmitted them downward, sunward, toward Earth.

Three hundred miles above Earth, in *Alphatown,* there was precious little time or computer space to permit more than the most fleeting glimpses of *Darwin II*'s reports. Almost all of the town's computer memory, and all the efforts of its inhabitants, had been devoted to keeping the biomorph project, and the town itself, alive. Insect and spider genomes were being uploaded from the Azores, edited, and downloaded daily while the town itself, now completely self-sustaining, had evolved into something like a hammer thrown around the world, spinning end over end as it flew.

From a height of three hundred miles, Wynne and Michelle, now grown to adulthood, could see Leslie Wells's and Jackson Roykirk's spreading reinfection of street lighting. At night, the east coast of Australia was veiled in ghostly cobwebs; but as a general rule, the lights were restricted to higher, colder latitudes that were traditionally insect poor. The Falkland Islands still glowed brightly, and parts of upstate New York, and Saskatchewan, Canada. A few well-lighted communities were beginning to broadcast

music and even television via the old satellite uplinks. The
Earth below, after a long night of radio silence, seemed
to be taking its first hesitant steps forward; but there was
not a flicker of light, nor a whisper of radio chatter, from
the City of Dreams, nor anywhere else on Long Island.
Anywhere, that was, except from the single research/trad-
ing ship that had gone out from the Azores, and was anchored, now, within sight of Long Beach.

Tam stood on a lawn of rot-stained but otherwise fungus-
resistant grass, on the very same spot where the motes had
climbed up Daddy's faceplate nearly twenty years before.
There was no need for space suits, this time. Helicopter
reconnaissance had revealed very little still living on Long
Island. No arachnid swarms. No humans, either.

Her long black hair riffled ever so slightly in a light sea
breeze. She wore it just as Mommy had worn it—Mommy,
whose bones lay somewhere behind those fungus-rotted
window frames, somewhere beneath the sagging tile roof.
She had not decided, yet, whether or not to venture inside
and collect the bones for cremation, or to leave them
where they lay—to refrain from looking at them, and to
remember Mommy as she had last seen her during the last
days of the old world. To remember her alive and graceful
and reasonably happy, with no real troubles except those
which, by today's standards, seemed so trifling as to be
the substance of nostalgia.

Oh, to be worrying about mortgage payments . . . or
scheduling shopping into the evening . . . or to be stuck
in a traffic jam on the Long Island Expressway listening
to e-mail and country punk . . . or to have a carefully
planned picnic ruined by ants . . . it must have been
wonderful.

A few blocks behind her, the beach buzzed with activity. This was the first stop on what would, if the *R.V.
Appleseed* could avoid pirates and military entanglements,
be a circumnavigation of the world. The ship carried a
precious cargo: crates of biomorphs—hundreds of crates—
with which the governments of Iceland and the Azores
hoped, one coastline at a time, to repopulate the Earth
with insects.

Although Tam had never met the man, or heard his words, she was, in a very real sense, signing her name to Rabbi Freedman's new covenant, in which humanity was being called upon to go into the wilderness and become restorers.

Now, looking at the wilderness that was once her home, she drew in a deep breath and expelled it with force. Her mind could not quite make peace with the notion that, by and by, no one would remain even to miss the old world. It filled her with pique, for a moment, to realize that more than half of the *Appleseed*'s scientists and officers had not been born at the time, or were too young to remember when the old world fell. There was no trauma in it for them, only the thrill of exploration.

And when she, and all the generation of mourners had passed, what then? Tam wondered.

Then, they would probably look back on the end days not as a horrible loss but as the beginning of legend, mystery, and high drama—as with any extinct civilization. Another lost Atlantis. Nothing more. Nothing less. Tam found it impossible to deny. No one walking down Telchines Road had ever wept for six million vanished Minoans and Egyptians. There was only marvel over the homes they had left behind—multistoried apartment complexes equipped with hot and cold running water, flush toilets, showers, and central heating—more than sixteen hundred years before Antony met Cleopatra at Alexandria. Minoan cities crushed under volcanic cocoons—they were the stuff of dreams, the stuff of endless wonder, not mourning. So would it be here, whether Tam liked it or not.

"Just another lost empire," they would say. "And good riddance, too," they'd probably add.

What arrogance! What reckless indifference! What . . .
What else could they say? Tam asked herself.

Could she really blame them? They could not know, from experience, what had been lost. They did not know the equal and opposite emotions that warred within her: remembrance of so much that was good in the old world, remembrance of so much that was bad. Much as Tam had loved laser television and cyber gloves, a part of her was forced to remember that much of the world that was erased was a bad world; and a part of her had learned to hope, along with the rest of the *Appleseed*'s crew, that the end days had provided a brave new opportunity to build the world brave and new.

A better world, she hoped—a world in which the people would never again give even five minutes of their time to the likes of Jerry Sigmond. A bit unrealistic, she supposed, but a miracle worth wishing for nonetheless. The last time anyone had put a Sigmond in authority, the result was a noose for humanity. Maybe—just maybe—the process of restoration was a chance to learn from the mistakes of the past, in order to build a future worth having.

Go into the wilderness and become restorers. . . .
They had been making preparations for a very long time. They had toiled. They had watched. They had waited.

They had no choice.

The Sigmond attack and the *Bluepeace* disaster had knocked the biomorph project back to the Stone Age. Building new mainframes had been relatively easy, as had reproducing the DNA scanners. Getting fresh supplies of ancient insect DNA was the hard part. The largest collections of Dominican amber had been housed at the American Museum of Natural History in New York, at the Smithsonian Institution in Washington, D.C., and in two private collections in Jersey City.

Today, almost nothing remained of the three cities. New York and much of northern New Jersey were simply flat, blackened by fire and fungal blooms, interrupted only here and there by splashes of green: by fungus-resistant grasses or by a cluster of cottonwoods on high ground. From the helicopter, Tam had seen evidence of the mysterious "shock bubbles" in which certain objects inexplicably survived a tornado, or a plane flying into a mountain, or a nuclear explosion, while all around them was total disintegration. The Verrazano-Narrows Bridge and the old twin towers of the World Trade Center were still standing, though the sides of the towers looked much like mowed grass spray-painted black.

Hoboken was the apparent epicenter, though no one

could figure out why. The town was reduced to a level plain on which not a single brick stood upon another brick. All the high-rises and churches and shopping centers had simply disappeared, except for steel boxes sticking out of the earth, marking places where bank vaults once stood.

Even before the *Bluepeace* fell, everyone knew that the four amber collections had become a vapor in the heavens, part of the very air that people breathed. So five expedition ships were sent to the Dominican Republic, in search of new amber supplies. The first three never returned. The fourth returned with a list of needed equipment, to be traded with a local warlord in return for amber-encased insects. The fifth expedition returned with the amber. And now a sixth expedition, as promised to the warlord, would unload twelve crates of live insects, to be followed by a seventh expedition, and an eighth, if the warlord honored his promise of safe passage. It was the beginning of trade routes, of what Leslie Wells, Tam's semi-adopted mother, had called the metastasis of civilization.

A clear, loud drone crossed the sky—the beating of helicopter blades. The tiny craft sped north without wasting a moment's time, or an ounce of fuel, to circle its support ship. It was headed in the direction of the radio signal Tam had recorded the night before, almost dead center on the AM band. The speaker had announced his location as Delmar, then signed off with an ancient Elvis tune: "Heartbreak Hotel."

Funny, Tam thought, *how the past can sneak up and bite you in the ass.* She looked across what had once been her backyard and, as she thrust one hand into a pocket and curled her fingers around a faded bit of Figment's ear, and as she held back the tears and her eyes stung, she noticed that her birdhouses still hung in the trees, and that the trees themselves were still in leaf. The leaves looked strange and depressingly brown, but the trees had survived nevertheless.

And Delmar was still alive! Delmar, New York. If only it were true that civilized people still lived here. If only.

The question that troubled her was: Why would they shout their presence on the airwaves? The Azores had decided long ago that when, by everything you knew, the world was a jungle, it was good policy to go radio silent and listen very carefully. Watch very carefully. And never, never shout, "I'm here!" You might wake the tigers.

Delmar.

Wynne and Michelle, following coordinates radioed up, on a narrow beam, from the *Appleseed,* had aimed *Alphatown*'s telescopes at upstate New York and, during their predawn flyby, mapped a large settlement surrounded by electrically lighted greenhouses, extensive—but not particularly healthy—farmlands, and a great wall.

The Delmarans.

Were they a dying people with nothing left to lose by attracting attention? Tam wondered. Or were they the have-nots trying to bait the haves into a trap? Or were they the beginning of a nation-state—very efficient greenhouse builders, perhaps?

They were a mystery that could not be left unexplored. But the people were far inland, and reaching them would be expensive, in terms of fuel. The *Appleseed* was a wind-driven vessel whose sails were three large, computer coordinated airplane wings mounted vertically on the deck. Her electrical power came from thin-film solar collectors, supplemented by two wind-driven generators. Save for possible getaways using the ship's rear-mounted water jets, all fuel was reserved for the helicopter; and during a round-the-world voyage in which it seemed unlikely that the fuel tanks could be replenished until and unless a supply of coconut oil was collected and refined, or until people willing to barter kerosene or gasoline could be found, every excursion inland had to be carefully debated and planned.

Every ounce of fuel was priceless. But the crew of the *Appleseed* had decided that finding the source of the broadcast was worth the price—worth that price and more: the helicopter, its two pilots.

Delmar. A newly discovered people. A first contact. It was hope and fear rolled into one.

(If only . . .)

The leaves on one of the birdhouse trees fluttered strangely, and Tam noticed that they were not leaves at all but a tremendous roost of butterflies. Painted ladies.

And again the past snuck up and smacked her across the back of the head. Daddy's painted ladies. So something had lived through that terrible night after all . . . then Tam took notice, for the first time, of the dandelions on the lawn. And she asked herself: *Are the butterflies pollinating the plants, slowly bringing their little corner of the world back? And is this why we have discovered that we are not alone in New York?*

Daddy's butterflies. A wise man once said that any sufficiently advanced technology was indistinguishable from magic. Well . . . Daddy had worked magic, and it lived here, now, at the old house. But the magic of science was not enough, not for Daddy.

Tam wished she could have worked *real* magic, and made it better for him. If only it had been possible for him, all these years, to know that something of his efforts had survived the Sigmond raid and was, perhaps, all these years, laying the foundations of restoration. It might have been a little easier for him, then. He might have blamed himself a little less, burdened himself a little less, if only . . .

For Tam, the two decades since the *Bluepeace* crash had been paved with the joys and defeats that time and chance bring to all people. The first and most hope-filled of those joys had been quite unexpected: the realization that, as Daddy and Leslie tried to restart the biomorph project, they were discovering that their relationship went deeper than spiders, roaches, and past rivalry. Tam encouraged it, hoping she might one day have a family again; but the first joy was also the first defeat.

With the loss of the *Bluepeace,* Daddy had lost something of himself. There was a deep wound in his heart, through which something of his spirit bled, taking with it that joyful spring in his step—which Tam last remembered seeing as they walked together across the lawn, to Mommy's Jeep, never to return. Daddy did not believe, could not believe, that he had any right to personal happiness. Not after the *Bluepeace* decision.

There was the job.

There was Tam.

And there was healing now—for all the world, maybe. But not for Daddy.

No, Tam thought. No one under the age of thirty would ever understand the peculiar horror and joy that warred within her. Remembrance. Restoration. Remembrance. The past was always a trap for her, and she found it difficult to believe that there ever was such a time when she had ridden with Mommy and Daddy all the way to Orlando on the interstates—ridden in the family car, faster than the wind—and that people once took such miracles entirely for granted.

The last days of the old world were the best time for us, Tam told herself—*as far away, now, as another galaxy.* And yet there were moments when she felt as if that time were only a gnat's breath away, that she could reach back and touch it—how warm and secure she once felt to have Mommy washing her hair in the kitchen sink, or to be playing video games with Daddy. She wished that she really could touch it, that with a wave of a magic wand she could put back the clock and make it all end happily. There would never have been a need to put off her wedding for a mission of restoration. Mommy and Daddy would have danced together on her wedding day and they would still be living in that beautiful house. Daddy would be retired now and she would meet him for lunch every week at Loui's Pancake Cottage. And her children would have come to know Grandma and Grandpa, and they would build sand castles on the beach. And the now chipped and rotted birdhouses would have sparrows in them.

"But, Daddy," she whispered to herself. "I don't have a magic wand."

And there was the magic of science. And the magic of remembrance. Good magic. Bad magic. Good. The Earth noticed neither. It did not answer Tam with its voice.

It simply moved onward and onward at its planetary scale.

Uncaring.

Unknowing.

Forever.

Afterword:
Reality Check

About 1953, the legendary British naturalist J.B.S. Haldane was asked by a priest what his years of studying Earth's creatures had taught him about God. Recalling, in that moment, that although the Earth was two-thirds covered with water, three quarters of all known species were insects, and a third of *them* happened to be beetles, he replied, "For one thing, He has an inordinate fondness for beetles."

Let's stop, you and I, and think about that for a moment. Let's think about all those insect species, just for a moment . . .

I don't know for a fact that most scientists walk this Earth in a state of endless wonder over the diversity and resilience of life. I know I certainly do. As far back as I can remember, I have been awed by (and haunted by) the insects. Even when my thoughts turn to how we might one day harness enough energy to cross the gulf between the stars, the insects seem to follow me. A case in point: Somehow, the brain of an ant, working far more efficiently than any automaton now on the drawing boards, is capable of performing all of the essential tasks that make possible the production of self-replicating machines. This is a reality, not a fiction: Within that tiny bundle of nerves lies the key to a technological advance that will make giant engineering projects (including an array of solar panels around the moon's equator) both feasible and inexpensive. It is the key to the universe—literally.

Perhaps we should all be awed and haunted.

All of the background facts about insects, as given in this story, including how they sustain our lakes, rivers, forests, the soil, and ultimately us, are reality. There was indeed a Kansas Grasshopper Act offering a five-dollar bounty on a bushel of severed grasshopper heads. Termites and cockroaches do indeed rank among nature's most efficient recyclers. They have been with us for more than 400 million years, and they are so good at what they do that every carbon atom in your body has, during those years, passed through their stomachs—repeatedly.

Equally real: The very different fates of two forests, one irradiated by gamma rays (a potent cousin to X rays, as described in chapter 9), the other cleansed of its ants. The implication of these tests is that a forest will be damaged more severely by the absence of ants than by the radiation effects of a nuclear war. God, Haldane might have observed, also has an inordinate fondness for ants. They make up more than 10 percent of the total animal biomass in most terrestrial habitats, including our forests and our cities.

All of the machinery that clicks through this novel is similarly grounded in reality. The Powell launcher (referred to in chapter 1, and intended to launch building materials into orbit) is a cheaper, more efficient version of Dr. Richard Bull's "space gun," first envisioned by Jules Verne. The particle bed propulsion system, so skillfully used as a bludgeon by The Don Peterson in chapter

23, was designed by BNL physicist Jim Powell, and was first tested in 1990. The single stage vehicle, into which Powell's (non-polluting) engine would have been fitted, was originally designed (by Powell and Pellegrino in 1984) for Senator Spark Matsunaga's U.S./Soviet Space Cooperation Initiative. The *Darwin* space probe, too, is a Powell/Pellegrino design, dating from 1985, and it did in fact become the primary reason for my involvement with the deep sea robots that first probed the Galapagos Rift and the *Titanic* (the former was practice for the ice worlds circling Jupiter and Saturn, the latter was a pause en route). The *Bluepeace* blimp is an unfinished Pellegrino/ Powell design, and micro-MRIs exist, at this time, only on our drawing boards—but stay tuned.

What else in this book is grounded in reality? Are such wonders and terrors as giant parasitic worms, the cloning of extinct species, swarms of *Desmodus,* oceans hidden in space, and cycles of mass extinction real possibilities? Yes and no, as follows:

1. All background historical details, including where the tradition of christening ships with bottles of champagne came from and why the man who organized America's blood banks bled to death, are real.

2. The biomorphing recipe (presented in chapters 16 and 17), through which ancient life forms may be resurrected from extinction by modifying DNA (primarily regulator genes) in embryos of their closest living relatives, is the latest version of my still-evolving "Jurassic Park Recipe" (characterized by Arthur C. Clarke as heading ultimately toward "Add water and run!"). Biomorphing simplifies the "cloning" process enormously, bringing such marvels as living, breathing dinosaurs closer to reality—which makes the question raised by Crichton and Spielberg ("Just because we can do it, should we?") all the more timely. While the bridge we are about to build (that is, redefining the word "extinct") is still a fiction, now is the time to consider what trolls may be hiding under that bridge—before we actually get there and have to deal with them. A case in point: Since the genetic distance between human and chimpanzee is less than 1 percent, were we to obtain a complete blueprint of DNA from, say, the bones

of an Australopithecine man-ape, a chimp embryo could be biomorphed into one of our ancestors merely by stitching in edited sequences of human DNA . . . less than 1 percent. With all that this portends in terms of sheer cruelty (not to mention resurrecting the ugly spectre of slavery), this is an experiment that should never, under any circumstances, be carried out—a troll that should never be approached. And it speaks well of scientists that there is 100 percent agreement on this point.

Ancient butterflies and dinosaurs, however, are a very different matter, and a possibility brought even closer to reality by paleontologist Mary Schweitzer's extraction of apparently ancient blood products (in very fragmentary form) and other organic substances from the femur of a *Tyrannosaurus rex*. Our attention has since turned to "mummified," paper-thin bones contained in a deposit of dinosaur eggs from China. Preliminary results from Schweitzer's lab have suggested that, at least insofar as the large, bipedal, flesh-eating dinosaurs are concerned, approximately 80 percent of the dinosaur genome may still be running around today—in ostriches (most of the remaining 20 percent probably resides in other animals, including reptiles). At the American Museum of Natural History, I have an ongoing bet with a colleague: By September 12, 2015 (Ashley Jane Amber Pellegrino's 21st birthday), we will have living saurian biomorphs. Riding on the bet: Sixty-five cases of Mars Bars—one case for each million years since they last walked the Earth. I estimate a 50/50 chance of winning.

"What good is that?" you may ask. "Who needs saurian biomorphs?"

The answer is that comparisons of the human genome with dinosaurs, birds, reptilelike mammals, reptiles—even insects and yeasts—will (and are) teaching us how to read DNA. Presently we can easily print copies from any genetic code we choose, but we can actually read and understand just a few sentences from the book of life. We are in a position very much like the first Egyptologists, who came upon hauntingly beautiful hieroglyphs but could not read them until the discovery of the Rosetta Stone. With a little help from extinct species, we are learning how to carve the Genetic Rosetta Stone. We are beginning to understand the words. Within that new understanding lies the cure for virtually every known disease, including aging. It seems likely that within the lifespans of people living on Earth today, we will be able to artificially boost human intelligence, and perhaps even *reverse* the aging process. Theoretically, there is no limit to how long humans may be able to live—which brings great promise and equally great responsibility into the world. I am reminded of this every time someone says, "Sounds great. If we can live so long, perhaps we can *really* go out there and colonize space—use the 'high frontier' as a pressure valve for our growing population."

WARNING: Earth is not a disposable planet, and it is not wise to behave like a spreading cancer in the galaxy.

Bridge ahead.

Trolls ahead.

Watch out for—

3. The genetic time bomb theory is highly speculative and was used, in this story, to provide one of several possible explanations (ranging from scientific to religious) for what appears, to those caught in the shockwave, to be an inexplicable outburst of evil. However, the Earth's approximately 33-million-year cycle of mass extinctions (which puts us just about due for another) is an apparent reality. The census of ancient insects before and after the last two mass extinctions (as described in chapters 1 and 11) was begun during my internship at New York's American Museum of Natural History in 1977, and was being expanded in New Zealand in 1980 when Luis and Walter Alvarez discovered an "asteroid ash layer" buried a few million years beneath one of my fossil crab beds. After some heated correspondence (which to a fly on the wall might have appeared to be bickering but was really brainstorming at its best), we arrived at a consensus that whatever killed the dinosaurs had impacted the insect class every bit as severely as the reptiles. That realization started a train of thought (or rather, a flight of abstract fantasy: What if the insects died first?). As I said, I was always haunted by and drawn to the insect world. What more

could I have asked for? Sex, violence, and a cast of trillions.

Although no one has yet discovered a time bomb ticking away in a fungus gnat's genome, the periodic resetting of forest ecology in China (every 120 years) by a genetic clock hidden somewhere in bamboo DNA is every bit as real as it is devastating and mystifying; and nature seems to be providing us with plenty of hints that (as was originally suggested by Charles Darwin in *The Descent of Man*) natural selection acts not only on individuals, but also on groups.

One of my favorite hints, or clues (second only to a bacterial consortium named *Rusticalus titanicus)* is *Pepsis marginata,* a large black wasp that spends its adult life as a vegetarian, but whose larvae are carnivores. The wasp has a very complex relationship with an equally large, insect-eating tarantula species, the kind of relationship that leads one to wonder if perhaps evolution does shape entire ecosystems all at once. The spider's body hairs give it one of the most delicate senses of touch in the animal kingdom. Any moth, cricket, mantis, or wasp reveals itself as soon as it approaches close enough to disturb the air currents, whereupon the spider spins, pounces, and sinks its fangs in with surgical precision. And yet for *Pepsis,* and for *Pepsis* alone, there is a special dispensation. When the wasp alights nearby, the insect predator unaccountably turns into a prey species, letting her walk all over its body without striking, and even standing guard while, inches away, the wasp digs the spider's grave. Once the prey is entombed, the wasp lays a single egg, walls the spider in, and leaves. Then the relationship begins to get really strange . . . and nasty.

When the egg hatches, the larva does not simply eat the spider and move on. No, the interaction between wasp and spider is a bit more complicated than that. The hatchling is much, much smaller than the spider and needs weeks of further development before it can fend for itself outside the tomb. During those weeks, it has no source of food and fresh water except the spider; so if it kills the spider quickly, by biting into its brain or respiratory ducts, the hatchling will starve before it matures. As far as we know, this never happens, because the wasp is born with a culinary program—at once obscene and wonderfully diabolical—that first targets the tarantula's bodily fluids, leg muscles, sensory and reproductive organs before focusing on and slowly taking apart the digestive tract. The growing larva kills the spider by inches, just a little piece at a time, keeping it wet and warm and alive by saving the central nervous system and circulatory organs for last. By the time the program has run its course and the wasp is ready to leave the tomb—ready to replicate the program in a new generation—nothing remains of its prey except hair and caved-in bits of chitinous shell in the shape of a spider.

We have, in this picture, a tarantula that is twice as large as the mother wasp and equipped with poisonous fangs. You would think that, drawn from the realms of pure chance, at least some of the spiders would eventually hit upon the right behavior (*If you come near me, I'll kill you*) and break the cycle, spreading its increasingly-likely-to-survive-genes into succeeding generations. Yet the precision with which the larva carves up and consumes the spider's organs, in just the right order, hints that this has been going on for millions of years.

While competition between individuals is clearly a powerful force in nature, it is not likely the whole story of natural selection. David Sloan Wilson (of SUNY at Binghamton) suggests that units of selection "are nestled in one another, like Chinese boxes. Genes compete with other genes within an animal; animals compete with other animals within a group; groups compete with other groups; and megagroups compete with other megagroups." In this sense, a beehive, or an entire reef ecology, or the biosphere itself, can be viewed literally as organisms.

If the Earth is a biological consortium whose activities are interrupted by occasional mass extinctions, then we are far from explaining how our little corner of the universe works. This is no cause for despair. It should fill us with great joy to be living in a Discovery Period (or, as some would have it, an Age of Ignorance), with unsolved mysteries strewn in every direction. If we begin to think of the whole interlinked ecology as a consortial lifeform, we raise new questions about whether or not the genomes of separate species may in some way be "communicating" with one another, in much the same manner as your nervous system communicates with free-roaming cells of the immune system. Add to these questions evidence from high-resolution sonograms that as many as one-third of human pregnancies begin with serious defects (often called "transient phenomena") that quickly self-correct, as if regulator genes are responding to some sort of feedback, as if DNA is a computer capable of at least rudimentary calculations . . . As within, so without? Is it possible that trillions of little self-preserving biocomputers, out there in the wilderness, are, to one degree or another, shifting this way or that in response to probability curves hidden in changing environmental conditions? Like most strange speculations, these will probably prove false, but that should not stop us from exploring the questions they raise. If you begin to perceive that the interplay between species might be more complex than we have imagined, if the next time a lowly ant crosses your path it arouses in you a measure of curiosity—perhaps even a sense of gratitude and wonder—then this book will have served up at least some small measure of what I had hoped to convey.

4. As this story was being written, many events that were entirely fictional actually made headlines shortly after the chapters were submitted. For example, a new prion variant made "mad cow disease" a household word and there did indeed follow "barnfires of cows" in England. Then, in April 1996, forty people in a Brazilian village were bitten in their sleep by none other than *Desmodus* (there were no fatalities, and, as stated in chapter 8, the overabundance of cattle in the region made this an entirely predictable, if not inevitable occurrence). In August 1996, a spectacular and somewhat terrifying bloom of the North Atlantic's bacterial and planktonic biomass was discovered off the Grand Banks, while in America concerns were raised about the mass death of honeybees. Then, during the winter of 1997, as a handful of media-savvy crisis-criers pointed to a leak of "radioactive heavy water" (failing to mention, of course, that you could drink water directly from "that poisonous leak" and receive only one two-thousandth the dose you normally receive from your envi-

ronment [make that one six-thousandth, if you happen to have granite floors or tabletops in your home]), and as they called for the shutdown of Brookhaven National Laboratory, Long Island's north shore became the site of a *Sarcoptes* outbreak—mites. (Editor's note: I can verify this, and sometimes I wonder if, maybe next time, Charlie should write a book about flowers.)

It's all just odd coincidence, I say—not at all unlike Sharon's "statistical anomlay." The so-called "Sharon effect," by the way (statistical anomaly or not), is an apparent reality, named after a certain acquaintance of Arthur C. Clarke and Father Mervyn Fernando (the name has been changed to protect the innocent from the innocent until proved guilty).

5. The blushing ostrich dinosaurs in the Prologue were actually created some years ago, as part of a children's book I was planning with the incomparable SF illustrator Bob Eggleton *(The Other Ark:* the one with all the dinosaurs aboard . . . and it's still out there . . . somewhere). While the blushing tool-makers are fictitious, they are based on very real questions about why ostrich dinosaurs and octopi, in spite of having the necessary manipulative limbs and a high nutrient feeding strategy, did not develop bigger, tool capable brains before we did. Anthropologists tell us that man's greatest evolutionary step was the one taken on two feet (it freed the hands to do work). I think dinosaur eggs and octopus eggs tell a different story: Man's greatest evolutionary step was *really* the one taken by woman, with her consumption of meats and other high-nutrient foods, with her high nutrient throughput to the developing young through an umbilical cord and, later, through milk glands. Big brains are energetically expensive. Though occupying less than 2 percent of the body's volume, your brain consumes more than a quarter of your oxygen and nutrients. The columns of your neocortex are essentially giant parasites living inside your body, and such growth can be sustained, during our formative years, only by the right kinds of mothers (for more on this subject, see chapter 4 of *Return to Sodom and Gomorrah,* Avon Books, 1995).

6. The two-step dinosaur extinction hypothesis, de-

scribed in chapter 1, can be blamed on me. The puzzling findings on which this speculation is based—including post–KT boundary (that is, *after* the approximately 65 million B.C. asteroid/comet ash layer) dinosaur egg fragments and large mammal bones unearthed in China—are real.

7. The New Jersey amber deposits (those thus far uncovered) date to approximately 90 million years ago (as determined by such evidence as datable volcanic rocks, and how far above or below these volcanic sequences the amber beds lie, and how far above the amber beds lie the last dinosaur bones). It was my introduction to the New Jersey amber beds, by paleontologist Gerard R. Case in 1977, that directly gave rise to the infamous dinosaur "cloning" recipe. You will recall that a scene in the first *Jurassic Park* film showed a lawyer rafting down a jungle stream toward an amber mine, and gave the impression that insects from the Age of Dinosaurs must be unearthed Indiana Jones style—from hostile jungle habitats. I'm sorry, but I do not have an Indiana Jones story to tell (this time). In reality, more often than not, Case and I carried out our excavations in the shadows of housing developments, shopping malls, and smog-shrouded freeway overpasses.

8. Prey-switching, disease vector-switching, death of the waterways, death of birds, terrifying replacement events (of insects by arachnids and other not-yet-dominant invertebrate groups), poisoning of the oceans, massive crop failures, and global economic collapse are just a few of the changes we could expect if even a handful of insect families (groups comprising related genera) were to disappear tomorrow. Although the background facts I have given (in chapter 3) on the millions of mites that live in our homes and on our skin are real, I took a liberty or two while using them to illustrate the sorts of population surges and resultant behavioral shifts that would undoubtedly occur in the absence of known natural controls (no one has yet been eaten alive in his sleep by bed mites . . . not yet). Almost everyone I know looks upon insects as the world's most annoying pests, but none of us fully comprehends, yet, what even nastier pests they may be keeping at bay. The "mote" outbreaks, while still a fictional example, are

in all likelihood less extraordinary and less horrifying than the surprises that nature would actually throw at us in the event of an insect die-off.

9. The Long Island slime plague of 1973, the wasp plague of 1979, and the mite plague of 1994—reality.

10. The President's encounter with a shark in chapter 8: Reality. That was me.

11. An evil mentor's attempt to force a student to perfect a pulsed laser, so that he could sting horses from afar and fix the outcomes of races—never mind.

12. All of the "culinary delights" mentioned in this book are real. I've eaten (and rather enjoyed) most of them myself, including certain insect treats. Fried grasshoppers, by the way, taste an awful lot like popcorn, while large grubs compare favorably with sweet shrimp. I have it on good authority that queen termites are sweetest of all. As for Mars Bars deep-fried in batter, the secret is in freezing them before frying.

13. Dr. Bill Schutt (who seemed real to himself, the last time he looked) is still alive—or at least undead. I am extremely grateful to Bill for a vast amount of technical information about bats in general, and *Desmodus rotundus* in particular. He actually spends much of his time teaching zoology at Bloomfield College in New Jersey and researching bats at the American Museum of Natural History's Department of Mammalogy. His research interests include the biometrics of bat locomotion and the evolution of vampire bats. In addition to publishing original research on bats, he is currently writing his first novel and plans to work with Richard "Tuna" Sinclair on a future collaboration.

Bill is an old friend and a good sport. It was he who suggested that I find a way to bring his favorite animals— vampire bats—into the story, and he requested that I make them kill him.

I was unsure of that, at first. I did not believe I could really find a legitimate reason for bringing bats into the tale, and weaving them throughout. But in my sleep I kept getting this picture in my head, a picture of a woman trapped in a school bus or a lighthouse, trying to press her palms over a crack in a pane of glass, and there was

a silent, seething mass of fur and fangs on the other side—
Desmodus. And in my dreams the Plainview Jesus pro-
jected itself toward Bill with a hideous grin, and there
were prions on its teeth and blood in its eyes, and I realized that I was attending a Christmas mass in Dante's hell.

"Oh, God—sounds like you've had a couple of really
bad nights," Bill said, when I told him of the dream.

"No," I said. "These were good nights. I think I know
how to kill you now, and how to send a really nasty
pattern of recoil out from a church."

After many long discussions about what Bill would and
would not say or do in certain bad situations (we actually
acted out those situations), the vampire bat scenario began
to take shape, with Bill pointing out at least two or three
overly dramatic "Pellegrinoisms" that needed to be
dragged out and shot. He also begged me not to harm
the bats, but he was okay with me blowing up Hoboken
thirty times.

Wherever possible, I wanted the bats in this story to
look and behave just like the real McCoy (for what I got
right, thank Bill; for any bat heresies that might have
squeaked through to publication, blame me). It should be
noted that vampire bats have never been known to descend
upon sleeping towns and bleed people to death. In fact,
not a single person is known ever to have died this way.
It happens in *Dust* only by means of an extraordinary
biological crisis. One of Bill's concerns with developing
horrible scenes of Death by Vampire Bats was that this
would feed the public's general conception that bats are
evil, monstrous creatures. Dr. Schutt points out that, like
insects, they are anything but monstrous, and he empha-
sizes the importance of bats to many of the world's ecosystems. Intelligent, unique, and highly beneficial, many bat
species have been destroyed or threatened because of ignorance and fear. Even vampire bats, whose ranges are limited to certain regions of Mexico, Central America, and
South America, are more timid than intimidating. "I'd still
walk into a church full of vampire bats," Bill says, "but
I guess I'd pass on the kneeling."

14. The World War II Bat Bomb, described in chapter
9, was actually built and tested, and America's first at-

tempt to construct a smart cluster incendiary bomb actually did work too well. An entire U.S. Air Force base and much of the surrounding countryside were burned to a cinder. Because the project was highly classified, the base commander was never told why his base had burst spontaneously into flames. Indeed, he went to the grave never learning the truth.

15. Prions easily rank, for me, among the top three in the Hit Parade of the world's most fascinating diseases—especially when they force us to consider (as in chapter 14) where these apparently infectious "Stanley" proteins (named after Stanley Prusiner) came from. They are perhaps the most ancient enemy of all, and yet at the same time they may hold the key to the origin of life—a process that has never entirely ceased. New prions must be emerging all the time, given the fact that we shed cells, and DNA, and random scraps of protein as prodigiously as a cat sheds hair.

16. The story of the harmless, filter-feeding sponge that evolved hooks and became carnivorous—reality.

17. The story of Los Angeles and other cities degenerating into "archaeologically invisible" populations and warlord leadership can be seen today in the economic collapse of Haiti, Albania, numerous African nations, nuclear-armed North Korea, and much of the former Soviet Union. If we are unwise, these will be coming attractions for much of the world during the next fifty years. Some of the more horrifying urban *Dust* scenes actually have occurred, and for these I owe much, in addition to my own collisions with mob rule, to eyewitness accounts (particularly from SUNY archaeologists Elizabeth Stone and Paul Zimanski) of Iraq before, during, and after the 1991 Gulf War. The Washington deathscape, through which Father Elton walked, was drawn from numerous (and unforgettable) conversations with Hiroshima survivors. Among these were a man whose nearsightedness was permanently corrected by the pressure wave (he does not, however, recommend nuclear explosions for corrective eye care), and a woman who came through the Hiroshima bombing unharmed, fled home to Nagasaki, and happened to be describing the "silent blue flash" to her family when the

second atomic bomb exploded. Knowing what that flash was, and responding to it immediately with a call to get under cover, probably saved her entire family. I also knew a priest who spent the rest of his life wondering what became of the children he had seen standing atop a demolished building in Hiroshima. I saw no need to embellish eyewitness accounts. The stranger and more disturbing the phenomena Father Elton witnessed—black fire sizzling forth from a body, people disintegrating as they waded into the river—the closer they are to reality.

18. The born sociopath, Jerry Sigmond, was inspired, in part, by numerous chance encounters with such personalities, raising enduring questions about where these creatures come from. Among these personalities was the reverend Jim Jones, whom I blundered into on my first archaeology expedition in 1975, and who was keenly interested in the fall of past civilizations. Looking back, I cannot recall the slightest hint on his face or in his words that the man had deceit and mass murder on his mind. I have never again looked on with a sense of incredulity as the neighbors of a newly discovered serial rapist or killer stood before newscameras and described the monster as "friendly," "gentle," or "normal." That's what makes them so scary. They don't grow hair on their palms. They don't foam at the mouth. They don't *look* like monsters. If they did, they would not be able to cause us such endless trouble.

In 1994, while on a lecture tour, I crossed paths with entomologist and behavioral scientist Edward O. Wilson and asked him what childhood events he thought could create a Jim Jones or a Saddam Hussein, a Ted Bundy or a Joel Rifkin. Wilson raised the possibility (and I have come to suspect he was right) that some people are simply "born rotten."

19. The story of the first glycerin crystal, and the chain reaction of crystallization that swept around the globe, is real. In 1969, a descendant of that crystal infected a very special coolant additive and replicated itself so thickly that the coolant began to resemble orange juice. The coolant in question was needed for electrical equipment aboard the *Apollo 11* lunar module, and Neil Armstrong's mission to

destiny came within a gnat's breath of ending before it ever really began.

20. Paleontological evidence that the continents were littered with dead, fungus-encrusted forests during the Permian extinction—reality. (For more on this subject, see Richard Kerr's report on Henk Visscher *et al.* in *Science,* vol. 270, 6 October 1995.)

21. The hatching of wheat seeds after more than 3000 years in the tomb of Tutankhamen ("King Tut")—reality. The hatching of beetle eggs after more than 3000 years in the same tomb was reported but remains to be proved (beetles, unlike wheat, can move into a sealed tomb and exist for multiple generations, even if the eggs are able to lie dormant for long periods of time). Evidence for extreme longevity of insect eggs is at best scant. Aside from a few strictly anecdotal reports of eggs hatching in apparently well-sealed museum containers after more than a century, this is, somewhat like the field of exobiology, a science that has yet to prove beyond serious dispute that its subject matter exists. We do know, however, that a New Zealand weta (a large cousin to the common cricket) can freeze solid and survive in this condition for at least several years. We also know that certain deep ocean shrimp eggs can drift for centuries before hatching, and that the eggs of frogs, fish, and aquatic insects can lie dormant for more than a decade in dried lake beds.

22. The grim details of life in an underground missile combat crew capsule, including equipment operation procedures—reality. I *have* made some changes with regard to food storage and life-support capability (where deletions or alterations were requested, I took those as opportunities to redesign and slightly improve the capsule environment). The "Sole Survivor/Soresport" equation, also known as the "Doomsday Machine," whereby missiles, upon losing contact with some of the capsules, would switch control to the surviving capsule(s), and upon losing contact with all capsules would begin a countdown to automatic launch against their last designated targets, actually existed during the height of the Cold War. This was the height of bravado and folly—not to mention blind trust in our machines. America's "Soresport" protocol was discontinued in the

aftermath of the Chernobyl and *Challenger* disasters. Similar protocols were reconsidered in Russia and China in 1986, and as of this writing (according to the latest available evidence) are still in effect.

23. The manner in which scientists speak to each other in this novel (and in real life) when they are trying to solve problems often sounds like sniping and bickering, but most often it only sounds that way. It's really just a matter of playing devil's advocate to each other, holding an idea up to criticism and seeing if it can stand the test of time (or if it can stand at all). Every good scientist understands that an idea profits nothing from someone who merely nods and says, "I like it." Harlan Ellison (the wise man whose words the President recalls in chapter 3) encapsulated this process most effectively while observing the *Voyager* scientists in 1980. Although best known for his fiction, his essay, *Saturn November 11,* is the finest (not to mention the most humanistic) account I have ever read of scientists at work (catch it in Ellison's *Stalking the Nightmare,* Berkley Books, 1982).

24. The disappearance of the Rocky Mountain grasshopper (formerly a plague organism whose swarms blotted out the sun and shattered American agriculture) is a real mystery that towers over the vanished Roanoke Colony and the *Flying Dutchman.*

25. Dr. Sandra Shumway's "dinoflagellate from hell"—reality.

26. The pain-dealing life cycle of dracunculiasis—reality.

27. The ravages of scurvy—a reality with possible influences on a legend: King Arthur is said to have died, finally, of an old wound that reopened.

28. The story of the lost World's Fair capsules (in chapter 18) and the role of landfills as anthologies of our civilization—reality. Environmentalists and politicians recently became concerned over reports that old newspapers and magazines in Long Island's Oceanside landfill were not decaying and might still be readable 4000 years from now (among other items, the Oceanside landfill entombs jet aircraft parts, lunar module construction logs, and the unfinished *Apollo 20* moonship). The powers-that-be are now

planning to inject chemicals into the mound to hasten decomposition. We've all heard the old refrain: "I'm from the government and I'm here to help you." Environmentally, this is senseless (materials that previously did not interact with the environment at all will be made to do so—which is bad news for air and water). Archaeologically, this is senseless (somewhat akin to burning the library at Alexandria).

29. On the fate of ships in the bacterial environment of the deep ocean, an irony arises: More than 90 percent of the world's iron deposits were precipitated out of the oceans between 2.5 and 1.8 billion years ago by cyanobacteria (blue-green algae), which consumed carbon dioxide and released iron-binding oxygen. Humans drew iron ore out of the Earth and fashioned it into the steel plates of the *Yorktown,* or the *I-52,* or (in our story) the *Nimitz.* Now, on the abyssal plains, bacterial consortia are dismantling the hulls of our sunken ships and returning them to the Earth as iron ore. Microbiologist Roy Cullimore (who appears in chapter 24) points out that Marcus Antonius, in the second century A.D., seemed to have anticipated this discovery when he wrote: "Substance is like a river in constant flow, and the activities of things are in constant change, and . . . work in infinite varieties; and there is hardly anything that stands still." So it is with the bacteria that digest (or recycle) our ships, and with the termites that digest (or recycle) our homes. So it is with almost everything else.

Are you beginning to get the feeling that the universe is rather larger than most people suppose? Good. Even the remotest iron-munching bacterial colony two-and-a-half miles down on the bed of the Atlantic seems to be hitched to everything else in the biosphere—as if the largest organism on Earth really is the biosphere itself . . . or the Earth itself. The theologians and poets really could have had it right all along: We live on the surface of a parent, not just on a planet.

But, as Roy Cullimore is quick to point out, "Earth is not a doting parent." Driving the point home, he notes that the world would be in just as much trouble—perhaps even more trouble—if the bacteria (instead of the insects) were plucked out of the equation. As with the insects, many people would at first take the disappearance as good news . . . and then they'd notice after a few days that beer was no longer fermenting . . . and that their intestines did not feel exactly right . . . and that all of the crops were beginning to die because nothing was fixing nitrogen in the soil and . . . *Dust* . . .

30. The French Research Vessel *Ocean Voyager,* which really exists, is a rebuilt and renamed ice-breaker, originally christened *Pandora II.* While aboard the *Voyager* (yes, the French really did send along a class 1-A chef nicknamed "Neelix") we discovered, during a 1996 expedition, an approximately fourfold increase in the amount of "sea snow" (organic debris consisting primarily of the dead bodies of copepods and other microscopic animals) falling to the floor of the North Atlantic. Over the course of ten years, the snowfall had literally become a blizzard. Roy Cullimore and I are presently exploring two probable causes for what is undoubtedly a massive plankton bloom: (1) The North Atlantic has been so severely overfished that precious little remains alive in near-surface waters (within a quarter mile of sunlight) to eat the plankton, and (2) Oil drilling on the Grand Banks has released methane into the base of the planktonic food chain (i.e., bacteria).

Determining which of these two causes accounts most for exploding planktonic populations will require comparisons with other overfished regions in the Pacific and Indian Oceans, as well as visits in submersibles to the deep scattering layer (a sonar-scattering layer of fish and plankton that rises to the ocean surface at night, and descends about a quarter mile by day). If the plankton are feeding on increased bacterial populations, then there is relatively little cause for concern. If, however, removing too many plankton-grazing fish and whales from the oceans has produced a plankton bloom that feeds primarily on one-celled plants (called phytoplankton) near the ocean surface, then we might, by diminishing an important element in the biological equation, be creating, by our own hand, a biological chain reaction that, while not as severe as the *Dust* scenario, is both analogous to it and severe enough. Most of the oxygen we breathe comes not from the Amazon rainforest (or even from all the forests of the world combined), but from those microscopic plants living in the top few inches of the ocean surface. They also absorb most of the carbon dioxide given off by us, and by our fossil fuels. If their numbers are in danger of being diminished, then the greenhouse effect (assuming the atmospheric chemists are correct about an already alarming trend toward carbon dioxide build-up) will impact us even faster than anticipated.

The good news is that if we restrict fishing, there is a huge plankton bloom for the remaining stocks to eat, and they should recover fully within a decade. But who would have believed that pulling too many fish out of the oceans could accelerate global warming, shift trade winds and agricultural belts, amplify summer and winter temperature extremes, bring forth encroaching seas and increase the strength of hurricanes?

Rule Number One of learning to live with your planet is simply this: Never, ever pull a major element out of the equation (or, put another way: When you pull the pin, Mister Hand Grenade is no longer your friend). As in the *Dust* scenario, the most forceful impact of (in this case) overfishing will be economic. As in ancient Babylon, as here and now: Economic collapse is the cause most likely to bring down any civilization, and economic collapse is reasonably easy to bring about. The horror of collapse is that our civilization really does have good reasons to go on living. If we are wise, and pay attention, we can build a future that anyone living today would be proud of. We can do much better than merely survive. We can excel. (Do you know, for example, that interstellar spacecraft, now on the drawing boards, should be flying by 2050?) Though we have a long way to go, one need only read newspapers from the turn of the 19th century to see that we actually have been getting better. (Do you know, for example, that lynchings were once so commonplace as to be a socially acceptable form of entertainment?) Human beings are perfectable, and I do believe we are moving in that direction.

But if anything is clear, anything at all, it is that we must move with caution. How fitting that a warning—a deep-ocean blizzard—should have smacked me in the face just weeks after this book was written, and that it should have come, of all places, from the decks of the *R.M.S. Titanic.*

"Pay attention!" an old friend once said. Her name was Eva Hart. She had been eight years old when she saw her father for the last time, waving from the deck of the ship they said not even God himself could sink—sinking the first time it sailed. In my photo file of the wreck I can pick out the very spot where Eva's father told her, "Take good care of Mommy. Shhhh . . . it'll be all right." That spot is covered with "snow" now.

"Pay attention," she said to me. "It was arrogance that sank that ship—the kind of arrogance that made men believe they could sail through the dark, at full speed, into an ice field they had been warned was ahead. If we keep behaving that way, then I'm afraid there will be an even bigger *Titanic* in our future—for the whole world, maybe. And next time there may be no lifeboats—for anybody.

"So pay attention," she warned me again, and again. "Move forward, yes . . . but temper arrogance with wisdom, and pay very close attention."

31. The reduction of the world's wheat crops from thousands of ancestral types to what now threatens to become a universal hybrid is a reality. Worse: It is a frighteningly arrogant reality. The spreading hybrid simply waits for the first resistant fungus that comes along. The same can be said of the world's other twenty top food crops. By breeding and cultivating only the most desirable (that is, the most profitable) seeds, our civilization plays a game of agricultural Russian Roulette (or, rather, we are ignoring the lesson of the Russian botanists who, during World War II, chose to starve rather than eat the genetic gold in Leningrad's seed bank). Until and unless we begin to pay more attention to genetic diversity, our best defenders of agricultural prosperity are fungus gnats. But history teaches us that they cannot always be relied on. One small case in point: During the winter of 1692 (fungus gnats are not particularly active in cold weather), a rye-infesting fungus, known to cause hallucinations and convulsions if ingested, is believed to have contaminated storage bins

in colonial Massachusetts—giving rise, apparently, to the Salem witch trials.

32. The minor role played by insects in the ecology of New Zealand (relative to the rest of the world)—reality. In fact, when colonists first introduced sheep to New Zealand, and (as a food source for the sheep) clover, they realized, almost too late, that there were no native bees to pollinate the clover—which necessitated the importation of European honeybees.

33. The possibility of life in icebound seas circling Jupiter, Saturn, and other iceworlds (kept warm and wet under the ice by the same tidal forces that cause the spectacular sulfur geysers seen on Jupiter's moon Io), originated as models proposed by me and Jesse A. Stoff. The models had existed with only a very low (next to zero) probability of life forming in those ice-covered seas until a team led by explorer Robert Ballard found a hydrogen sulfide-based food chain thriving near volcanic vents on Earth's East Pacific Rise. Such vent ecologies are now known to spread along more than 40,000 miles of the Earth's ocean floor. As below, so above—probably.

The 1996 discovery of a remarkably ancient lifeform two-and-a-half miles under the Atlantic—the *Consortia* (wherein independently living bacteria are arranged into actual tissue layers), teaches us that we should not expect to find mere, single-celled bacteria living beneath the ice of Europa, Ganymede, Enceladus, or Titan. Given more than 4 billion years of warm, wet environments, simple bacteria will not remain simple bacteria for very long. There is probably a great deal of multicellular life out there, beyond Earth. You just have to know where to look.

Given the number of tidally flexed iceworlds in our own solar system (at least four at last count), and given a growing body of evidence that our solar system is not unusual, it would appear that oceans inside iceworlds far outnumber Earth-like worlds (that is, worlds with just the right amount of mass located just the right distance from just the right kind of star). Aside from providing a good motive for a real *Darwin* mission, the "Oceans Above" theory would seem to shoot down all those humanoid UFO abduction myths. When we really do encounter intelligent life, the odds are greater than a thousand to one that it will be an aquatic iceworlder. Life as we know it is probably a galactic minority, if not downright freakish.

34. The rise of anti-science and the march against the City of Dreams . . . As with the emergence of "mad cow disease" from obscurity, another of the fictions presented here is threatening to become outdated by parallels in the real world before the ink is quite dry. (And, yes, it *is* true: Uncle Charlie buys pens by the case and writes his first drafts longhand, about which the late Isaac Asimov once remarked, "I've heard of writers who do that, but I always thought they came from other planets.")

There have, as of late, been all sorts of rumors about Long Island's Brookhaven National Laboratory. For the record: no one is hiding crashed UFOs at the lab (that's just where we designed the Valkyrie starships). Brookhaven is in reality, as in this story, one of the world's leaders in biomedical research—especially with respect to advanced preliminary design of such future magic as micro-MRI scanners and methods of reading and deciphering the genetic code. It is the place where maglev trains, the neutrino telescope, and a great many rocket designs originated. Clean energy for all humanity, from solar power, is a main research objective there. And the Shroud of Turin was dated there. B.N.L. is indeed "the best bar in town," endangered now by what seems to be the Age of Irrationality.

During the past week, I have seen placards declaring, "B.N.L. stands for Bogus Nuclear Liars," and heard two men on the boardwalk in Long Beach discussing how "the scientists have poisoned all of our drinking water with radiation . . . and we should round them all up and kill them." Sounds like the Dark Ages to me, when people used to accuse Jews of poisoning wells. Sounds an awful lot like Jerry Sigmond.

Now, about that "poisoned drinking water" . . . there is a machine at B.N.L. called the High Flux Beam Reactor—which produces a very powerful beam of neutrons that can be used to reveal the structure of molecules, or to produce medical isotopes, or even to probe the structure of an embryonic skeleton in a dinosaur egg. Such capabilities make much of today's (and tomorrow's) medical science possible. The problem: a water tank near the reactor has leaked tritium, the same element that makes the dial on my Casio watch glow. It is an isotope (or "heavy" form) of hydrogen, consisting of one proton and two neutrons. Enough tritium has escaped to produce readings undetectable with ordinary geiger counters: in the range of 3 billionths of a curie (the curie is a measurement of radioactivity). The average movie theater exit sign gives off about twenty curies. This is approximately 6.7 billion times more potent than the "B.N.L. tritium plume." In 1996, the tritium-illuminated dials of Flight 800 released 100 curies into the waters off Long Island's south shore—and that was not sufficient to make a shrimp sick.

Unfortunately, local politicians and media personalities do not speak in terms of billionths of a curie. After all, people might understand that a billionth of something that is already quite small must in fact be *really* small. So they elected to announce measurements in *pico*curies. A picocurie is a trillionth of a curie, and under this measurement, 3 billionths of a curie can be announced as 3000 picocuries. Cute trick. You can make anything sound dangerous, simply by reducing the unit of measurement and cranking up the number of zeros.

Using these cranked up zeros, one of our more prominent local politicians declared that he would not rest until there was a Congressional investigation, because "no amount of radiation can be acceptable," and "all of it" would have to be removed from the environment. Okay. Let's not argue with him. Much as it might be fun to strip every atom of carbon-14 out of his (naturally) radioactive DNA, let's not argue. Rather, let's build a huge shield in space to block out all radiation from that big fusion reactor in the sky—the one that rises in the east every morning. Let's see how Congress is feeling after they have protected us and the plants from the damaging effects of solar radiation for about two weeks.

"This [the future of science at B.N.L.] is not really a scientific question," laments one physicist. "We live in a political world."

We frown upon our ancestors because they lived in a

Dark Age of superstition and were all but scandalously ignorant of nature; and we fail to see that our descendants shall frown upon us for the same reasons.

Charles Pellegrino
New York, New York
April 15, 1997

Selected
Bibliography

Alvarez, L., *et al.*, "Extraterrestrial Cause for the Creta-
    ceous-Tertiary Extinction," *Science*, Vol. 208, p. 1095,
    June 6, 1980.

Alvarez, W., *T. rex and the Crater of Doom*, Princeton
    University Press, 1997.

Bakker, R.T., *The Dinosaur Heresies*, New York, William
    Morrow and Company, 1986.

Berenbaum, M.R., "Spin Control: Synthesizing Spider
    Silk," *The Sciences*, Vol. 35, p. 13, October 1995.

Boesch, D.F., *et al.*, *Harmful Algal Blooms in Coastal
    Waters: Options for Prevention, Control and Mitigation*,
    National Oceanic and Atmospheric Administration
    (NOAA) Coastal Ocean Program Decision Analysis Se-
    ries No. 10.

Broad, W.J., "Magnetic Fields on Distant Moons Hint at Hidden Life," *The New York Times,* p. C1, May 20, 1997.

Braiman, Y., *et al.,* "Ordering Chaos with Disorder," *Nature,* Vol. 378, pp. 444, 465, November 30, 1995.

Burkholder, J.M. and H.B. Glasgow Jr., "Interactions of a Toxic Estuarine Dinoflagellate with Microbial Predators and Prey (the Toxic Ambush-Predator Dinoflagellate *Pfiesteria piscidia*)," *Archives for Protistenkunde,* Vol. 145, p. 177, 1995.

Burkholder, J.M., *et al.,* "New 'Phantom' Dinoflagellate is the Causative Agent of Major Estuarine Fish Kills," *Nature,* Vol. 358, p. 407, July 30, 1992.

Buvet, R. and C. Ponnamperuma (Eds.), *Molecular Evolution: Chemical Evolution and The Origin of Life,* North-Holland, Amsterdam, 1971.

Cohen, F.E., *et al.,* "Structural Clues to Prion Replication," *Science,* Vol. 264, p. 530, April 22, 1994.

Coher, E.I., "Cave-Associated Tropical American *Neoditomyia* (Diptera: Mycetophilidae)," *Pan-Pacific Entomologist,* Vol. 72, p. 152, 1996.

Colbert, E.H., *et al.,* "Temperature Tolerances of the American Alligator and Their Bearing on the Habits, Evolution and Extinction of the Dinosaurs," *American Museum of Natural History Bulletin,* Vol. 86, p. 327, 1946.

Craig, *et al.,* "Arachnomania Issue," *Natural History,* Vol. 104, March 1995.

Cullimore, R., *et al.,* "Deep Ocean Bacterial Consortia," *Nature* (in preparation: a living fossil from the good old, old, old days).

Darwin, C., *Journal of Researches into the Natural History and Geology of Countries Visited During the Voyage of the H.M.S. Beagle Round the World,* J. Murray, London, 1845.

Delgado, J.P., *et al.,* *The Archaeology of the Atomic Bomb* (Bikini Atoll Sunken Fleet); U.S. Department of the Interior; Southwest Cultural Resources Center Professional Papers, Number 37, Santa Fe, New Mexico, 1991.

Eldredge, N., *The Miner's Canary: Unraveling the Mysteries of Extinction,* New York, Prentice Hall, 1991.

Fenton, M.B., *Bats,* New York, Facts on File, 1992.

Fernando, M., *This Piece of Planet Earth: Sri Lanka,* Subodhi Institute for Integral Education, Sri Lanka, 1994.

Folsome, C.E., *The Origin of Life: A Warm Little Pond,* W. H. Freeman and Co., 1979.

Gould, S.J., "The Belt of an Asteroid," *Natural History,* August 1980.

Gould, S.J., "Reversing Established Orders," *Natural History,* Vol. 104, p. 12, September 1995.

Greenhall, A.M. and U. Schmidt, *Natural History of Vampire Bats,* Boca Raton, Florida, CRC Press, 1988.

Holldobler, B. and E.O. Wilson, *Journey to the Ants,* Cambridge, Massachusetts, Harvard University Press, 1994.

Hopson, J., "Relative Brain Size in Dinosaurs," in Roger D.K. Thomas and Everett Olson, eds., *A Cold Look at the Warm-Blooded Dinosaurs,* Boulder, Colorado, Westview Press, 1980.

Kerr, R.A., "A Volcanic Crisis for Ancient Life?" *Science,* Vol. 270, October 6, 1995.

Margulis, L., *Symbiosis in Cell Evolution,* W.H. Freeman and Co., 1981.

Margulis, L., *Ghia in Oxford II: The Evolution of the Superorganism,* Oxford, 1997.

Nuridsony, C. and M. Perennou, *Microcosmos* (VIDEO: a documentary about "the planet below the planet," as seen through a day in the life of insects on a French meadow. The most exquisitely recorded and edited film ever on this subject, it truly takes you by the hand and leads you into a hidden world).

Pellegrino, C.R., "The Trouble with Nemesis," *Evolutionary Theory,* Vol. 17, p. 219, December 1985.

Pellegrino, C.R. and J.A. Stoff, *Darwin's Universe: Origins and Crises in the History of Life.* (Originally published: New York, Van Nostrand Reinhold, 1983; 2nd edition Blue Ridge Summit, Pa., TAB Books, 1986; 3rd edition in preparation.)

Pellegrino, C.R., "Dinosaur Capsule," *OMNI,* January 1985 (10th anniversary *Jurassic Park* recipe update Vol. 17, Fall 1995 issue).

Pellegrino, C.R. and R. Cullimore, "The Rebirth of the R.M.S. Titanic: A Study of the Bioarchaeology of a

Physically Disrupted Sunken Vessel,'' *Voyage,* June 1997.

Prusiner, S., ''The Prion Diseases,'' *Scientific American,* Vol. 272, January 1995.

Rampino, M. and B.M. Haggerty, ''Mass Extinctions and Periodicity,'' *Science,* Vol. 269, p. 617, August 4, 1995.

Rathjc, W. and C. Murphy, *Rubbish! The Archaeology of Garbage: What Our Garbage Tells Us About Ourselves,* New York, HarperCollins, 1992.

Raup, D.M. and J. Sepkoski Jr., ''Periodic Extinction of Families and Genera,'' *Science,* Vol. 231, p. 833, February 21, 1986.

Raup, D.M., *Extinction: Bad Genes or Bad Luck?* New York, W. W. Norton, 1991.

Safina, C., ''The World's Imperiled Fish,'' *Scientific American,* Vol. 273, November 1995.

Schutt, W.A., Jr., ''The Chiropteran Hindlimb: Evolutionary, Ecological, and Behavioral Correlations of Morphology,'' in T.H. Kunz and P. Racey, eds., *Bats: Phylogeny, Morphology, Echolocation, and Conservation Biology,* Washington, D.C., The Smithsonian Press, 1997.

Schutt, W.A., Jr., *et al.,* ''Functional Morphology of the Common Vampire Bat, *Desmodus rotundus,''* *The Journal of Experimental Biology* (in press).

Shumway, S.E. and A.D. Cembella, ''The Impact of Toxic Algae on Scallop Culture and Fisheries,'' *Reviews in Fisheries Science,* Vol. 1 (2), p. 121, 1993.

Silleck, B. and J. Marvin, *Cosmic Voyage* (VIDEO; IMAX/Smithsonian: To date, the finest film available depicting time and space and our place in it).

Stone, E. and P. Zimansky, ''Mashkan-shapir and the Anatomy of an Old Babylonian City,'' *Biblical Archaeologist,* pp. 212–218, December 1992.

Tresedor, K.K., *et al.,* ''How Ants Help Plants: Absorption of Ant-provided Carbon Dioxide and Nitrogen by a Tropical Ephiphyte,'' *Nature,* Vol. 375, p. 137, May 11, 1995.

Vacelet, J. and N. Boury-Esnault, ''Carnivorous Sponges,'' *Nature,* Vol. 373, p. 284, January 26, 1995.

Wade, N., ''Chemical Traces of Blood Found in Bones of

Tyrannosaurus Rex," *The New York Times,* June 10, 1997 (see also M. Schweitzer, *et al.,* in The Proceedings of the National Academy of Sciences, beginning June 1997).

Waldbauer, G., *Insects Through the Seasons,* Harvard University Press, 1996.

Wooley, L., *Dead Cities and Living Men,* New York, William Morrow and Company, 1956.

Acknowledgments

My first thanks, as always, must go to Mom, Dad, Adelle Dobie, Barbara and Dennis Harris—five very special teachers who believed in a hyperactive, "ride-the-shock-wave," school-hating little boy who could barely read but who (paradoxically) loved science and art. Your belief meant a lot to me. Add to these five blessings, two other extraordinary teachers who came aboard as I entered my (narf!) teenage years: Agnes Saunders and Ed McGunnigle, of the Nassau County 4-H Club.

Next, my appreciation to John Douglas and Russ Galen, who really brought sperm and egg together on this thing and then sold it; to Lou Aronica, who bought it; to Jennifer Brehl, who nurtured it. All four acted as—well, midwives, I guess you could say. It *needed* midwives. This would have been a very depressing story without their guidance through the rewrite, and the rewrite to the rewrite (for a

start—just for a start: in the original draft everybody died).
My thanks also to Amy Goldschlager, who put up with my
endless telephone conversations about the creepy crawlers,
Enceladus, Europa, and other things that go bump in the
night. (Our conversations often went something like this:
"Hi, Charlie. How are you?" To which I'd reply, "Fine.
I've been thinking about superstrings. Never really believed in all those multiple quantum dimensions, but Arthur faxed me something last night about the latest
palladium experiment and I'll be damned if they're not
really tickling a few strings. So maybe fusion is not the
only thing that heats the sun. Now, about this neutrino
deficit . . ." And the really fun part is that Amy *understands* this stuff.)

Bruce Berman and Kevin McMahon (Plan B Entertain-
ment/Warner Brothers) were kind enough to read (and
buy) an earlier draft and make detailed comments that
have improved the book's final form. Thus have they become a refreshing challenge to "Harlan's Law" (which
Harlan himself had already seen disproved by J. Michael
Straczynski).

Thanks are also due to:

Akihiro Takahashi, "Father John," Dr. "Reese" (Hiroshima), Eva Hart and Michel Navatril *(Titanic),* Elizabeth
Stone and Paul Zimanski (Iraq), and Mr. Unger (Auschwitz) for recollections of civilization at some of its darkest
moments. Mr. Unger, especially, has seen how ordinary
human beings can sink far lower in a mob than any individual can sink by himself.

For tours of the stock exchange and discussions of probable economic impacts, I am indebted to Carol Roble (Cer-
tified Public Accountant), Marvin Tobis and Marty Roberts
(Prudential Securities).

For the *Nimitz* Control Van (based on our actual experi-
ences with the *Argo* Control Van): Tom Dettweiler, Robert
Ballard, Jean Francheteau, Roger Hekinian, and, of course,
Angus, Argo, and *Jason.*

For operations and procedures: *The* Don (Peterson), Ed
Bishop (Lucent/Bell), Felix Limardo (Pulsar), Mary Leung
(Paine Webber), Greg Benoit, Fred Haise, Al Munier,
George Skurla (Northrop/Grumman), General Tom

Stafford, Bill Muller, Tommy Attridge (USAF and Grumman), Bob Hartenstine, Rhoni Katz (U.S. Navy), Harrison Schmitt, Deke Slayton (NASA), and Gregory Grechko (CCCP).

For wide-ranging conversations spanning several years and most of the scientific and theological subjects encountered in this book: Jim Powell, Hiroshi Takahashi (B.N.L.), Cyril Ponnamperuma, Arthur C. Clarke (University of Moratura, Sri Lanka), Father Mervyn Fernando (Subodhi Institute, Sri Lanka), Father Robert A. Mcguire (Spirit Life Center, New York), Stephen Jay Gould (the natural source, Harvard University), Edward I. Coher (a natural resource, L.I.U.), Walter Lord (national treasure and all around nice guy), Rabbi Zuscha Freedman (salt of the Earth), Bill and Janet Schutt (AMNH: friends to vampire bats), Pierre Noyes (Stanford Linear Accelerator; friend to antiprotons), Kevin Pang, Carl Sagan, Torrence Johnson (NASA/JPL), Daniel Stanley (Smithsonian Institution), Luis and Walter Alvarez (Berkeley), Mary Schweitzer (Museum of the Rockies, Montana), Michael Rampino (NASA), Mike Hammer (S.O.P.I.), Senator Spark Matsunaga and Harvey Meyerson (Washington), Claire Edwin Folsome (University of Hawaii), Sandra Schumway (L.I.U.: friend to the dinoflagellate from hell), Gerard R. Case and Donald Baird (AMNH, Carnegie Mellon), Paul Wygodzynski (AMNH), Joshua Lederberg (Rockefeller University), Joshua Stoff (Cradle of Aviation Museum), Jesse A. Stoff (Solstice), Edward O. Wilson (Pellegrino University Professor at Harvard and friend to ants), Alan Branch (Wounded Knee), George Tulloch, Matt Tulloch, Alex Lindsay (of R.M.S. Titanic Inc.), and Roy Cullimore (Droycon Bioconcepts Inc. and friend to bacterial sludge).

Finally, I am indebted to Richard "Tuna" Sinclair for his help and inspiration. This novel could not have been written without him. (P.S.: Meesha the cat got away.)

Charles Pellegrino
Vancouver, Canada
March 13, 1997

HER NAME, TITANIC
The Untold Story of the Sinking and Finding of the Unsinkable Ship
by Charles Pellegrino

On the evening of April 14, 1912, the awesome ocean liner *Titanic* struck an iceberg and vanished into the sea.

Seventy-three years later, a dedicated group of scientists set sail in search of the sunken behemoth—an incredible mission that uncovered shocking secrets buried two miles below the ocean's surface.

Author Charles Pellegrino combines two enthralling modern adventures in one—re-creating the terrible night the *Titanic* went down as well as providing a first-hand account of the remarkable expedition that found her final resting place.

70892-2/$6.50 US/$8.50 Can